# CROW'S FATE

## CARNIVAL OF MYSTERIES

## KIM FIELDING

D1737886

Tin Box
— PRESS —

This is a work of fiction. Names, characters, places, and incidents are either the product of the author's imagination or are used fictitiously. Any resemblance to actual persons living or dead, business establishments, events, or locales is entirely coincidental.

Crow's Fate

First edition

Copyright © 2023 Kim Fielding

Cover Art by Dianne Thies, LyricalLines.net

# CHAPTER 1

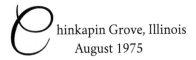

*C*hinkapin Grove, Illinois
August 1975

THE SCREAMS CAME and went like the refrain in a song, always so high-pitched that it was impossible to tell whether they came from male or female throats, from children or adults. They tickled inside Crow's ears and made him squint up into the bright, moth-ringed lights. There was actual music too, runs of notes that he recognized from a long distance away. The Jackson 5. Elton John. The Eagles. Queen. Lynyrd Skynyrd.

Although the sun had set, the day's heat still hugged the trampled grass, wet and heavy and scented with popcorn and beer. He walked slowly, perhaps slightly dazed, one hand clutching the damp little wad of bills in one pocket.

"Come *on*, Crow!" Julie grabbed his arm and tugged hard. "There's a haunted house and the world's strongest man. And I bet there's bumper cars. I definitely want to ride those."

Crow squeezed his small stash of money even more

1

tightly but allowed himself to be pulled along. Sandy and Marty were already up ahead, standing at the brightly painted entrance booth and looking back with impatient expressions. They were likely eager to find a ride that would give them an excuse to squish close and make out. They could never seem to get enough of touching each other. Marty said he stole so many rubbers from the vending machine in the bowling alley, where he worked after school, that his boss had noticed them missing and was considering taking the machine away. "Then I'd have to go to Blair's Pharmacy and buy them," Marty had complained. "Can you imagine?"

Crow had never used a rubber. Had never had sex—a fact that for some reason seemed especially salient on this sticky August night, with Julie's skin hot against his. He'd be eighteen in October, and that was an ancient age for a virgin. His mother had been eighteen when he was born. He didn't want to have sex with Julie, though. He liked her just fine, but he'd mostly ended up with her by default because she was Marty's cousin and Crow was Marty's best friend.

Now he and Julie stood at the booth, where a large man with an unlit cigar sat inside, grinning at them. "A buck each to get in, kids."

Julie immediately plopped a dollar bill onto the little wooden counter, but Crow hesitated. He hadn't realized it would cost money just to get into the carnival. Then he'd have to pay for food, for rides…. His meagre little savings, a gift from his Aunt Helen, wouldn't stretch far.

But Julie was waiting, and Sandy and Marty were already inside.

"Don't worry, kid," said the man in the booth. "Your ticket includes admission to all the shows, so it's a good deal. You'll find it a dollar well spent. You'll see." He chuckled, as if at some private joke.

Crow put a dollar on the counter.

The man took it with a solemn bob of his head, as if they were undertaking an important transaction, and placed a paper ticket in its place. Crow slid the ticket into a back pocket.

"Have fun, kid," said the man.

Walking side by side, Crow and Julie approached a red-and-white-striped archway. *Welcome Traveler* was painted on the arch, which made Crow cough a bitter laugh. Unless you counted the journey he'd made in infancy, which he'd been too young to remember, he'd never been more than a few miles from Chinkapin Grove.

As he passed under the archway, an odd tremory feeling passed over Crow, making his hairs stand on end. *Someone walked over my grave.* That was what Gran said when she shivered a little for no reason. So now Crow pictured a face-less person striding through the Chinkapin Grove Cemetery, moonlight threading through the branches of the old oaks.

That image might have stopped him in his tracks, but Julie had his arm again and was pulling him forward.

A steady stream of people moved along with them, chatting and laughing. Little kids darted ahead and were chased by older siblings or parents. Couples strolled hand in hand. One man stood motionless along the edge, watching. He was tall and slender, dark-haired and dark-eyed, dressed in black-and-white clothing far too glamorous and strange for Chinkapin Grove. His gaze caught Crow's, and for a split second—or maybe it was an hour—everything else faded into the background and went totally out of focus. Crow was suddenly chilled and he felt flayed, as if everything inside of him was now plainly visible to this man. But something about the man was also... well, *familiar* wasn't the right term. *Fitting*, perhaps. Crow was ready to pull himself from Julie's grasp and walk toward him.

But then the man gave a very slight nod and the spell was broken. The surroundings became normal again, and Crow allowed himself to be moved along.

The midway was a single grassy lane lined with tents in a rainbow of colors. Outside of each tent, a sign announced what could be found within, usually with elaborately painted illustrations. There was Gentleman Jim, Master of Knives. Darius the Wonder Dog. Parcifal the Juggler.

Crow would have liked to see any of these—he'd paid his dollar, after all—but Marty was clamoring for food first. They followed their noses to an area where tents and trucks sold all manner of treats. People were clustered thickly here, eating oversize corn dogs, funnel cakes, caramel apples, and sno-cones. The thick aromas of hot oil and sugar made Crow's stomach grumble. *You can only afford a little*, he reminded himself, *so choose wisely.*

He followed his friends to a truck with dancing clowns painted on its side, and when he saw the menu board, he exhaled in relief. The prices were much lower than he'd expected. A turkey leg, fries, and a Coke slushy cost him only a dollar fifty. He'd even be able to afford ice cream or popcorn later, if he wanted.

Marty found them a picnic table nearby, which they shared with a young couple and their baby. Crow had gone to school with the parents, but they were a few years ahead of him and he didn't know their names. They seemed happy with each other and with their child, a placid-faced little being in a diaper and tiny T-shirt.

"Hey, guys," Marty said in a stage whisper. When he was sure he had his friends' attention, he surreptitiously pulled a flat metal flask from his back pocket, hidden by his untucked shirt. "It's the good stuff from my dad's liquor cabinet. He doesn't think I know where he hides the key."

Sandy gave him a skeptical look. "That's not a great idea, Mar. Not here."

"Sure it is, babe. We'll just wait until it gets later." He wiggled around, returning the flask to its hiding spot.

Instead of booze, Julie produced a small notebook and pencil from one of her pockets. "We need a plan. We only have tonight, so what are we going to do and in what order?"

A lively discussion followed, but Crow chipped in only occasionally. That was his style most of the time: go with the flow unless he found something entirely disagreeable, which was rare. It wasn't that he didn't have opinions or preferences. For the most part, though, pushing for them felt like more effort than it was worth, especially when the chances of getting his way were slim. *Be grateful for what you got, boy*, Grandad liked to tell him. *It coulda been nothing at all.*

It was mutually decided that going on rides immediately after eating wasn't such a great idea, so when their food was gone, they headed for the shows. More people had arrived, making it feel as if the entire town were there. It was disorienting to see familiar faces among capering clowns, exotic-looking roustabouts, and vivid scenery. It was like that old TV series, the one Crow sometimes caught in reruns. *The Twilight Zone*. Yes, this felt like an episode in which an entire drab Illinois town has been somehow transported to another dimension.

Crow wasn't sure what he thought of that idea. This dimension was a lot more interesting than his usual one; that was for sure. But it made him as uneasy as standing at the edge of a diving board at the community pool. Worried about what was about to happen, but also excited. As if that one leap might change everything forever.

The small group of friends sat for a while inside a black tent, watching the Amazing Mephistopheles perform magic tricks.

Crow had seen magicians on TV, where their tricks always seemed hokey. Although he couldn't figure out the details of how they did their schtick, the generalities were obvious. Trap doors. Hidden compartments. Marked cards. Objects tucked up sleeves. But when Mephistopheles blew on his cupped palms and a large bird with glowing-ember plumage appeared —a phoenix, he said—that felt like real magic.

After making the phoenix disappear, Mephistopheles invited old Ernie Selby—stooped and withered—onto the small stage and caused a three-dimensional scene to appear overhead. The characters in the scene, a group of muddy soldiers moving through a blackened forest, were as fully detailed as Crow himself. One of them, he realized, was a young Ernie Selby, not much older than Crow and his friends. As the crowd watched, young Ernie heaved a fallen comrade over his shoulder and, crouching low to avoid flying bullets, carried him away.

"Séchault," said old Ernie as the images faded away. He was standing straighter now, his cloudy eyes gone bright. "September 1918."

Mephistopheles nodded. "You saved that man's life. He had six children and now over twenty grands and great-grands. All of them here because of what you did that day."

Ernie went back to his seat amid thunderous applause. He looked like a man who now recognized himself as a hero.

That felt like real magic too.

Crow and his friends went into other tents, watching a juggler and then a fire-eater. Julie and Sandy made goo-goo eyes over Samson the Strongman, a blond giant in a loin-cloth. Crow also—

No.

They all went to the Big Top, where the Flying Galliers spun and soared as if they had a special exemption from the laws of gravity. When that show was over, Marty announced,

"I want to try the games. I'll win you a stuffed animal at the milk cans, Sandy." As a pitcher for the high school team, he probably would. He'd been scouted by a couple of minor league teams, although nobody had made him an offer.

While the others seemed keen on this idea, which aligned with Julie's written plans, Crow held back. He wasn't sure why. True, he'd never been particularly good at aiming at things, he didn't want to win any toys, and if he spent his money on games, he wouldn't have any left for rides or more food. But none of those reasons were the root of his hesitation. He simply felt... unwilling. As if an invisible fishing line were tied around his insides, holding him back.

"I, uh, need to do something," he muttered.

Julie looked alarmed. "Is something wrong?"

He shook his head. "I just.... It's a thing. I'll meet you by the carousel in half an hour, okay?"

His friends wanted to argue, but he set his chin stubbornly and they backed off. "Half an hour," said Julie. She gave him a quick kiss on the cheek, like butterfly wings dusted in powdered sugar, and then the three of them hurried off.

Crow remained standing in the center of the midway, an unmoving island amid a rushing river of people. And suddenly the crowds felt like too much, the colors too vivid, the sounds clashing, the scents a gooey mass. Although the temperature had become noticeably cooler as soon as he entered the carnival, sweat now tickled his neck and made his thin T-shirt cling to his body. He looked past his faded cutoffs and down at his legs, which were too long and skinny, as if he were transforming into a bird. His frayed old tennis shoes felt too tight.

He needed to sit down somewhere quiet, but there wasn't a whole lot of quiet to be found in a carnival.

He made his way down the midway on shaky legs, as if

he'd been sick for a while and hadn't fully recovered. Sometimes someone who knew him called his name and he automatically waved, but he didn't really register their identity. They were real and he was a dream, a ghost moving among them.

Down at the far end of the midway, a little distance past its nearest neighbor, was a small tent the exact shade of the purple irises that Gran liked to grow. Although there were bright lights above it, nobody but Crow was nearby. The sign out front showed a beautiful, voluptuous woman with knowing eyes and a kind smile. A crystal ball hovered above one of her outstretched palms, while her other hand held a tarot card depicting a yellow wheel. *Madame Persephone* the sign said.

He was afraid of the tent, although there was nothing obviously sinister about it. Grandad sometimes called him perverse, and maybe he was right about that because, despite his fluttering heart, Crow stepped closer to the tent. He put his hand on the soft cloth that shrouded the opening. And then he pushed it aside and stepped through.

It was dark inside, much darker than the midway, so Crow's first sensory information was the scent: a mixture of floral and spice, a little like the incense Aunt Helen had brought back from her honeymoon trip to Chicago. But this aroma was deeper, more complex, and probably wouldn't fade away after an hour or two, like the incense. In fact, he had the sense that the odor had been here for a very long time and was as much a part of the tent as the fabric itself.

A single lightbulb hung from the peak of the tent, and fairy lights outlined the ceiling where it met the walls. Crow blinked a few times in an attempt to help his eyes adjust. Which was when he saw another person in the tent with him. Madame Persephone, he presumed, although her back was to him. She was broad-shouldered and as tall as he was, which surprised him because few women were. A colorful scarf covered her head and back.

Crow made a small noise, not quite a throat-clearing, at which point she spun around, the scarf dropping to the floor.

It wasn't Madame Persephone.

It was, in fact, a startlingly handsome man, perhaps in his mid-twenties. With the scarf gone, Crow could see that he wore old blue jeans and a short-sleeved button-down shirt. His long dark hair was bound into a ponytail; his eyes, also dark, glittered with humor. He grinned as if doing so came naturally, as if smiling was his usual response to almost everything.

"S-sorry," Crow stammered.

The man laughed, scooped the scarf from the floor and settled it on the back of the chair. "No need to be sorry. I was the one doing something he oughtn't."

He had an accent. English, Crow was pretty sure, although he'd never met anyone with an English accent. In fact, he had never met a single person born anywhere other than Illinois. The unfamiliar vowels sent a shiver across Crow's heated skin and gave him a clenching feeling low in his gut; neither of those sensations was unpleasant.

"I... I...."

"She'll be back in a bit. You can wait here if you fancy." The man waved toward the tent's only other chair, which faced a cloth-covered table.

Crow took a step backward. "It's okay. I don't...." He wasn't sure how to finish.

"It's fine. The boss just wanted a brief natter. She won't be gone long. You don't want to miss out on a reading with her —she's the best. Have a seat and I'll keep you company while you wait."

Keeping company with this man was terrifying and also the thing Crow most wanted in the world. He took a few deep breaths before sitting down. When the man didn't say anything, Crow took a longer look around. The inside walls of the tent were draped in a great variety of fabrics. Whether due to the dim light or the fabrics themselves, Crow couldn't tell, but the colors seemed to swirl in a way that reminded him of the lava lamp Aunt Helen had also bought in Chicago. The effect made him a little dizzy, and staring at the man made him dizzier, so Crow focused on the furnishings instead. They turned out to be minimal: the table in front of him, the two chairs, and a smaller table off to his left. Both tables held a variety of objects: a crystal ball like the one on the sign, decks of cards, crystals, and some other things he couldn't identify.

"Nice, isn't it?" asked the man. "Quiet."

Crow noticed then that the sounds of the carnival were completely absent inside the tent. He could hear his own breathing, a little harsh, and the man's, which was calmer and more even. It made the space feel so intimate that Crow's cheeks heated. He hoped the dim light would prevent the man from noticing.

Still smiling, the man sat down in the empty chair with an easy grace Crow could never hope for. "I come here sometimes when I need a few minutes away from everything. Madame Persephone doesn't mind as long as she's not with a local."

"You work here?"

"'M a roustabout. Help set things up and take them down again. In between I carry things about and put in a hand wherever it's needed. Like just a bit ago when Mr. Ame told me to send Madame Persephone to him. He's the showrunner—the bloke who owns the carnival."

That made sense. This man looked strong, and Crow could easily imagine him hauling heavy loads and hoisting... whatever needed to be hoisted. "Is it a good job?"

"Ah, lovely so far. But it's been only a few weeks for me, hasn't it? I expect I'll need more time before I decide whether I'll stay for good."

"Am I interrupting one of your, um, quiet times? 'Cause I can go."

The man shook his head. "Stay. Madame said I'm to keep an eye on the place while she's away. Entertain any locals who stop by. None did until you, though, and I was bored. Which was why I was playing with her scarf when I oughtn't."

He didn't look at all repentant, however. In fact, he reached back and stroked the fabric draped over the chair as if he were considering putting it on again. He had big hands, Crow noticed, his fingers long and broad.

Crow tore his gaze away. "I don't even know if I was going to, uh, get my fortune told. It's bullshit anyway. I'd rather spend my money on rides."

If the man was offended by this, he didn't show it. He cocked his head instead, as if studying Crow. "Where are you from?"

"Here." That was only a whisker away from the truth. Slightly emboldened, Crow crossed his arms. "You?"

"There." Laughing eyes. "And whom do I have the honor of meeting?"

It could be some kind of scam, some carny trick to glean private information and thereby empty Crow's pockets. But Crow had nothing to lose but a couple of dollars, and he didn't want to go back out onto the midway again. "Crow."

"Is that a nickname?"

"It's the one my mother gave me." It was almost the only thing she'd given him: Crow Rapp, a strange name on a birth certificate that didn't list a father. She'd given him her good looks too, or so people said. Neighbors said she'd been a beauty, and Aunt Helen claimed that Crow was her spitting image. He didn't know if that was true because his grandparents had no photos of her and wouldn't speak of her at all.

Sometimes Crow would look in the bathroom mirror, past the diagonal crack, and wonder which of his features might be her legacy. The butter-gold hair that bleached almost white in summer, or maybe the storm-cloud eyes. The squarish face with the wide, serious mouth. Perhaps the long-limbed frame, lean and wiry.

"You don't look much like a crow," said the man, "with that pale hair and those pretty eyes. The name would suit me better, love. Maybe I ought to steal it."

This felt dangerously like flirting, and Crow's cheeks burned again. A man shouldn't be flirting with him. And Crow shouldn't be enjoying it. Shouldn't be hoping the man would push a bit farther.

"You can't steal a name."

"Can't I? I'm a bloody good thief, I am. Or used to be. And look." He pulled out the tie binding his hair. Released from its prison, the hair flowed over his shoulders, black and glossy as, well, a crow's wing. His eyes were shining and black—or close enough to it that his pupils blended into the iris—and his nose was just a *little* sharp.

Crow's name would suit this man well.

"I should go," said Crow, but he didn't move.

"Oh, don't. Tell you what." The man's eyes glinted with mischief, but he didn't seem cruel. He pulled the scarf off the chair, draped it carefully over his head, and tossed one end over his shoulder. Framed in silk, his face was even more striking, with a slightly cleft chin, lush lips, and thick eyebrows that almost seemed to have a life of their own. It was the kind of face that made Crow wish he were a painter or photographer.

And wasn't that the dumbest thing a Chinkapin Grove farmer's grandson ever thought?

Crow decided to take the man's bait. "Tell me what?"

"Tell you your fortune. Madame Simeon at your service. And I won't even charge you a fee, so you can save your dosh for the galloper. Or perhaps you're a Ferris wheel man?"

Crow knew with complete certainty that he ought to get up and leave the tent. Ought to leave the carnival, in fact, and go home, crawl into his bed, think nothing but Chinkapin Grove thoughts, and dream nothing but Chinkapin Grove dreams.

He did none of those things.

Instead he raised his chin the same way he did when people called him a bastard, when people called his mother even worse. When the air around him felt both sticky as sorghum molasses and sharp as the thorns on Gran's rose-bush. When the hostile thoughts and malevolent wishes buffeted him like an April tornado.

"Tell my fortune," Crow said.

Simeon made a gleeful sound and rubbed his palms together. He had pale skin, a contrast to his dark hair and eyes. It would look especially white against Crow's late-summer tan, a bronze baked into him from helping his grandparents tend to the soldiered ranks of corn. Crow wondered how Simeon could stay so white after hours spent erecting tents. Unless maybe the roustabouts worked only at night.

"Your future," Simeon said, "it's an important thing, but it's unreliable. Not as unreliable as the past—the past trans-forms constantly or fades away completely. But the future twists away across this bend and that, and when you reckon you know where you're going, you end up somewhere completely unexpected."

"Does this mean you won't tell me?"

"Nah, love, I'll give it a go. Could start by saying you'll

13

meet a stranger, tall, dark, and handsome. But now that's past instead of future, innit?"

Oh, those laughing eyes. As if delight ran through Simeon's veins instead of blood. There was a depth there too, a knowledge of the pain that life could bring. But didn't bitterness make the sweet even more intense?

Bravely, Crow leaned forward. "So what *is* my fortune, then?" Hoping and not-hoping that Simeon would say the right thing. Would grant him the future—just a few breathless minutes—that his heart begged for so piteously. Crow and his heart weren't asking for forever. The future could be *now* and only now, a few stolen minutes in in the arms of a man with crow's-wing hair.

And if those few minutes tore Crow apart, what of it?

Simeon raised his hands and let them hover over the crystal ball as if he were about to pick it up and toss it through a hoop. They didn't actually touch the glass, however. That was a boundary he seemed unwilling to cross.

"A carnival comes to town," Simeon said. "Yeah, that bit's past now too. And the tent at the end of the midway, that's present. But what happens next—"

Simeon froze. His expression slowly shifted from teasing to surprised and then to horrified. His eyes widened as he stared into the ball. His throat made a clicking, dragging noise. Impossibly, he paled.

And then he shot to his feet, almost knocking over the chair, and threw the scarf onto the ground. He backed away until he nearly touched the tent wall, his hands out in front of him as if warding off an attacker.

He started to cry, large tears trailing down his cheeks, his chin trembling as he worked his mouth without parting his lips.

"Simeon? What—?"

A slow shake of the head before Simeon spoke, low and

soft. "Go home, Crow Rapp. Go back to your farm. The corn will be ready for harvest soon, and school will be starting. Embrace your family. Stay safe, love. Stay safe." A deep breath and then he said it a third time, as if it were an incantation. "Stay safe."

Fortunetelling was bullshit; Crow knew that already. And Simeon wasn't even a fortuneteller—he was a roustabout playing around while Madame Persephone was off on an errand. This was all just jokes and fakery.

But that was a lie.

Whatever Simeon had seen—a vision Crow desperately did not want to know—was as genuine as rows of corn awaiting the combine harvester and as real as the splintery floorboards in Crow's bedroom. Whatever Simeon had seen was nothing but a confirmation of the dark truth that Crow felt but had refused to acknowledge for his entire life.

Without another word, Crow stood and fled the purple tent.

# CHAPTER 2

*P*ortland, Oregon
Nearly ten years later — April 1985

"HEY, man, wanna score some weed? It's good shit."

Considering, Crow stopped walking and looked at the man seated on the low stone wall. He wouldn't mind getting high after work, and a joint or two would be cheaper than rotgut and easier on his digestive system too. But if he had the joints in his pocket while on the job, he'd be tempted to smoke them on break. Then he'd probably end up fired, and he wanted to keep this job for a while longer, shitty as it was.

"I'll pass," he said.

The man—who was really a kid, probably a decade younger than Crow—shrugged as if it didn't matter. Maybe it didn't. Maybe he was too stoned to care. "Suit yourself, man."

So Crow continued across the street to Pioneer Square, his rubber-soled boots slapping against the damp bricks. The chilly mist didn't prevent a small cluster of skinheads from loitering near the fountain. They sneered at him but without much effort, as if they were simply performing a task expected of them. They always noticed Crow but never truly messed with him. Maybe they figured he wasn't worth the bother, or maybe they simply preferred easier prey.

He wondered what they'd do if he crossed the square holding hands with Cameron, Dee, or any of the other guys he sometimes fucked. Not that Crow was likely to hold hands with any of those men; they didn't have that kind of relationship. But still, it would be interesting to see the reaction.

Crow snorted at that thought as he climbed the steps to Broadway. Apparently at some point he'd concluded that violence was a nice break from the ordinary, even if it was aimed at him. He didn't like to fight and would run away when he could. But sometimes he couldn't, and then…. He turned his thoughts away from that.

He could have taken a bus—fares were free downtown—but he enjoyed his walks, even in the rain. Maybe especially in the rain. It made him feel cleaner. He liked to vary his routes, zigzagging through the streets in a different pattern each day. Now he turned right on Broadway, then left on Morrison and right on Tenth, skirting the Galleria shopping center. Dee went there sometimes to buy clove cigarettes from the stand on the third floor, and if Crow accompanied him and their wallets weren't too empty, they might caffeinate at Coffee Ritz or have a meal at Souvlaki Stop or Bogarts. They hadn't done that in a while, though. Dee hadn't felt well enough.

Now, of course, Crow didn't go in. He continued to plod up Tenth all the way across Burnside, past Powell's Books and through the yeasty smell seeping from the Weinhard Brewery. The east-west streets in this part of town were named after founding fathers and arranged in alphabetic order, so that Couch led to Davis, which led to Everett. Crow continued north all the way to Overton and then turned west until he passed under the freeway and emerged a block from work.

He was pretty damp by now, droplets running from his hair down the back of his neck and under his collar. He was shivering a bit, but that was nothing new. No matter the ambient temperature, he hadn't been truly warm since an August night a decade earlier. Despite the drizzle, he paused for a moment outside the entrance to CorruCorp, bracing himself. The letters of the company name, painted on the other side of the glass door, were scratched—as if something had tried to escape.

As soon as Crow stepped inside, the din assaulted him. Giant machines rumbled and roared nonstop, silent only on Christmas Day. Forklifts hummed as they moved forward and beeped when they reversed. Men shouted to one another. Boots stomped across concrete floors. Metal clanked. Heavy boxes thunked. High overhead, fluorescent lights delivered their lifeless glare. The heavy odors of grease, paper, and glue seemed to permeate everything.

God, he hated this place. Not just the miserable conditions and low pay but also his schedule—either second or third shift—which left him constantly at odds with a first-shift world. The work itself consisted of standing on the production line, manipulating the product into place, and carrying stacks of cardboard. It left him aching by the end of his ten hours and gave his mind too much room to wander.

As Crow trudged to the locker room, he remembered toiling on his grandparents' farm. That had been hard work too, hot in summer and cold during the fallow season. But at least he'd breathed fresh air and felt honest sun on his back. And he was helping to produce something important—food —not just cardboard boxes. Containers of nothingness.

The locker room was crowded with other people coming on shift. They joked and laughed as they put on their coveralls and steel-toed boots. Some smoked cigarettes, which was technically forbidden inside the building due to the presence of chemical fumes, but the rule wasn't enforced. Crow nodded and greeted a few people but mostly kept to himself.

He got in line, grabbed his timecard, and clocked in. The cha-chunk sounded like an executioner's axe.

"Robertson!" And then a pause. "Hey, Robertson!"

It took those two tries before Crow remembered that Robertson was him. In Portland, he was Cliff Robertson. In Phoenix he'd been Chuck Reynolds. In Shreveport, Chris Reed. In Kittanning he— Well, that didn't matter. This was Portland, and he was Cliff Robertson.

He trotted over to his supervisor, a man so thin and pale that he looked as if he'd been caught in one of the presses and had peeled himself away, like a cartoon character. His name was Melnyk, and he wasn't a bad sort. Although he wasn't especially great either; the personality had been pressed out of him as well.

"I'm moving your schedule around. You'll be third shift starting on Sunday." If Melnyk's body had been through the press, his voice had been subjected to the grinder. Years of shouting over the machinery had left it rough and jagged.

Crow did a quick mental calculation. "That means I'll work twelve days without a day off."

Melnyk shrugged. "It's what we need."

Need. Years ago, in some city he couldn't now name, Crow had rented a room in a houseful of hippies—back when such people still existed. One of his housemates was a woman who called herself Zen, a name that was no more genuine than whatever Crow was using at that time. Perhaps because Crow was young, she decided to subject him to what she called Teachings with a very audible capital T. She said that life was comprised of suffering. He could have told her that. And she said that the cause of that suffering is need. Stop needing things and you stop suffering. Which he supposed made sense, but she was never clear on how to stop needing, probably because she had no idea. Zen also got into screaming matches with anyone whose food entered her designated spot in the refrigerator.

CorruCorp was a company and therefore it could not suffer, no matter what or how much it needed. Crow envied it. Zen would likely preach that envy was another serious fault.

"You got it?" Melnyk rasped.

Crow had to take a moment to remember what he was supposed to be getting, and then he gave a grudging nod. "Sunday. Third shift."

Apparently considering the matter settled, Melnyk headed purposefully toward the single-facer machines. Crow headed for the flexo.

By the time Crow made his slow way home after clocking out at one, the kids in plaid, leather, and studs were long gone from the Galleria, and the skinheads had abandoned Pioneer Square. Even the dealers had left the low wall in front of the old courthouse. A few Tri-Met busses rumbled by like orange-and-gray dinosaurs grudgingly on their way to extinction. A handful of homeless people slept in doorways or wandered in their own private purgatory, but for the most part, Crow had the city to himself.

He was hungry. A few places were open this late, but none were nearby. Besides, he wasn't in the mood to join the club kids at Quality Pie or the truckers, college students, and sex workers at the Hotcake House across the river. Maybe he'd pick up something at the Plaid Pantry—a plasticky sandwich, a bag of chips, a carton of milk. Or maybe he'd just head straight home and go to sleep.

Home. Now there was a flexible concept.

He'd lived in a lot of different places over the years and they shared a few characteristics. They were cheap. They were reasonably close to wherever he could find work. And they had landlords who weren't picky about their prospective tenants providing IDs or references. Here in Portland he was staying in what had likely been a fine house when it was built a hundred years earlier but had long ago been chopped into tiny apartments with creaky floors and a pervasive smell of onions and mildew.

He occupied a single room in the basement, and although it was always damp and chilly, it was also dark and quiet when he had to sleep during the day. Furnished with a narrow bed, a sagging couch, and a dresser with one of its drawers broken, the room also included a heavy coffee table with carved wood doors, which doubled as a rather awkward dining table. The kitchenette boasted a wheezing fridge, a pitted sink, a few cupboards, and a microwave. No oven or stove. But he had the luxury of a private bathroom and was planning a hot shower tonight before bed.

He wondered if Dee was still awake and whether he'd eaten.

Until recently, Dee and a roommate had shared a two-bedroom apartment on the east side. He'd dropped out of Portland State a couple of years earlier and had worked two jobs, saving up so he could back.

Then Dee got sick.

He said he wasn't surprised when the night sweats and weight loss began. In fact, he claimed it was almost a relief; the waiting had been as painful as the symptoms. He'd been able to hide it for a while, until the purple lesions appeared on his nose and at the corner of his mouth. "The mark of the beast," he said, laughing. But his eyes were furious as well as bereft.

Both jobs fired him. The roommate, whose name was on the lease, kicked him out. Dee's savings were magically transformed—poof!—into medical bills, motel rooms, medicines. Friends evaporated too; family broke away.

And although Crow didn't want to, he invited Dee to stay in his hole in the ground. They didn't love each other, and sharing a room was dangerous for reasons Crow could never explain to Dee. But alone was a terrible place to be when sick, when your own mortality was chasing you down, and Crow felt that if he turned away from Dee's desperate need, he'd shed whatever tiny bits of goodness remained in him.

Lately, Dee pretty much sat on the couch, wasting away and raging. He wrote letters and tore them up, the fragments of paper accumulating around him like bitter snowfall. It was mid-spring for the rest of Portland but late winter for him. For a few minutes every day, though, he'd talk with Crow and smile and make up funny lyrics to songs he'd heard on the radio.

Crow was thinking about that, how this morning when he'd awakened to Dee riffing off "Like a Virgin" and "Girls Just Wanna Have Fun," for one groggy moment Crow had thought that if loving Dee wasn't a possibility, perhaps some cousin of it was. *Close enough for government work*, Grandad used to say. Crow said it now in a low growl, a counterbeat to his footsteps as he walked between the pools of streetlight. When he turned the corner and saw the flashing lights parked in front of his house, he knew.

"No," he said, but like every prayer he'd ever uttered, it went unanswered.

He didn't immediately flee. Instead he lurked behind a

rhododendron and watched as men in blue uniforms milled around. Saw two men in a different uniform emerge through the basement door, carrying a shrouded figure on a stretcher. Nobody was in a hurry. When the ambulance pulled away a few minutes later, its lights and sirens were off.

Neighbors clustered nearby with arms crossed, watching. If not for the pajamas and coats, they might have been the audience at a theater.

More uniformed people went into the basement, maybe to puzzle over the red symbol that Crow knew would be scrawled on one wall. It would be a hieroglyph, a feather painted in still-wet blood. Crow wondered grimly if the artist had been aware of the risks of touching that blood.

"I'm sorry, Dee," Crow said from his hiding spot behind the bush. "You never even knew my real name."

That might be the only benediction Dee would receive.

Eyes stinging, Cliff Robertson melted into the darkness and was gone.

# CHAPTER 3

*M*areado, California
Four months later — August 1985

HE SLEPT NAKED, starfished on his back across the lumpy mattress, the bunched sheets beneath him. He'd been dreaming of rain lately, and of landscapes frozen in grays, whites, and dull browns. But once awake, he'd be swaddled in heat despite the swamp cooler wheezing hopelessly in the window.

He woke up slowly.

The original purpose of the little building that he rented had never been clear to him. It squatted at the far back of a weedy lot behind a small stucco house that had probably been built in the twenties. It might have been a garage, he supposed, or a workshop of some kind. Or maybe it was built to house the sort of relative that an owner didn't want under their roof.

The stucco on the exterior of Crow's building had been painted a pale ochre. A broken plastic chair sat on the tiny cement slab outside the front door. The structure inside was simple: a bare concrete floor, whitewashed walls, and a ceiling of wooden roof trusses. One window housed the swamp cooler and the other overlooked a rickety fence. There were a few basic pieces of furniture. No kitchen, although he did have a tiny refrigerator. He had a bathroom with toilet, sink, and jury-rigged shower but without hot water. At this time of year, he didn't miss it.

He got up slowly and stretched, then tried to remember whether there was anything to eat. With a slight lift of spirits, he realized it was his day off. He could grab a meal out, maybe from a taco truck, and go to the little market nearby. He might even walk downtown and spring for a movie at the Gem Theater. The old heap had seen far better days, but the AC worked just fine. Besides, it reminded him a bit of the Cairo, where he and Marty used to spend their scant pocket money. He wondered if the Cairo still existed.

A quick shower cooled him off, and Crow put on shorts, a T-shirt, and tennis shoes, grabbed his thin pile of disposable income, and ventured out into the oven.

One consequence of working the graveyard shift was that he slept until four in the afternoon even on his days off. That was the hottest part of the day here, the merciless sun hovering in a sky that hadn't produced a single drop of rain since Crow had arrived in late May. It was different than the humid summers of his childhood; this air baked you, the Midwest parboiled.

Few other people were foolish or desperate enough to be outside right now. Even the children were hidden away, likely transfixed by television screens as they sweated out the last days of their summer vacations. But the few pedestrians he passed gave him polite greetings. As a blue-eyed blond, Crow stood out in this neighborhood, just as he did in the tomato cannery where he worked. Everyone was cordial, however, and patient with his rudimentary attempts at Spanish.

As Crow ambled, he decided to skip the taco trucks, at least for now. He could have popcorn at the theater and grab something more substantial later. Or he could go to a bar and drink his dinner instead. But he stopped now at the market for a can of Coke to tide him over for the rest of the walk.

"Hello, Carey," said the woman behind the counter. In Mareado he was Carey Rhodes. She was Ximena—probably everywhere, not just in Mareado—and she always seemed pleased to see him. She and her husband owned the place, which also had a gas station and a few outdoor tables where patrons could sit and eat.

Crow crabbed a can from the nearby cooler and took it to the cash register. He set two quarters on the counter and waited for Ximena to give him a nickel in return, but he wasn't in any hurry to go back under the sun. "Cómo estás hoy?" he asked, because she had been helping him learn a few phrases.

She smiled. "Muy bien." Then, no doubt realizing she'd reached the limits of his linguistic abilities, she switched to English. "Are you on your way to work?"

"Nope. Day off."

"Oh, that's nice. You know, when it cools off a little, you should go to la feria."

Crow's chest became tight. He didn't know that word, but it sounded a lot like an English word he *did* know. "La feria?" he asked carefully.

"Yeah, the carnival. About half a mile west of here on Sloane Road. I think they're here for only one night, so you picked a good day to have off."

His hand was starting to crumple the can. He made an effort

to relax his fingers and the tight muscles around his mouth. Ximena was being friendly. She wouldn't know. Besides, this couldn't possibly be the same carnival—there must be dozens of the things across the country. Hundreds, even.

Crow knew better. He had a ruthless little place inside his brain that knew all the things he'd rather deny.

"Gracias," he said, hoping his voice didn't sound tight. He considered making another purchase, one of the cheap bottles of booze Ximena kept on the shelves behind the counter. But he'd spent a decade relying too heavily on that crutch. He'd stay sober tonight.

Outside, he drained his Coke in one long swallow, tossed the can into a trash bin, and headed east toward downtown. Definitely not west to Sloane Road.

The movie at the Gem was a comedy—or so he thought. After it was over, he remembered neither the title nor the plot, but he thought he might have laughed at some parts. The popcorn had been bits of Styrofoam and the Coke—his second of the day—had no taste at all. The longed-for air conditioning had instead raised goosebumps on his flesh and frozen his bones.

He left the theater and headed west as if chasing the setting sun. Delicate pinks and oranges tinged the sky like one of those paintings Mrs. Davis had shown in a vain attempt to bring a little culture to a classroom of fourteen-year-olds in rural Illinois. Back then, Crow had liked the paintings. He had thought that when he grew up he'd temporarily escape Chinkapin Grove and visit some art museums to see them in person. Aunt Helen had said there were some in Chicago. He'd escaped all right; he'd gone far beyond Chicago and the borders of Illinois. But he'd never seen any of those paintings.

On another night, in a better mood, he might have

concluded that the sky was just as good as pigments brushed on canvas, if not better.

The highway that ran like a north/south spine through Mareado separated the downtown and the middle-class neighborhoods from the cannery, auto shops, tire stores, and small machine shops on the west side. Walking the underpass beneath the highway was like crossing an international border into a much poorer nation that couldn't afford sidewalks, streetlights, or road repairs. The west side had residents who toiled hard but never prospered beyond the next month's rent. It had clusters of boys and young men who strove to look tough but mostly, Crow thought, looked sad, as if someone had broken a promise to them. It had old, rusted cars and trucks that spewed fumes as they rattled past; front yards encased in chain-link fences with barking dogs and plastic toys trapped inside; and bougainvillea running wild on front porches near little gardens with herbs, tomatoes, peppers, and sometimes even a few rows of corn.

Crow marched west, turned south to Sloane Road, and then west some more.

Dusty little houses like his landlord's grew farther apart, their backyards parched landscapes containing collapsed sheds and long-dead vehicles. Sometimes there were chickens; twice he saw goats. After several blocks, the houses gave way to hardscrabble little farms. He doubted anyone could make a living off these pieces of land, yet still people grew things.

He approached a long row of Italian cypresses running perpendicular to the road, cutting off his view of what lay beyond. They didn't stop the familiar sounds of delighted screams and blasting music. The same songs he'd heard a decade earlier, in fact. "Bennie and the Jets." "Killer Queen." "Sweet Home Alabama." "Witchy Woman." The traffic was heavier here, with cars rumbling slowly past him, their windows rolled down.

The space beyond the cypresses had, until recently, been a bean field; he could still spot a few scraggly, overgrown plants near the edge of the road. Now, though, there was the carnival, with a steady line of people heading toward the ticket booth from the improvised parking lot across the street. Couples and families and groups of teens and young adults laughed and chattered loudly. Although the sun was almost fully set by now, tall lights illuminated the area to an almost daytime level, making the colors seem unnaturally bright.

*Go home*, he told himself firmly. *Eat something. Drink yourself into a stupor. Sleep. Go to work tomorrow.* Rinse and repeat, until he was forced to leave this town and find a new depressing residence and a new mind-numbing job. Or until whoever had been chasing him for so long finally succeeded in destroying him.

"I'm still Crow Rapp," he said out loud. "In Mareado and everywhere else."

As he stood there, trapped in the amber of indecision, an unfamiliar emotion crept under his skin: anger. He was used to sadness, loneliness, boredom, exhaustion, fear, desperation, resignation. But this was entirely different. This had fangs and claws that wanted to burst from their hidden places to destroy the thing that had destroyed him. The *person* who had destroyed him.

Crow marched forward, steps heavy on the hard-packed soil.

He reached the ticket booth at a lull between other visitors and was somewhat surprised to discover a woman within. She was sharp-angled, her hair arranged in elaborate braids, a cigarette dangling between long, thin fingers.

"A dollar to get in and see the show." Her accent made

Crow think of palm-treed islands and music played on steel drums.

"Prices haven't changed?" Crow asked.

She held out a hand. "It's one dollar."

He pulled a bill from his shorts pocket and she waved him on.

The archway was still there, still painted red and white. *Welcome Traveler.* Ten years ago he'd scoffed at that. Back then, he'd never gone far beyond Joutel County. Ever since then, however, travel had been one of the few constants in his life, and now the sign fit perfectly.

The midway was exactly as he remembered it, with colored tents and signs advertising various attractions. The flow of people wasn't too different either. Sure, the clothing styles had changed and many of the conversations were in Spanish, but the essentials remained. These were people who rarely spent money on entertainment and who were hungry for a few hours tinged with magic and flavored with strange spices. And—speaking of spices—he could smell the enticing aroma of fried foods. He'd eaten nothing today but popcorn and found himself craving a giant corndog, a cardboard basket of fries smothered in cheese, and a cone topped by a tottering swirl of vanilla-and-chocolate soft serve.

But Crow didn't turn toward the food concessions. He didn't pause to watch the acrobats or see the world's strongest man. He had no interest in the carousel or the house of mirrors.

As he made his way toward the far end of the midway, a phalanx of clowns temporarily blocked his way. They were blowing bubbles, squeezing the rubber bulb on giant horns, twisting balloons into poodles and flamingos and handing them to delighted children. The clowns paid no attention to Crow, but he had the sense that they were aware of him and that their smiles and laughter were directed at him. Perhaps mockingly; perhaps not.

Finally the clowns moved away, only to be replaced by an ageless man even taller and thinner than Crow. He was dressed in spotless black and white and he examined Crow with an inscrutable expression.

"The future is unreliable," the man said in a soft voice that was almost like singing. "It's a matter of probabilities."

Crow remembered someone else telling him the same thing, and the anger surged again inside him. "I have no future. I'm here about the past."

The man shrugged. "It is so easy to misunderstand our own needs." And then he stepped aside.

As before, there were no people near the purple tent. Walking toward it brought a vivid case of déjà vu, except this time Crow carried an enormous burden. Back in Chinkapin Grove, he'd worried about ordinary, mundane horrors like being stuck on the farm forever, like falling in love with the wrong person, like poverty and rejection. He'd been so innocent.

After a few steadying breaths, Crow pushed aside the fabric door and stepped into the tent.

Someone stood with their back to him, head covered by a scarf that seemed bright even in the dim lighting. "Simeon," Crow said.

But even as the name left his throat, he knew it was wrong. And when the person turned around, it was not a handsome man with eyes like polished obsidian but instead a beautiful woman with generous curves.

"Ah," she said as if she'd expected him. She stepped to the larger table, flipped over a single card, and nodded. Looking up at him, she said, "The hanged man."

All Crow's confidence fled; he felt like a small child. "I-I'm sorry."

"Don't be. You haven't interrupted anything important."

"Are you Madame Persephone?"

Her laughter was rich. "Who else would I be? Would you like a divination?"

Shaking his head almost frantically, he backed toward the exit. "I was looking for someone."

"Simeon."

"He told me he was a roustabout. But that was a long time ago."

This brought more laughter, which he didn't understand although it didn't seem cruel. "This time in the evening you're likely to find him around the food concessions."

Crow's anger was still there, but uncertainty threatened to extinguish it. He mumbled a thank-you and made to leave.

"Crow?"

Keeping one hand on the fabric flap of the doorway, he turned to look at her. A large candle flickered on the table even though he felt no air movement against his skin. The shadows cast by the flame danced and leapt like living creatures along the tent walls. Looking at them made him dizzy, but it was hard to turn away.

"A soothsayer only *sees* the truth and perhaps tells about it, Crow. She doesn't create it."

He had no answer for that, so he simply nodded and left. He was a fair distance up the midway before he realized she'd used his name twice. A name he'd never told her and that nobody had called him in ten years.

HE WAS HUNGRY. He admitted that to himself as he skulked near the booths and trucks selling food. And after about thirty minutes he gave up on telling his stomach to stop chewing on itself and bought a sausage in a bun. It came with potato chips and a drink, all for a dollar, which couldn't possibly be enough to make the seller any profit. Until he took a bite, he'd almost forgotten how delicious food could taste. He devoured it quickly and bought another, and when that was gone he snacked on various deep-fried delicacies until his belly was rounded and tight and his fingers fragrant with grease and sugar, even after he wiped them clean with napkins.

Although he saw many people while he ate, including a few that he thought were probably roustabouts, he didn't see Simeon. Maybe Madame Persephone had lied. Not that she owed the truth to an irate stranger. Crow sighed and went to drop his last wad of napkins into a nearly overflowing trash can. When he tossed them in, however, they tumbled right back out again, so he bent, retrieved them, and dropped them in more carefully.

"Thank you, sir."

Crow spun around to find himself face-to-face with a black-haired man.

Simeon looked exactly as he had a decade earlier, except when Crow had first met him, Simeon had appeared older than him and more sophisticated by far. Now Simeon looked years younger than Crow. And God, still every bit as handsome.

Simeon still wore his shining hair tied back in a slightly messy tail. His short-sleeved cotton shirt seemed specially cut to show off his muscles and trim waist, just as his faded jeans displayed his rounded ass and long legs to advantage. He grinned the same grin, the one he'd worn the moment Crow first saw him. It was impersonal, an invitation he might send to anyone—and probably did—to join in his fun.

But then Simeon's eyes widened and his jaw dropped. "When is it?" he rasped.

That wasn't the response Crow had expected. "What?"

"The date. No, that won't help since I don't know.... How long has it been since you saw me, mate?"

"Ten years."

Simeon shook his head slightly. "But it's been three months since I saw you."

That didn't make any sense. But neither did a lot of other things in Crow's life, and he was almost accustomed to it. Still, he hadn't come here to solve temporal mysteries. He curled his hands into hard fists and spoke through clenched teeth. "What did you do to me, you son of a bitch?"

Crow had expected Simeon to respond with similar aggression or to at least become defensive. Instead, those corvid eyes filled with sadness and compassion. "Oh, love, I'm sorry."

"You're fucking *sorry*? Do you know—"

Simeon gently settled a hand on Crow's shoulder. "Let's go discuss this somewhere quieter, yeah?"

Giving a quick glance around, Crow remembered that other people were here. Children. Locals just wanting to spend a few hours having fun and forgetting about their burdens. Crow had already brought pain to far too many people: his family, Dee, the middle-aged couple he'd rented a room from in Dayton, and.... Too many.

So Crow gave a stiff nod and followed Simeon away from the food carts, across the midway, and into a shadowed area well behind the big top. A collection of vehicles was parked there, and although it was hard to discern details in the dark, Crow was confused by what he saw. Several semis, a few big busses, a handful of RVs and trailers, a lot of smaller trucks, some cars, and... enclosed wagons? In fact, Simeon led him to one of those wagons, where a single lantern hung over the door at one end, revealing elaborately carved wood painted scarlet and gold. The wagon had large wheels with many spokes, and there was some sort of yoke thing at the far end that Crow supposed was used to hitch it to… what? Surely this couldn't be towed on a highway.

Simeon climbed four steps, opened the door, and gestured at Crow to follow. But Crow hesitated. "What is this?"

"My home, of course. Nicest place I've ever lived. Come in and see."

Maybe this time Simeon would do more than forecast doom—maybe he'd simply slit Crow's throat. Crow wasn't sure whether that would do the trick, but he wasn't eager to find out. On the other hand, it turned out that he *was* curious about the interior of the wagon.

With much trepidation and very little common sense, Crow followed Simeon inside.

# CHAPTER 4

*T*he interior of Simeon's wagon was like a well-organized acid trip. Hanging lanterns provided warm illumination on carved wooden walls and on a ceiling painted in a variety of crayon-box colors. A raised bed at the far end of the wagon sat atop a storage space, the mattress covered in richly embroidered blankets. Another bed, mounted near the ceiling on the left, had a wooden bench beneath it, inset with silk brocade. Well-worn Persian carpets layered the painted floor, and shelves and clever little cabinets were tucked in everywhere.

"Lovely, isn't it?" Simeon said proudly. "I share with only one other bloke—another roustabout, named Pete. All this luxury for just the two of us, and I've been with the carnival for less than six months."

It was nicer than anyplace Crow had lived as an adult, but he wouldn't have called it luxurious. He wondered about Simeon's background, to judge the space so generously. But that was another mystery he was not here to solve.

Simeon walked to the far corner and began doing something, but his body blocked Crow's view. Crow tensed until

Simeon turned, smiled, and waved a blue-and-white teapot. "Fancy some tea?"

"I— No."

"Suit yourself. I'll have some, though. A carnival is thirsty work, you know. Loads of hauling things here and there, and the air's dusty. Not that I'm bothered, mind you. It's honest work and I'm treated well. I meet interesting people. The dosh is only so-so, but I don't need much, not with room and board provided."

Crow stood awkwardly, feeling entirely out of place while Simeon puttered around as if this were a pleasant social call and they might pay a visit to the queen when they were done. After filling a delicate-looking cup—and offering some to Crow again—Simeon sprawled on the brocade bench. Because the wagon was somewhat narrow and his legs were so long, his feet nearly touched the cabinet built into the opposite wall. "You can sit, you know. You look as if you've been walking for some time."

Which of course Crow had; the theater was over three miles away. But Simeon's assessment didn't require prognostication, because Crow's shoes and lower legs were dusty and his shoulders sagged slightly with fatigue. He remained standing and pinned Simeon with a steady gaze.

"What did you do to me?" he growled.

Looking deeply unhappy, Simeon set his teacup on a nearby shelf. "Wasn't my doing, mate. I'll admit I was in the wrong. I messed about with Madame Persephone's things when I ought not to have done, and I teased you a bit when you were… too young. Too unready, I expect. But I didn't think I'd truly foresee anything. Certainly not—" He broke off and looked away, the corners of his mouth tight.

"You did something to me."

"I didn't. Your future was already there. I didn't create it. I haven't that power."

"Why didn't you tell me what you saw?" That came out more anguished than Crow had intended.

Simeon sighed. "I didn't know how set that future was. I'm no expert on any of this. I was afraid that if I told you, then you'd do things to put those events in motion."

"You thought I wanted those things?" This time the question was a roar, and Crow moved a few feet closer, almost looming over Simeon.

"No, no. I never thought that. But self-fulfilling prophesies, yeah?" Simeon stood and reached slightly toward Crow, palms up, as if pleading for understanding.

"I would have stopped it. I would have done something. They're dead! Do you understand that? They're all dead because of me and because of you!"

"No, mate." Simeon shook his head. "I've done loads of things I'm ashamed of now, but you can't lay this weight on me. Your destiny would have happened regardless, even if we'd never met."

"I have free will." But even as he said this, Crow wasn't sure he believed it.

"We all do, but within limits. I can't will myself to be a bird and fly away, although Christ knows that when I was younger, I wished I could. You can't will yourself to be other than what you are either."

"I don't fucking know what I am!" Crow surged forward and pushed Simeon hard, sending him staggering back. His elbow hit the teacup, which flew off the shelf and landed on the rug, hot liquid sinking into its surface. Simeon lost his balance and fell, bashing his head against the wooden edge of the bench. The impact was shockingly noisy inside the small wagon.

Everything was still and silent, like a crime scene photo: a smear of scarlet on the wood, Simeon staring up at Crow.

A small voice spoke inside Crow's head. It was a familiar

voice because it was his own. *This is what you are. This is what you do.* He could embrace that identity, could be a predator instead of prey. He would be powerful. Feared. Not a bird who flew away again and again, but one who would dive in and grip with dagger talons, tear with knifelike beak. He could choose this.

Or he could choose otherwise.

Crow fell to his knees beside Simeon. "I'm sorry. My God, I'm so sorry. Is there a doctor here? Do you have a phone?"

Simeon blinked at him a few times before slowly sitting up. He pressed a palm to the back of his head, winced, and looked at the bright blood on his pale skin. And then, shockingly, he managed a small smile. "I'll be fine."

"But—"

When Simeon made an effort to stand, Crow scrambled to his feet and offered a hand. Simeon's skin was warm, and some of his blood must have transferred to Crow's palm, which was only fitting. But once he regained his footing, Simeon didn't let go, staring intently into Crow's eyes. "You're strong," he finally said.

"I'm sorry. I didn't mean—" Crow stopped himself, unsure whether he'd be lying if he finished the sentence. He swallowed. "You're hurt." Well, that was inane.

"I've a hard head. It's been knocked about worse than this. Didn't make me any wiser but I doubt it's done much harm."

"You don't have to be so forgiving about it."

"I'm the forgiving type."

And God, even with his hair mussed and his head bleeding, Simeon was so goddamn beautiful that Crow wanted to cry.

After a long moment, Simeon gave Crow's hand a gentle squeeze, as if Crow were the one who needed comforting. "I'm going to fetch some water and ice, get myself sorted. You'll wait here, yeah?"

"You could call the police."

Simeon laughed. "That's unlikely on several counts, mate. The coppers and I aren't really on speaking terms. Just... stay. Please."

Crow didn't make any promises, but after Simeon hurried out the door, Crow didn't leave. He picked up the teacup and put it back on the shelf, and then he found a small towel and knelt to dab up the spill. He wiped the blood from the bench as well, and then worried that the towel would be stained. As if, in the larger scheme of things, that mattered.

Simeon returned only a few minutes later, an ice pack held to the back of his skull. He seemed relieved that Crow was still there, which was a mystery; he should have wanted Crow far away. But no, he poured tea again, this time two cups without asking, and he explained cheerfully that minor injuries were common among roustabouts and there was always a first aid kit somewhere nearby. "You'd think it was the performers who got hurt, yeah? Throwing knives, swallowing fire, spinning through the air. But I've never seen it. My mates and I, though, we collect bumps and bruises and scrapes like postage stamps."

He sat on the bench and gestured Crow to follow suit. Crow couldn't refuse, nor could he say no to the little china cup filled with fragrant liquid.

"I hope you don't take milk and sugar," Simeon said. "I haven't any."

"I... no."

They were sitting close, Simeon angled slightly toward him and Crow facing dead ahead. His hand was big and awkward. His tongue was tied. Honestly, he was unused to conversations, especially with someone he'd recently attacked.

Simeon, on the other hand, seemed as comfortable as if

they were chatting at a garden party. "I have some biscuits, I think, if you'd fancy some."

"I'm not hungry."

"That's right, you were at the food concessions earlier. Did you try some of Tam Wakefield's jam doughnuts? Those are bloody brilliant."

Crow started to answer and stopped himself. "Why are you being so nice to me?"

"Dunno. I reckon somebody ought to."

Simeon set down his teacup. He had set down the ice pack before pouring the tea, and now he touched it to his head for a moment, winced, and shrugged. He tossed the pack aside and spent a few fascinating moments straightening his hair into a neat ponytail. Finally, he sighed. "Do you want to know what I saw?"

"What about self-fulfilling prophesies?"

"Bit late to worry about that, innit?"

That was true enough. Crow gave a little huff, then drank some tea and leaned back with his eyes closed. As if that would somehow protect him. "Okay, yes."

"I'm not Madame Persephone. Never had a vision before yours, hope I never have one again. I don't know if it came to me because I was messing about in her tent, with her things, or if it was some sort of...." He waved a hand between himself and Crow. "Dunno. Synergy. I used to be a thief, you know."

"You mentioned that."

Simeon grinned as if pleased that Crow remembered. "Yeah. Bloody good one. Perhaps I stole some of Madame Persephone's talent, just for a few seconds. By accident."

"Is it theft if it's accidental?"

"Ah, mens rea! Criminal intent. Had a solicitor explain that to me once, when I was a boy. Said I was too young to have any. Judge didn't agree."

Now Crow wanted to ask about that: why Simeon had stolen something when so young, what had happened to him because of it, and how he'd ended up as a roustabout instead. But Crow hadn't come here tonight to gather Simeon's biography. "What did you see?"

"Death."

"Details."

"I saw flames reaching tall into a jewel-box sky. Poison flowing invisible into a house through the vents. Bullets shattering first a window and then the man inside. A blade dripping red. And I saw you."

Crow gripped the teacup so hard that he feared he might break it. He tried to loosen his muscles, but everything inside him was as tight and tense as if one of the carnival clowns had filled him with air and was twisting him into a poodle shape before handing him to a child. "You saw me killing people."

"No."

Crow whipped his head to the side, incredulous. "You did."

"I saw you burnt. Gasping for air. Riddled with holes. Bleeding. I saw you escape those deaths by sprouting feathers and flapping away, but you were red, not black like your namesake. It was the most horrible thing I've ever seen, and believe me, I've seen horrors. You were alone, again and again."

Crow let out a long, reedy breath that wanted to transform into a sob. He didn't let it. "Did you see *why*?"

"No, mate. That's the problem with fortune-telling. Like those oracles in the old Greek stories, yeah? Forever nattering on about things without being bloody clear about what they meant. Prophecies as riddles. I think the whole mess raises more questions than it answers. You know, those

Greek tragedies happened when men attempted to escape their fates. I saw *your* tragedy, but not the reason for it."

Of course there were no answers. Crow shouldn't have expected any, and Simeon certainly didn't owe them anyway. Crow's existence wasn't so much a tragedy as a farce. A man keeps thinking he can escape his destiny. He runs away, tries to hide. Goes to big cities and tiny towns all over the country. Changes his name. But always his destiny finds him. And then the man tries again, lesson unlearned. Isn't that hilarious?

"Crow? Are you all right?"

Laughter tasted bitter, like nasty medicine, so Crow chased it with some tea. "I am not all right. But that's not your problem. I'm sorry for... everything. I'll go."

He started to stand, but Simeon pushed him firmly back into his seat. "By my calculations, you owe me a story, mate. Ten years, you say. You can pay me with just a bit of that."

Crow had never told anyone truths about himself. Not even his name. But maybe Simeon was right—maybe he did owe something. In compensation for hurting him today. In exchange for a cup of warm tea and a little sympathetic companionship.

"All right," Crow said slowly. "You want a bit of me? Here's the most essential piece: I don't think I'm human."

# CHAPTER 5

*S*imeon left the wagon for about fifteen minutes, saying he had to tell his boss he'd be indisposed for a while. "Boss won't mind. While the locals are here, that's a quiet time for roustabouts. It's the before and after when we're kept hopping." He returned with two bottles of beer and a paper plate of doughnuts. "Sustenance."

Why did Crow feel so comfortable in this very strange place, with this very strange man? Why did Simeon's wagon feel more like home than anywhere Crow had lived for the past ten years? A delusion, no doubt. An attempt by his mind to calm him before he shared—for no rational reason—his most essential secret.

The beer was a brand that Crow had never heard of, and it tasted so good that he moaned after his first swallow. It made him remember the first beer he'd ever had, pilfered and consumed with Marty inside Marty's family barn one hot summer evening. They'd been thirteen years old. After the beer was gone, they lay on a patch of lawn and stared up at the stars. For an hour or so, Crow had believed that all kinds of things were possible.

Now Simeon sat beside him, nibbling on a donut and not saying a word, as if all of this were totally ordinary and completely expected.

"How's your head?" Crow asked.

"Good as it ever was. Don't worry—I've been beaten much worse than that."

Thinking of Simeon being beaten bothered Crow, which was stupid considering he'd been the most recent abuser. And then Crow realized that spitting out his tale wouldn't be any easier if he postponed it any longer, so he drained the bottle and set it aside.

"I don't think I'm human. At least not entirely."

Simeon, after waiting a moment for an explanation and not getting one, asked, "Why not?"

"You don't think it's a weird thing to say? Or that I must be crazy?"

Simeon shrugged. "Not much for judging others, yeah? I expect you've a good reason for thinking this, and I'm curious to know what it is."

It wasn't a single reason at all, really, but rather a stack of them. Like the evidence Perry Mason had collected every Thursday night when Crow was a kid, although this case wasn't going to end with a falsely accused suspect going free.

"When I was in Chinkapin Grove, I never really felt like I belonged. Even though I'd spent almost my whole life there. I used to figure that was on account of my mother. My grandparents adopted her when she was a baby, so she was sort of an outsider too. She was real smart, though. Graduated high school when she was only sixteen, and when my grandparents didn't pay for her to go to college—don't know if that was a wouldn't or couldn't—she ran off to Chicago. Got a job at a department store. She came back to Chinkapin Grove two years later with a newborn son. Wouldn't say who the father was. Left the baby with her parents, ran away, and…."

He made a gesture with his hands as if he were a magician performing a disappearing act in one of the carnival tents.

"She disappeared?"

"She sent envelopes with money orders for a few months, I guess to help pay my keep. Then the envelopes stopped."

"You don't know what happened to her?"

"Maybe my grandparents knew something, but they refused to talk about her. Anyway, everyone in town knew I was a bastard whose mother had abandoned him, so I figured that was reason enough to feel different. And then when I was older, I realized"—even after all this time it was still hard to say the next part out loud—"well, I realized I was queer."

Simeon didn't shy away or look appalled. In fact, he nodded slowly. "Yeah. Where I come from, that could get you hanged."

"Well, I don't think anyone would've hung me if they'd known, but they sure wouldn't have been happy about it. So I didn't tell a soul. But *I* knew. It made me feel like a freak, like there was something fundamentally wrong with me. And there was, but that wasn't it."

He hadn't imagined that Simeon would be such a good listener, intent on Crow's words and expressions, willing to wait patiently when Crow paused. Shit. He knew nothing about this man aside from a few details that didn't seem important just now. Crow was positive that Simeon had a fascinating backstory, and he found himself wishing that he could learn it. And that was interesting too, because Crow was usually so caught up in his own story that he gave little thought to anyone else's.

To gain courage for the next part, Crow ate a donut. There was something almost unbearably innocent about its sticky sweetness.

"The night we met for the first time, I ran home and buried myself under the covers, like a little kid hiding from the bogeyman. Freaked out my friends a little because I was supposed to meet back up with them at the carnival and I never showed. When I saw them next, I lied. Told them I had been feeling sick. I pretended like that night never happened."

And the pretense had worked, more or less, when he was awake. When he slept, however, he dreamed about the carnival. Sometimes about Simeon specifically. Crow would wake up from those fitful sleeps achingly hard, and he'd jerk off while imagining what silky black hair would feel like as it brushed against his skin. In a way, those nights had been worse than the ones with the nightmares, because they left him feeling dirty. Sinful.

"I was waiting," Crow admitted in a whisper. "Every day, like my head was in a guillotine and knowing the blade was going to drop… eventually. I pulled away from my friends because I couldn't stand to face them. They didn't understand why. I think I hurt them." It was only one transgression among many, but it weighed heavily. He and Marty had been best friends since first grade, and Julie was a sweet girl who deserved much better than Crow, or at least deserved an explanation. But what could Crow have said?

"You were trying to protect them," Simeon said.

A hint of relief ran through Crow's bloodstream, like the first warm breeze of spring. Simeon understood. "I was afraid if I stayed close to them, something horrible would happen." And more than that, he was certain that he wasn't worthy of them. "But I didn't move away from my grandparents."

"You were still a child."

"Bullshit. I was almost eighteen. My mother was sixteen when she left, remember? I could have run away. But I was too fucking scared."

"It's terrifying to be completely on one's own." Simeon

said this with the authority of personal experience, and again Crow wondered what paths Simeon had wandered in his life.

Crow looked down at his own hands, folded neatly in his lap as if in preparation for prayer. "There was a fire." That phrasing was passive and almost benign. A fire was where you and your fellow Boy Scouts cooked hot dogs and s'mores. It was a place where you gathered with other high school students after a football game, knowing the cops would pretend not to notice your illicit beers as long as everyone behaved reasonably well. It was a cozy flickering in the living room fireplace, the mantel above displaying photos of you and your aunt (but not your mother; never her) while the aroma of a chicken dinner lingered in the air.

Also, the statement was a lie, because another event had happened first. And if Crow had reacted appropriately—not that he knew what that meant, even now—perhaps the fire would never have happened.

Simeon's expression was open, expectant, and Crow lurched to his feet. What the hell was he doing here, and why was he spilling his guts to this stranger? He moved toward the door, but Simeon was lightning-quick and bolted to block his way.

"Will running away again solve anything?" Simeon asked.

"Will telling you?"

When Simeon shrugged, Crow very nearly hit him again. Then he uncurled his tight fists. "Let me go," he growled.

After a moment, Simeon shrugged again and stepped aside. There wasn't much room in the narrow trailer, so when Crow reached to open the door, their bodies brushed. An electric thrill coursed through Crow's nervous system, but he shook it off and rushed down the steps. He didn't look back.

The darkness outside seemed to contain a maze of vehicles. He got lost, which was stupid. The rides were nearby; he could hear the music and the screams. But no matter which way he turned, his route dead-ended in a semi trailer or RV or a painted wagon similar to Simeon's. He felt high or drunk, despite having consumed only a single beer. He felt as if he were floating above the carnival in the cooling night air, watching his little body bounce this way and that like a pinball. He felt as if he'd been living in a dream—or a nightmare—for a decade and had just now realized it.

Finally he stumbled out into the midway. It was later than he'd thought, and now there were few young children among the visitors. Groups of teenagers, yes, and pairs of lovers, every person with a gleam in their eyes that suggested they were experiencing something remarkable. Something they would remember for the rest of their lives.

And why shouldn't they? Crow had certainly remembered his first visit to the carnival. That one evening, those few minutes in Madame Persephone's tent, felt more real and more vivid than anytime before or since. It was etched into his brain like a tattoo. Although he had no ink on his skin, he said aloud, "I'm the tattooed man!" But nobody heard him.

He made it almost to the ticket booth before he stopped and turned around.

Of course he couldn't find his way back to Simeon's wagon. Simeon probably wasn't even there anymore; he'd likely gone back to work. Which meant he could be anywhere. Crow wandered around, seeking him out although he didn't understand why.

Crow was standing outside a green tent, feeling more exhausted than he should have, when a dog appeared. Medium-sized, with a coat like Marty's old golden retriever, the dog looked at Crow expectantly.

"I don't have any food," Crow said.

Could dogs roll their eyes impatiently? This one seemed to. He then gave a single hoarse bark that sounded almost like a word—"Come!"—and trotted down the midway. Bemused, Crow followed.

Behind the carousel, a group of workers sorted through a stack of metal pipes, although Crow couldn't discern their objective. A slender man with a mustache seemed to be issuing instructions, but Crow couldn't hear his voice over the calliope music. What mattered most, however, was that one of the men was Simeon, and when he glanced up and saw Crow, he stopped what he was doing. He nodded at the dog—who barked again before trotting away—exchanged a few words with his supervisor, and sauntered over.

"Second thoughts, or have you decided you ought to hit me again?"

"I didn't hit you. I pushed."

"And I expect that's an important distinction."

Crow scowled. "Thank you. For the donuts and the beer and the tea." And the patience and forgiveness and willingness to listen.

"I'll listen to the rest, you know. Can't give you solutions, but it might feel better to say it out loud to someone."

"You don't have to be nice to me. I'm an asshole."

Simeon grinned. "And we're both bastards. Anyway, I'm always a sucker for a story, even when the bloke telling it is a bloody tosser." He stepped close and whispered in Crow's ear, making Crow shiver. "Tell me why you don't think you're human. You've been a terrible tease."

Fair enough, Crow supposed. "Here?"

"No. Come with me."

Crow expected to be led back to the wagon, and he wouldn't have minded that. But this time when Simeon took him into the darkness, they ended up in an empty space behind the haunted house. The front of the attraction was painted with ghosts, giant spiderwebs, and dancing skeletons, but the back was plain wood and metal. Shrieks came from inside but only dimly, and there was so little light here that Simeon had to grab Crow's wrist and tug him over to a pair of sturdy crates, where they sat. This was the edge of the carnival, apparently, but Crow couldn't see what lay beyond. A fence? An empty field? A row of trees? Or simply... nothing.

"My eighteenth birthday was the October after I met you." Crow began speaking without preamble or hesitation, letting the words flow before he got scared again and stopped them. "October tenth. It was a Monday, so I would have been in school, but it was also Columbus Day so we were off. Usually I'd be up early to do chores, but Gran said I could sleep late as a special treat." That had been his only gift aside from a couple of T-shirts. He hadn't minded; he knew money was tight.

"I woke up early anyway because I had a terrible dream." He couldn't make out Simeon's expression in the dim light, which made this easier. "But it wasn't really a dream." He had to take several deep breaths before he could go on.

"I slept in the attic. I didn't have to—there were a couple of empty bedrooms below—but the attic was bigger. And the window gave me a view out over the fields even when the corn was tall. It was like standing at the bow of a ship, gazing out over the ocean. You know how the sky looks just before dawn, indigo with the thinnest strip of orange? That's when I sat up in bed and saw three birds fly in through my window. It had been cold the night before, almost cold enough for frost, so I'd closed that window before I went to sleep. But now it was open and the birds flew in."

"Crows?" Simeon's voice was soft, like a flannel blanket.

"No. Yes. I don't know. They looked like crows, except they were red instead of black. Dark red, like old blood. I sat up in bed, trying hard not to scream, and they landed on the floor beside me. Then they weren't birds anymore. They were… people?" He thought of a term he'd read when he went through a sci-fi phase as a kid. "Humanoid, but not human. Tall and thin and bald, wearing cloaks made of those dried-blood-colored feathers. I don't know if they were male or female. Or something else."

His heart had risen up in his chest at the sight, blocking his throat and making it hard to breathe. His limbs were boiled-noodle weak; he couldn't have stood if he'd tried. For the first time since he'd been very young, he was dangerously close to wetting his bed.

"I think they all spoke at once, but I'm not sure. 'Join us,' they said. It sounded more like bird cries than speech. And the weird thing—well, it was all fucking weird, wasn't it?—was that I didn't ask who they were. I wasn't even surprised to see them, not in my heart of hearts. I'd been expecting them, I guess."

"Since you'd met me."

There was a note of bitterness there, so Crow reached out blindly until he touched Simeon's arm. He squeezed it. "No, before that. My whole life, in fact."

"Ah."

"I had no idea what they were. I still don't. But I *did* know that they were…." He tasted the word for a moment on the tip of his tongue and wasn't sure it was the right one. But he couldn't find better. "Evil."

Crow didn't admit to the rest of what he knew that early morning: that if he obeyed their command, he would finally and indisputably belong somewhere. No more isolation, ever. And Jesus Christ, that had tempted him so badly, even though he'd been aware of what joining them would do to him.

"So you said no?" Simeon asked.

"I said no."

"That was bloody brave of you."

"No." It hadn't been bravery that made him refuse but rather a hard core of self-preservation. He'd never valued himself much, but he didn't want to lose what worth he had. "But I did say no, and they were furious. Hissing noises. I could see little sparks in the air around them. 'You will take your proper place among us. Until you do, death will come to those who are close to you.' Then they were birds again, and they flew at me with their talons and sharp beaks. They left my face and arms bleeding. They flew out the window and were gone."

That hadn't been the end of it. It was just the beginning, in fact. But Crow gasped for air as he remembered the stinging scratches, some of which had barely missed his eyes. Gran had asked him about them over breakfast, and he'd mumbled some excuse that he couldn't remember now and that she couldn't possibly have believed. But she'd let the subject drop, perhaps chalking it up to boyhood mischief or the unsolvable mysteries of teenage boys.

"I couldn't go back to sleep after that. I helped Grandad with the chores, and he thought it was on account of me finally discovering responsibility now that I was an adult. After that, it was a pretty ordinary day."

On previous birthdays, Crow had hung out with Marty, but now they were barely speaking to each other, although sometimes Marty gazed at him across a classroom with bewildered hurt in his eyes. Crow spent his eighteenth birthday reading a book—the title of which he no longer remembered—and tinkering with the old Ford truck Grandad said he could have if Crow could ever get it running. Crow didn't know much about vehicles and wasn't especially good with them; that was Marty's forte. But since there was no more Marty, Crow banged around with a wrench on the principle that he couldn't make the truck any worse.

That night Gran made some of Crow's favorite foods and served a chocolate cake for dessert. Grandad told him he was growing into a fine young man. "You'll have a family soon, Crow, and the farm will be yours. Maybe you'll make a better go of it than I did."

After dinner they'd sat in the living room and watched the Bears beat the Rams while Gran worked on her basket of mending. And then they all went to bed.

Dragging his mind back to the present, Crow realized that he'd been silent for a long time and that Simeon still waited beside him. "There was a fire." The words carried as much weight this second time. "That night. I woke up and... smoke and flames everywhere. I couldn't find the stairs leading out of the attic. My eyes burned. I couldn't breathe. I was.... It *hurt*. I couldn't even think. I was just battering myself against things, desperate to escape. I fell. I think through the window. I landed hard on the ground below, with glass and broken things inside me and my skin blistered and my lungs a furnace and I was blind and deaf and I....." Crow took a deep, whooping breath that made him cough as if he were still expelling smoke.

"And?" Simeon asked after a full minute.

"And then I felt myself coming back together. Like Gran mending a tear on Grandad's sleeve. I was between the house and the barn, only there wasn't much left of the house by then. Just flames and charred wood and ashes. I screamed for my grandparents, but I knew the truth. They were gone. I was standing there naked, and there was a red feather laying at my feet.

"The fire department showed up, along with a lot of neighbors. Somebody wrapped me in a blanket. The police were asking questions and I don't know how I answered. I guess I was in shock. After a while, Aunt Helen took me to her place and gave me some of her husband's clothes to wear.

She must have been falling apart too, but she looked after me, putting me in their spare bedroom and telling me to get some sleep. Instead I waited until she left the house—back to the farm, probably, dealing with the aftermath—and I ran. Haven't seen her or Chinkapin Grove since."

Crow fell quiet. A small night creature rustled through dry grass not far away, and then there was a very brief high-pitched squeal. A sad event, he supposed, but it also meant that a predator would eat tonight. A death like that he could understand, but he could never wrap his mind around the senseless ones that brought no benefit, only shattering loss.

"I don't know what words of comfort to offer you," Simeon said after a while.

"There aren't any." And then, because he might as well finish the tale, he continued. "Ever since then, if I stay anywhere long enough to care about someone, they die. I've often been with them when it happened, but every time I've survived. I've been poisoned. Shot. Stabbed. Hit by a car while crossing a street. It hurts like fuck each time, but I heal almost immediately and walk away, while whoever I was with stays dead. I've wandered all over the country. I change my name, but it doesn't matter. They find me."

"Are you tempted to give in and join them?"

"Always," Crow sighed. "It would be so much easier."

"Why don't you?"

That was an excellent question. It wasn't courage or strong morals. It wasn't even fear, because he was already good friends with that emotion. "My grandparents... they weren't perfect. But they did the best they could for me. I can't become the thing that murdered them."

"Ah. Loyalty, then."

Crow kicked his heel against the crate. "More likely just stupidity."

"Have you made any effort to find out if there's a way to stop them?"

"Who the hell would I ask about something like that?" Crow shouted. "People would just tell me I'm nuts. When I saw the carnival was here tonight, I hoped you'd have answers."

Simeon answered calmly. "I don't."

"Nobody fucking does!"

"Except your mother."

Once again Crow very nearly punched Simeon. The only thing that stopped him was the darkness. And the fact that Simeon was right.

"My mother," Crow spat.

"Your name can't be an accident."

Crow snorted. "No, it's a totally obvious name for a blue-eyed blond. And did I tell you my last name?"

"No." Simeon paused for a moment. "But I know it, don't I? It came to me as part of that horrible bloody vision. Rapp."

Amid all the other terrors ten years ago, Crow hadn't even noticed that Simeon had used his full name. "The Chinkapin Public Library had this book, *Surnames and Their Meanings*. I looked up Rapp once, when I was thirteen or fourteen." He'd snuck between the shelves to do it, obscurely feeling as if he were looking at illustrations of naked men in the anatomy books or reading the racy parts of romance novels. The research had felt somehow disloyal to his grand-parents, whose last name was Storey.

"Don't keep me in suspense, mate."

"It's German. One of its meanings is *raven*."

"Ah."

Crow gave a bitter laugh that, truth be told, sounded a lot like one of his namesakes. "I thought it was some weird joke of mom's. Or a sign that she was crazy."

"But perhaps it was a message."

Rage momentarily sparked red at the edges of Crow's vision. "Not one I can understand. Not one that would make sense to *anyone*. She couldn't have just left me a fucking note? Or, I don't know, stuck around to explain it to me?" What he meant was, *to protect me.*

"She might have had reasons."

"Reasons," Crow scoffed. "She knew what I was and so she didn't want me. She abandoned me."

"But she didn't dump you in a ditch, did she? Or leave you at a foundling home. She took you to your grandparents, a place she knew was safe because it had been safe for her."

Crow didn't want to hear a defense of his mother, even though what Simeon said made sense. He wanted to be angry, to cherish his grudge as if it were something precious. "Then she's responsible for their deaths too. It doesn't matter anyway. She disappeared and took the meaning of her stupid message with her, and that's the end of it."

He leapt to his feet. "This was all pointless. Everything is. And if I spend more time with you, I'll probably end up hitting you again."

"A lot of people have. I've a talent for attracting fists." Simeon stood too, then moved so close that his warm, sweet-scented breaths puffed against Crow's face. "But I'm often lucky and attract something else instead."

It was hard to tell from Simeon's voice whether he was joking or flirting. Even if Crow could have seen his expression, it wouldn't have helped. And even if Simeon was flirting and Crow understood him correctly, Crow wouldn't have known his own mind. It was as if they were in the House of Mirrors, where everything was infinitely reflected and the truth was impossible to sort out.

Simeon settled things—from his perspective, at any rate—by grasping Crow's forearms, tugging him nearer, and kissing him. His grip wasn't hard; Crow could easily have pulled away. But he didn't. Because it turned out that the contact settled his own desires too, at least in part, and it turned out that he'd been aching for this kiss all evening. Hell, he'd been wanting it for ten years, and every other kiss in the interim had been a pale imitation of what he truly desired.

Eventually Simeon moved his lips away, but only so he could whisper in Crow's ear. "Stay, Crow Rapp. There's room for you in my bunk. Pete won't mind. I'm certain Mr. Ame could offer you a position of some kind."

It felt like hope. The first glimmer of hope that Crow had experienced since the fire. But much quicker than those flames had died, the emotion was doused, leaving him with the bitter taste of ashes. "I told you what happens to anyone I get close to."

"It wouldn't happen here at the carnival. It couldn't."

Simeon sounded so certain, and Crow wanted to believe him. God, he'd sell whatever soul he possessed for a safe haven. For… a friend. But Simeon himself had admitted that he had seen the future only that one time, and Crow couldn't risk bringing disaster to another person's door.

"I have to go," Crow said and squirmed out of Simeon's gentle grip.

"It's not likely you'll encounter the carnival again."

"I know."

Silence lay between them, and the helplessness of dreams.

Crow turned and walked toward the sounds of the midway, and Simeon didn't follow.

But Crow paused just before stepping around the curve of the Big Top and into the lights and sounds. "What's your last name?" he called into the darkness, not sure whether he'd receive a response.

A voice came to him as if from very far away. "I'm Simeon Bell."

A bell could be a warning or a summons. It could celebrate a wedding or mourn a death. It could be a call to arms. Or it could be nothing but a pleasant chime, a small distraction from life's daily cares.

"Goodbye, Simeon Bell," Crow whispered before turning back toward the midway.

# CHAPTER 6

*C*row very nearly left Mareado the next morning. He went so far as to shove his few belongings into a backpack and open the door. But then he stood there, seeing nothing but blinding morning light and feeling the promise of heat. He couldn't move. If he made it as far as the sidewalk, he'd be frozen forever, with no idea where to go next.

So after a few moments he turned and went back inside.

He spent the day in a stupor on his bed, not moving and not sleeping. Not thinking. He watched a line of ants make its steady way from the windowsill, across the wall, and into the corner behind the dresser. He listened to the swamp cooler wheeze like a dying man. He ignored his hunger and thirst.

When the time came, he stood, stripped, and took a shower. He didn't feel the cold water, although it gave him goosebumps. He got dressed and ate something out of the refrigerator, immediately forgetting what it had been. He took a few breaths and tried to settle his brain into the correct grooves for a night at the cannery. He stepped outside onto his tiny porch.

Simeon sat on the plastic chair, waiting.

All of the oxygen fled Crow's lungs in a noisy bark.

Simeon wore jeans and a simple buttoned shirt, his hair in a neat tail down his back, but he was as incongruous in this place as a pterodactyl or a Martian. In fact, Crow now realized he'd harbored the implicit odd notion that Simeon couldn't exist outside the confines of the carnival, as if he were a kind of mirage.

Crow tried to ask several questions at once, the words melding together into an interrogative squawk that raised a familiar grin from Simeon.

"You sleep late." Simeon stood and stretched as if he'd been on the chair for a long time.

"Graveyard shift. How... how are you here?"

"Madame Persephone, of course. That woman's a treasure, she is. Course, she didn't give me your precise address, but I got enough clues to suss out where you live."

That answered the *how* well enough but not the bigger question, which Crow was afraid to ask. Especially when he noticed the small duffel bag lying near Simeon's feet. And Simeon, damn him, didn't seem inclined to help him out. He simply stood there on the little porch, the afternoon sun picking up glints in his hair. Even in bright light his eyes were as dark as pools of ink.

Crow's pulse beat hard in his neck, and he still wasn't breathing properly. He felt as if he were standing at the edge of a fathomless abyss. His next step was inevitable, but he didn't know whether it would send him soaring high, strong-winged, or plummeting into the void.

And yet the situation was, objectively, so ordinary. He was on the little porch of his rental, the stifling heat causing a trickle of sweat down the back of his neck, the smell of dust and dried grass in the air. A jay called somewhere near, harsh and strident. Possibly a warning or perhaps simply making its presence known.

"Why are you here?" Crow asked at last. Getting the words out didn't make his pulse any steadier.

Simeon kept his expression neutral. "I'm going to help you."

"Help me how?" Crow asked, even as he shook his head.

"Solve your mysteries. Find a way to safety."

*Safety.* There was an ambiguous term.

"Why would you want to do that? You barely know me. I yelled at you and pushed you."

"You've got my curiosity going, and I never can shut the bloody thing up. You may be a bird, but I expect I'm a cat. I've run through several of my lives already. And as for the other…." Simeon shrugged. "Loads of people hit me sooner or later, and now we've got that bit over with, haven't we?"

"I'm not going on some kind of goddamn quest."

Simeon eyed him for a moment. "Tell me something. When those… whatever they are… asked you to join them, did you want to? Do you still want to?"

Crow had a great many weaknesses, including that he was a poor liar. When he tried to deny Simeon's accusation, the words shriveled in his throat. "Yeah," he rasped. "Sort of."

"Right. How much longer, then, until you tire of this game and give in?"

"I'm shocked I've lasted this long."

"So, find the answers. Which will it be, mate—defeat them… or *become* them?"

Suddenly, Crow remembered evenings on the farm just as spring was turning into summer, after everyone had put in a long, hard day of work. He and his grandparents would sit on the front porch—much larger than his current one—with iced tea and a cobbler. Gran and Grandad might chat about politics or current events or local gossip or things around the house that needed work, but Crow would gaze out over the fields with their promising rows of new green shoots. He'd look at the dirt under his fingernails, a reminder of the good soil that sustained him. He'd hear the soft back-and-forth of conversation, and he'd love his family and his home so deeply that it hurt. And just a few years later, all of that became soot and ashes, charred wood and bones.

"Defeat them," Crow said.

"Right." Simeon bent, picked up his bag, and slung it easily over his shoulder.

"But you can't come. I told you what happens—"

"Death and disaster, yeah. I've faced those things before. And I'm making this choice, not you, which means only I am responsible for whatever becomes of me."

"But… your job. The carnival."

"I loved that place. First true home I ever had. But they've packed up and gone away, and I couldn't find them now if I tried."

"And you'd give them up for…?"

"Already have. Told you—for curiosity's sake." His lips curled into a smile. "And perhaps another kiss like last night's. That was bloody brilliant."

Now Crow was just as hot internally as externally. But he took a step back. "I don't necessarily need the monsters to kill you. I might very well have AIDS."

Simeon's brow furrowed. "What's that?"

"AIDS." When comprehension didn't dawn on Simeon's face, Crow made an impatient sound. "The disease? You catch it from contact with infected blood or by having sex, and then you die slowly. My friend Dee had it, although the monsters got to him first. He and I used to fuck, so…." He spread his arms, palms up, wondering how any man who kissed other men could be so oblivious. Surely the carnival had access to news sources.

"I'm sorry about your friend. Are you sick as well?"

"Dunno." Crow had heard something about a test, but it was only available if you tried to donate blood. Which was something he'd never do, in case his blood was clearly not human. If he did have the disease, it likely wouldn't kill him; nothing seemed to. But that didn't mean he couldn't pass the virus to someone else.

"I'll take my chances," said Simeon.

"But—"

"Look. We can make this work, you and I. But we need an understanding. My choices lead me to my consequences, and that's not your burden. Ditto for you. We can be companions, not encumbrances."

Crow considered this for what felt like a very long time. The jay was still cawing, but if it was speaking to Crow, he didn't understand its message.

"I have no idea where to start," he admitted at last.

Simeon beamed like a man who'd won a contest. "That's easy. We start at the beginning."

"And where's that?"

"We start where you began."

As far as Crow knew, he was born in Chicago. That was what his grandparents had said on one of the rare occasions they were willing to discuss it. Aunt Helen said so too. Crow had gotten a good look at his birth certificate only once. It gave his name and his mother's but was accusingly blank for the father. The certificate also said he was born at Mercy Hospital.

But Crow wouldn't have known where to begin his search in Chicago, whereas he did have an inkling about a potential source of information in Chinkapin Grove. "Aunt Helen," he said to Simeon, who watched as Crow stuffed a few changes of clothing into his backpack.

"Who's she, then?"

"My mother's sister. Also adopted. She was nine years younger than my mother and only nine years older than me, so she was more like a sister than an aunt. She never talked much about my mom, but maybe she knew more than she said." He'd gotten that impression on a few occasions when unspoken words seemed to hang heavy over both of them. But he'd never pushed, and she always changed the subject. He didn't know if that was due to her preference or a request from his grandparents.

"Is she in Chinkapin Grove?"

"She was ten years ago." And it was hard to imagine her anywhere else.

"All right."

Crow shoved another pair of socks into his bag and looked around. A few of his belongings remained in the dresser or on top of the lone table, but he didn't have room for them, and none were irreplaceable. Nothing he owned was irreplaceable, in fact. Everything in his bag could be bought at a Kmart.

The rent was paid through the end of the week. He didn't bother leaving a note for his landlords, and he wouldn't ring their doorbell either. They'd figure out soon enough that he was gone, and if they were lucky, they'd quickly find someone else to fill the bed. Crow also wouldn't give notice at the cannery. It was both freeing and sad to know that he could disappear suddenly and few people would notice; fewer still would care.

Crow took a final look around, determined there was nothing left worth taking, and stepped outside. Simeon followed closely behind.

It was a nice change to be leaving a place of his own volition and not because the birdmen had arrived. No deaths in Mareado could be added to Crow's conscience. But it was strange to have a destination. For ten years, Crow had run away from, not toward. One problem with having a destination was that you needed a plan of some sort. A roadmap.

Out on the sidewalk, Crow stopped and looked up at the sky as if it might offer guidance, but it remained dazzling and unhelpful.

"Is it far to Chinkapin Grove?" Simeon asked.

Crow did a quick mental calculation. "Couple thousand miles."

Simeon whistled. "Bloody big country you have here, mate."

"Only if you have to get somewhere fast."

In fact, each year the United States had felt increasingly confining, a cage with eternally shrinking space. It was like the trash compactor scene in *Star Wars*, with the walls moving relentlessly inward. Crow had been expecting that someday soon he'd be crushed.

"How will we get there?"

Well, that was the sixty-four-thousand-dollar question, wasn't it? Most often Crow traveled by hitchhiking. Truckers especially were often willing to exchange a ride for someone to talk to, making the long miles roll by faster. But two men traveling together would likely make it much harder to catch a ride. People wouldn't have space, or if they did, they might feel uneasy about being outnumbered.

"Greyhound, I guess," Crow said with a sigh. He had a little money saved and could afford tickets to get them that far.

Simeon looked puzzled. "A dog?"

"A bus. Greyhound is the name of the company. How long have you been in the US anyway?"

"Don't know. I've been with carnival less than six months, but you and I met ten years ago. Time's funny that way." Simeon shifted his feet and appeared uncomfortable.

"How?" Crow demanded.

"No idea. I was bloody lucky to land a position with the carnival, and I took care not to ask too many questions while I was there."

That was fair enough, and Crow had enough weird things in his own life without worrying about anyone else's mysteries. He'd long ago reached the conclusion that the world was a much stranger place than most people understood; if you scratched the surface often enough, you were bound to find surprises. Some less pleasant than others.

"We'll take the bus," Crow said and headed toward downtown and the station.

Simeon didn't say much along the way, but he seemed to take in their surroundings with great interest, as if this dusty little town were exotic and fascinating. Once he paused to pet a skinny orange cat that had meowed at him and later plucked a pink blossom from a crape myrtle tree, sniffed it, and tossed it aside. He moved easily, strides loose and long, as if his bag weighed nothing and he could walk all day.

When they were almost to the station, Crow stopped. "Do you have any money?"

"Mr. Ame gave me some when I told him I was leaving. I've no idea of its worth."

"Can I see?"

Shrugging as if unconcerned, Simeon pulled from his front pocket a worn leather purse with a metal clasp. Crow's Gran used to have one very much like it, and sometimes she'd take out a few coins so Crow could catch a matinee with Marty or buy an ice cream at Blair's Pharmacy. Simeon handed the purse over and Crow peeked inside to find a small stack of crisp paper bills totaling a hundred and fifty dollars.

He handed the purse back. "It's not a lot. I hope he didn't cheat you."

"He wouldn't." Simeon tucked the purse away.

"How do you know that? You said you used to be a thief— I'd expect you to be more careful about money."

Simeon laughed so hard that a middle-aged man across the street stared at them. "Thieves aren't careful about money, love. We know that it's nothing but bits of paper and worn metal, that it flows in and out like the tide and ultimately has no value at all. When I needed something, I took it. No need to bother with nasty currency."

That was one way of looking at it. Crow had never paid money much attention either, other than to make sure he had enough to cover the necessities. Even if he'd somehow managed to collect a lot of it, which was highly unlikely, wealth would only have made him easier to find. And what would he spend it on? He could only carry so much in his backpack.

Still, it was nice to be able to fill his belly and have a comfortable place to sleep.

At the bus station, which reeked of old sweat, it took several minutes of consultation with the agent before Crow shelled over the money for two tickets. It would be a long slog, with bus changes in LA, St. Louis, and Springfield, but he'd expected that.

"We've got half an hour, if you want to grab something to eat first."

Simeon liked that idea, so they walked to a nearby market, where Crow paid for the kinds of things that would travel well: apples, cheese sandwiches, crackers, candy bars. Simeon acted as if he'd never seen any of the brands, and he contemplated the cookie selection as seriously as a child with a strict snack budget.

And then they were sitting next to each other, halfway down the bus with Simeon in the window seat. He bounced his legs as they rumbled out of the parking lot.

"It's not that exciting," Crow said. "You're gonna see mostly blacktop and desert, then farms. A few shitty-looking downtowns."

"I've never seen a desert."

One of the very few benefits of Crow's life was that he'd been just about everywhere in the country, just like in that old song. When Aunt Helen was fifteen, she got a job at Rory's Burgers N Stuff, and she bought that record with one of her first paychecks. She used to sing along with Hank Snow—although not very well—and she'd claimed that when she grew up, she'd visit all of those towns for real.

But Crow didn't like to think of the wisp of family he'd left behind, so instead he turned his attention to Simeon, who was gazing out the window at a strip of car repair places.

"Where are you from?" Crow asked.

Simeon turned to look at him, one eyebrow cocked. "You've some curiosity too?"

"If we're going to sit next to each other for two thousand miles, I might as well know something about you."

"Aside from my previous employment and my skills with my mouth?" Simeon flashed white teeth that were charmingly crooked. God, everything about him was charming, even his faults. Maybe especially his faults.

Crow glanced around to see if anyone had overheard, but the bus was fairly empty and nobody sat near them. He could put his hand in Simeon's lap and nobody but Simeon would notice. Crow kept his hands to himself. "Yeah. Aside from that."

"I'm from the East End." Simeon must have sensed Crow's puzzlement, because he snorted. "London, mate. Bethnal Green. Do you know it?"

"I've never left the country." He didn't have a passport or any other proper form of ID. From a bureaucratic standpoint, Crow Rapp had ceased to exist the night of the fire.

"And I'd hardly been outside London until I joined the carnival."

"Is your family still there?"

Simeon gave one of his rare frowns. "No family. You don't know who your father was, and you barely met your mother, and I reckon I'm the same. Copper found me squalling in the street as a newborn and took me to a foundling home."

Crow felt sick. He might have been parentless, but for eighteen years he'd had his grandparents and aunt. Simeon had lacked even that much. He hadn't even had a mother who cared enough to abandon him somewhere safe.

"Do you ever think about them?" Crow asked. "Wonder who they were?"

"Used to. I'd stare at people in the streets to see if I could find myself in their faces. I'd dream of them too—dreams where they were birds who rousted me from the nest before I was fledged." He sounded very young and forlorn and far away, and for the first time in his life, Crow wanted to take someone into his arms and comfort them.

Instead, Crow sat on his hands and looked across the aisle, past empty seats to a landscape of parched-looking orchards.

# CHAPTER 7

*S*imeon made a surprisingly good travel companion. He didn't talk much, never complained, and sometimes pointed out something he found interesting. He got hold of a book somewhere, a battered paperback of Ray Bradbury stories, and made his way slowly through it. "Not much of a reader," he said, blushing a little. "Didn't spend much time with schooling."

"I didn't graduate high school. Wasn't a very good student anyway." A few teachers had claimed that Crow was smart enough, if he'd only apply himself, but he never saw the point. He knew how to farm, and he figured that was what he'd be doing with his life. In any case, his grandparents couldn't have afforded to send him to college.

"Sometimes I'd go to Westminster, to the pubs the King's College lads liked to frequent. I'd smile at them, they'd buy me a drink, I'd pick their pockets. A bit of fun and profit for me, and they could afford to lose the dosh. They'd take the piss with me on account of me being beneath them, but that didn't stop them from fancying a snog or a grope in an alley.

I didn't mind them looking down on me, but I envied them a bit."

"Did you go there for profit or for the chance to hang around with educated people?"

Simeon smiled. "Bit of each, I expect." Then he returned his attention to the book.

At times Simeon would fall asleep, his head lolling onto Crow's shoulder—a heavy weight, yet a welcome one. They both had to make do with bus station restrooms for quick cleanups, but somehow Simeon still smelled like popcorn and hay and freshly sawn lumber.

Every now and then Simeon would tell a little story from his past. His version of London seemed much more antique than Crow expected. Horse-drawn carriages, women in long skirts, men in tall hats. He could have been making it all up just for the hell of it, but the tales felt true. If they were, he'd been born a very long time ago. More of that weird time-slip stuff, and it was probably best not to inquire too deeply.

It took almost three days to get to Chinkapin Grove, and their interactions remained entirely platonic—not even hand-holding or a quick kiss—and yet incredibly intimate. Crow knew what Simeon looked like when he slept and the small sounds he made while dreaming. He knew that Simeon had a sweet tooth and made a face when he drank coffee. He knew how the strands of Simeon's hair worked their way loose from their tie like living things seeking freedom, and how Simeon would gentle them with his fingers before confining them again. He knew that Simeon could strike up an easy conversation with anyone he met, leaving them smiling and content. He knew that when Simeon walked under a clear night sky, just a short stroll between bus and station, he'd direct his gaze upward as if counting the stars, as if considering how to steal a few of them.

Crow wondered what little nuggets Simeon was

collecting about him. Maybe none. Maybe Crow had nothing worth collecting.

They arrived in Chinkapin Grove at ten thirty in the evening. There was nobody else at the bus stop, which wasn't a proper station, and all the businesses downtown had long since closed for the night. Humidity made the warm air feel heavy, and cicadas droned from the trees lining Main Street. Although Crow recognized Blair's Pharmacy and many of the other places he used to pass all the time, they didn't feel familiar. This place felt no more like home than Mareado or any of the dozens of other places where he'd briefly stayed.

"It's empty," said Simeon, his tone neutral. He brushed a palm against the lamppost outside the Lincoln State Bank.

"Typical for this time of night. There's a Fourth of July parade that brings everyone downtown, but aside from that, it's pretty quiet even during the daytime."

"It's never quiet where I come from." Simeon looked around. "Where does your aunt live?"

"Assuming she hasn't moved, about a mile from here, right where the town's giving way to cornfields. We'll have to walk there. But it's pretty late." Although that was absolutely true, he actually needed more time to gather his courage. The journey halfway across the country hadn't been long enough. *One more night*, he promised himself. *Then I can do it.*

If Simeon sensed the true reason for Crow's hesitation, he didn't comment. "Do you reckon there's somewhere we can sleep?"

"The Grove Inn is a couple blocks from here. Or it was, anyway."

They strolled past Berger's Hardware, the Elks Lodge, the Farmers Insurance office. If they kept going straight, they'd see the police station and the library, and beyond that, the elementary school where Crow and Marty used to get in trouble for passing notes. But they turned right on Fourth

Street instead. The laundromat was still there and the barbershop, but King's Family Diner was gone and Mary-Lou's House of Fashion had been boarded up.

They finally reached The Grove Inn, a three-story pile of bricks that claimed to be the oldest building in the city. The ground floor housed the lobby and a restaurant that was Chinkapin Grove's closest kin to fine dining, the place where locals went for special occasions. At one point, there had been an assumption that Crow would take Julie there before the prom, and Marty would take Sandy. But of course Crow was gone long before then. He wondered now whether the others had kept the plan, and who had been Julie's date.

The door to the lobby was unlocked and a bell jingled as they entered. There were a couple of old upholstered chairs, some bad landscape paintings on the walls, a rack of tired-looking brochures, and a polished wood counter with a cluster of knickknacks at one end. A man stood up from behind the counter and looked at them with mild suspicion. "Can I help you?"

Crow recognized him. This was Darrin Spiegel, who'd been a year behind Crow in school. Back then, Darrin had a rusty old Chevy that he'd steer slowly around town on weekends, his girlfriend beside him, his left arm hanging out the window with a cigarette between his fingers. Now he was paunchier, his hair shorter and thinning. He didn't seem to recognize Crow, which was a relief.

"We'd like a room," Crow said.

Darrin looked back and forth between them, eyes slightly narrowed. "How many nights?"

"Just tonight."

Now Darrin was frowning. Crow didn't know whether it was because of the late hour, or because he and Simeon looked travel-worn, or because they were two men trying to get a room together. Or maybe Darrin just frowned

74

frequently. He had one of those faces that seemed to have experienced a lifetime of disappointments.

Simeon stepped closer to the counter, let his duffel fall to the carpeted floor, and leaned on his elbows. "My mate here's giving me a grand tour of your fine country, he is. I was going to visit only the big cities, but he steered me here as well. Says places like this are the *real* America."

Darrin's eyes had widened as soon as he heard Simeon's accent. "He's right. This is the Heartland, you know? Where real people live, not those fakers from New York and Los Angeles."

Crow, who would have bet everything he owned that Darrin had never been within a five hundred miles of either of those cities, nodded in feigned agreement.

"I'm looking forward to exploring in the morning," Simeon said. "What would you recommend I see?"

That question threw Darrin for a bit of a loop because Chinkapin Grove was thin on tourist attractions. He drew his brows together in a tight vee and gnawed on a chapped lip. "We have brochures." He gestured. "But none of those things are really right here in town."

"I don't want brochures. You're the real expert, mate. Tell me what you know."

Darrin puffed out his chest. "I *have* lived here my whole life. We've got a real pretty mural inside the library, and the post office is a nice building. There's the Gregg Mansion— you can't go in, but it's cool to look at from the outside. We used to have a replica log cabin, you know, like a little museum on pioneer prairie life? But it got busted up in a tornado."

"That's too bad," Simeon said as if he meant it.

"Yeah. The cemetery's interesting, though. And just at the edge of town is Lick Run, which I guess is bigger than a creek but smaller than a river. It's a good place to sorta sit and enjoy a little nature. You can cool off your feet if it's hot, and some folks go fishing."

A bend in Lick Run formed a peninsula that was prone to flooding and so had been left undeveloped. When Crow was in high school, local teenagers would gather there on Saturday evenings to build bonfires, get drunk or stoned, play music on transistor radios, and make out. Sometimes boys got into fistfights. Crow had experienced his first kiss there, sitting on a felled log with Julie and watching the flames crackle, and although it hadn't gotten his blood rushing, it had been sweet nonetheless.

"Sounds lovely," said Simeon to Darrin. "Peaceful, like."

Darrin continued to extol the virtues of Chinkapin Grove, and Crow would never have guessed there was so much to say about his hometown. And even though most of what Darrin talked about was far from exciting, Simeon gave an excellent impression of being fascinated and clearly won him over. By the time Darrin ran out of things to say, he practically had stars in his eyes as he looked across the counter at Simeon.

"Yeah. So, uh, the room will be thirty dollars."

For the first time since they'd left Mareado, Simeon paid. Then he carefully wrote his name in the guest book, his signature spidery and old-fashioned-looking. He handed the pen to Crow, who wrote *Carl Rogers* on the line below and made up an address in Arizona.

Darrin handed over a key with a large wooden fob. "Three oh six. It's our nicest room. I've given you an upgrade, on account of you being a foreigner."

Simeon literally bowed. "Thank you for your generosity, sir."

The stairway was creaky and the wallpaper had been marred by hundreds of hands and suitcases. The close air smelled like a century's worth of cigarettes. But the room itself wasn't bad; it was certainly an improvement over the bus and also over most of the places that Crow had temporarily called home. The paintings were as bad as the ones in the lobby, and the pastel bedspread looked out of place with the heavy antique furniture. There was an air conditioner, however, and a spacious bathroom with a tub, and even a little sitting area with a loveseat and tables.

"We'll have to share the bed," Crow pointed out, rather unnecessarily.

"It's a bloody big one. Could probably fit half the town on there with us."

They took turns showering and came out smelling of Ivory soap and floral shampoo. Simeon's hair, loose and damp, trailed down his bare back like a short silk cape. He stood at the window, looking out at the empty street. He wore nothing but an odd-looking pair of loose boxers with a drawstring waist; his broad muscled back showed a few small scars on the pale skin, and his waist narrowed above a rounded ass.

Although they'd spent a few days sitting shoulder to shoulder and thigh to thigh, this man was still a stranger. Yet despite the gulf of knowledge between them, and despite having shared only a single kiss, Crow felt as if they were connected. Tied together with invisible ropes. Those ropes were made of silk, however, and Crow didn't mind them at all.

Simeon turned, caught Crow staring, and smirked. "Like what you see, love?"

Crow only shrugged. He knew he cut a far less impressive figure in his Fruit of the Looms. He tended toward skinny—sometimes even scrawny—rather than bulky. His skin was milky except when he blushed pink or had a tan, and although he had some body hair, it was sparse and so pale as to be nearly invisible.

But he wasn't here to be a model. "I'm going to sleep."

"All right. Early start tomorrow?"

Crow had to think for a minute about what day tomorrow would be. Friday. So if Aunt Helen's schedule was anything like it had been a decade ago, her husband would be at work at the title company and she'd be home doing chores with the radio turned up loudly. "Not too early, but nine or so. We can eat before we go see her."

"All right."

After waiting a moment—for what, he had no idea—Crow got into bed and turned out the light. Now all he could see was a silhouette of Simeon with a faint halo around him, almost as if Simeon wasn't truly there, as if he were a figment of an overactive imagination. When Crow was young, he'd sometimes lie in the near dark, looking at his shirt hooked over the back of a chair and making himself shiver as he pretended it was a monster coming to get him.

He should have known better; the real monsters had wings.

Crow had nearly dozed off by the time Simeon climbed in next to him. There was plenty of space between them—more than there had been on the bus—yet Crow was acutely aware of the nearly naked body beside him.

Simeon moved around a bit, rearranging pillows and blankets, and then let out a heavy sigh. "I'd very much like to fuck you right now." The somewhat coarse statement was made in a tone of tender regret.

After a hard swallow, Crow managed to speak. "I told you. AIDS. I don't know if—"

"That's not it. I think if we fucked, you'd be done with me. You'd walk away from me tomorrow morning, and I'd never learn what your answers are. So I'm going to be patient, which is bloody difficult for me."

Although Crow's first instinct was an angry retort about

not being that much of an asshole, he kept silent and considered Simeon's words. Maybe Simeon was right—Crow might walk away. Run away. He was good at that.

In the darkness, he asked a question instead. "Has there ever been anyone who hasn't walked away from you afterward?"

"No."

Then Simeon rolled over and did a terrible job of pretending to snore.

THAT NIGHT, Crow dreamed of flames. In the dream he wasn't afraid of them because although they burned, they didn't hurt. They also didn't consume the space around him, which was an enlarged version of Simeon's carnival wagon. Crow sat on the rug with a cup of tea, and all around him the fire swooped and soared like red birds. Dream-Crow knew that if he willed it, the flames would destroy the wagon and the carnival, and they'd keep on consuming everything until the entire country was scorched gray and black and ashes fell in an endless blizzard. Dream-Crow sipped his boiling tea and tried to decide whether to release the fire. In the corner of the wagon, Simeon watched and waited for his decision.

WHEN CROW WOKE UP, Simeon sat beside him on the bed, knees drawn under his chin, staring at Crow expressionlessly.

"Wha'?" Crow sat up and rubbed his face.

"You put me in your dream."

It took a few moments for Crow's groggy brain to process that, at which point he gaped.

"You were burning things," said Simeon. "You trapped me there. I couldn't move, couldn't speak."

"I can't trap people into my dreams. That's...."

*Crazy?* No more so than dozens of other things that had happened to him.

"But you did, didn't you? What did you mean by it?"

"Mean— How the hell do I know? It was a fucking dream. I can't control those."

Simeon gazed at him. "If you're not controlling your dreams, who is?"

"I.... I...." Crow made an impatient growl. "It's my subconscious."

"Still *yours*. Still you."

Crow had no idea what to do with this conversation. He got out of bed, almost stumbled over his own feet, and rubbed his face again. His eyes burned. "I'm sorry I did it," he muttered, because he truly was.

"I'm not angry that you put me there. Just trying to suss out why."

"I don't know why. I don't know anything, okay?" Crow shuffled into the bathroom, where he took another shower because God knew when he'd have access to one again. There was no more shampoo, however; Simeon must have finished off the tiny bottle on his long hair.

Simeon was dressed by the time Crow emerged. Wordlessly they packed up their belongings and trudged downstairs. Crow didn't recognize the older woman who'd replaced Darren behind the counter, and he exchanged only a few words with her as they returned the key and checked out.

Chinkapin Grove was a little more lively in daylight, but not much. A few cars and trucks rolled down the street, none of them in any hurry, and a couple of kids sat outside the library, probably waiting for it to open. Crow now realized how much the downtown had changed. Many of the shops and businesses he remembered were gone, their windows entirely covered in curling newspapers, faded For Rent signs tucked in the corners, and glimpses of dead flies and dust on the windowsills inside. Although not yet a ghost town, it was diminishing gradually in hospice care and patiently awaiting its final heartbeats.

"It didn't used to look this bad," he whispered.

Simeon nodded. "Looks as if it's almost given up."

But the B&R Café was still there, unchanged. Even the clusters of old farmers hunched over coffee mugs and newspapers looked the same. Crow led Simeon to a table in the corner, where a waitress he vaguely remembered took their orders for pancakes and sausages. Crow asked for coffee, black, and Simeon wanted tea. She didn't seem to recognize Crow, but her eyes were distracted, as if her mind were somewhere far away while her body was stuck on autopilot. The unremarkable food filled their stomachs, at least, before they ventured out into the growing heat.

"We don't have all this sun back home." Simeon shielded his eyes with a palm as they walked down the sidewalk. "Sometimes we've air so thick you can chew it, or a fog so dense you can't see your fingers in front of your face. And the cold—it's damp and creeps into your bones. I think I spent my whole childhood shivering."

Crow was relieved that Simeon had, at least for the moment, moved on from the dream hijacking. "Do you miss it?"

"A bit, yeah. It wasn't a nice home, but I knew it. Knew my place, I expect. Here and now...." He shrugged.

"Can you go back if you want to?"

"Dunno." Then Simeon suddenly smiled and shoved a

hand into his pocket. He held his palm flat to show Crow a small porcelain figure of a blond boy in overalls and a straw hat. "Look what I have."

"Where did you get that?"

"Our lovely inn. There were several of them on the end of the counter, but I chose this one because he looks like you."

"You stole that from the Grove Inn?" Crow asked incredulously.

"Nicked it, yeah. I told you: I'm a thief."

"But… why?"

"The urge struck me." Still grinning, Simeon shoved the little figure back into his pocket.

Crow didn't know what to say, so he held his tongue.

CHAPTER 8

*L*ike Crow's mother, Aunt Helen had hoped to go to college, but again it had been beyond the family's budget. Unlike Crow's mother, she'd remained in Chinkapin Grove after high school and married a local boy who'd earned an associate's degree at the community college. They'd moved in with his widowed mother near the edge of town, he'd gone to work at his uncle's title company, and Aunt Helen had become, she liked to say, a happy housewife.

Before her marriage, she used to talk about how much she was looking forward to becoming a parent. But she and her husband were still childless several years later, and it hadn't occurred to Crow until he was grown that the lack of children might have been a source of grief.

But now as Crow and Simeon neared the little tan-colored house where Aunt Helen had lived, a little girl was riding a Big Wheel in the driveway. She looked to be five or six, Crow guessed, her strawberry-blonde hair escaping uneven pigtails, and she had Aunt Helen's knobby chin. She stopped to stare in the frank way that small kids often do, not alarmed but clearly intrigued by the two strangers looking back at her.

"Jamie Ruth Fowler, you better not be riding in the street again." A woman stepped out of the open garage, caught sight of Crow and Simeon at the end of the driveway, and froze.

Aunt Helen's hair was cut short, and she wore an old pair of denim overalls and a T-shirt. She was heavier than when Crow had last seen her, but the weight sat comfortably. She stood motionless, a garden spade in one gloved hand, her mouth slightly open, the sunlight bright on her face.

"Mama, who are these men?" Jamie hadn't ridden any closer, but she looked as if she wanted to.

Shaking herself, Helen gave the little girl a weak smile. "Honey, can you do me a favor and bring me the rake? I think it's out back somewhere. You can stop and get yourself a couple of cookies along the way."

If Jamie had considered arguing, the cookies changed her mind. Abandoning the Big Wheel, she sprinted to the house's front door and slammed it behind her.

"She's beautiful," Crow said. "I bet she's smart like you too."

Helen visibly collected herself, but her question still came out as a whisper. "Crow?"

"Yes. I...." He paused because there were no right words for a moment like this. Then he remembered who stood beside him, and manners gave him an excuse to stall. "This is my friend, Simeon Bell."

Even shock couldn't overcome Midwestern politeness. "Nice to meet you," she said to Simeon with an admirable attempt at a smile.

He bowed without irony. "The pleasure's mine, madam."

She didn't seem surprised by his accent, maybe because she was still overwhelmed by Crow's arrival. "I don't know what to do."

"I'm sorry," said Crow, who truly was. "I didn't come here to upset you. If you tell me to leave, I will."

For a terrible minute she seemed to seriously consider it. Then she shook her head hard, dropped the spade onto the driveway with a clatter, and ran to envelop him in a strong embrace that smelled of crushed leaves and earth and coffee. He hugged her back, and they both sobbed a little. In those moments, he privately admitted that some part of him had hoped he might make Chinkapin Grove his home again. But that tenuous dream was dead now; he couldn't endanger Helen and her family.

They had to separate eventually, Helen wiping her eyes with the back of her arm and Crow wishing he had a Kleenex. Simeon had apparently waylaid Jamie upon her return, because now he knelt in front of her doing something with his hands that she watched raptly.

"Mama, this man is magic!"

Simeon rose to his feet looking slightly sheepish. "I hope you don't mind," he said to Helen. "I only thought perhaps—"

"It's fine. I'm going to…. Can you guys give me a few minutes?"

"Of course," said Crow.

She nodded and, after putting her gloves and spade into the garage, took Jamie's hand and walked her to the house next door, a tiny cottage not much bigger than Crow's rental in Mareado. The front door opened before she had a chance to knock, and Helen had a brief conversation with an older woman who shot curious glances at Crow and Simeon. Then the woman ushered Jamie inside and shut the door.

Helen returned to her own driveway. "Mrs. Schmidt will keep Jamie busy for a while. They like to spend time together. Mrs. Schmidt's grandkids live in Peoria, and Jamie doesn't have any grandparents." She swallowed thickly. "Come inside so the neighbors will stop staring."

Crow and Simeon followed her into the house.

Crow had been here plenty of times, but it had been redecorated in his absence and didn't feel familiar. The living room furniture looked fairly new, everything in beige, dusty rose, and teal, and there were toys scattered around. The rake lying in the middle of the floor had most likely been abandoned in the search for cookies.

Helen moved the rake aside and tossed some stuffed animals off the couch. "Sorry the place is such a mess. Do you want something to drink? I've got some coffeecake too—Mom's old recipe." She looked down at her hands and gave a ragged laugh. "I should wash up first, though."

There was a depth to her eyes that Crow had never noticed before, their blue color more like the sky just after sunset rather than on a breezy April afternoon. She had lines at the corners, too. He remembered one Saturday afternoon when he had been seven or eight and she had some pocket money from her job at Rory's. She'd taken him to the Cairo Theater to see *Help!*, and she'd bought his tickets and paid for popcorn, and the two of them had sung aloud during the entire film. She'd come out of the theater so giddy, spinning on the sidewalk and gushing over how dreamy Paul was. Crow hoped that girl was still inside her.

Crow shook his head. "We had breakfast. I don't care whether your hands are clean. I just want…. Helen, I can't stay long. Can we talk?"

After a brief hesitation, she gestured them to the couch and took the armchair for herself. Crow suspected that the orange-and-brown afghan draped over its back might have been one of Gran's creations. She could churn one of those out in a matter of days.

"I can leave," Simeon said quietly. "Wait outside."

But Crow said no, and Simeon stayed.

They all looked at one another. Where to begin this

conversation? Crow settled on a safe topic. "How old is your daughter?"

"Six last month. She'll be starting first grade soon, but she already knows how to read. I didn't…. She doesn't know about you. It was too much for a little kid. I figured I'd tell her when she's old enough to understand. Except I'm plenty old, and I don't understand."

A decade's worth of sorrow settled on Crow so heavily that he couldn't breathe. He felt pressed into the couch, two-dimensional like a cartoon character run over by a steam-roller, his heart struggling feebly to beat. Helen had gone without seeing him, and her daughter, who should have been Crow's beloved little cousin to entertain and spoil, didn't know him at all. He was less than a ghost to his own family; it was as if he'd never existed at all.

Except for the harm he'd done. And really, that was true of his entire life. Nothing to show for it, nothing accomplished, no acts to be proud of, no memories to fondly look back on. He was a void, a black hole.

"You've grown up looking hard," Helen said. Not an accusation, just a matter of fact.

"Yeah."

"When you were a boy, you always had this sweetness to you. And those big blue eyes, all shiny like something from Disney. That's gone."

"I know."

She regarded him evenly. "Did you start the fire?"

It felt as if she'd stabbed him. But then, wasn't it deserved? "No. But I'm responsible for it."

"Why? Were you careless? Foolish? I don't believe you were malicious."

"I was…." He couldn't find the words. Maybe there weren't any. God, after all this time he should have had a better handle on this thing, but it had been so much easier to not think about it. To run away whenever he was forced to face it.

Crow tensed in preparation for running away again, this time because he couldn't explain. But Simeon set a hand on Crow's knee and said, "D'you want my help, mate?"

Jesus, Crow certainly did. Jaw clenched, he nodded.

"Ma'am," Simeon began, but Helen stopped him with a hand.

"Helen, please. I'm not really the ma'am type."

"What happened to your people wasn't because of what Crow did or even what he wanted. It was because of what he was. What he still is, I expect. And he can't help that."

Her mouth worked for a moment. "What is he, then?"

"A bloke with a tale to tell."

And just like that, as if Simeon had uttered an enchantment, Crow's tongue worked again and he found himself capable of speech. He gave Simeon a grateful look before turning to Helen. "Do you want to hear it? You'll probably think I'm crazy. Or making up wild excuses."

"Even crazy is better than nothing," she said.

So Crow told her about the red birds that had flown through his window on the morning of his eighteenth birthday. He told her about everything that had happened since, the string of deaths, the times he should have died too and didn't.

Helen didn't interrupt. Her expression was grave but not judgmental, her hands laced together as if she were praying —or as if she held something caged inside.

When Crow stopped speaking, she cleared her throat. "So you left Chinkapin Grove because—"

"Because I was terrified. And I stayed away because I was terrified."

"And why have you come back?"

He laughed raggedly. "Because I'm still terrified. I need to know if I can end this somehow. I hoped I'd find some answers here. I won't stay long."

"Answers," she repeated. And then for the first time she turned her full attention to Simeon, who'd remained silent yet very present for the entire telling of the saga. "And who are you, and what's your role?"

Crow had already made it clear that he'd had male lovers, and Helen hadn't flinched. It wasn't especially significant compared to threatening red birds, deadly fires, and ten years' worth of absence. When Crow was young, he'd thought that being queer was his deepest and most shameful secret, but it turned out that it had become as unimportant as the fact that he liked his coffee black or that he sometimes wished he knew how to play the guitar. Just one of the quirks that made him unique and that shouldn't be of interest to anyone else.

Still, Crow waited for Simeon's reply to Helen's question.

"I'm a roustabout. Or was, until a few days ago. Crow and I met at the carnival where I worked. And he intrigued me. A priest once told me that while I have many sins, curiosity would be the end of me. The rest of my sins would determine what happened to me after."

"Aren't you worried that you'll die too? Like my parents and Crow's friend Dee and the rest?"

Simeon gave a gentle chuckle. "I know I'm going to die—only question is when and how. But it's never concerned me overmuch. It's a gloomy subject, innit? Not much to my tastes."

Escapism, Crow thought. Simeon escaped by not thinking about troubling things, and Crow escaped by running away from them. Problem was, those things would always track you down in the end.

"What answers do you want?" Helen finally asked Crow.

"My mother. What happened to her? What did she know about me? Where did she go?"

"Sara." She sighed.

Crow had very rarely heard his mother's name mentioned, and even then, it had usually been by somebody outside the family. One neighbor whispering to another and then glancing his way. A teacher saying something to his grandparents and then being silenced by Grandad's glare. When Crow was a kid, he'd always thought it unfair that when these adults said the name, an image came to them of Sara the person. They knew what she looked like, sounded like. How she wore her hair and whether she'd been the quiet girl in the back of the classroom or the eager one sitting in front. He had nothing.

Helen stood. "I'm going to check on Jamie. Then we can take a walk. I don't have all your answers, Crow, but maybe I have a few."

She left them alone in the living room. Crow could tell that Simeon wished he could prowl around and inspect everything, this very average little Midwestern home that must have seemed so exotic to him.

Helen was smiling a little when she returned. "They're making cookies, and then they're going to watch *The Price Is Right*. I think they'd be perfectly happy if I left Jamie there all day." Her expression turned more serious. "Let's go for a walk."

Of course Simeon leapt to his feet, and Crow was intrigued too. They followed her out the front door and to the public sidewalk, where she turned left, away from town.

"When did you arrive?" she asked as they walked past modest houses.

"Late last night. We stayed at the Grove Inn."

"I always wanted to do that when I was a girl. I thought it

was fancy." She laughed softly. "I guess it was, for us. But you saw what the town looks like now."

"Boarded up."

"Yeah. So many people have left. Not as suddenly as you, but they're just as gone. Families work a farm for generations and then fall on hard times and lose it to the bank. Crop prices are low, land's not worth much of anything anymore, everyone's up to their neck in debt. They're doing a concert next month in Champaign, you know. All kinds of famous musicians. I don't think it'll help much, though. Places like Chinkapin Grove are never going to recover."

"I'm sorry," Crow said.

"Well, I guess complaining doesn't help. I'm pretty lucky, actually. Paul got a good paying job in St. Louis when his office closed here. We decided Jamie's better off in Chinkapin Grove, though, at least for now, so she and I stay here and Paul comes home on weekends. We're thinking Jamie and I will probably move soon. But that's okay. She'll be in school then. I want to take some classes, maybe get a degree. Assuming my brain's not too ancient."

She sounded cheerful about it, and maybe she really was.

While they were talking, Crow realized their destination. Hell, he'd probably had an inkling even before they walked out the door. After all, he'd traveled this way a thousand times, running the mile or so to Aunt Helen's to visit or to bring her something from Gran or to carry a message that could have been shared via telephone. Then he'd mosey back along this exact same street, sometimes with Marty at his side or sometimes singing songs he'd heard on the radio or mentally reenacting scenes from the last movie he'd seen. Gran would be waiting for him at home, usually with chores to do. But she'd also have cookies or a bread-and-butter sandwich or celery sticks smeared with peanut butter.

"Does Marty still live here?"

Helen shook her head. "He died in a car wreck the year after he graduated high school. He was driving too fast down Willford Road. His family's farm got foreclosed on a few years ago and they moved away."

Well, there it was: a new flavor of grief. Crow almost doubled over with the pain yet he somehow kept walking.

"Not your fault," Simeon said quietly.

Not directly, no. But what if Crow were a normal person who'd stayed in Chinkapin Grove and remained friends with Marty? Crow might have been with him in the car, might have warned him to slow down. Or they might have been away from the car and doing something else entirely.

"Julie?" he asked.

"Went to UI Urbana-Champaign, got a degree, never came back. Her folks are still here, though. Super proud of her. I think she got married a couple years ago."

That eased a little of Crow's pain.

By now the town had petered out and they passed small farms. Some of the houses were boarded up and forlorn, but the fields were in use. They'd probably been bought by one of the big agricultural corporations. This made Crow wonder what would have happened to his family farm had all the bad things not occurred. His grandparents had been struggling to get by for their whole lives, even when other farmers were doing well. So maybe the bank would have taken over, and he had no idea what would have happened then. Grandad had an eighth-grade education. He knew how to raise corn and soybeans, how to care for cows and chickens and tractors.

"So much space," Simeon said, interrupting Crow's thoughts. "Where I come from, we're crammed together like rats in a nest. Here you could go hours—perhaps even days—without seeing another soul."

Crow couldn't tell whether Simeon approved of this or

not, only that he found it astonishing and maybe overwhelming. "It's never quiet, though," Crow said. "Day or night, you hear the wind rustling the trees and the rows of corn, in winter rattling the windows and pounding against the shingles. You hear birds—ordinary ones, I mean. Might hear a cow calling or chickens clucking. Rain falling. Sleet pelting the windows. Snow making its own hushed music, kind of like church. When a car goes by on the road, you hear it, maybe even recognize the sound of the engine. You hear the diesel rumbles of the combines."

"You miss it," said Simeon.

Helen watched Crow as she walked, waiting for the answer.

Crow spoke honestly. "Sometimes. I think when you grow up in a place, it's always in your blood."

"In your lungs, more like, if you're from London."

"So even if you couldn't wait to get out of there, some part of it is always gonna call to you. And some of the people there will too."

For the first time, Helen gave one of her big, warm smiles, and she reached over to give his arm a friendly squeeze.

Crow almost didn't recognize his old home when they arrived. There was no sign of the house, just thick weeds over what had once been the foundation. The barn listed dangerously to one side, parts of its roof missing entirely. The ravages of weather or simple neglect; Crow couldn't discern the cause.

Helen gazed out at the rows of corn almost ready for harvest, the golden leaves whispering secrets. "I still own it. I'm not sure why. I mean, I bring in some money from leasing it out, and that sure helps, but that's not all. Just too hard to give it up. Sometimes I like to imagine Jamie building a little house here for her family when she grows up, but that's just plain crazy. By then there'll be nothing left here but ghosts."

"So leave it to the ghosts then," Crow said. "Let them be content."

The three of them stood silently awhile, each alone in their thoughts. Then Helen squared her shoulders and lifted her chin. "I brought you here for a reason, not just nostalgia. You know, Sara and I weren't real close as sisters go. I was still pretty young when she graduated and moved away. But she used to send me postcards from Chicago almost every week."

Crow hadn't known that. "What did they say?"

"Nothing important. Something funny she saw somewhere, or what somebody at work said, or what it was like to ride the 'L'. She shared an apartment with a bunch of other girls, I think, and she told me about them. It sounded like such a huge adventure to me. Then the cards stopped. I asked Mama about it and she told me not to worry, Sara was just busy, but I could tell she was bothered too. She had that tight look around her mouth. Remember that?"

"Yeah." It meant the bills were piling up, or Grandad's gout was flaring, or Crow's grades weren't what they should be.

"Maybe six, seven months after the last postcard arrived, Sara showed up on the front porch with a baby in her arms."

"Gran and Grandad must have been furious."

Helen looked thoughtful. "Not really. They were shocked, of course, but I think they were also relieved to see her. And there was you. I remember being a little jealous, actually, watching my parents pass you back and forth like you were the most precious thing they'd ever seen. And you were an ugly baby, Crow Rapp. All red-faced and bald, with your little eyes all squinted up like you were suspicious of everyone."

Simeon chuckled. "I can picture that right clearly, I can. He still makes that face often."

Crow was able to ignore the teasing because he'd just experienced an unexpected lightening in his soul. He'd always been confident that his grandparents loved him, but what a gift to know that they'd welcomed him from the start. That they'd never viewed him as an intruder or a burden or a source of shame.

"What happened next?"

"I don't know. I was too little to be allowed near the grown-up conversations, so they shooed me away. Anyway, I thought Sara was going to stay. She spent a couple nights here, I think. She wouldn't tell me who your father was. 'Just a boy I met.' Maybe she told Mama and Papa, I don't know. I was happy to have her home. But at some point I realized her suitcase was full of baby stuff and she had almost nothing of her own. One morning she kissed me on the head at breakfast, and when I came home from school, she was gone."

"And I wasn't," Crow said.

"No, you were squalling. Cried for a week straight, it seemed like. But my parents were awfully glad she'd left you with them, Crow. They always were."

"Nobody heard from her again?" Simeon asked after a long silence, seeming to be as engrossed in the story as Crow was.

"No." Helen hesitated slightly. "I guess I oughta be used to people I love just disappearing, right? Most of them have, one way or another." She sniffled and wiped impatiently at her eyes. "The day before Sara left, I was sitting out on the back porch playing with a kitten, and she came out of the house carrying her jewelry box. It was her thirteenth birthday present, and she used to threaten me with death if I even thought about touching it. I don't know what she kept in it. That afternoon, she asked me to help, so I followed her to the barn."

Helen would have been about nine then—only a few years older than Jamie was now. Crow had seen photos and knew that at that age, Helen wore her hair in braids that always looked on the brink of unraveling, and her clothes always seemed as if they'd gone on neatly that morning but had been through adventures in the meantime. He could picture her eagerly tagging along behind her older sister, wondering what was up.

Now Helen started walking toward the remains of the barn, and this time it was Crow and Simeon who tracked her, all of them avoiding overgrown weeds and bits of rubble left over from the demolished house. There used to be a small door on the side of the barn closest to the house, but now the door itself was gone and the gaping entry was festooned with spiderwebs.

"I didn't think to bring a spade, but I bet there's one in there," Helen said.

Before Crow could respond, Simeon darted inside. The darkness seemed to swallow him immediately. Crow started to follow, but Helen stopped him with an outstretched arm. "Two people in there are more likely than one to knock the whole thing down."

She was right, but Crow twitched nervously, imagining the entire structure collapsing and entombing Simeon. That death would be Crow's fault too. "Be careful!" he called.

"I'm rarely that!"

Simeon's answer would have been more comforting if it wasn't immediately followed by a loud clatter and some colorful cuss words that Crow had never heard before. Helen again stopped him from going inside.

Simeon emerged a few minutes later, grinning widely,

dust and cobwebs and bits of ancient hay caught in his hair. He triumphantly held aloft a small shovel. "Will this do?"

Helen gave a businesslike nod as she took it, but Crow had to look away. He recognized the shovel. The handle had once been painted green, but toiling hands—including his own—had worn away much of the paint. This was the light-weight tool that Gran used in her vegetable garden. Crow had used it to scrape old bedding and debris out of the chicken coop and to clear a pathway through the snow when he felt too lazy to fetch the snow shovel for the front walk and driveway. It had been one of a number of shovels in the barn, including one used for digging trenches and another for making fencepost holes.

Leaning on the handle, Helen continued her story. "That afternoon, Sara had me dig a hole right outside the barn. She watched with that box in her hand. It was a warm day for October, and the sunlight was that particular orangey shade that only comes in autumn. Her hair glowed like spun gold, and I thought about how pretty she was and that I'd never be as pretty as her. And I dug that hole. Right here." She tapped a spot with her foot. It was just to the right of the doorway and close to the barn wall.

"Did she put the box inside?" Simeon asked.

"Yes. Real gently; I remember that. Then she made me bury it, and afterward she stomped all over it, making sure the soil was packed in tight. I kept asking her what was in that box, but she wouldn't say."

She paused, waiting for Crow to state the obvious. Which he did. "But there was a reason why she wanted you there. And why you're holding that shovel now."

"Yeah." Helen pressed her lips together for a moment. "Maybe you think she abandoned you because she didn't love you, but that's not true. She loved you so much. Anytime you weren't in Mama's or Papa's arms, you were in hers, and she was going on about how pretty her squishy-faced baby was, and how strong, and how she could already tell that you were the smartest person in Joutel County."

Of course Crow couldn't remember her holding him and cooing at him, and he wanted to rail against the unfairness of it all. He should be entitled to at least a small memory of her. But even as he silently raged over this, he remembered that Simeon had been treated even more cruelly. Crow had experienced those moments of tenderness; Simeon never had.

"I wish I'd known her," Crow said quietly.

"You have so much of her in you. Did you ever catch Mama and Papa staring at you as if they'd seen a ghost?"

"I figured it was because they were wishing I wasn't there."

"Don't you dare say that, Crow Rapp! Don't you dare!" A rush of color appeared in her cheeks. "They loved you, and you know it. They were just seeing your mama in your face or your actions, and it hurt them a little."

"Seems like all I've ever done is hurt people."

Helen shook her head fiercely. "You keep on thinking that about yourself and you might as well crawl into a grave right now. You're no villain, Crow, and you never have been." She took a few heavy breaths. "But I need to tell you what Sara said after we buried the box. That's the important part. She said she had a real important job for me. If she wasn't around on your eighteenth birthday, I was supposed to help you dig up the box. And I was going to, but that morning Paul had to take me to the hospital in Carbondale."

"Hospital?" asked Crow, stricken.

"I was having a miscarriage."

"Jesus, Helen, I'm sorry."

She gave a tired smile. "It was my third. Paul and I never told anyone. It's all right, though. Now we have Jamie."

It seemed ironic: one sister having a baby she certainly

hadn't planned and the other desperate to have a child but unable to. Another of life's cruel jokes.

"I would have told you about the box the next day—I hadn't forgotten my promise to Sara. But that night...."

"Everything burned."

"And then you were gone. I should've told you on your birthday, just like Sara told me to. Maybe then the fire—"

"Don't. Don't make my burden yours, please."

After a few seconds, she gave a small nod. Then she handed him the shovel. "Go ahead and dig, Crow."

He did. The soil was hard, as if actively resisting him, and the sun was hot on the back of his neck. Then a shadow slid over him very fast, and when he looked up he saw three birds wheeling overhead. It was hard to judge their species, silhouetted against the light, and although they weren't making a sound, he knew they were crows. Common enough birds, and they often liked to follow people with ploughs or shovels in hopes they'd be spared the work of digging up tasty bugs. Grandad used to joke about it while they worked the farm. "There's your flock," he'd say. "Now don't you go sprouting feathers and flying away from your chores."

Simeon watched alongside Helen but didn't offer to help. They all knew this had to be Crow's job.

One of the birds called out, followed by the others. The harsh sound had always reminded Crow of raucous laughter. He wanted to shout back at them to leave him alone, but instead he put more energy into his task until the blade scraped against something hard.

A wooden box buried for years might be fragile, so Crow leaned the shovel against the barn, knelt, and began scrabbling with his hands. It was strange to once again handle the soil on this farm. Satisfying, somehow.

The box was in surprisingly good shape. Crow sat down before opening it, and Simeon and Helen sat as well, both craning their necks to see. Meanwhile, more crows appeared —a dozen or more, all of them circling and cawing. Helen scowled up at them. "It's like that old movie. *The Birds*. Have you ever seen it?"

"I've never seen a moving picture." Simeon sounded wistful.

"*Never?*" Helen asked. "How is that— Never mind. Let's see what's in the box."

Crow had never seen the film either. He didn't need Hitchcock to make him wary of birds. After casting a nervous look upward, he held his breath and opened the lid.

# CHAPTER 9

*C*row's hands were shaking. In fact, his whole body trembled, so he set the box in his lap, where it felt heavier than it should have, and looked inside.

There were three envelopes. Two bulky manila ones, the first with his name written on it and the other with Helen's. The third was a plain white envelope, flat, with his name. It occurred to him that he was seeing his mother's handwriting, was holding items that had last been held by her, and for the first time in his life he felt a true connection to the shadowy woman.

"Yours first." He handed the appropriate envelope to Helen.

She held it in her palms for a few moments, staring at it. "She didn't tell me there was anything in there for me."

"Perhaps she thought you might dig up the box if you knew," Simeon suggested. "You were only a child, yeah? I would have had that box up the moment her back was turned."

"Helen's not a thief," Crow pointed out, perhaps cruelly.

Simeon simply shrugged. "All of us are thieves under the right circumstances."

Helen had ignored this entire interchange. She took a few steadying breaths, ripped her envelope open, and reached inside. And then she burst into tears.

It was a necklace. Choker length, pearls alternating with glittering rondelle beads. Helen clutched it in her palm and tried hard to calm herself. Simeon surprised Crow by pulling a fabric square from his pocket and handing it to her; she nodded and used it to dab her eyes and blow her nose.

"It's not as valuable as it looks," Helen said, sniffing. "Rhinestones and freshwater pearls. But it cost a lot, considering Mama and Papa's budget back then. It was their graduation gift to Sara."

Simeon gave a soft smile. "So it's actually quite valuable, innit?"

"She never once let me touch it. The most I was allowed was to admire it when she wore it, but that was only a couple of times. She took off for Chicago pretty soon after she graduated."

"She loved you too," said Crow.

"Yeah."

Helen carefully clasped the necklace around her neck, smoothed the envelope, and tucked it into a pocket. She seemed to consider returning the handkerchief to Simeon, but when he chuckled wryly, she tucked that away as well.

And now it was Crow's turn. The birds seemed louder than ever, and it felt as if every crow in the county circled overhead. Weird magic aside, could that many birds kill a person? Maybe. Beaks aimed at eyes, claws tearing at skin. It could be enough.

"Maybe you should both leave. It'd be safer."

But Helen shook her head firmly and Simeon scoffed. "Not bloody likely, mate."

After a moment's consideration, Crow opened the manila envelope first. It also contained jewelry, but his was a ring. A man's ring, gold and heavy. The center was blue enamel with a gold crest, with the numbers 19 carved on one side and 55 on the other. Inside the ring were faint initials: LMW.

"That looks like a class ring, but not from around here," said Helen.

"Do you know who LMW is?"

She thought for a moment. "There's Louis Wall. He's my dentist in Carbondale. But I have no idea what his middle initial is, and he's too old to have graduated in '55."

With some trepidation, Crow slid the ring onto his right ring finger. It fit perfectly. He folded the empty envelope and placed it in the box. Then he held the remaining envelope and stared at it, as if that were a functional way of revealing its secrets. Some of the crows settled on what remained of the barn roof, and others perched on the oak tree that had once grown in Crow's backyard and had escaped the fire. They watched him, their black eyes glittering. Simeon's eyes glittered similarly, while Helen's were wide and blue.

Fuck.

Crow slit open the envelope and pulled out a folded sheet of unlined paper. A piece of yellowed newspaper fell out, which he caught before it reached his lap. After a moment of indecision, he decided to read the letter's girlish handwriting first. And since Helen and Simeon were as eager to know the contents as he was, he read it out loud.

DEAREST CROW,

I need to leave to protect you and everyone else I love. It hurts. I'd rather rip my heart out. But I know your grandparents will take good care of you and raise you well. And Helen too—she's going to grow up to be such a fine person.

Your father was a kind man. He worked the counter of the diner where I used to go for lunch sometimes, and he was sweet and funny. We fell in love. We didn't have the money yet to get married and find an apartment together, and I guess we were a little foolish. You're eighteen now, so you know what I mean. Don't ever let anyone tell you there's something wrong with you just because your parents weren't married, because there isn't. And Larry was so excited to meet you.

You can read what happened to him, although the article doesn't tell the whole story. All I have of him is you and this ring.

This is so hard to write. Today you're eighteen. I hope so much that you're celebrating with family and friends and maybe opening a few presents. But maybe the same thing's happening to you that happened on my eighteenth. Crow, if I could do something to keep that from you, I would. But I don't know how. I just know I need to go. And if this thing happens to you—you'll know what I mean—you need to leave too. No matter how hard it is. You need to leave *now*.

I'm going to look for a solution. If I find one, well, I'll come rushing home so quick and scoop you up and hold you in my arms so tight. And you'll never see this note.

If I don't find one, well, just know how much I love you, my Crow.

Keep safe. Be happy. Be loved.

—Mama

CROW COULDN'T BREATHE. He lurched to his feet—heedless of the box, the letter, and the newspaper clipping—and staggered several feet away. He vomited up his breakfast and, seemingly, everything else he'd eaten for the past year. Blessedly, Helen and Simeon remained where they were, leaving him alone in his misery. When he was confident that he wasn't going to puke up his stomach itself, he spit several times to clear some of the sour taste, wiped his mouth with the back of his hand, and returned to the others on wobbly legs. The crows, which had been strangely silent since he opened the box, simply watched.

"Sorry," he mumbled as he sat down again. He almost told them that he'd never once been sick since his eighteenth birthday—not so much as a sniffle—and how he'd forgotten how awful it felt to barf. But he didn't want to talk about that now, and they probably didn't want to hear it. So he nodded thanks to Simeon, who'd taken custody of the letter and clipping and now handed them over.

Helen had the jewelry box in her lap. "What do you want to do now?"

"What does the newspaper say?" Crow asked.

"We didn't read it."

Had he been in their place, he wouldn't have shown such restraint. And yet he couldn't bring himself to look at the fragile scrap. He stared up at the sky instead, as if it might bring an end to his troubles. He remembered watching that same stretch of sky from his bedroom window one June afternoon when he was a boy, seeing a steel-gray wall of clouds moving in from the west. *The clouds are going to eat the sun*, he'd thought, and he wasn't frightened. Just fascinated.

He'd heard an eerie wail and thought it might be the sun screaming in terror.

And then Grandad had come thundering up the stairs, shouting about tornadoes, and had dragged Crow down to the storm cellar where Gran was waiting. They'd all sat there in the dim light with the spiders, listening to the hiss of the transistor radio and the shriek of wind, until the announcer said it was safe to come out.

There'd been a little hail damage but not enough to cause

his grandparents much grief. The twister, they'd learned later, had touched down several miles away and had collapsed somebody's barn. Crow had been a little disappointed, hoping for more excitement.

Watch what you wish for.

He looked down at the newspaper clipping and began to read aloud. It was a short piece, and there was no way to know what paper it had come from.

### Lincoln Park Man and Mother Murdered

Late Tuesday might, unknown intruders broke into a home at 2016 N. Kenmore Ave. and attacked the sleeping residents. Mr. Lawrence Michael Willemsen, 20, died immediately. His mother, the widowed Mrs. Bernard Willemsen, 48, died early Wednesday in the hospital from her wounds. Both victims appeared to have been attacked with knives.

Also present in the house was Mr. Willemsen's wife, who is expecting and was not injured. She was too traumatized by the events to give a description of the intruders.

The motive for the attack is unknown. Any citizens with information about these murders are urged to contact the Chicago Police Department.

This time Crow didn't throw up. He felt blank, like a cement floor swept clean of debris.

"How awful for Sara," said Helen, her eyes unfocused. "To lose so much when she'd been so hopeful about her future."

Crow's family history was, apparently, nothing but losses. He almost envied Simeon, who might never have belonged to anyone but who'd also never felt the agony of loss. But when he glanced at Simeon to see how he was taking it, Simeon was staring at the sky, wide-eyed.

A thousand crows whirled. Maybe several thousand. They didn't caw, but Crow could hear wingbeats and the rush of air through their feathers. If the sun had been directly overhead, the flock would have blocked it out like a storm cloud. Even still, there were enough of them to cast waves of shadows onto the ground. Although the air was warm and sticky, Crow shivered. "I think we should leave."

No one argued the point.

Moving slowly, like sleepwalkers, they gathered the letter, clipping, and box; they stood and brushed themselves off; they looked around as if lost or perhaps seeking something. They had taken only a few steps toward the road when the birds began to dive.

The terrifying thing wasn't the reality of talons and beaks, because the crows swooped up again just before contact. And it wasn't even the sheer number of them, or the way they seemed to be plunging down in organized squadrons. It was their silence. The only sounds were the wind whistling through their feathers as they descended and then the beat of their wings as they rose. They came down again and again until Crow, Helen, and Simeon retreated inside the ruined barn.

"I'll run out," Crow said. "Away from town. They'll follow me and then you two can get to safety."

Simeon crossed his arms. "Like hell you will. Besides, there's no point making a martyr of yourself when there are enough of them to go after all three of us."

That was true enough, but Crow didn't have another plan. He set down the box and peered into the dusty shadows to see if there was anything they could use for defense. There was a pitchfork and at least one other shovel, but that wouldn't do much good against such an enormous assault force. There was a big lump of rusting metal that had once been Crow's Ford truck. Also not useful. Meanwhile, Helen and Simeon eyed the barn roof warily. So far, none of the crows had come through the large hole, but they circled just above it and whirred past the gaping doorway.

Helen stood with her hands on her hips and scowled. "This is the stupidest thing that has ever happened to me. Who gets trapped in a barn by birds?"

Crow sighed. "People I care about. Jesus, Helen, I'm so sor—"

"Can it. Not your fault. We need solutions, not blame."

That was true, but Crow had no solutions. His entire life was one big fucking question mark, and even when he went in search of answers, all he got was more mystery. He shook his head miserably.

Simeon looked worried but not freaked out. "How long until nightfall? They won't fly in the dark, will they?"

"The ones that came on my eighteenth birthday came at night."

"Oh. Forgot that bit."

"You forgot—" Crow stopped himself before he said anything nasty. None of this was Simeon's fault, and the guy had been pretty solid considering how much change his life had recently gone through. When he'd been a kid in London, he'd probably never envisioned himself threatened by a flock of crows in Illinois.

After a moment, Simeon pulled a coin from his pocket and began playing with it, flipping it between his fingers in ways that seemed to defy the laws of physics. Sometimes it caught a sliver of light, and sometimes it disappeared entirely. He didn't even seem to be paying attention to what he was doing—his nimble fingers like creatures separate from him—but the tense lines around his mouth eased a little. This was how Simeon calmed himself, Crow realized enviously. Crow wished he had a similar trick.

"Rats," Simeon said suddenly, making Crow and Helen jump and scan the floor. Then he shook his head. "Sorry, not here. Was just remembering something from a long time ago. I was very small and there were rats that would bite you in your sleep. I used to have nightmares about them. But at least the bloody things couldn't fly."

That brought a long-buried memory to Crow. "Roaches. I was sleeping on a mattress on the floor, and I woke up with them all over me. On my goddamn face even. And some of them *can* fly." He shuddered.

"Right. So the good news is we're not being set upon by rodents or cockroaches. Or snakes. Or mad dogs. Or a herd of panicked horses pulling omnibuses. That's the bright side."

And the dumb thing—the silly thing—was that Crow smiled a little and so did Helen. If the world was going to be absurd, then Crow ought to appreciate it, the way he sometimes enjoyed watching old *Monty Python* episodes on late-night TV. Maybe there were no answers at all, only riddles that folded in on themselves like origami. If you tried too hard to make sense of things, you only ruined the beauty of the creation.

Grinning, Simeon stepped closer and pretended to pull the coin out of Crow's ear. Acting on instinct, Crow retaliated by tugging him nearer and giving him a fierce, breath-stealing kiss. It was the kind of kiss that Crow had rarely experienced, where his knees went weak and the universe disappeared. He was convinced that if they could just keep on kissing forever, no harm could come. Simeon might have felt the same; he locked his fingers through Crow's belt loops and hung on tight.

If Helen was horrified, Crow couldn't manage to care.

But then she screamed his name, and when he opened his eyes to the world again, he saw that the barn was collapsing.

They all darted for the doorway, but a portion of the roof fell, blocking their way. It was impossible to see clearly through the dust, the air so thick with it that they all coughed and hacked, feeling blindly for a way out. Helen grabbed Crow's hand and Crow caught Simeon's, and at least that was something. At least they hadn't lost each other.

The wood rumbled and roared, the crows screamed, beams snapped and crashed.

And then the whole structure came tumbling down upon them with a roar, pinning them to the hay-strewn floor.

Insanely, Crow remembered Simeon's list of things that were worse than a flock of homicidal birds. "At least it's not fire," he whispered.

THEY DIDN'T DIE.

Crow wasn't shocked at his own survival; he was accustomed to emerging relatively unscathed from the shadow of death. He *was* surprised, however, to discover that Helen and Simeon were still alive. Filthy. Bloody. Bruised. But they managed to collectively dig out of the ruin and stand beside it with the guileless sky bright above them. Not a bird in sight.

Helen's nose had been bleeding but wasn't anymore, and she spit a few times to get the dust out of her mouth. "Oh," was all she said.

Crow couldn't manage even that single syllable, and Simeon, who'd somehow kept hold of that coin through everything, was tumbling it between his fingers and staring at nothing at all.

"I'm sorry." Those were the only words that made it past Crow's throat. He repeated them as if that might somehow make them mean more, and with an impatient shake of his head he took a few steps toward the road.

Simeon caught his arm. "Don't run."

"What then? Stay until they come back and kill you both? Maybe this time they'll take down the whole goddamn town."

He thought Helen would agree with his fears, would be crazy with worry over the little girl currently baking cookies and watching game shows with the neighbor. But she took Simeon's side. "Will running away do you any good? You can't keep it up forever, Crow. You're not even thirty and you look ancient."

"Can't stay. Can't run. You want me to join those fuckers?" Appallingly, his voice broke and he had to fight back tears.

Simeon squeezed Crow's arm. "You can't. You're a good man at heart. And if you give in now, what was the point of all the fighting, all the deaths?"

"I've never fought."

When Crow was a boy and others had teased him about his mother, about his strange name, about his awkwardness, about the otherness that everyone could sense but not name, he didn't fight. Occasionally Marty did on his behalf. Mostly, though, Crow simply walked away. That was all he was good for.

"Love, what if instead of running away, you ran *to*?" Simeon's voice was gentle.

"To where? Unless you're going to put in a call to Madame Persephone, I don't have a clue where to go next. I was hoping I'd figure things out here in Chinkapin Grove. You see how that turned out." He waved his arms to encompass the current mess.

"But you did learn something, didn't you? You know who

your father was and what happened to him. That's far more than I'll ever know about mine."

Reluctantly, Crow nodded. Then he twisted the ring, still on his finger. His father was no longer a shadowy monster but instead a young man who worked at a diner and fell in love with the pretty blonde farm girl.

"I've always assumed that whatever I am, it came from him. Like he tricked my poor, innocent mother into thinking he was human. Or worse. But now it turns out that she was the…." He stopped and looked apologetically at Helen, who had loved her sister.

"Sara was no monster either, and neither are you."

"But what *am* I then?"

Helen had no answer, and Simeon only shrugged.

But as Helen touched the pearls around her neck, she said, "I can tell you one thing. Sara was adopted from the same agency that I was. Mama and Papa told us when I was little, before Sara went away. They said they had such luck with her that when they could afford it, they went back. It made me feel a little like that good brand of boots you always buy because you know they'll last, but that's okay. I always figured there was something pretty great about being someone's intentional child and not just an accident of genetics."

"Gran and Grandad were proud of you."

She smiled. "I know. They never let me doubt it. Anyway, I can tell you the name of that agency. Maybe they have records about where Sara came from."

"Did you ever look up your own?" asked Simeon softly.

"Never wanted to. I know who I am: Helen Storey Fowler." She lifted her chin high. "But Crow, if you want to know who you are, I think you need to go to Omaha."

It might be a dead end. It might end up being a place where more people were endangered because of Crow. But a slim possibility was better than none, and a vague direction was better than wandering aimlessly.

"I guess I'm going to head back west a ways."

Simeon, who had never let go of Crow's arm, gave it a tug. "Westward ho, love."

# CHAPTER 10

*T*he jewelry box, letter, and newspaper clipping were buried somewhere in the rubble of the barn. Nobody felt like digging for them, and anyway, Crow had what little information those papers could give him, along with his father's ring, and Helen had the necklace. That was good enough.

They walked back to Helen's house, Crow vaguely grateful for the town's sparse population because it meant that they didn't encounter anyone. If a few neighbors stared through their windows at the dusty, battered trio, those spectators remained hidden and silent.

Crow, Helen, and Simeon were silent too, although the inside of Crow's head was noisy enough to make up for it. The late summer sun shone over them, its light a specific hue that Crow had never seen anywhere else. If he were an artist, he'd call it Chinkapin Grove Gold.

Helen insisted that Crow and Simeon clean up at her place, so they each showered and changed into more presentable clothes. She made sandwiches and packed them into bags, along with apples, bananas, and an assortment of snacks that had probably been originally intended for Jamie. Then she gave Simeon a hug. "I hope we can get to know each other better someday."

"I hope the same."

She turned to Crow. "Write letters when you can. Or at least send postcards. Don't disappear on me again."

"You saw…. I kissed Simeon."

"It was hard to miss."

"It doesn't bother you?"

She gave an impatient little huff. "Honey, I've found a lot of things in this life to be bothered about. That isn't one of them."

They hugged hard and long, and he thought about how strong she was. Then she stepped back. "Figure things out and come back. I miss you. I want Jamie to get to know her cousin Crow."

After another hug, Crow and Simeon left Helen's house and headed toward the bus station.

Welcome
Traveler

"DOES THIS FEEL MORE LIKE HOME?" asked Crow as they walked down Chicago's Adams Street.

Simeon gave him a puzzled look. "Why would it?"

"Chicago's a really big city. So's London."

"Ah, but we've nothing like that." Simeon gestured at the Sears Tower, which loomed a block ahead. "You've mountains of steel and glass, yeah? And you haven't the horses and the wagons, the reek of soot and tide and sewage and horseshit."

While Crow was well aware that his home and Simeon's were separated by an ocean, he tended not to dwell on the fact that they were also, apparently, separated by a century or more. It didn't make any sense. But then, neither did crows that turned into people and killed everyone you cared about.

"What do you think of Chicago, then?"

"Oh, it's a jolly place to spend a day or two, I reckon. But I don't belong here."

Crow nodded in understanding. He didn't belong here either, although he had no idea where he *did* belong. Maybe nowhere.

They'd arrived by bus too late to catch the train—the daily California Zephyr—so they'd bought their tickets for the next day, stored their bags at Union Station, and taken the opportunity for a little tourism. They'd have to sleep rough tonight on the station benches, so Crow figured they might as well try to wear themselves out a little by tromping around the city. Besides, it was fun to watch Simeon's reactions to new things, his eyes full of wonder.

Then Crow had an idea. "Do you want to go to the top of that building? It's the tallest in the world."

Simeon grinned like a delighted child. "Can we?"

Admission was expensive, but this felt worth the splurge. It turned out that Simeon had never been in an elevator, and he was ill at ease until he got chatting with the middle-aged woman who operated it. By the time they reached the 103rd floor, the woman and Simeon were best pals and he seemed entirely relaxed.

At least until he stood near a window and looked out, at which point he gasped and fell back a few steps. "Bloody *hell!*"

Crow had never been up here himself and had never flown in a plane. He'd been on buses and trains over mountain passes, although that was a different experience from this. But for Simeon's sake, he feigned nonchalance. "Quite a view, huh? If the air was a little clearer, we could see three other states across the lake."

"It's so… so much." After a moment, Simeon moved back to the glass and stared out. Cars scurried beneath them, tinier than ants, and Crow had the insane urge to break the glass, spread his arms, and see whether he could fly like his namesakes.

Simeon turned to him, his expression earnest. "You have to understand. London's big all right, but not my corner of it. I spent my life essentially in a cage, with everything pressing in close. No escaping it either, not for a bloke like me. D'you see?" It seemed important to him.

And Crow *did* see. Simeon, like Crow, had been born with an unalterable fate, doomed by his parentage to a desperate existence. Then the carnival had come along and offered him a golden key, a once-in-a-lifetime chance to escape.

"Why would you give up the carnival to get stuck with me?"

"Dunno exactly. I've always followed my whims, which has put me in trouble more times than I can count. But it's also led me to everything good that I've ever had. I expect I'm gambling that you're one of the good things."

"I'm not, though. Jesus, I've already got you almost killed once, and—"

"And you've brought me to the top of the world." Simeon indicated the view. "This is a wonder, it is. Like soaring through the clouds in a dream. I'm willing to take some risks if it means rewards like this. I can't help that living is a nasty business that always comes to an unhappy end. But I can steal some joys along the way."

Something inside of Crow shifted suddenly, like when he adjusted a pack on his shoulders and it sat more comfortably. Fragmented memories bobbed to the surface of his mind: sitting on the front porch with his grandparents and Marty on a July evening, drinking iced tea and watching fireflies. Catching sight of a bear and her cubs ambling through trees.

Listening to an impromptu concert in a city park, with adults and children laughing and dancing. Seeing the sun rise over one ocean and, a couple of years later, set into another. Eating a perfectly cooked burger and fries after a day of fasting. Listening to Dee laugh at something silly, the illness and sorrow momentarily fading away. Noticing the fond way Aunt Helen tugged gently on her daughter's pigtail.

There had been joys along the way. But he'd tossed those experiences aside like empty wrappers, not recognizing how precious they were.

"You all right, love?" Simeon looked concerned.

Crow gave himself a mental shake. "Just spacing out. Sorry."

They spent a long time slowly circling the observation floor, looking down at the thin ribbons of streets and toy buildings. Crow wondered where his mother had ventured when she lived here. Had she ever taken the elevator to the top of the Sears Tower, perhaps on a date with Crow's father? Had they gazed out at the city together and imagined that someday one little piece of it would be theirs?

Possibly sensing Crow's thoughts, Simeon stood close. "You know the address where your father lived, yeah? D'you want to go there?"

Crow twisted the ring on his finger. "No."

"The hospital where you were born? Or the shop where your mother worked?"

"None of those places matter anymore."

Simeon nodded and set a sympathetic hand on Crow's arm. The contact felt good, grounding Crow to the planet despite their current aerie.

"Faggots."

Crow spun around and saw a florid man in his thirties, his lip curled in distaste. Usually Crow didn't care what anyone called him, but today heat spiked in his belly and through his veins. "Mind your own fucking business," he growled.

The man took a step forward. "They oughta put all you diseased scum in a camp somewhere."

Crow had formed a fist and was raising his arm when Simeon stepped between them. "Ah, you'll have to excuse my friend, mate," he said to the man. "He's had a rough day. We'll just be on our way and then you can enjoy the views you paid so much for, yeah?"

Astonishingly, the man relaxed his posture. Crow wasn't sure whether it was because Simeon and Crow both towered over him or because nobody could resist the charm of Simeon's smile. "Shouldn't do that faggot shit in public," the man muttered. "Kids might see."

Before Crow could retort that a comforting arm tap was hardly "faggot shit," Simeon nodded. "Right. Don't want to scar the kiddies. Accept our apologies?" He held out a hand.

The man still wasn't happy, but he gave a grudging shake, and when Simeon grinned and clapped him on the back, the man almost smiled.

"C'mon," Simeon said to Crow, jostling the man a bit as he towed Crow away.

When Crow and Simeon emerged onto the sidewalk, Crow was still miffed. "You didn't have to be so nice to that asshole."

"Would it have been better to hit him and end up in jail?"

"No," Crow admitted. "But there's a happy medium somewhere."

"Madame Persephone's rather jolly most of the time."

For a moment Crow stood blinking, trying to process the non sequitur. And then he understood Simeon's pun and snorted an involuntary laugh. Simeon laughed too, and that set Crow off until he was guffawing what felt like a decade of suppressed mirth. Not that Simeon's joke had been all that funny, but he had been so deadpan about it, the sparkle in his eyes so bright, that Crow couldn't help himself. It felt good.

"How about a nice dinner?" Simeon suggested when their chuckles finally died out.

"We just bought expensive tickets. We can't afford a nice dinner."

"Today we reunited with your only family, learned who your father was and why your mother left, almost got murdered by crows but didn't, and stood on top of the world. I expect all that deserves a celebratory meal."

He had a point. They'd be worrying about money soon enough; one decent dinner would give them something nice to look back on. "What are you in the mood for?"

Simeon shrugged. "Dunno. I've never eaten in a proper restaurant."

That brought Crow up short. "*Never?*"

"Wasn't really an option for me back home. And once I joined the carnival, I never strayed far from it. Didn't want to lose it."

"You strayed with me."

A flash of white teeth. "I've told you I'm foolish, yeah?"

Well, goddammit. They might as well go somewhere nice, or at least as nice as their very casual attire permitted. Crow thought for a few moments and then recalled a place Aunt Helen had mentioned after her honeymoon, a German restaurant that had impressed her as exotic. She'd said it was in the Loop.

"I know a place. But you'll have to ask for directions."

"You can't?"

"I tend to creep people out."

"They're not paying proper attention, then. What's the name, love?"

"The Berghoff."

Crow hung back and watched as Simeon loped over to a

woman waiting to cross the street. He envied Simeon's easy way with people. Within seconds the woman was smiling, touching her hair, and ignoring the walk signal.

Simeon returned quickly. "It's just a bit down this street, she says."

She hadn't lied; the restaurant was just four blocks down Adams Street. Simeon gawped at the spacious, wood-paneled interior. Crow was relatively blasé until he looked at the menu and spied the numbers. "Uh, this is pricier than I thought."

"Don't worry about it."

"But—"

Simeon held up a leather wallet. "We've plenty of dosh now."

For a moment or two Crow was so astonished that all he could do was goggle. When he tried to speak, it came out as an unintelligible sputter, and Simeon waited, grinning, until Crow managed real words.

"You stole that!" Crow hissed, hoping nearby diners couldn't hear.

"Didn't pluck it from a tree."

"You can't do that!"

"I can. I'm actually quite good at it." Looking extremely smug, Simeon tossed the wallet across the table to Crow. "We've enough for a lovely dinner, a bed softer than a train-station bench, and some left over. Seems our friend from the tower's well off."

"You—" Defeated, Crow stopped abruptly. The deed was done, and trying to undo it would only bring trouble down on their heads. Besides, the man had been an asshole. Yes, that was a crappy rationalization, and it wasn't as if Crow's soul were immaculate. Pickpocketing a bigot was nothing compared to the harm Crow had brought to people.

For once looking serious, Simeon leaned forward and

spoke quietly. "I was straight with you from the start—told you what I am. I didn't steal when I was with the carnival, but that was because I didn't have to, and anyway it wouldn't have been right considering Mr. Ame treated me so well. But I'm still a thief, Crow, and I don't fancy reforming myself. If that's too wicked for your sensibilities, I'll go now."

What Crow should have done at that moment was throw the wallet back and order him to leave. Their separation would be safer for Simeon. But Crow couldn't force himself to do it. Jesus, he'd been alone for so long that he should be accustomed to it, yet when he imagined never seeing Simeon again, something dark loomed inside of him. *That's it,* said a screechy voice in his head. *Leave the thief and join us at last.*

Crow shuddered. "Stay. Please."

"Why?"

*If you leave, it'll destroy me.* But that kind of honesty wasn't fair to Simeon, so Crow sighed and gave a different version of the truth. "I want you to. I don't care if you stole from that bastard."

"And when I do it again—which I will—you won't get your knickers in a twist?"

"No."

Simeon relaxed and sat back in his chair. "All right, then. How about you help me order some dinner?"

THEY ENDED up eating too much food and enjoying every bite. They each ordered a beer, and when Simeon gave a toast to their involuntary benefactor, Crow joined in. He had only the one glass, though, and realized it was the first alcohol he'd touched since the night he'd sat in Simeon's wagon. He also hadn't reached for the sweet, smoky numbness of a joint either, and that was interesting and new.

Somehow Simeon charmed the waiter so much that the man brought two free apple strudels for dessert.

"How do you do that?" Crow asked after he and Simeon had left the restaurant. They'd decided to spend some time strolling before retrieving their bags and finding a place to spend the night.

"Do what, love?"

"Make everyone like you so easily?"

"Survival trait. Where I came from, death was easy, yeah? You might live if you had a family to support you, but I didn't. Brute strength worked too, but I was undersized as a lad. That left me with nothing but a pretty face, a skillful tongue, and quick fingers. I learned to use what I had."

In the warm, humid darkness, with pools of light providing only brief clarity, Crow thought about this. He tried to inventory his own survival skills but couldn't come up with any, aside from a willingness to run and a seemingly supernatural imperviousness to death. He would have preferred Simeon's gifts.

They stopped when they reached the Chicago River, its turgid waters bound by bridges and penned by skyscrapers. When Crow was small, Aunt Helen had told him that the river used to flow into Lake Michigan but engineers had reversed it. Now he wondered whether rivers had some type of primitive emotions, and if so, whether this one resented the enforced change of its nature.

"Sometimes I walked to the Thames." Simeon's voice was soft, his gaze thousands of miles and a hundred years away. "Stinking old bitch, she was, but the city's lifeblood nonetheless. I'd see the ships go out and wonder what it'd be like to be on one of them. To watch the world opening up before me."

Crow moved slightly closer to him. "But you never did."

"I reckon I'd have made a bloody awful sailor. And I was scared. My home was a rathole, but it was *my* rathole. I knew how to get by. Anywhere else and I'd be lost."

This confused Crow. "But you're doing so well now. Since you left the carnival, everything you've faced has been brand-new to you and you've taken everything in stride."

Simeon turned his head and gave Crow a long, serious look. "It's you, innit? I follow your lead."

Nobody had ever followed Crow before. Why would they? So Simeon's announcement was both surprising and unsettling. But there was a little thrill in there somewhere too, the power of mattering to someone. And of *doing* something.

# CHAPTER 11

 he hotel was far more modern than the Grove Inn, and their room had two beds. Simeon knew what a television was but had never watched one, so Crow showed him how to switch on the set and change the channels. But its entertainment value quickly waned. "Nobody truly acts like that," complained Simeon, pointing at a sitcom.

"None that I've seen. But I guess people watch TV to escape reality, not to relive it."

Simeon huffed and turned off the set. He seemed restless. The Gideon Bible made him snort, the tourist guide to Chicago didn't interest him, and their uninspiring view of a brick building didn't hold his attention either. While Crow paged through a spy novel that Simeon had picked up some-where during their journey, Simeon ended up lying on his back with his hands pillowing his head, staring up at the ceiling.

Finally Simeon grunted, stood, and stripped naked, then gazed at the abstract painting on the portion of wall between the two beds.

Crow tried very hard not to stare, but it was a losing

battle and he ended up tossing the book aside. "What are you doing?"

"Nothing."

"With no clothes on?"

"It's warm enough. Don't need them."

If Simeon was handsome in jeans and shirt—which he certainly was—he was breathtaking without them. His pale skin almost glowed in the lamplight and his muscles formed intriguing shadows. Unbound, his hair flowed over his shoulders. He had a triangle of hair on his chest and another at his groin, where his soft cock somehow managed to seem… jaunty.

Crow chuckled drily at the last thought.

"I'm funny?" Simeon seemed amused rather than offended.

"No, I'm stupid."

"Ah. A sharp intellect's good enough if it gets you somewhere, but far too many people misuse it." Simeon bent his head a little. "I could join you in your bed, you know. It's big enough for two."

"No."

"Well, *that's* stupid then. I want to shag you. You want it as well. But you sit there with your arms crossed as if that'll accomplish anything."

Crow's arms *were* crossed; he hadn't realized that. Although he unwound them, he couldn't find a comfortable way to arrange them. It was as if he'd never had arms before. "I don't want to make you sick."

"I was ill when Mr. Ame found me, you know. Consumption. Coughing my bloody lungs out. It wasn't too bad yet, but I don't expect I had much of a future waiting for me."

"Did they give you antibiotics at the carnival?" When Simeon looked puzzled, Crow clarified. "Medicines?"

Simeon shook his head. "When I got to the carnival, the

cough disappeared. I asked Mr. Ame about it, but all he said was, 'Can't have our roustabouts ill, can we?' and that was that. I decided it was better not to pry—a good rule about the carnival in general, in fact."

"All right, so they magically cured you. But you don't have the carnival now, and—"

"And it doesn't matter. I keep telling you. I don't mind a risk when the payoff looks promising."

It was a convincing argument and Crow almost gave in. But then he remembered that this was Simeon, who could sweet-talk the stars out of the sky. Crow turned off the bedside light and lay flat. He closed his eyes. "No."

After a few moments, Simeon padded into the bathroom.

DESPITE HIS BEST EFFORTS, Crow couldn't fall asleep. He told himself it was due to the city's nighttime noises—sirens and garbage trucks and revving engines—but he'd slept in far noisier places than this. Maybe it was that big meal, sitting heavy in his stomach. Or simply the aftershocks of a very eventful day.

But he knew better, and he couldn't help tensing when Simeon crept out of the bathroom, tiptoed to the other bed, and settled himself in. Some time passed, and Crow was certain that Simeon remained awake too.

Finally, Crow spoke. "Thank you."

"For what?"

"Dinner. This hotel room." And a lot more than that, but Crow couldn't voice those things. He hoped Simeon, ever-perceptive, knew anyway.

"It's good to share an adventure with someone. You're an interesting bloke."

*Interesting.* That was one word for it.

Sometimes truth came more easily in the dark. At the beginning of the summer when Crow was seventeen, he and Marty had snuck out to the barn one night to smoke cigarettes and talk about girls. In that close, warm space, with the scent of hay thick in his nose and the glowing tip of his Marlboro hypnotizing him, Crow had come very close to revealing the secret that had been tormenting him for a couple of years already.

"Julie talks about getting married sometimes. But what if I don't want to marry her?"

"Then don't," Marty said blithely. "She'll go away to college and you'll marry someone else. I hear Carol Hansen has it bad for you."

"But what if I don't want to marry *any* girl?"

"Then you can wait. You ain't an old maid yet, Crow." Marty had paused for a moment, and when he spoke again, he sounded hesitant. "Do you think that you're….?"

The question had hung there, heavier than the smoke lingering in the still air. *Yes,* Crow had almost said. *I think I am.* He could have bared himself that way to his best friend, there in the obscurity of night. But Crow had coughed instead, and Marty called him a good-natured name, and the moment had passed.

Marty was dead now, Crow remembered. Marty would never know who his childhood best friend really was.

"Truth or dare," Crow said.

"What?"

"It's a game. You ask the person *truth or dare?* and if they say *truth,* they have to honestly answer whatever question you give them. If they say *dare,* they have to do whatever you tell them to do."

Simeon chuckled. "Ah. Questions and commands."

"Did you play that when you were a kid?"

"Didn't have much opportunity to play anything. But I heard about it."

Shit. Crow kept getting so caught up in his own problems that he forgot Simeon's life hadn't exactly been a bed of roses. "You go first." He waited, heart beating faster than it should.

For a very long time, Simeon said nothing. Then, very softly, "Truth or dare?"

And Crow chickened out. "Truth."

"All right. Give me a mo."

Crow tried not to squirm. The game had been his idea, after all, although he didn't know what twisted corner of his mind had offered it up. He'd played it with his friends when he was twelve or thirteen, that awkward stage between child and adolescent, and usually he'd opted for dares. The challenges had been mild things such as ding-dong-ditching someone's house or running across the road—trafficless late at night—wearing only his underwear.

"Tell me," Simeon said, "what it's like to be a part of a flock. To belong to someone."

Crow's first instinct was to respond that he belonged to nobody. But that wouldn't be the truth, at least in the spirit of the game, because once upon a time he truly had belonged. His family had been small, but they'd loved him. So had Marty, in the way best friends do. And after everything, Helen still cared about him even now.

Simeon had never had any of that.

"It feels... safe. Like even if times are rough, you know you have people on your side. And they understand you. They forgive you if you do something stupid, like when I was fourteen and borrowed Grandad's truck even though I didn't have a license and one of the local cops saw me driving out near the edge of town and called my house and told Gran what I was up to."

Simeon's laughter was warm. "What happened?"

"My grandparents yelled at me. I had to do extra chores for a week. And then Grandad took me way out in the sticks where there was nothing much to hit, and he made sure I knew how to drive well." Crow couldn't help but smile at the memory.

"He loved you."

"Yeah. And I wasn't always easy to love. But you know, belonging to someone is a burden too. Because you care about them, and you can't always fix their problems. And when you fuck up, that affects them too."

"Is it worth it?"

Crow answered without hesitation. "Yeah."

A long sigh came from the other bed. "I used to think about it a lot, when I was small. Some kind couple stumbling into the foundling home or catching sight of me on the street and finding me irresistible. It never happened, not to me or to anyone else I knew, but it was nice to imagine."

"But what about when you grew up?"

"'M not trustworthy enough for friends and haven't anything to offer a wife. And as for blokes, well, some found me fizzing enough for a quick brush, but that was all."

Ignoring the confusing slang, which he presumed had something to do with sex, Crow said, "We're friends, though. Aren't we?"

"We are." Simeon's smile was audible. "Cheers. And now it's my turn, I expect."

"Truth or dare?"

"Dare."

Well, that was cheating, because somehow Crow felt as if *he* were the one being dared. And what was he supposed to say? He didn't exactly want Simeon to run down the hallway and knock on strangers' doors, and running half-naked through Chicago was apt to get him arrested. It was hard to think of a challenge for a man who cheerfully quit his job to bum around with a mysterious, dangerous stranger and who almost got killed by crows in a barn and barely even flinched.

"I dare you to join me in my bed tonight."

"Love, that's hardly—"

"But no sex."

Simeon was silent for a few moments. "None at all?"

"Nothing. No touching."

Crow didn't know why he was suggesting this, but now that the words were out of his mouth, he realized that he very much wanted to sleep with Simeon. Maybe he'd become too used to the proximity of Simeon's body after a couple of days on a bus and one night at the Grove Inn—as if Simeon were a giant teddy bear. Or maybe Crow was just plain perverse.

Simeon's sheets rustled, and a few seconds later the mattress dipped as he climbed in beside Crow. He tugged the covers over both of them and, true to the dare, didn't make contact. The queen-size bed gave them plenty of room. But unlike on the bus or even in their bed at the Grove Inn, Simeon was entirely naked. And Crow, wearing a pair of cheap boxers, was acutely aware of Simeon's nudity.

"I won the game." Simeon sounded entirely pleased with himself. And maybe he was the winner, but Crow felt like one too.

THEY HAD a hearty brunch the next day, again courtesy of the asshole from the Sears Tower. Then they boarded the train and chugged through suburbs and past cornfields.

"Blimey," muttered Simeon when they crossed over the Mississippi.

"Big river, huh?"

"Bigger than the Thames, I reckon. But the Thames banks are crowded. Here there's nothing on the other side."

"Of course there is. There's Iowa."

Simeon elbowed him. "You've a sense of humor after all. I was beginning to wonder."

Naturally that made Crow scowl, which made Simeon laugh, and then Crow couldn't help laughing in return. Simeon's good cheer was too infectious. When he was amused by something, his entire face lit up and his eyes sparkled as if he were a child receiving a wonderful surprise.

Iowa was more corn, and pig farms, and junkyards, none of which Crow would have considered scenic. Yet Simeon gazed out of the window with rapt attention. Iowa probably seemed exotic to him, a concept that made Crow smile. And if Crow put a little effort into it, he could imagine that instead of riding Amtrak, he and Simeon were aboard a magic conveyance taking them to wonderful adventures—not murderous bird-creatures.

Occasionally Simeon got up to stretch his legs. He managed to make friends with everyone in their car: a young couple going to visit relatives in California; an old man who'd traveled to every continent, including Antarctica; three teenagers on their way to college in Wyoming; an Iowa family returning from vacation; a middle-aged woman who knitted as she wandered the continent by train. Crow watched him, trying to figure out Simeon's secret to charming people. All he could discern was that Simeon smiled a lot and listened intently to what other people said, making them feel fascinating.

Delays along the tracks meant it was nearly midnight when they pulled into Omaha. The small station was new but definitely not an improvement over the old one. Across the lobby, a sleepy-looking station agent sat at the counter, staring at some paperwork.

"How far to the adoption agency, love?"

Crow pretended not to notice the endearment. "I don't know. But it's not going to be open now anyway."

"We could break in, take a peek at the paperwork."

Not sure whether Simeon was serious, Crow shook his head. "Let's try the legal routes first."

"Do the legal routes involve a lovely hotel bed? If so, I'm agreeable."

Simeon zoomed over to the agent at the counter, who seemed disinterested at first. But within moments Simeon had cast his spell, and the guy was grinning, nodding, and waving his arms around. He scribbled something on a piece of paper and handed it to Simeon, who gave him a small honest-to-God bow.

Simeon hurried back. "Dan's given us his advice on where to stay tonight."

"Has he, now?"

"Says it's close, cheap, and clean. Gave me a tip for breakfast as well."

Traveling was a lot easier with Simeon. On his own, Crow had to figure out the details for himself, usually by trial and error. Experience had helped him make better guesses about potential lodgings, but he still often spent a lot of time trudging sidewalks or wondering whether the resident vermin infestation might get to him before the crow-creatures.

Maybe this area was nice enough in the daytime, but now it was dark and deserted, as if someone had misplaced this part of the city and hadn't bothered to look for it. He and Simeon walked across the tracks and along a few easy blocks toward downtown, where they found the motel that Dan had recommended. It was small, old, and slightly dilapidated, but the rate was low and the room clean. There were two beds again, but neither of them was big enough to hold a pair of grown men. Which, if Crow was honest, disappointed him. Although last night Simeon had been faithful to the dare and hadn't brushed so much as a fingertip against Crow, it had been good to know that he was right there. To share his body heat and breathe in tandem with him.

"You all right, love?"

Crow realized he'd been staring blankly at one of the mattresses. "Tired, I guess. You can watch TV if you want, though. I'll sleep through it."

"I'm not sure I fancy televisions. Everything is so small and flat, and the people just natter at you. You can't talk back."

"You can, but they won't hear you. Grandad used to yell at the news announcers." Crow smiled at the memory and at how Gran would call her husband a crotchety old man and tell him to hush.

Simeon huffed and stomped off to the bathroom. Crow fell asleep before he emerged.

He dreamed of being atop the Sears Tower, only the view was of endless farms instead of city and lake. Simply mile after mile of cornfields in orderly rows, without a single road or house or other structure in sight. And as Crow watched from his perch in the sky, the rows rippled and warped and then grew haphazardly—a wild jungle of corn, with some stalks reaching heights far beyond what was natural.

"You can't efficiently harvest that," said dream-Crow. "It'll all go to waste."

"No, it won't."

A man had appeared at Crow's side. He didn't have a face, just a beige blur like an out-of-focus picture, but he wore a set of cook's whites stained a rusty-red with dried blood. He had a familiar ring on one finger.

Crow frowned at him. "What do you know about farming? You're from Chicago."

"This isn't farming, son. It's life."

Before Crow could ask what the hell that meant, an enormous flock of black birds darkened the sky. Tens of thousands of them, maybe more, swooped down to eat the grain. Each bird grabbed an ear of corn before flapping up and away and—faster than in real life—over the horizon.

"No!" Crow pressed his hands against the window. "They'll take it all. We'll have nothing." He looked to the ghost of his father for help, but the man in white had disappeared and was replaced by Simeon, nude and unhappy.

"Stop banging the glass, love. You'll break it."

Crow hadn't even realized he was doing that, but now he curled his hands into fists and hit harder. The tower shook with every blow, but the birds paid no mind, just continuing to arrive in their uncountable masses and stripping the crop before flying away. Already entire sections lay bare, the stalks rapidly withering and then disappearing, leaving nothing but parched earth.

"They're stealing it all," cried Crow. "Can't you see?"

"But it's not even yours. It's not even *real*. You're dreaming."

Dream-Simeon tried to put a consoling hand on Crow's shoulder, but Crow didn't want to be soothed. He wanted to escape this cage and attack those fucking birds. Tear their fragile wings from their bodies, wring their necks, dash their broken bodies against the ground they'd ruined. He wanted the world to be filled with their bloody feathers.

"Crow—"

But Crow punched the glass again, and this time it shattered. Simeon unsuccessfully reached for him as Crow fell forward through the gaping hole. It was so far down to the ground, and he couldn't fly. He spread his arms anyway, uselessly. The air rushed past, too fast for his lungs to fill, too fast for him to scream.

The birds rose up from the field all at once, a living, moving landscape of shining black. Crow prepared to be destroyed.

But the birds came up beneath him and lifted him. Gently. Their soft wings tickled his skin, and it was like lying on the world's most luxurious bed. Simeon flew with them, his arms outstretched and his hair rippling in the wind. The birds carried Crow up and up, back to the top of the tower, where they wafted him inside before depositing him carefully onto the tile floor.

Then they were gone and Simeon stood over him. "I don't think—"

CROW WOKE WITH A START, almost falling out of bed. Neither of them had closed the drapes, so enough streetlight came through the window that Crow could clearly see Simeon sitting upright on his own bed.

"How are you doing that?" Simeon sounded frightened.

"Doing what?"

"You dragged me into your dream again."

Crow shook his head, not to negate what Simeon had said, but because he couldn't make sense of it. There *wasn't any* sense to it.

Simeon stood and came to sit on Crow's bed. "We were in the tower. You fell. The crows—"

"Saved me. I don't understand. What does it mean? Is it another way of getting me to join them? Does it mean that eventually I *will* join them? Fuck, I'd rather plummet to my death." Crow pulled his knees into his chest and wrapped his arms around them, as if trying to protect himself.

"Are you certain the dream's prophetic? Mine never are."

"I don't know."

Simeon put his hand on Crow's arm, and although Simeon was naked and Crow nearly so, and although they were sitting together on a narrow mattress, there was nothing sexual in the contact. It was one friend comforting another.

"Have you ever pulled others into your dreams, love?"

"No."

"You and I have spent less than a week together. Have you spent longer with others?"

Crow had to think for a moment. "Yeah. A few times. Dee had been staying with me for over a month when he— When they came for us. And I've had roommates now and then. Or people I worked with every day."

But he hadn't spent every moment—awake and asleep—with those people. Not even Dee. Since Simeon had showed up on Crow's little porch in Mareado, however, they'd never been more than a room away from each other.

After chewing his lip thoughtfully, Simeon sighed. "Let's get some sleep, yeah? And hope we get some answers in the morning." He returned to his own bed, where he spent considerable time arranging pillow and covers.

"Simeon? I'm sorry."

"For what?"

"Whatever I'm doing to you. The dreams."

"You're not doing it intentionally, and it's not harming me. It's just... odd. The same way it was odd when I briefly became a soothsayer and glimpsed your future. The carnival's full of interesting people, but you're the most fascinating bloke I've ever met. By far."

Crow wasn't sure whether that was a good thing. But

then, he found Simeon fascinating too, with his charm and his light fingers.

Although he tried, Crow didn't get any more sleep that night. He remained quietly in bed, however, staring into the darkness and trying to think of nothing at all. Simeon didn't stir, so maybe he, at least, got a decent rest.

They both rose early and took turns in the bathroom, in what now felt almost like a routine. When they stepped outside, the morning sun was already baking Omaha and the few other pedestrians moved as if through warm honey. When Crow was a boy, this was the kind of day when he'd rush through morning chores as quickly as possible, and then he and Marty would head to Lick Run and spend a good part of the day alternately splashing in the water and dozing on the grassy banks. After dinner they would eat big bowls of ice cream on Crow's front porch, listening to music on Marty's transistor radio and hoping for a cool breeze.

But Marty was dead, Crow was grown, and today he headed to the agency that had arranged the adoptions of his mother and aunt.

Helen had given him the name of the place, and a call to the Omaha telephone operator had produced the address. After breakfast at the diner that Dan had recommended— very good as well as cheap—Simeon got directions to the Murray Family Agency. It wasn't a long walk, although it felt farther in the heat as Crow's body grew heavier with every step. If Simeon hadn't been there, cheerfully chattering about everything they passed, Crow would have given up.

The agency was at the edge of downtown in an old two-story brick building. The first floor housed a furniture store with living room sets behind the plate-glass windows. To reach the agency, Crow and Simeon went through a glass door and up a set of grimy narrow stairs that smelled like a high school locker room. It was even hotter in the stairway than outdoors, and Crow gasped for air.

A tax-preparer's office was at the top of the stairs on the left; the agency was on the right. After a few deep breaths and a final urge to flee, Crow stepped inside. What he found was nicer than he expected. Someone had clearly made the place as pleasant as possible for potential clients. The waiting area contained a handful of comfortable-looking chairs, a water cooler, peaceful landscapes on the wall, and a small table with slightly out-of-date magazines. Behind a half-height wall, a woman sat among a small forest of filing cabinets.

She looked to be in her twenties and wore a lavender satiny blouse with puffy sleeves and a big neck bow. Noticing them, she stood up from her desk and came over to the short wall. A spool of grape-colored thread was in one of her hands, as if she'd been about to sew on a button or mend a tear. "Can I help you?" She looked puzzled about what two men were doing in an adoption agency.

Crow opened his mouth, but not a single word came out. The woman raised her eyebrows. Crow gave Simeon a desperate, pleading look.

And of course Simeon stepped up to the plate.

"Good morning, miss. I'm hoping you can help my friend."

She gave Crow an extremely doubtful look. "If he's interested in adopting, he'll have to come back with his wife."

While Crow tried to disguise a hysterical snort of laughter as a cough, Simeon simply smiled. "It's not that. His mother was placed by this agency, you see, and he's hoping for some information about her background."

It was clear that the woman wanted badly to return Simeon's smile, but she also seemed concerned. "We can't do that, I'm afraid. Our records are confidential."

"Understandable. But this is quite important. It's to do with my friend's health."

That wasn't a complete lie, Crow supposed. And standing here under the fluorescent lights, he probably looked ill enough to be convincing. He was too thin despite a few days of eating well with Simeon, and his pale skin was clammy.

The woman gave him a long, assessing look before turning her attention back to Simeon. "I need to check." She scurried away to somewhere behind the bank of filing cabinets.

And it was like a magic trick, because when she returned a few minutes later, she had aged two or three decades and changed into a floral-print dress with shoulder pads and a high-buttoned neck. Her hair, instead of being teased and sprayed into high bangs, was a few shades darker and done up in a short perm. For some reason, she held a ruler in one hand. She must be the younger woman's mother, Crow surmised. They looked too much alike not to be related.

"Yes?" asked the second woman. She seemed to be trying to look at Crow, but her gaze kept straying to Simeon.

And it was Simeon who answered. "Good morning, ma'am. My friend is searching for information on his mother's original family. We understand that you can't share this freely, but it's rather important."

"His health depends on it," she said drily, as if she didn't believe it.

"His wellbeing and future are very much at stake, ma'am."

"And he can't speak for himself?"

Crow cleared his throat. "I'm.... Sorry. I'm a little nervous."

The woman seemed to soften a bit at his admission. "I can't guarantee you a thing. But tell me your mother's name, and I'll see what I can do."

"Um, Sara. I don't know the name of her birth family, though."

She frowned. "If you get that from her, my task will be much easier."

"Um." Crow shifted from foot to foot. He had no idea why he was finding this so difficult, except that he'd rarely discussed his mother with anyone. Until recently. "She's... gone. She left when I was a baby. I don't know what happened to her."

Now the woman seemed genuinely sympathetic toward him. "I'm sorry. Women are often in very difficult situations when they have a baby. Leaving doesn't necessarily mean they were unloving. Often it's the kindest and the hardest thing they can do."

Her words weren't especially surprising, considering that she worked at an adoption agency, but they eased Crow's mood a bit. She wasn't judging him or his mother.

"I can tell you the name of the family who adopted her. They later adopted another daughter through your agency too, if that helps."

She nodded. "All right. We can start with that, I suppose. Name and hometown of the adoptive family?"

"Storey, with an *e-y*. Chinkapin Grove, Illinois."

The woman's expression went blank.

"Ma'am?" Simeon prompted after a few seconds of stony silence.

She looked coolly at both of them. "Just a moment." And then she disappeared behind the filing cabinets.

Crow took a few steps toward the exit, but Simeon caught his hand and dragged him back. He didn't say anything, but he gave Crow's hand a squeeze and smiled at him, which was enough to rebuild some of Crow's courage. Simeon let go just as a third woman appeared.

She closely resembled her colleagues but was at least in

her seventies. Her steel-gray hair was in a tight bun, and she wore a polyester pantsuit and an eggplant-colored cardigan. She carried a very sharp pair of scissors, which was slightly alarming. And judging from the look in her brown eyes, she knew exactly who Crow was—and his mother's family.

"You are Sara Storey's son," she said as soon as she reached the low wall separating them.

"Yes."

"And you want to know where she came from."

"Yes."

"Why?"

Crow wasn't sure how to answer that. He almost looked to Simeon for rescue again, but that wasn't fair. This was Crow's problem.

"I think... I think there's something unusual about her birth family. Dangerous. It's made me dangerous too."

She cocked her head. "And you wish to join them?"

"No."

After a moment, the woman sighed. "What about your father? Who is he?"

"He was murdered before I was born."

"And how old was your mother?"

"Eighteen."

She nodded as if this was meaningful. "It was hoped that things would be otherwise with her. She was an aberration. Don't bristle at me like that, young man—it's the simple truth. Her father was a very ordinary man, and it was hoped that watering down the stock would help. Which it clearly hasn't, even after a second generation." She waved her free hand in Crow's direction.

"Watering down *what* stock?"

A big clock on the wall, like the ones that had hung in Crow's elementary school, ticked loudly. That was the only sound. No traffic noise from the street, no humming air conditioner despite the cool office air, no voices or type-writers or telephones or other clerical noises.

Finally, the woman gave a small shrug. "I'm Miss Aisa. Follow me."

Crow indicated Simeon, hoping Simeon wouldn't mind. "Him too."

"Well, of course. You two are twined together, aren't you? Birds of a feather."

What did that mean? Did she think they were lovers? And if so, was she truly so indifferent to it? Simeon and Crow exchanged confused glances before trailing her deeper into the office area. There was no sign of the other women behind the file cabinets—just large wooden desks piled with papers, and spools of thread scattered everywhere. The papers made sense; the thread would have been more sensible in a tailor's shop. But neither Crow nor Simeon asked for an explanation, and Miss Aisa took them behind more file cabinets, made of wood and so tall that they nearly reached the ceiling. A ladder would be needed for the top drawers.

At the far back of the office stood a round wooden table, ancient-looking and with an inlaid mosaic top. When Crow tried to discern the pattern of the tile, he felt dizzy. There were three wood chairs at the table, elaborately carved and upholstered in crimson velvet.

"Sit," Miss Aisa ordered, and they obeyed. After she sat down, she spent a long time staring intently at Crow. Her scrutiny made him want to squirm; the scissors in her hand didn't make him any more comfortable.

"Tell me what you know," she said at last.

This wasn't at all the way things were supposed to go. He'd come to get answers, not to be interrogated by a slightly terrifying old woman. But if he refused, she'd likely turn him away.

"I'm going to sound crazy," he warned.

Her laugh was sharp. "I very much doubt that. Simply tell me what you can, boy. Your thief can help you."

While Crow tried not to choke on his own tongue in response to her statement, Simeon leaned forward, eyes full of wonder. "Cor blimey," he said quietly. "You're not who you appear to be, are you?"

"Young man, I am *exactly* whom I appear to be." She opened and closed the scissors a few times, creating a *snip snip* as she cut the air. "But you do have a knack for finding yourself in unusual company, don't you?"

"I do indeed."

So Crow told her... well, pretty much his life story. Which ended up being longer and more complicated than he'd anticipated, especially when he got to the most recent parts and Simeon chimed in. Simeon was an excellent story-teller, which shouldn't have surprised Crow at all. The sunbeams and shadows shifted across the room as they spoke, and twice Miss Aisa stood and fetched them glasses of juice—Crow couldn't identify what kind of fruit, but it was delicious—and she never seemed bored or impatient. The telephones never rang to interrupt them. Nobody else entered the office, and the two younger women never reappeared.

Finally all the words were out and Crow and Simeon waited.

"Well," said Miss Aisa. She opened and shut her scissors without looking at them. "I'd like to point out that this wasn't our fault. Despite what some people say, we don't *control* most things. Not nowadays. We have become firm believers in free will."

"I don't think I understand."

She waved her free hand as if his statement didn't matter. "And also, in most cases we don't watch closely. How could we, with so many lives at once? Oh, a long time ago it wasn't so bad, but the numbers have risen like a Malthusian nightmare. We can't possibly keep up. But we do our best with what we can." *Snip-snip.*

While Crow tried to make sense of all of this, Simeon leaned forward, his folded arms on the table. "Ma'am, Crow doesn't want to place blame. He's just hoping for answers, yeah? And perhaps solutions."

She gave a brisk nod. "Solutions are not within our bailiwick. But I can tell you some things that may prove useful."

That was something, anyway, and a bit of weight seemed to lift from Crow's shoulders. Not that he should be getting too optimistic, but anything would be better than nothing. "Please. I'd really appreciate it."

The smile she gave him was surprisingly warm and sympathetic. "It is a shame things didn't work out for you as hoped. But there's still time, young man. Until the thread is cut, things can still change." She stood, disappeared behind some file cabinets, and quickly returned with a tray containing more juice and several small dishes containing olives, dried figs, crackers, and a crumbly white cheese. "Help yourself, boys."

Crow hadn't realized he was hungry until he began to nibble, and the snacks were delicious. Simeon seemed to be enjoying them too.

Miss Aisa didn't eat or drink anything, but she nodded approvingly at the two of them. "This agency is quite special, as you may have surmised. We handle very unusual cases, ones that ordinary agencies wouldn't know what to do with. We started it on a whim, I suppose, a way to pass the time, but it's also fulfilling. We find homes for those who are exceptionally hard to place."

"Like my mother," said Crow.

"Yes. And others as well. Yesterday, for example, we

placed a charming changeling boy into a loving family. His biological parents couldn't care for him—the fae can sometimes be too reckless in their child-rearing—but his new parents will take good care of him."

Simeon worked his jaw and looked away, but when Crow patted his leg with clumsy comfort, Simeon managed a smile.

"But my mother?" Crow prompted.

"I can't tell you about her people. It's not my tale to share, you see. But I can say that most of them are not any more dangerous than human beings. Which, frankly, isn't saying much, but they're not generally *evil*. There's a strain among them, however, that runs bad. I suppose it's like certain inherited illnesses among humans. This strain runs in your mother's family."

"And in me." The peculiar thing was how normal it felt to be having this very odd discussion with this very odd woman, in a weird office in Omaha with Simeon at his side and the taste of briny olives on his tongue.

Miss Aisa shrugged. "So it seems. Your mother's mother hoped that she was free of it. She chose a human father for her child to even further reduce the risk. But then your grandmother was struck—quite a bit later than the norm—when her daughter was still an infant. There was no immediate family who could care for the babe. It was decided that the best course of action would be to place her with a human family. Which we did." That was followed by a deep sigh.

Crow suddenly had a terrible thought. "Aunt Helen."

"Oh no, dear, don't worry about her. She's entirely human and ordinary."

Although Crow wanted to argue that his Aunt Helen was *not* ordinary and was in fact very special, that wasn't the important point at the moment. "But you placed her too."

"We did. Your grandparents came to us looking for a second child. They likely couldn't have afforded an adoption through most agencies, but they were good people, so we found them your Helen. Whose mother was a young waitress in Scottsbluff and whose father was a truck driver—already married—who sometimes drove through."

That was a lot better than Sara's background. Just normal human imperfections of the sort that were enacted by millions of good people every day.

"Placing my mother with the Storeys was not a great course of action. They're dead."

Miss Aisa narrowed her eyes. "They loved your mother, yes?"

"Yes."

"So deeply that when she abandoned all of you, they were deeply wounded."

Crow sighed. "Yes."

"They loved you as well?"

He knew the answer deep in his heart. "They did."

"They had your mother to love for eighteen years and then you for eighteen beyond that. Thirty-six years is a good stretch by human terms. Do you think that, given the choice, they would have given up those years in exchange for... what? Another decade or two of life?"

It wasn't a fair question because, of course, they'd had no such choice. And hadn't Miss Aisa been going on about free will just a few minutes ago? But then, people almost never had the opportunity to make those sorts of decisions. Even Crow, who'd been given a terrifying hint about his future the day he wandered into Madam Persephone's tent, hadn't been able to clearly see the consequences of his actions. Hindsight is twenty-twenty, they said, but the future is always a myopic blur.

"I don't think they would have traded us away like that," Crow said.

"So then perhaps the placement *was* the best among many bad options."

Crow slumped in his chair. He wanted to rail against the unfairness of it all, but he knew that was a fool's game. Of *course* life was unfair. Who promised anything different? And with Simeon next to him, Crow could also understand the gifts he'd been given, unearned. He hadn't had to grow up in an orphanage or try to survive on the streets of a slum. And even during the past decade of drifting and fleeing, he'd always carried a sense of home in his heart because he knew that long ago he'd been loved.

His voice was scratchy when he spoke. "I don't want to be"—how had she put it?—"*struck*. I want to be free of this strain. Is that possible?"

"I don't know. You've escaped it thus far—"

"Escaped? They've killed people I cared about. They almost killed Helen and Simeon just yesterday!" God, had that only been a day ago?

"But you haven't joined them. And as I've already said, until the thread is cut, hope remains."

Hope had been in short supply for his entire life.

"What do I do?" Crow asked.

"It's not my place to advise you. But I can give you information. I can tell you where your mother was born."

"Yes. Please."

She opened a cleverly hidden drawer in the side of the table and pulled out a little spiral notepad and pen. She wrote something on the top sheet, tore the paper out, and folded it into quarters. Then she reached over and handed it to him. "Look later. After you leave here."

"Okay." He slipped it into his pocket. She might not have given him what she promised, but he couldn't force her to reveal things. He'd just have to draw on that hope she was talking about.

She stood and then guided them back into the reception area. Just in front of the door, she paused and looked at Simeon. "You haven't asked anything about yourself, young man."

"Do you have anything to tell me?"

"No. I don't often look at the past. It's murky. But I can point out that cast iron is often tempered to increase its strength. The tempering process can be difficult. But without it, the iron could not withstand nearly as much."

Simeon gave one of his rare frowns. "I'm not metal, ma'am."

"Unruffle your feathers. The principle is sound."

On that note, she opened the door for them.

"Thank you," said Crow, feeling awkward again. "For—"

"Your gratitude is noted."

But before they could step out, she stopped Simeon with a hand to his chest. At least she didn't poke him with her scissors. "Young man, you may keep that item in your pocket. Consider it a gift from me and my sisters. But use it carefully." She dropped her hand and ushered them out the door, which shut firmly as soon as they were in the hallway.

Crow waited to speak until they were out on the sunbaked sidewalk. "I've never met anyone who talked in so many riddles. Who do you think she really is?"

"Dunno. Sphinx? Oracle? Mad old lady?"

"Or none of the above. What did you steal this time?" Crow wasn't even angry—just curious.

Grinning, Simeon pulled a spool of purple thread out of his pocket.

# CHAPTER 12

*A*lthough they'd had snacks at the Murray Family Agency, they decided coffee and a little something to eat wouldn't go amiss. Besides, it was brutally hot; Crow's shirt stuck to him and sweat dripped in itchy trickles down his nape. Luckily they happened on a diner only a couple of blocks away. It looked like the sort of place where nobody would mind if they loitered, and the frowsy interior was blessedly air-conditioned.

After some coffee and strawberry pie, they stared at each other across the Formica table.

"You don't want to look at the paper she gave you?" Simeon asked.

Crow scrunched up his face, remained silent, and stared at the bits of pie that remained on his plate. The truth was, he didn't know whether he wanted to look. The paper might not have the information Miss Aisa had promised. Or it might, and he'd go to the place where his mother had been born and then hit a dead end. Or he might go, only to discover that he could no longer control the monster within him.

"I want to just quit," he admitted. "Be a normal guy with a regular job, worry about stuff like taxes and elections and whether my roof's gonna last through another hailstorm."

"Can't."

"I know."

That didn't mean he couldn't sulk about it, though, so he did, using his fork tine to draw pictures in the smears of pie filling on his plate. When he realized that he was making a crude sketch of a bird, he pushed the plate away.

Simeon grabbed the plate and, grinning, stuffed the last bites of pie into his mouth. "Have you wondered what else might exist?"

"What do you mean?"

"Well, there's you, and we don't know who your granny was, but she wasn't human. I've seen some odd types at the carnival as well. Nice blokes, but not… not human, I expect. It stands to reason, then, that the world contains others as well. The creatures our ancestors believed in but that us modern sorts consider nothing but fairy tales."

It was a little distracting when Simeon licked the fork—a fact which he probably knew perfectly well. Crow tried to focus. "Like… what? Unicorns and ogres?"

"Miss Aisa mentioned the fae."

Yes, she had. But what had felt plausible within the weird confines of that office seemed crazy here, where the bored-looking waitress refilled his mug and the high school kids in a corner booth tossed french fries at one another.

"I'd fancy meeting a unicorn. Not that I've the prerequisite to attract one." Simeon gave a playful leer. "Or merfolk. Dragons? Not sure about that one. Rocs. Griffins. Perhaps a phoenix, arising beautiful from the ashes. You're a bit of a phoenix yourself, aren't you?"

"Wrong kind of bird. And I'm hardly beautiful."

Simeon's expression turned earnest. "You are, though.

The first moment I saw you, I found you handsome. A bit young, though. You're still handsome at first glance. But when I watch you over time and see the shadows and lights in your eyes, the careful way you hold yourself, the way you stumble over your own tongue at times.... Beautiful."

Crow blushed, something he rarely did. His face must be scarlet, judging by how his ears burned. "I'm not a good person. Or a good... whatever I am."

"Of course you are. Not a saint, but you keep saying no to those bloody birds. You hurt over every death they've caused. You could have lived your life any number of ways, but you've tried not to harm others. You don't even fancy it when I steal."

Fine. Looking at that stupid piece of paper had to be less painful than this. Crow drew it from his pocket and set it on the table, still tightly folded. It reminded him of when he and Marty used to play paper football during study hall. The teacher was an old guy who'd nod off over the newspaper, leaving the students to their own devices. Some of them actually studied, while others drew pictures in their notebooks or read novels or took naps of their own. As long as they were quiet, Mr. Steiner didn't notice. So Crow and Marty would flick a bulky triangle of paper back and forth, and Marty would keep score on a page of his geometry textbook.

"You've gone away from us, love."

Crow blinked. "Sorry. Just remembering something."

"Was it good?"

It was. Crow smiled as he recalled how eventually Marty would be unable to restrain his laughter, and Mr. Steiner would awake with a start and glare at them. And when everyone was finally released from study hall, Crow and Marty would thunder down the hallway to the cafeteria, cackling like a pair of madmen.

"Do you have any happy childhood memories, Simeon?"

"Yeah. Wasn't all gloom and doom. One year the foundling home had a new director, a bloke with progressive ideas. He brought in his wife and had her teach us to sing. I quite liked that. It sounded pretty, yeah? And if we did well, she'd give us boiled sweets after. One afternoon she had me sing 'Abide With Me'—a solo—and everyone listened and clapped after, and she told me I sang like a bird and gave me an entire bag of boiled sweets that I didn't have to share."

Simeon's eyes shone. Crow understood how important it would have been to an orphan child to get those moments of attention and approval. To feel special for that short time.

"Can you still sing?"

Simeon laughed. "Not much for hymns nowadays, but I expect so. In the carnival, I'd lead the chants when we were doing the heavy work like putting up the big top."

"I'd like to hear you sometime."

"Might do."

At that moment, what Crow wanted most in the world was to drag Simeon to the nearest motel, tear off their clothes, and lose himself in the heat of Simeon's skin. Instead he simply unfolded the paper.

"Where are we going next, love?"

Crow heaved a sigh. "Have you ever been to Washington state?"

THEY WENT to the public library first, an imposing modern building of white concrete and dark windows. Simeon barely had to flirt with the librarian before she fetched an appropriate atlas, from which they learned that Bayaq was a tiny town at the northern edge of Washington's Olympic Peninsula.

"How far is that from here?" Simeon traced his finger along the route, lifting it as he passed over the Rockies as if the peaks were real.

Crow had traveled enough to be able to guesstimate distances fairly well. "About two thousand miles."

Simeon whistled; the librarian didn't seem to mind.

But Crow was scowling. "We can't afford train or bus tickets that far. Even sleeping in our seats, we'd still need to eat, and—"

"Not to worry."

"But—"

"We've enough dosh for another night here in Omaha. You're going to make yourself cozy in a motel room, and I'll go out and collect funds." Simeon lifted a silencing hand. "And I promise I won't break your moral code in the process. Might bend it a bit, perhaps."

Until recently, Crow hadn't been aware that he *had* a moral code. It likely wasn't especially strict, but he didn't need more weight on his conscience. "What if you get caught?"

"A risk of the trade. But I won't."

And then he changed the subject by waving the librarian over and asking her questions about the Olympic Peninsula. Having visited there herself, she was delighted to answer them all. Crow didn't really pay attention—he was too busy worrying about everything—but Simeon hung on every one of the librarian's words, as if she were telling him the secrets of the universe instead of about seaports and rain shadows.

When they left the library, Simeon was practically skipping. "Mountains with snow on them! I've never seen that. Nor a rainforest. Nor—"

"We're not going there to sightsee."

Simeon huffed good-naturedly. "Perhaps not, but if we're going there, we might as well see the sights, yeah? Unless you'd rather that I blindfold you to ensure you don't possibly enjoy yourself even a bit." He laughed at Crow's predictable scowl.

With time on their hands, they wandered the Old Market area, with Simeon scoffing at the name because he didn't find the brick buildings all that old. "I'll wager none of them were built before I was born," he said. But he liked the converted warehouses anyway, window-shopping with such attentiveness that Crow wondered whether he was casing the joints for potential larceny.

When the heat became too oppressive, they ducked into a bar and nursed a beer each. Simeon gave a long speech on the merits of air-conditioning—and on central heat, which left Crow imagining what London winters had been like for him as a boy shivering in worn-out clothing, hungry and miserable.

During the depths of winter, when the wind rushed down from the Great Plains and made the Storey farmhouse shudder, Gran used to tuck Crow into bed under a mountain of quilts, a hot water bottle nestled against his feet. He'd lie on his mattress, wrapped like a burrito and with only his nose and upper face exposed, listening to the windows shake and, sometimes, the sleet rattle against the glass. He'd been grateful then for his home and for the knowledge that he'd wake up in the morning to a big bowl of steaming oatmeal, a mug of milky tea, and bacon still sizzling on the plate. If it was a school day and the weather was especially bitter, Grandad would take him in his old truck, saving Crow from having to walk a mile and a half.

"You're far away," Simeon said quietly.

"Sorry."

"Don't be. When you get like that, your face softens. You

look remarkably like the boy who caught me messing about in Madame Persephone's tent."

Crow shook his head. "That boy died in a fire."

"No, he's still in there. You ought to let him out more often."

Welcome Traveler

THEY HAD dinner at a cavernous Italian place, where they both ate too much garlic bread and spaghetti with meatballs. Simeon had never had spaghetti before. They both laughed themselves hoarse at his fledgling attempts to wrangle it and at the number of times the young waitress had to bring him more paper napkins. "All food should be this much fun," he declared.

"There's lots of fun food at the carnival," Crow reminded him. "Fried things on sticks, for example."

"Yeah, but those don't pose such a challenge to eat."

Somehow Crow ended up singing "On Top of Spaghetti," which amused Simeon and the family at the next table. The kids even joined in for the final stanza, and for once it was Crow who received big smiles from the waitstaff. He'd only consumed a single beer today, a couple of hours before dinner, but being in Simeon's company made him feel a little drunk.

They returned to the motel where they'd spent the previous night and ended up in the same room with its pair of twin beds and view of the unremarkable building across the street. Simeon left almost immediately and Crow didn't ask where he was going.

Only after he'd left did Crow realize that this was the first time they'd been apart since Mareado. The room wasn't especially big, but it now seemed empty and too quiet, and the television made a very poor substitute for Simeon's company. Swearing under his breath for allowing himself to get attached to someone, Crow washed a few things in the bathroom sink, hung them over the tub, and hoped they'd be dry by morning. Then he spent a long time staring at the paper Miss Aisa had given him, with its scroll penmanship and two words separated by a comma—city and state. He thought about her enigmatic comments to Simeon about cast iron needing to be tempered.

Crow had been tempered too, literally passing through a fire. The process may have hardened him, but he didn't believe it made him stronger. Perhaps he'd grown more brittle.

Simeon came back late, smelling of cigarettes, although Crow had never seen him smoke. Crow had been sitting in bed and fretting. He refused to admit to himself how relieved he felt at Simeon's return.

"Fruitful?" Crow asked drily.

"Quite. Did you know that certain gents around here fancy going to pubs and watching sporting events on the televisions? And that, furthermore, some of those gents become entirely bladdered and treat their waitresses like shite?"

Crow had a good idea where this was going. "And they lose track of their wallets along the way?"

"Precisely. There were loads of men like that where I came from as well, only without the televisions to distract them. Louts. There's no good reason to take liberties with some poor girl just trying to do her job."

After a moment of internal prodding, Crow determined that his conscience wasn't twinging at all.

Grinning, Simeon dumped a wad of bills onto Crow's bed. "Still haven't sussed out the costs of things here. Have we enough to get to Bayaq?"

It took Crow a few minutes to sort and count, and then he whistled. "This would get us there and back, no problem. How many people did you steal from tonight?"

"Enough. But they won't learn a lesson from it. I'm just a thief, not a priest or their mother. Someone else can teach them proper behavior." Simeon said this with a different accent than usual, sounding every inch the Victorian gentleman. Then he insisted on splitting the cash between them because, he said, it was always safest to spread one's wealth among different locations. Still looking pleased with himself, he hummed as he got ready for bed.

Crow fell asleep quickly and dreamed he was back in the Murray Family Agency offices, except the filing cabinets were gone and there was no sign of the women who worked there. The spools of thread *were* there, however, some of them much bigger than in real life. And there were hundreds of thousands of them. Millions, maybe. If he stared at any one of them for too long, it would writhe and pulsate a bit, making him uneasy.

He sat at the round table. A moment later a door appeared and Simeon strolled through it. Like Crow in this dream, he was naked, and although he didn't seem to care about that, he sighed loudly. "Again."

"I'm not doing it on purpose. I don't know how to stop."

Simeon took the seat next to his. "It's not so bad, really. More interesting than my dreams. Mine have rats in them, and shrieking rooks, and angry bobbies, and air so thick and gray that you choke on it."

*Mine have birds too.* But Crow didn't say that aloud for fear of summoning them. Evidently, though, the thought was enough. A flock of black crows swooped through an open window and settled among the spools to preen themselves.

"They don't seem hostile," Simeon pointed out.

Crow gazed at the shining feathers and intelligent, glittering eyes and saw that Simeon was right. The birds were unruffled, and some of them even seemed to be falling asleep. "What do they want?"

"The ones we saw in Chinkapin Grove—"

"*Those* were hostile. They almost killed us. Or you and Helen, at least. I probably would've survived."

One of the nearest crows, a particularly large specimen, made a noise that sounded remarkably like a human chuckle. Then it used its beak to mouth gently at a spool of lilac-colored thread, although it disturbed neither the spool nor the thread.

"Did they almost kill us?" asked Simeon. "I got the impression they herded us into the barn."

"Which they destroyed."

"We didn't see that bit. What if they shooed us in there to protect us, and something else made the building collapse?"

Crow opened his mouth to protest and then stopped. It was true that they hadn't witnessed the actual destructive acts. And when the three humans were outside, the birds hadn't directly harmed them.

"Miss Aisa said most of your grandmother's folk aren't bad. What if the good ones are trying to look out for you?"

That strange thought was surprisingly comforting. For a decade now, Crow had been under siege. It would certainly be nice to have allies. But then he frowned. "If they're so helpful, where have they been all these years? People have died."

As if in answer, the nearby large crow tapped its beak, hard, on the top of the spool. It looked at Crow expectantly, as if he ought to know what this meant. But when Crow shook his head slightly, the bird made a raspy caw and hopped away.

# CHAPTER 13

The bus ride from Omaha toward Seattle was a form of torture. For one thing, the first leg of the trip began shortly after dawn, the early start making Crow groggy and out of sorts. Simeon, of course, was an early bird, sprightly and cheerful, which by all rights should have grated on Crow's nerves but didn't.

The second form of torture was sitting next to him on the bus and watching him gaze out at the scenery as if endless acres of corn and soybeans were remarkable. Again, Crow did not find this annoying. He was instead entranced, drawn to Simeon like a drab moth to bright flame. Crow couldn't get enough of watching his dark eyes sparkle, his agile mouth lift into a hundred versions of smiles, his broad fingers move across the window glass as he traced the shapes that he saw. Simeon's hair seemed extra glossy today. He smelled like coffee and the chocolate pastries they'd grabbed for break-fast. Crow wanted to melt into him and feel their nerves sing together.

"You look as if you're starving and you fancy me for dinner," Simeon said somewhere near the western edge of

South Dakota, where golden wheat fields rolled like sea swells.

Crow blushed and looked down at his feet. "Sorry."

"Wasn't complaining." Simeon leaned in closer, although nobody was sitting close enough to overhear. There were only a few other passengers and most appeared to be dozing, except for a woman a few rows behind them. "We could get off at the next stop. Spend the night at a motel. Catch another bus tomorrow."

A part of Crow was badly tempted by the idea, but he wanted to get to Bayaq as soon as possible. He shook his head and changed the subject. "I spent a little time north of here a few years back. There's a national park with bison and about a zillion prairie dogs."

"I'd heard that hunters had killed all the American bison."

"Most of them, yeah. But before they were completely wiped out, somebody stepped in to save them."

Simeon looked pensive. "I heard stories about the Wild West when I was a boy. Labored my way through reading stories about it in the newspapers. It sounded so entirely different to my life. Better, yeah? With the wide-open spaces and clean, hard work."

Although Crow didn't want to burst Simeon's bubble, he felt obligated to give a dose of reality. "You're right about the spaces. But white people slaughtered many of the Indians who were here first. The settlers did a pretty good job of killing each other too. Or they died of dysentery or cholera, or froze to death in blizzards, or drowned when the rivers flooded."

"I saw death nearly every day in London. And cruelty born of twisted hearts and stunted souls."

"How did you come out of that so... buoyant?"

That earned Crow a sweet smile. "Perhaps I came out of it *because* I'm buoyant. There was a woman who came into the foundling home when I was small. Toffs would do that now and then, I expect so they could tell their friends they were doing something to help the downtrodden poor. Or maybe they were simply bored. They'd come in and gawk at us, give us a Bible lesson or teach us a hymn, and then they'd go. Sometimes they'd take a girl home with them to work in the scullery or learn to sew, but they hadn't any use for the boys."

Crow remained shocked by Simeon's casual descriptions of his childhood but didn't say anything. He wanted to hear the rest of this story.

Simeon's eyes were focused on a time and place far away. "This particular woman was young and plump and pretty, but her hat was the grandest thing about her. It held an entire garden of silk flowers, all of them so bright among the ribbons that they seemed like a mirage inside our gloomy walls. I wanted to touch those flowers but knew I daren't. I stayed close to her, though, and I expect she found me charming instead of grubby, because she didn't seem to mind that I hung on to her skirts.

"She gave us a little lecture about how we ought to be quiet and obedient and diligent, and then we might lead happy lives despite our humble origins. A load of bollocks, of course—I knew that even then. But as she nattered on, I was able to slip in close and nick one of those flowers. She never noticed."

"What happened?" asked Crow.

"Nothing much. I kept that fake rose hidden in my clothing for days. I'd look at it now and then just to enjoy the brightness. Then one afternoon another boy caught me looking and fought me over it. I beat him bloody, I did, but when a monitor arrived, the boy told him about the flower and it was taken away. I got a caning over it, too."

"Simeon—"

"Don't." Simeon chucked Crow's cheek. "I got a lot of

canings, I did. Part of the tempering that Miss Aisa mentioned."

Crow wasn't comforted by Simeon's easy acceptance of brutality. "But you lost the flower."

"I didn't, though. Not really. Because by then I knew exactly what it looked like, what it felt like when I tickled the silk against my nose. They couldn't take *that* from me. So I learned a lesson: if you hold things close enough they'll always be yours. You can bring them along with you everywhere you go, no matter how miserable those places are. And then they're not so miserable."

A space opened up in Crow's chest and he breathed freely again. "Those joys you mentioned at the Sears Tower."

"I carry them with me. I've quite a collection now, and Crow, nobody has added more to it than you have."

They didn't kiss, not with the woman a few rows back staring gimlet-eyed. But they did interlace their fingers and that was nice as well.

The bus pulled into the Billings station past midnight, and they had an hour to spend before the connecting bus arrived. Luckily the depot's diner counter was open, so they ate burgers and fries and then bought enough packaged snacks to tide them over until they reached Seattle in the early evening. It wasn't a big station and there wasn't much to see, but it felt good to walk around, exercising muscles that had been idle for too long.

The next bus was even emptier than the last. The driver, a gray-haired man with deeply-etched frown lines, grunted at them as they boarded, but it was nothing personal. He also grunted at the college-aged boy, the grandmotherly woman with the overstuffed bag, and the work-gnarled man in grimy blue jeans.

Crow expected to fall asleep quickly, but somehow the blackness outside beguiled him. Once they left Billings—

which didn't take long—there were very few other towns and virtually no traffic. Just the bus on the highway, and the dark sky and dark ground meeting seamlessly, as if they were one and the same. Montana was known as Big Sky Country, but this emptiness felt strangely claustrophobic. Crow found himself yearning for a city, where even late at night there were bright lights and rumbling engines and pedestrians on mysterious errands.

Simeon had dozed off with his head on Crow's shoulder, his hair tickling Crow's cheek. Crow hoped he was having good dreams, free as they were of Crow's influence: dreams about colorful flowers and incense-scented tents, about spaghetti and french fries, about a Western landscape in which nobody was murdered and cowpokes gathered companionably around their campfires to sing plaintive songs.

Lightning flashed in the distance, startling Crow, but nobody else seemed to notice. Not even when another bolt came, and another, imprinting his retinas with their afterimages. A summer thunderstorm, maybe caused by a cool front sliding down from the mountains. It was too dark to see the clouds and judge the size of the storm. Crow hoped it would be one of the small ones that swept by quickly.

But there was a lot of lightning. Soon the sky was lit up almost constantly, the jagged bolts like a demon's neon signs. It was hard to judge distance, but it seemed as if the storm was moving closer—or that the bus was driving toward it, which was functionally the same thing. Maybe they were rushing to meet each other like long-lost lovers.

Soon Crow could hear the storm. The thunder seemed to travel through the metal sides of the bus as a barely audible deep, low rumble. The sound made the hairs on Crow's arms stand on end and set his teeth on edge.

*Just a storm*, he told himself. Not uncommon in this

region at this time of year. He'd experienced blizzards, and they were a lot more dangerous.

But the lightning continued and the thunder grew louder. A bolt touched down so close that he was momentarily blinded, and its cracking boom followed almost immediately after.

Everyone on the bus sat upright, startled and blinking, including Simeon. "What?" he asked.

"Thunderstorm."

Crow needn't have answered, because it was obvious what was going on. In front of them and on both sides, the sky sizzled and bellowed.

And then a moment later, the hail began.

Pea-sized, mothball-sized, penny-sized, or larger—Crow couldn't tell. But the din of the ice pummeling the roof was loud enough to compete with the thunder. It was like being inside a drum. All of the passengers were pale and grim-faced, their backs stiff and hands clenched.

But when a hailstone hit the window next to Simeon's head with enough force to crack the glass, Crow knew what he had to do. Lurching from his seat, he made his way to the front of the bus.

"Sit down, sir," growled the driver.

Instead, Crow bent in as close as he dared and lowered his voice, hoping nobody else would hear. "This is my fault. Stop the bus and let me out."

"We're in the middle of nowhere with fucking Armageddon going on out there. I ain't letting you off his bus. Go sit down!"

The driver's hands had a death grip on the wheel, his eyes trained doggedly forward. He looked like a man who'd just driven through the gates of Hell.

Crow considered forcing open the door himself. He'd probably survive the fall from the moving vehicle; he'd lived through much worse. But he was afraid that the driver would struggle to stop him, which might cause the accident that Crow was trying to avoid. Knowing he'd sound insane, he opened his mouth to plead with the man. But Simeon grabbed Crow's wrist and dragged him back to their seats.

"What in the bloody hell do you think you're doing?" Simeon kept his hand wrapped tightly around Crow's wrist. It hurt, although that hardly mattered.

"It's them. The ones who are after me. They're doing this."

Simeon, who'd accepted everything so far with equanimity, looked incredulous. "They can control the *weather*?"

"Sure. Why not? Jesus, Simeon, they're gonna kill you all." Crow tried without success to yank his arm free.

The other passengers had observed this unfolding drama, engrossing enough to slightly distract them from the storm. But they'd also heard what Crow said, and their expressions grew even more uneasy.

"Young man, young man." The grandmotherly woman was clearly addressing Simeon. "Does your friend have his medications available? If so, he needs to take them."

Crow laughed at the absurdity, which of course made him seem even more unhinged. Simeon might have attempted his charm trick on the woman, but he was too busy keeping Crow in his seat. "You can't go out into this," he hissed at Crow.

"I can't stay here!"

The lightning was now a constantly flashing sheet and the thunder a continuous banging. The hail provided a contratempo. It was a concert composed by the devil himself and Crow's racing heartbeat added to the chorus. Crow was frantic. He couldn't catch his breath and his skin felt on fire.

A hailstone struck the righthand side of the windshield, creating a spiderweb of cracks near the door. Just a moment later, another hit Simeon's window. This time the glass shattered, sending pebbled shards and a torrent of rain inward. In his shock, Simeon loosened his grip and Crow wrenched free.

He started to stand—

And a scream reverberated. He couldn't tell if it was human or rending metal. The bus lurched, forcing Crow to fall painfully into a row of seats, and then something impacted the bus with tremendous violence.

Tumbling through the spinning vehicle, Crow felt bones break: his right arm, his ribs, his right lower leg. His skull. Some object pierced his torso and ruptured something deep inside. He couldn't see anything, couldn't discern what direction was up, couldn't hear anything but an unearthly shrieking. He felt as if he were falling and flying at the same time, as though he were being flayed, as if he were being smothered by a blanket of feathers.

"Simeon!" He tried to shout but couldn't tell whether he said anything at all.

A wall of nothingness collapsed on him.

# CHAPTER 14

*oo many stars*, he thought.

Helpless, he fell up into them and tumbled through the diamond-speckled firmament. Sometimes his hands brushed through a cloud of space dust, tickling him, and sometimes he momentarily caught a planet like a lobbed softball and then let it go.

The stars sang to him in a language he couldn't comprehend. He couldn't control the movement of his body. But he didn't hurt.

Then Crow felt soft damp grass prickling under him and a hand on his cheek, and he realized he was still alive, lying on his back, staring up at a clear night sky. There were sirens nearby. Dancing red and blue lights. And directly above him, Simeon's blood-streaked face.

"You're hurt." Crow tried to reach up but his arm didn't want to obey. Fine. It could stay where it was.

Simeon made a wounded sound masquerading as laughter. "You were dead," he rasped.

"No."

"I saw you. Broken. Nobody could have survived—" His voice caught and he closed his eyes.

"I could," said Crow wearily. "I always do. I told you. It's the people around me who die."

Crow saw Simeon cut his eyes away, toward the spot where the lights and the noise were coming from, and Crow knew that more deaths had been added to his conscience. But not Simeon's. God, it was selfish to be grateful, but Crow was.

"Tell me," he commanded, although he knew the important parts.

"We collided with a lorry. A big one. We... I believe the bus rolled. It was confusing. By the time I crawled out of the wreckage, the storm was gone, almost as if it had never been there at all, except the ground was wet. And I found you here. Not breathing. There wasn't enough of you left intact *to* breathe."

"Oh." Crow managed to move one arm and then the other. He was about as coordinated as a newborn, but aside from a general dull ache, he wasn't in pain. "And the others?"

Simeon winced. "Both drivers dead. The emergency crew is working on the others. They took one look at you and decided you were far past helping."

That was probably just as well. Crow didn't know what his regeneration process entailed, exactly, but he figured the fewer witnesses, the better. He didn't want to end up being experimented on in some government agency's lab.

"But you're hurt," Crow pointed out again.

"Nothing important. A few cuts and bruises."

"You're covered in blood."

"Mostly yours, love."

Ah. Crow mustered all his strength and determination and managed to sit up. Simeon looked alarmed but didn't try to stop him; in fact, he held a steadying hand to Crow's shoulder.

Up a gentle embankment, the bus lay on its side in the grass, like a great beast done in by hunters. The truck—a semi—was nearby, the cab crumpled inward and the trailer jackknifed at a painful angle. And beyond that were police cars, fire trucks, ambulances—a surprisingly large number of emergency vehicles considering their remote location. He wondered who had alerted the authorities to the accident and how long it had taken them to arrive. There were about a half-dozen cars and pickup trucks on the side of the highway and what looked like the population of a small city standing around or kneeling over bodies on the ground.

Crow and Simeon watched silently as someone was transferred to a stretcher and placed into an ambulance, which sped away into the night. A few minutes later, the actions were repeated with a second patient. The third one managed to walk to a police car with assistance from a paramedic. But nobody seemed in any hurry to move the three remaining bodies, two of which had blankets draped over them.

"I did this," Crow whispered.

"Bollocks. Stop blaming yourself, mate. It's too close to self-pity."

Shame stabbed at Crow. Simeon's words, though perhaps harsh, were correct. People were injured and dead while he was fine, and once again he was making it all about him. "Are you really okay?" he murmured.

"I'm fine." Simeon slung an arm around Crow's shoulders. It felt good. "A bit shook up after seeing you dead, but…."

After a while, a cop wandered over. He looked young and somewhat overwhelmed. There probably weren't a lot of storm-related mass casualties in his jurisdiction. When he saw Crow sitting upright rather than going into rigor mortis, his jaw dropped. Recovering, his voice came out as a squeak. "I thought—"

Although Crow had no idea how to explain his resurrection, Simeon came to the rescue. "He looked a right mess, didn't he, guv? I thought the same myself."

"But he was…. I saw his insides."

"Trick of the light, I expect. Casting all kinds of odd shadows, and of course he was soaking wet from the rain as well, and there was a good bit of blood. I reckon he scraped his noggin. Those wounds bleed more than they ought to."

The cop blinked a few times before seeming to accept that Crow really was alive; and since people couldn't just rise from the dead, there must have been a mistake earlier. "I'll need a statement from you, sirs. It shouldn't take long. Then I can take you into town so you can get cleaned up and catch some sleep. I guess you can catch the next bus tomorrow night."

That sounded like an excellent plan to Crow, who badly wanted a shower. He was hungry too; regenerating took a lot of energy. Also, he wanted to get a closer look at Simeon in decent light to make sure his injuries were as minor as he claimed.

The cop's name tag said Deputy Stone, but by the time he finished asking questions, Simeon was on a first-name basis and calling him Wyatt. He was younger than Crow and trying hard to be professional, but sometimes he stumbled a bit and then blushed. Crow and Simeon told him the basics: there had been a fierce thunderstorm, the driver tried to steer through it despite some damage from hail, and then they'd crashed into something—the truck, they knew now—and rolled.

"That storm was the damnedest thing," said Wyatt. He'd taken off his cap to scratch his head. "Not a word about it in the forecasts, and not a drop of rain in town. That's less than ten miles from here."

"You Yanks do have interesting weather." Simeon said it as if that were something to be proud of.

"Guess so."

When Wyatt was satisfied with their answers, he walked them to his cruiser and settled them into the back with some fussiness, like a grandmother making sure the kids were comfortable. Then he loped off, presumably to talk to his colleagues and to let the paramedics know that the final victims had refused treatment.

"Well, this is loads better than a Black Maria." Simeon petted the upholstery. "As if being hauled off to jail isn't bad enough, the bobbies'll do it in a wagon reeking of piss and puke."

"Were you hauled off to jail often?"

Simeon shrugged. "More often than I preferred, love." He squirmed a bit in his seat. "I've something to show you. Found it next to your bod—next to you."

Although Crow knew exactly what Simeon had found, he didn't say so, instead nodding mutely for him to go on. Simeon pulled something out of his jeans pocket and placed it on his open palm. A feather, of course, its barbs crusted together into clumps. It was too dark in the back of the patrol car to discern colors well, but Crow knew that the feather was coated in dried blood—his own or Simeon's. And that the feather itself was the same hue as the blood.

"As if there were any question of the cause," Crow muttered. "They leave their sign just to taunt me."

Simeon held the feather's shaft between finger and thumb and twirled it slowly, contemplatively. "It's a sign of weakness," he finally said. "They wouldn't do it if they were confident of winning."

Crow only sighed and shook his head.

By the time Wyatt returned, Crow was leaning, half-asleep, against Simeon's shoulder. If the deputy objected to that, he didn't say anything. Instead, he got into the driver's seat, shut the door, and pulled smoothly out onto the highway.

ACCORDING to the sign at the city limits, Lemont had a population of 577. This early in the morning, there were few indications of life among the handful of businesses, and the windows were dark in all of the houses. But a middle-aged couple was waiting at the Stewart Family Motel when Wyatt pulled into the parking lot. He must have radioed ahead and told them what to expect, because they appeared only a little shocked at the dried blood that still liberally covered both Simeon and Crow.

"Oh, you poor things!" said the woman. "That must have been such a terrifying experience! A couple of years ago I was driving out to Three Forks to visit my sister, and my truck blew a tire, and—"

"Doris," interrupted the man. "I think our guests need rest more than they need your stories."

Unoffended, she laughed. "Of course. I *do* go on sometimes. Boys, your room is all set. I put in extra soap and towels."

That sounded like one version of heaven. But Crow had other concerns as well. "Ma'am, is there somewhere we can get food? Doesn't have to be anything fancy."

Doris looked thoughtful. "Well, the grocery store won't be open until eight. The Conoco opens at six, and they have candy bars and Twinkies and the like. And Lemont Grill—they have real good breakfasts—they open at seven. But I'll tell you what. You go get settled and I'll have Frank bring you some sandwiches."

"I'd appreciate that, ma'am." Crow felt as if he ought to tip a hat like in a Western. Too bad he didn't have one.

Doris headed off to the little house at one end of the L-shaped motel, while Frank and Wyatt accompanied them to a room at the other end. Wyatt carried their bags, which he'd apparently retrieved from the remains of the bus. There was just a bit of awkward shuffling while Simeon and Crow thanked Wyatt, and Wyatt told them to have their hosts call the sheriff if anything was needed. Frank demonstrated how to work the television and the climate control, and as he left, promised a food delivery soon.

The room was blessedly silent once Crow and Simeon were alone, but under the bright overhead light, Simeon looked awful. Dried blood stained his clothing and flaked from his face and hair. Crow likely looked just as bad, if not worse, and it was a testament to Doris and Frank's fortitude that they hadn't freaked out. "I want to check you over for injuries," Crow said.

Simeon's face lit up. "You fancy playing doctor?"

"I fancy making sure you're going to survive until breakfast. I bet Doris and Frank have a first-aid kit we could borrow. They seem like the type, don't they?"

"Go wash up, love. You can have a look at me later."

Deciding it wasn't worth arguing over who showered first, Crow made his way to the bathroom. It felt wonderful to get the blood and grime and fuck-knew-what-else off his skin. There were a few small pinkish scars scattered on his limbs and a larger one near the center of his stomach, but he knew from experience that they'd be gone within hours and he'd be good as new.

Fuck.

He emerged from the bathroom in a cloud of steam, a

towel wrapped around his hips. Simeon was sitting at the room's small table, now covered in plates. "Doris is a treasure," he announced. "And Frank brought first-aid supplies as well."

"Good. Let me—"

"Eat. Doctoring later." Simeon stood and hurried to the bathroom before Crow could complain.

And anyway, eating sounded like a wonderful idea. As promised, Doris had sent sandwiches—four of them, each piled high with meat and cheese and tomatoes. There was also a bowl of baked beans and another of macaroni and cheese, along with a couple of apples, two big wedges of chocolate cake, a quart of milk, and a pitcher of iced tea. Crow dug in immediately.

Simeon returned fairly quickly, dressed identically to Crow, and took the other chair. He seemed as enthusiastic about the food as Crow was, and between the two of them they demolished everything. "Being nearly killed works up an appetite, it seems," said Simeon after wiping his mouth with a paper napkin.

"It does for me because I heal—" Crow stopped himself with a grunt as a realization hit him. If he hadn't already been sitting down his knees might have given out.

"What's wrong? You look as if you've seen a ghost."

*I might have, or close enough.* "You're really not badly hurt, are you?" There were a few scratches on Simeon's body, and some interesting bruises were forming here and there, but that was all.

"Told you I wasn't."

"Yeah, but why not? That wreck would have killed me. It *did* kill three people, and it looked like the others were in bad shape. But you don't even need Band-Aids. How come?"

Simeon frowned slightly. "Just lucky, I expect."

"What do you remember about the accident itself?"

175

"Er… the storm. You were being mulish and trying to get out of the bus. That woman thought you were barmy. Then…." He thought for a moment, brow creased. "Thud? I may have hit my head on something. What I recall next is kneeling on the grass with your corpse in my arms." Simeon shuddered and wrapped his arms around himself, although the room wasn't cold.

It could be nothing but luck, as Simeon said. Maybe his part of the bus was better reinforced or had somehow avoided the worst of the impact. Except Crow had been inches away from him, and he certainly hadn't escaped serious damage.

Crow had been dragging Simeon into his dreams, which meant that Crow had some kind of metaphysical connection to him. What if that connection extended further? What if it meant that Crow's resistance to death was now shared with Simeon as well? The idea filled him with an equal mixture of horror and exultation. Horror because Simeon had never consented to be engulfed by Crow's spooky weirdness. And exultation if it meant that Simeon was now protected from harm.

Turning over how best to broach this subject, Crow glanced up at Simeon—and saw that he was still trembling, his skin paler than usual. Alarmed, Crow lurched out of his seat to crouch beside Simeon. "What's wrong? Is it internal injuries? I can call—"

"Dead."

"What?"

Simeon sounded very young, and Crow remembered that he *was* very young in terms of actual number of years lived. "You were dead," Simeon said.

"But I'm fine now. And, um, not a zombie or anything."

"I thought I'd lost you forever. I can't— I couldn't abide that."

Crow's breath hitched when he caught Simeon's meaning. "I'm *fine* now," he repeated, but this time more gently.

And then somehow they were standing, clutching each other in a fierce embrace, Simeon half-sobbing, half-babbling into Crow's neck. "We've not known each other long," Simeon said. "I know that. And I'm only a thief, a man of no account at all, and you're— But I'm connected to you, don't you see? Never fancied being adrift before, but now I believe I'll sink without you. The world without you would be far too empty." He tried to pull away, but now it was Crow's turn to keep *him* close.

"I care about you," Crow admitted. "So much it hurts, and I haven't cared about anyone in a very long time."

Simeon locked gazes with him. "Don't lie to make me feel better."

"I have a lot of faults, but lying isn't generally one of them. How could I not care for you?"

"Because I'm nice to look at, yeah?"

Jesus. This wasn't an aspect of Simeon's personality that Crow had glimpsed before. He kicked himself for not noticing that a lot of that self-confidence was a mask. "You're the most remarkable person I've ever met, okay? The way you can make anyone feel comfortable and at ease. The way I keep slamming you with the weirdest shit in the universe— sometimes *deadly* weird shit—and you accept it all. The way you're up for any adventure and never complain. The way you make me see that sometimes there are glimpses of light in this dark world."

That was a speech. Crow had never made a speech before; it wasn't his style. But he meant every word, and now Simeon was staring at him as if *Crow* were one of those lights.

And then they were kissing.

Not their first kiss, but the most desperate, the most

passionate. The one that made Crow nearly forget everything except how badly he wanted Simeon. *Needed* him.

The towels had fallen away from both of them and they were chest to chest, hard cock to hard cock, fitting together like lock and key, all heat and mouth and tongue and hands and skin, glorious skin, and—

Ah, but Crow only *nearly* forgot.

"We can't," he groaned, going still.

"Why not?"

"What if I'm sick? Dee. He was so young and vibrant, and then he… wasn't, and—"

"Love. You told me the disease is spread in blood, yeah? I had your blood all over me tonight. If there's anything I can catch from it, I expect I already have."

Crow moaned. "Oh no. I didn't—"

Simeon cupped Crow's face. "We already had that chat about self-blame, didn't we? No more of it. I've made my choices knowingly. I choose you."

"Oh." Crow let out a long breath. Simeon had faced death twice since meeting Crow and he'd not run away; he knew and accepted the risks. And it was quite possible that Crow didn't carry the virus. And even if he did, it seemed increasingly likely that his immunity to its effects might carry over to Simeon as well.

"I'm not sure if I'm thinking with my brain or my libido," Crow said with choked laugh.

"Then stop thinking at all. Enough of that already today, innit? And too much fear and sorrow. We're both due for—"

"Joy."

Simeon's smile would have illuminated a stadium.

Crow stood there for a moment, made dizzy by Simeon's sudden shift from post-shock to passion to delight. Simeon was like a human storm bringing fascination and pleasure instead of destruction. Before Crow could decide what to do about it, Simeon launched himself against Crow, driving him back across the small room and against one of the beds, pushing him not especially gently onto the mattress, collapsing on top and making them both *oof*.

God, Simeon's strong back and rounded ass, the silkiness of his still-damp hair, the chocolate taste of his kisses. And his clever hands that somehow managed to touch all the right spots on Crow's body even though Crow was sandwiched thoroughly between Simeon and the comforter.

For the first time without the assistance of booze or drugs, Crow lost himself—and it was wonderful. He was no longer haunted and hunted, not for now. He was a creature whose only purpose was to feel good and to make Simeon feel good, and there was no dark past or uncertain future for either of them. Just the glorious now.

They'd landed on the bed without grace or calculation, and after nearly tumbling off for the third time, they stood— still somewhat entangled—stripped off the comforter, and collapsed back down in a more sustainable position. Crow was still underneath, which gave him the advantage of touching more of Simeon's skin. But Simeon could use his greater weight and superior location to direct how things went. Both of these things satisfied Crow. It was like a contest neither could lose.

Like a big cat, Simeon licked the side of Crow's ribcage. "You're a better feast than Doris's cooking," he purred before gnawing gently on a clavicle.

Crow, who'd never been much for talking during sex, was content to listen to Simeon whisper incomprehensible British slang into his ear. Crow did manage appreciative moans now and then, but his mouth was mostly busy with other things. He sucked and nibbled on Simeon's nipples, enjoying their flavors of salt and soap. Judging from the resulting blasphemies and thrusts, Simeon enjoyed it too.

At some point, however, a problem made itself known in Crow's befogged brain. "We don't have lube."

Simeon stopped what he was doing. "What?"

Shit. K-Y probably hadn't been invented yet in Simeon's time. "Lubricant. God, I want you in me, but—"

"Lovely." With considerable enthusiasm, Simeon scooted to the foot of the bed and knelt, hauled Crow's legs onto his shoulders, and demonstrated that his magic mouth could do more than charm strangers. Crow didn't know what was better. Was it his view of Simeon's dark head at his groin, the long line of Simeon's spine, the rounded mounds of his ass waggling teasingly? Or was it the hot, slick tongue inside him, the broad fingers probing until Crow clutched the sheet in his fists and tried to impale himself on whatever body part Simeon wanted to use?

No. What was better was when Simeon slid his cock into Crow. Slowly—somewhere between care and a tease—and with his polished obsidian gaze never moving from Crow's face.

"All right?" Simeon asked.

Crow managed a grin. "Fuck me."

And Simeon complied. His movements were long and slow and deep. Deliberate, like choreography. He stroked Crow's cock in synchrony. And he kept up a whispered, urgent litany of praise and bliss.

Crow's climax began deep in his core and spread like hot honey, loosening tense muscles and blinding him with sparkling lights. He might have cried out. He might even have sobbed.

Simeon followed a moment later with a string of inchoate oaths.

Then they were huddled together in the too-narrow bed with Simeon as the big spoon, his damp cock nestled softly in the cleft of Crow's ass. When Simeon chuckled, his breath tickled the back of Crow's neck. "D'you reckon that when we leave, Doris will suss out what's what and be scandalized?"

"Possibly." Crow didn't care. Right now he couldn't care about anything except for how very much he wanted to remain exactly like this for eternity.

Simeon kissed his nape. "You need to know something."

Uh oh. "What?"

"I always enjoy getting a leg over, and I've never especially minded who with. It's all just a bit of fun, innit? But this, with you? It means something."

Crow let out a long sigh of surrender. "What does it mean?"

"Dunno yet, do I? We'll have to work it out, you and I."

And suddenly exhaustion collided with Crow like an out-of-control semi. He yawned, and then yawned again. He thought about rolling out of bed and cleaning up a little. At least brushing his teeth. He was still considering it when he fell asleep.

# CHAPTER 15

*S*ince nobody disturbed them, it was nearly noon by the time they left the bed and got dressed. Grinning, Simeon did his best to make it look as if both beds had been slept in, but Crow wasn't sure that Doris and Frank would be fooled.

The travelers emerged from their room into glaring sunshine and stood there blinking, trying to get their bearings. There were only three cars in the parking lot, two of them from out of state. Over the roofline of the motel, off in the distance, loomed a sharp spine of mountains. A single black bird perched on the motel sign and watched them. Crow tried not to worry about that.

Doris emerged from the office, smiling broadly. "You boys look well rested. Just what you needed after that terrible accident, I'm sure."

No, what they'd needed was something quite different, but Crow wouldn't tell her that.

Simeon, naturally, rose to the occasion. "That delicious meal did wonders, ma'am. We're grateful for your kindness."

Doris's round cheeks pinked. "Well, I don't want you to have only bad impressions about Montana."

"It's a beautiful place, ma'am, with beautiful people."

The thing that made Simeon's charm work so well, Crow concluded, was that his words were sincere. Sure, he overplayed a little, and that accent didn't hurt either. But he wasn't lying, and people could tell.

"Well now," she said, a little flustered. "I have a message for you from Deputy Stone. He's off duty now, but he asked me to make sure and tell you." She pulled a paper from her jeans pocket, squinted at it for a moment, and then seemed to remember the reading glasses on a chain around her neck. She perched them on her nose. "There'll be seats for you on tonight's bus, so no worries there. The bus company will be paying your bill here, and wherever you eat today, you should keep the receipts and get them to reimburse you. You'll just need the incident report. And you'll need that, too, if you want to file a lawsuit. Someone from the sheriff's office will drop off a copy this afternoon."

Really, people ought to be suing Crow over the wreck, not that he had any assets for them to take.

"This means you boys have the whole afternoon and evening free. Maybe you just want to rest up after all the trauma, but if you want to do a little exploring, you have a few options."

"I'd fancy a bit of a tour," said Simeon.

She giggled like a schoolgirl. "Not much to tour, really. The historic city hall and fire station are a few blocks from here, and just beyond that is the old jail. It's mostly in ruins, but you can look if you want. Better yet, though, Lemont Reservoir is about a mile away. Lots of folks go there to swim or fish. Now, if you had a car you could get to Yellowstone, but—"

"That's all right, ma'am. We're content to spend the day in Lemont."

Returning to their room, they discarded the now-ruined clothes from the previous day, then washed a few items in the sink and hung them to dry. Afterward they wandered down the road into what passed for a downtown. The tavern served up some decent burgers, and the walking tour started with a quick look at the worn brick building that housed the fire department. They avoided the jail, and then walked to the reservoir. The temperature was warm enough to be pleasant but not overbearing.

There were quite a few people at the reservoir: families with young kids splashing in the water, clusters of teenagers listening to boomboxes, and a few groups fishing from small boats. But there was plenty of space, so Crow and Simeon picked a quiet grassy spot partially surrounded by low trees.

"The lake looks lovely," Simeon said morosely.

"I'm pretty certain Montana frowns on public skinny-dipping."

"Shame."

They took off their shoes and socks, though, and rolled up their jeans, letting the water lap gently at their shins. The slight breeze brought snatches of children's laughter and Bruce Springsteen. Dragonflies and butterflies darted and dipped in the air, while above them not a single cloud marred the blameless blue sky. If any ravens or crows were watching, Crow didn't see them.

Simeon let out a long, contented sigh. "I couldn't have dreamed of this when I was a boy. Didn't know it was possible to find such peace."

Out of long habit, Crow almost scoffed. Peace? Barely more than twelve hours ago, they'd been looking at corpses on the roadside. The rest of their journey was a cipher. Hell, a new storm could gather at any moment, maybe this time with hail big enough to brain them both.

But… it *was* peaceful, here and now. They weren't dead, and worrying about last night's deceased wouldn't bring them back to life. Crow could still feel a small physical twinge, a reminder that Simeon had been inside him. He could close his eyes and recall the precise sensation of that silky black hair flowing through his fingers.

"It's nice," he said, meaning… everything in that exact minute, which was all that counted right now.

Simeon grinned and bumped his shoulder.

ALTHOUGH IT WAS PAST MIDNIGHT, Doris stayed up to see them off. After she gave them plastic bags full of snacks, Frank drove them to the bus stop and waited, engine idling, until the bus rolled to a halt. They boarded, and he waved before driving away.

The bus driver gave them wary nods. He must have heard something about what happened the night before, but he didn't say anything. Nor did any of the dozen or so other passengers. Crow and Simeon found an open pair of seats near the back, settled in, and promptly fell asleep.

The next morning and afternoon slid by like an almost-forgotten dream. They switched busses in Spokane and passed through miles of sun-burnished wheat until they topped the Cascades and descended into a lush green. They were in Seattle before dinnertime. From there they took another bus and then a ferry across Puget Sound—which delighted Simeon.

It was cool and overcast in Kingston, but not raining. They ate dinner at a Mexican place, and Simeon—who had never tried Mexican cuisine—declared tacos his new favorite food. He reserved judgment on guacamole, however, and swore cheerfully at the chilies that heated the pico de gallo. Crow found the food tasty, but he enjoyed watching Simeon even more.

After dinner they stood near the ferry terminal and watched the small moored boats bob gently up and down in the marina. No corvids here, just a lot of seagulls who lost interest in Crow once they realized he had no food to share.

"How much farther to Bayaq?" asked Simeon.

"Forty-five miles."

"Bit far to walk, innit?"

Crow was tempted to say that it *wasn't* too far—that he was in no hurry to get to their destination and face whatever awaited him there. But he gave a quick nod. "I'll ask if there's a bus or something."

The thin man behind the ticket counter for the ferry was visibly bored, and Crow's presence didn't perk him up. "You can get a bus to Sequim," he said, monotone. "That's as close as you're gonna get."

"How far is Sequim from Bayaq?"

Although he looked put out by the additional question, the man answered. "Three or four miles."

Well, that was doable. "When's the next bus?"

"Five-fifteen tomorrow morning."

Shit. "Is there a motel nearby?" It was too cold to just camp out on the beach, especially when Simeon and Crow didn't even own a blanket.

The man stared out of the window for a while as if deciding whether to answer. Crow wondered if even Simeon's charm could have warmed this guy up, but in any case, Simeon had remained near the door, browsing a rack of brochures.

"Neap Tide," the man finally said before turning his back to Crow and starting to page through a catalog.

There was only one main road in town, heading inland, and it made sense that the motel would be along it. Or so Crow hoped. As they left the terminal, he updated Simeon with the plan.

"Smells lovely here, yeah?" Simeon observed. "The sea but also… I dunno. Woodsmoke. Growing things. Whatever those flowers are over there." He pointed to a weedy bush in front of a church.

Simeon was right, and as usual he lightened Crow's mood.

Which plummeted considerably when they reached the Neap Tide Inn. Crow had become spoiled during this journey, staying in places that were much nicer than his norm. But the Neap Tide—or more accurately, the *Eap Ti*, according to the sign with missing letters—looked fairly grim. The long, two-story building with white-painted walls was going scabrously gray. A few of the windows were boarded or taped, the parking lot was cracked and weedy, and the upper exterior walkway sagged visibly in spots. Despite the inn's location on a narrow peninsula at the edge of a rain forest, it offered a view of neither water nor trees. Just the parking lot on one side, an enormous pile of gravel on the other, and a crumbling cement wall across the road.

Crow understood. People landed here when they'd run out of money and hope, and maybe they battered themselves against the nation's border a few times before slumping down, getting covered with mildew and moss, and disappearing.

"You all right?" Simeon asked quietly.

"We could sleep on the beach instead."

"We could. But it's starting to rain."

Crow hadn't even noticed. It wasn't a downpour, and

certainly nothing like the storm in Montana, but it would be miserable to camp in. He took a few deep breaths and trudged toward the motel office.

It smelled like ancient cigarette smoke and onions inside. A massive man with a tangled tumbleweed of hair and an overgrown gray beard sat behind the counter, watching something on a grainy TV. He didn't turn to look at Crow and Simeon. In fact, Crow wasn't sure the man *could* move. It was like expecting to be acknowledged by a mountain.

"Pardon me," Simeon said. No response. He said it again, louder, "Pardon me."

Eyes still glued to the screen, the clerk made a rumbly sound. It seemed he was watching *The Love Boat*.

Simeon pressed up against the counter as if that might help. "A room for one night, please."

The man grunted again. Simeon and Crow might have stood there all night, but a commercial for McDonald's came on and he finally cut his eyes in their direction. "Thirty. Cash. Check out by ten."

Simeon put the money on the counter and they both waited. Finally the man gave another rumble. "One oh three."

"The key?"

"Ain't locked."

Well, that was interesting. It saved the clerk from having to fetch things, Crow supposed.

Outside again, Simeon huffed. "I miss Doris."

"We seem to have found the only human on the planet who's immune to your charm."

"What if he's not human? Could be one of those other things Mrs. Aisa mentioned. Perhaps he's a fairy."

Crow snort-laughed.

The room was as dismal as he'd expected. Only one light bulb was operational in the main room, the bathroom had mold growing in the corners, and Crow didn't want to know the source of the many stains on walls, carpet, and furniture. There were two narrow beds: one with a severe sag in the mattress that threatened to swallow the occupant and the other with the cushioning and comfort of plywood.

While Crow stood slump-shouldered, Simeon went back and forth between the beds, testing the mattresses as if he might somehow discover something satisfactory. "I feel like sodding Goldilocks," he muttered.

"Sorry."

"I've seen far worse."

"And you've seen far better."

Simeon stared at Crow for a long moment. Then he surged forward without warning, bearing Crow backwards and into the wall with a loud *thunk*. Crow was reminded quite suddenly of how strong Simeon was. And when Simeon settled his heavy hands on Crow's shoulders, pressing down just enough to make their presence really known, Crow's stomach gave a slight clench of fear.

"Listen to me, mate."

It was the first time Crow had seen him truly angry. Even back in Simeon's wagon, when Crow had pushed him and made him hit his head, Simeon had been bewildered and then a little amused. Now, though, his mouth was set in a hard line and his black eyes seemed flat and unreflective. He spoke in a raspy growl.

"I am responsible for myself," Simeon said. "Always have been. Sometimes I've made bloody terrible decisions, but that's on me, not anyone else. And *you* are not accountable for every bloody thing that goes wrong. The world doesn't revolve around you, Crow Rapp, and most of us can fuck things up quite well without your assistance. So stop with the sodding apologies!"

"I'm sor—" Crow shut himself up in time.

Simeon's expression softened immediately and he leaned

his forehead against Crow's. His voice grew gentle. "When I was nine or ten, I ran away from the foundling home. It was early spring and still bloody cold, especially at night. I spent days wandering, half-frozen and half-starved until I barely knew my own name. And then somehow—don't recall exactly how; I expect it was mostly good luck—I found an attic I could reach by a bit of climbing. The window wasn't locked or even fastened, so I could go right in. Place was full of spiders and dust, but it was nice and warm, especially near the chimney. And there were chests of old moth-eaten clothes and blankets so I could build myself a nest of sorts. As long as I stepped lightly, nobody in the rooms below would know I was there."

"That must have been awful, to be all alone so young."

"It was and it wasn't," Simeon replied. "Because in that attic I was warm and nobody was... harming me. I was lonely. Often I was still hungry. Sometimes I was scared. But I could look out across rooftops and feel for a time as if I was flying above the city's cares. I could almost imagine that someday I'd do better."

Crow decided not to pursue the "harming;" he had a fairly strong suspicion of what Simeon meant. Instead he emitted a shuddering sigh. "You did do better."

"Aye. I can abide a load of misery as long as I've hope for improvement. So uncomfortable beds. Omnibus accidents. Falling barns. Not my cup of tea, but look what I've gained. Adventure. A mission. A remarkable friend. A lover. Countless treasures, and worth every bit of suffering."

"You are the most glass-half-full person I've ever met." Crow reached up and put his hands on Simeon's back.

"Stewing over what I haven't got never did me any good. I'd rather celebrate what I have."

As if to make his point, Simeon kissed Crow.

It was not gentle or sweet. It was... hungry. Demanding.

And, trapped against the wall by Simeon's bulk, damned if that wasn't exactly what Crow needed. He didn't just accept it, however—he fought back. Well, maybe fight wasn't the right word, not when they both wanted the same thing. But it was definitely some kind of battle, each pushing into the other, each striving to achieve the other's surrender.

Crow bashed against the wall a few times, which didn't hurt but did bring an angry knock from the adjacent room. With a surge of strength, he shoved Simeon, banging him into the dresser. They didn't stop kissing and their hands were everywhere, squeezing, stroking, unbuttoning. Gasping breaths echoed in the small room.

Simeon was clearly still angry at Crow for being so self-absorbed. And Crow was angry too—not at Simeon specifically, but at the entire world... and mostly at himself. Which was nothing new, and this seemed like a perfectly reasonable way to deal with those feelings. It was another form of tempering, maybe. You take rage, heat it with a dose of burning passion, and end up with something else in the end. Perhaps something more useful.

At least Crow hoped so.

In any case, his body was delighting in the amorous conflict, and soon his brain had pretty much switched off. He and Simeon were grunting, panting beasts, all tongues and teeth and incoherent moans.

It was glorious.

Being bigger and stronger, Simeon eventually won the battle. He had Crow backed into a corner, both of them with their shirts hanging open and their unzipped jeans sliding low on their hips. Simeon pressed their chests together to keep Crow from escaping and, at the same time, yanked so hard on Crow's cheap boxers that they tore.

Even though Crow was less agile with his hands, he still managed to tug down Simeon's underwear.

Then it was hot sticky skin on hot sticky skin, hard against hard, and soft on soft. Fingers laced against scalps, hairs prickling, hips bucking, breath tickling, chests moving in and out in tango, the universe falling away as both gave and gave and took and took. No mercy, no regret.

Simeon squeezed one hand between them and wrapped it tight around both their cocks.

And what did it take after that to make them come undone? Nothing but a few thrusts and a bruising kiss.

They collapsed into a gasping tangle on the floor.

THE SHOWER WAS BARELY MORE than a tepid trickle, the tiny bar of soap produced no suds, and the towels were so thin as to be almost transparent. Yet Simeon and Crow managed to clean up anyway, after which they squeezed together into the too-hard bed. They could hear two different televisions battling from nearby rooms. Pipes rattled whenever anyone used a toilet. Whoever was upstairs stomped around like an irate rhinoceros.

It didn't matter.

Simeon was warm and pliant against Crow's back, and sometimes he pressed his lips softly to Crow's nape or shoulder.

"I've never done that before," Simeon said after a while. He sounded half-asleep.

"Had sex against a wall?"

"No, I've done that loads of times. I've spent far more time shagging in alleys and storerooms than in beds."

"Then what part was new?"

Simeon paused before replying. "The not-newness was

new." He made a sound that might or might not have been a laugh. "I've never shagged the same bloke twice."

It took a moment for his meaning to sink in, and not because of the Britishisms. What seemed impossible was that a man of Simeon's beauty and confidence had never experienced more than a one-night stand.

Crow turned over, putting them nose to nose in the darkness. "Is it less exciting when it's a repeat performance?"

"But it wasn't, was it? Tonight was nothing like last night. And next time—God, there will be a next time, yeah?—will be different as well. Because with someone I care about, every little detail matters."

IT WAS BARELY past dawn when they got ready to check out of the Neap Tide. Crow was a little sore from the uncomfortable bed—and probably from the previous night's sparring—and so anxious about what was to come that he couldn't stay still. They had some snacks with them, but he couldn't eat, and the overstimulation that coffee would bring might have killed him.

Before they walked out the door, Simeon stopped him with a hand on his arm. "Almost forgot. Nicked you a present yesterday."

"What?" asked Crow, at once pleased and exasperated.

Grinning, Simeon reached into his bag and pulled out a postcard with a pretty photo of mossy trees. He handed it over. "Thought you might fancy writing a note to Aunt Helen. You'll have to find a postage stamp, though."

"Where did you steal this?"

"While you were nattering with the nob at the ferry terminal."

Crow didn't understand why Simeon hadn't just bought the thing—he could have afforded the twenty-five cents. But now it was done and he couldn't find it in himself to be angry. He rooted through his bag until he found a pen and then jotted a few words:

*Dear Helen,*

*The Pacific is gorgeous. I hope you can see it someday. Hugs to Jamie.*

*Love, C*

He felt more settled when he was finished. "Okay. Let's go catch that bus."

# CHAPTER 16

$S$equim was, as Simeon pointed out smugly, within the rain shadow of the Olympic Mountains. Instead of rain and trees, the area around the small city consisted of gently rolling farmland and dairies. It was pretty, Crow thought.

The bus let them off a few blocks from downtown. It was still early, but they went inside a small grocery store and chose items for a walking breakfast. That much accomplished, they set out north for Bayaq. The road was narrow and without sidewalks, but there was very little traffic and the walk was pleasant. After finishing his food, Simeon sniffed at wildflowers and waved at cows. It was mostly Crow's fault that they walked slowly, however. His feet seemed made of lead this morning.

An hour and a half later, after a few twists and turns, they reached their destination. At least Crow assumed so. The town itself, if you could call it that, consisted of a single block of weathered buildings clustered near the banks of a tree-lined creek. There was a general store, a post office, a gas station with mechanic's shop, a café with a Closed sign in the window, a machinist shop, and a veterinarian. Only a car and a pickup were parked near the buildings, and although there weren't any people in sight, a dog was barking somewhere.

There were also hundreds of large black birds—all of them silent—perched in the nearby trees.

"I don't know what I'm supposed to do now," said Crow. He hadn't formulated a plan beyond this point, which was stupid. Had he really expected to be met by a welcoming committee?

"Could go inside the store and ask."

"Ask what? 'Hey, can you direct me to my possibly scary supernatural relatives?'"

Simeon rolled his eyes. "Something like that. Come on."

The store was crowded with shelves and boxes and bags. It smelled of honey and fresh-cut lumber, which wasn't at all unpleasant. A bulletin board just inside the door contained the sorts of notices that Crow might have found in Chinkapin Grove: people looking for extra work or selling cars or furniture. Dogs and cats for adoption. Babysitting services. Somebody named Sunflower was offering Reiki services, whatever that meant. Bob claimed he could clean gutters fast and cheap. He also had a truck and could haul away junk.

Pinned in one corner of the cork board was a drawing of a raven. No words, no phone number. Just a bird with a heavy black beak. At least the bird itself was black and not red. Crow hoped that was a good sign. He stared at the bird for a long time, looking for answers or hidden meanings but finding only ink on paper.

Finally he sighed and wandered further into the store, Simeon just behind him.

The only other person Crow could see was a young woman standing behind the counter. She couldn't have been long past her teens and—rather improbably for this location, Crow thought—she was dressed in full punk regalia. Bleached mohawk tipped with fuchsia dye. Nose ring. Dramatic eye makeup. Studded leather motorcycle jacket. Artfully ripped white T-shirt. The counter hid the rest of her, which was too bad. He was curious to see the rest of her outfit.

She was staring at them, but in a flat, disinterested way that suggested they were only slightly more entertaining than a shelf of canned vegetables. She watched as they approached the counter.

"Pardon me," Simeon began, for which Crow was deeply thankful.

"If you don't see it out, we don't have it," she said.

"I was hoping, actually, that you could give us some information about this area."

Her eyes had lit up as soon as he voiced enough words for his accent to be discernible. "Oh my God. Are you really English?"

Simeon executed a genuine goddamn bow. "Born and bred in London, I was."

"Oh my God!" Suddenly Simeon was much more fascinating than creamed corn. She put her elbows on the counter and leaned forward. "That's so cool! I'm gonna go there someday, when I save enough money. But what are you doing here, at the end of the earth?"

"I think this area is lovely."

She moaned dramatically. "It's boring. So incredibly boring. And the people here. They talk about stuff like logging and cows and the weather and I don't know how much longer I can stand it."

"It seems quite exotic to me, miss. That's the thing of it, yeah? Every place in the world is exotic to someone."

Although she looked dubious about that statement, she was otherwise besotted, now leaning so far forward that Crow—ignored in the background—almost expected her to crawl over the counter and fling herself into Simeon's arms. Crow wondered what Simeon would do. He'd made it clear that he was attracted to women as well as men, and he and Crow certainly hadn't made any promises about fidelity or monogamy. Hell, they'd known each other only a short time, had been thrown together by chance and whim, and Crow had already nearly gotten Simeon killed twice.

And he was making it all about himself again. Having a silent jealous fit when Simeon was only trying to help him.

Seemingly oblivious to Crow's inner turmoil, Simeon was still chatting with the girl, telling her a carefully curated version of things she should visit when she got to England. It must have been hard for him to keep his varying timelines in mind, but he was doing a good job of it. Anyway, at this point he could have told her anything and she probably would have eaten it up.

The shop door jingled and a middle-aged man strode in. He must have been familiar with the girl and her unlikely choice of outfits, since he simply gave her a small wave and continued on to a display of toothpastes.

But Simeon took advantage of that small interruption to steer the conversation back on course. "My mate here is searching for some distant relatives. He doesn't know their name, but he's been told they live in Bayaq. Do you think you can help?"

"There's only, like, four hundred people here. I know everyone."

For the first time, she truly focused on Crow. Since he generally preferred to remain unnoticed, her attention made him uncomfortable. And then her eyes widened. "Oh." She straightened up from the countertop and crossed her arms.

"Oh?" Simeon prompted.

"He looks like one of them."

Crow's heart thudded hard enough to hurt and he struggled to swallow past his desert-dry throat. What he wanted to do was demand more information—or run out of the store and keep running until he dropped. Instead he rasped, "Please."

The girl's eyes filled with compassion, and now she spoke to Crow instead of Simeon. "They're, like, some kind of cult? We hardly ever see them. Nobody seems to know exactly where they live, which is weird."

"But they do live around here?" Crow managed.

"I think so. Sometimes one of them comes into the store. And they always buy something small and specific, like one piece of candy or a couple of nails. Or they check their mail." She gestured at a bank of old-fashioned mailboxes built into one wall. "But they just sort of appear out of nowhere, right? And after they walk outside they disappear. I dunno. Maybe they walk down near the creek, but that's real rocky and weedy. There isn't a path."

While Crow was chewing that over and trying to decide what to do about it, the other customer approached with a box of toothpaste in one hand and a six-pack of beer in the other. He aimed an impatient glare at Simeon, who still stood close to the counter.

Simeon nodded. "Thank you, miss. It's been a delight to meet you. I hope you make it to London soon."

"Thanks." With a resigned expression, she addressed the man. "Can I help you, Mr. Cooper?"

Back outside on the store's front porch, Crow made a frustrated sound. "I don't know what to do next."

"Well, you've a good idea now that your mother's people are truly here, yeah? Mysterious folk who look like you."

"But how am I supposed to find them? I bet that girl's lived here her whole life and even she doesn't know where they are."

"But has she ever made the effort to look for them?"

Simeon's unrelenting optimism was both annoying and comforting, which didn't make any sense. But then, nothing made any sense anymore—if it ever had.

"Perhaps," Simeon said, "we could camp here and keep an eye open for them."

"For how long? She said they rarely come here. Even if we bought a tent or whatever, someone's going to object if we start squatting in downtown Bayaq."

"We've some dosh left. We could rent a room."

Crow pictured himself peering endlessly through a window, waiting for a glimpse of strange pale people. He'd go crazy. Besides, how long until his pursuers showed up and wiped the whole town off the map in order to get at him? He could easily picture the entire place in flames, a red bird painted on the road to remind him who was responsible.

Wait. Birds.

Ravens still crowded the nearby treetops. In fact, there were now even more of them. A thousand or so pairs of dark eyes regarded him. There was nothing threatening in the birds' behavior, although he fancied there was something judgmental about their beaks.

Jesus. He really was losing it.

Well, in that case he might as well act crazy too.

He stepped off the porch and onto the gravel parking strip that lined the road. Lifting his arms high as if they were wings, he shouted, "Hey! If you guys are really on my side, I could use some help. Where the hell are my relatives?"

The ravens all rose into the air at once, the sound of their beating wings like fast-paced drums. The birds swooped and dove in a choreographed dance, much like the murmurations of starlings he'd sometimes seen back in Chinkapin Grove. But this swarm seemed to have more intention, the individual animals forming one enormous beast, a sort of shifting dragon that might breathe fire at any moment. Crow was terrified but also fascinated.

And then he realized that, although each single raven was whirling and diving and ascending in dizzying patterns, as a group they were moving slowly but clearly north.

"They're leading us," Crow said.

"Then I expect we ought to follow."

THE FLOCK PROGRESSED SLOWLY but relentlessly while Simeon and Crow struggled along on the ground. They left the road and cut across a wide, grassy field. A pasture, perhaps, although it was unfenced and no cattle were in sight. Still heading north, they rose up a gentle slope and then down a steeper one, into a small ravine formed by the creek. As the girl at the general store had said, there was no path. Crow and Simeon had to pick their way carefully among stones, blackberry bushes, wild roses, and muddy rivulets.

Simeon stumbled over a small rotted log, his fall averted by Crow catching his arm. "This would be loads easier if we could fly," Simeon pointed out.

As if in response, a single raven hurtled down at them, making them both duck. It swooped their heads without quite touching them, then uttered a croak that sounded like a laugh before rocketing up to join its colleagues.

And then it started to rain—not as a polite mist, but rather in big squishy drops that almost immediately soaked through their clothing. And Crow's sneakers. He could only hope that his bag was somewhat waterproof.

He began to laugh. Because there was absurd, and then there was traipsing through weeds with a time-traveler from the past, being guided by birds, all because a weird lady in Omaha said this was how he'd find his supernatural relatives.

Simeon stood, his wet hair even longer and blacker than usual, and looked at Crow with puzzlement and a touch of alarm. "Love?"

"It's… just…." Crow tried to catch his breath, couldn't, and ended up waving his arms instead. If someone needed an illustration of a madman for their dictionary, he'd make an excellent candidate. "Crazy," he managed. Meaning himself, their situation, and the whole entire fucking world.

"Absolutely." Simeon strode closer, drew him into a wet and squishy embrace, and kissed him in the rain.

It felt kind of romantic, like in a movie, and it was glorious.

But then the ravens began to scold, and after a few of them had executed a dive-bomb, Simeon and Crow got the hint. They continued on their journey, shivering and half-blind. Even through the noise of the rain and the creek, Crow heard waves. That finally made sense when they rounded a tree-crowded bend and ended up on a cliff overlooking the ocean, undoubtedly a gorgeous view on a clear day. The creek had taken a turn too, and now there was a muddy path alongside it, leading steeply down the hill. Both men skidded here and there as they descended, although neither fell. There were a lot of trees on both sides of them—huge evergreens with thick trunks and a dense tangle of ferns and shrubs around their base.

No evidence of civilization. No signs or trail markers, no bits of trash, no power lines. It was the kind of place in which bigfoot—or perhaps something even more primeval—

seemed likely to make a sudden appearance. Crow could imagine this place looking exactly the same long before humans settled here. He wasn't sure how he felt about that.

As they reached the bottom of the hill, the rain petered out, though the sky remained steel-gray. The trees closed over them, the ravens moving from branch to branch, urging them onward. Luckily the path remained, but it was so narrow that Crow was forced to walk in front of Simeon rather than beside him.

The path ahead was flanked by a pair of massive trees, each so huge that someone could have bored tunnels for cars to drive through, as had been done with some of the redwoods in California. About thirty feet up, a wide horizontal branch connected the trees, forming a natural archway. Dozens of ravens perched there, while the rest landed nearby.

Crow passed under the arch. As he did, a shuddery sensation crawled over his skin and down his back. *Someone walked over my grave.* He'd felt that before, long ago, when he was still a boy with an entire tremulous future ahead of him, when he'd been side by side with a sweet girl named Julie and the scents of sugar and fried foods hung in the air, delighted screams echoing over the sounds of midway music.

He'd scoffed then at the words painted on the striped arch, but of course those words had proved as prescient as the handsome man in the fortune-teller's tent. *Welcome Traveler.* Well, he'd certainly traveled since then, hadn't he? Flying back and forth across the continent like a bird caught in a cage, never alighting anywhere for long, never calling anyplace home.

The carnival hadn't caused the things that happened to him afterward, and neither had Simeon or his vision. Crow knew that now—had always known, really, even though for a while Simeon had seemed like a handy scapegoat. But it was all connected. Some type of otherworldly chain of events that he didn't understand, a hidden mystical thread running through his life. Very much, in fact, like the spools of thread at Murray Family Agency.

But before Crow had the chance to puzzle this out, two people appeared out of nowhere and blocked his way.

# CHAPTER 17

It was not like looking in a mirror; the likeness wasn't that close. But Crow could see the resemblance between himself and the man and woman who faced him. They were both tall—taller than him, in fact—and very slender. Their long blond hair was only one shade removed from white. Their pale blue-gray eyes were the color of subtle shadows on icebergs, and their unlined and unblemished skin was as colorless as fresh snow.

They were beautiful in a cold, remote way—like marble statues. Both wore gauzy sleeveless shifts, also white, which seemed impractical given the cold and muddy conditions. Their feet were bare.

For the moment, all of their attention was on Crow, their stares frank and appraising. The woman said something in a language that had a musical lilt and a lot of vowels. It sounded like a question.

"I'm sorry," said Crow. "I only speak English."

The man and woman exchanged looks before she addressed him again. "Whose offspring are you?"

It was an odd question to ask, and for a moment he

puzzled over how to answer. "My name is Crow Rapp. My mother—" He stopped because as soon as he said his name, expressions of recognition settled on their faces.

"Why are you here?" asked the woman.

How to summarize? "To find out who I am. To learn what happened to my mother. To end the chase."

This time the man spoke. "The chase?"

"Red birds."

Now the pair looked alarmed. The woman lifted one long-fingered hand. "They pursue you?"

"Yes. They've killed… people I care about."

"But you have not joined them?"

Crow shuddered. "No."

After another silent exchange, the pair nodded. "Very well, Crow Rapp. Enter our home that we may converse."

His stomach roiled, either from fear or relief, and Crow started forward. But when Simeon took a step as well, the strangers held up their hands. "He does not belong here."

"This is Simeon Bell. He's my friend. I'm not sure I would've had the brains or the balls to come here without him, and he stuck with me even after I nearly got him killed. I'm not leaving him. He belongs with me."

Crow glanced back. It occurred to him that maybe Simeon didn't want to follow these weird people into a magical forest. But Simeon was staring at Crow wide-eyed and slightly open-mouthed, as if Crow had utterly astonished him. And Crow realized that there hadn't likely been many occasions when someone showed loyalty to Simeon, when someone indicated appreciation for what he'd done or the desire to remain in his company.

"Cheers, love," Simeon said softly.

Crow smiled and took his hand. If it turned out that his freaky relatives were also homophobes, they could go fuck themselves.

The people in white looked at each other and then at Crow and Simeon. A few of the ravens made quiet, hoarse noises that Crow imagined were meant to support his argument.

"Very well," the woman said at last. She and her companion turned and began walking down the path. Crow and Simeon followed.

AFTER A SHORT TIME, the trees became more widely spaced and the underbrush less dense. To his right, Crow caught glimpses of a broad sandy beach buffeted by waves and with a few rocks off in the distance. He didn't see any people on the beach, just driftwood and several species of birds. Once he watched, astonished, as an otter galloped out of the water, a fish grasped in its jaws. It stopped just past the reach of the waves and settled in to eat lunch.

The path widened, and it was dry, as if it hadn't rained here at all. No water dripped from the trees, although when they skirted a small bog, wisps of eerie mist floated past before dissipating. A few minutes beyond the bog, the path turned inland and into a ravine between tall sandstone cliffs. At first the ravine wasn't much wider than the trail, but then it opened quite suddenly into a flat valley, perhaps a quarter mile in circumference and with a cliff blocking the opposite side.

There were houses in this valley.

Crow hadn't spent any time trying to picture what his relatives' homes would look like. To start with, he wasn't very imaginative, and besides, how could he make any guesses when he had no idea who these people were? If he *had* thought about it, however, he wouldn't have come up with what he saw: small mounds that appeared to made of adobe or maybe stone, each inset with multiple panes of glass. The windows varied in size and shape and seemed set into the walls according to no particular plan. There were perhaps three dozen of these houses scattered at random throughout the valley. The ground between them was covered in a low-lying herb with tiny pink flowers. The plants had a pleasant smell, a bit like mint and honey.

"Bloody *hell*," whispered Simeon. He hadn't said a single word since the pale couple had allowed them in. Maybe he hadn't wanted to remind them he was there. But now his eyes were huge. Crow didn't know whether it was the houses that amazed him; or the thousands of corvids that perched everywhere; or the sky, which had a disturbing twinkle to it, as if the entire valley were domed by a sparkly crystal.

Or maybe Simeon was responding to the people who were coming out of the houses.

All had the same pale, ethereal look as the pair that had brought them here. They all wore white tunics, although the lengths varied and some were embroidered with abstract designs in metallic thread.

Simeon pressed in close to Crow as the people neared, and Crow didn't blame him. It was spooky—nobody was saying a word, and there was something *off* about them, something he couldn't quite put his finger on. Of course, if they turned out to be dangerous, there wasn't a damned thing Crow could do to protect Simeon or himself. He suspected that Simeon could hold his own in a fight, but even he would be easily outclassed by sixty or so... whatever these people were.

Nonetheless, Crow did what he *could* do, which was to tightly grip Simeon's hand while keeping his own back straight and holding his chin high. *Don't fuck with me*, his expression said. He'd used it plenty of times on human beings, and it usually worked. It was all he had.

The crowd fanned out, forming a semicircle about ten feet away. The woman who had greeted them at the arch gave a slight dip of her head. "This is Crow Rapp," she said. In English, which he supposed was for his benefit.

Still, he had to add, "And my friend, Simeon Bell."

It was hard to look at these people. They reflected light—or maybe radiated it—so that it was like staring at a sidewalk on a very sunny day. But even though Crow had to squint, and even though chills ran down his still-damp spine, he didn't glance away.

One of the figures stepped forward. He had a short beard and a tunic embroidered with silver flowers. While his eyes were as pale as everyone else's, they showed a hint of warmth. "Why are you here, Crow Rapp?"

It was a little like a job interview, and Crow felt a hint of hysteria. People asking questions and you weren't sure what they wanted to hear. He gave the same answers as before because they were the truth. "I'm looking for my mother and a sense of who I am. And more importantly, I want to know how to get rid of the red bird people for good."

Predictably, everyone seemed pretty upset by that last part. The woman who'd greeted them said a bunch of words in their language, which appeared to soothe the crowd a bit, and then the bearded man gave a grim sort of nod. "Follow me," he commanded.

With considerable trepidation, Crow obeyed, continuing to clasp Simeon's hand.

The man took him to one of the little houses, where the door stood open. He waved them inside, followed, and closed it. The interior was... dizzying. It was larger than it should have been, and the stone floor was almost completely covered in thick rugs and embroidered cushions.

There was no other furniture. The rugs and cushions were in rich jewel tones, and the walls were covered with patches of color. It was like standing inside a box full of giant puzzle pieces.

The man dropped gracefully onto a cushion and sat cross-legged, his tunic draped over his knees. When he gestured at Crow to do the same, Crow tugged Simeon down with him. He was a little embarrassed to be wearing muddy, squelchy shoes and grubby damp clothing, but the man hadn't really given them an opportunity to go barefoot or to dry off.

"Who sent you here?"

Crow shook his head. "Can you at least tell me your name? You know mine. I think you know who I am. But I don't know a damned thing about any of you."

The man appeared to consider this for a moment. "I am Lo'orush. And forgive my rudeness. We rarely allow outsiders here. Especially those who are not our kind." He shot a glance at Simeon.

"What *is* your kind?"

There it was, the sixty-four-thousand-dollar question. But it just lay there, flat and gasping, until Crow nearly screamed with frustration. Would have screamed, in fact, if Simeon hadn't been right there with gentle pressure on his hand. A calming presence.

Finally Lo'orush spoke. "I could tell you our name for ourselves, but it wouldn't mean anything to you. His kind call us many things, none of them accurate."

"His kind? You mean humans?"

Lo'orush made a small frown. "Yes."

"Okay then, what do humans call you?"

A long flat stare, followed by a tiny shrug. "Angels. Demons. Fairies. Spirits. Elementals. None of these are exactly accurate."

The list had made Crow's head spin, but he'd taken particular notice of the second item. "Demons?"

"We were once… somewhere else. But there were certain disagreements, and some of us were cast out. We came here, to this plane, where we endeavored to continue our lives as we chose. This has become increasingly difficult as humans have multiplied. We must resort to various means to remain hidden. Sometimes we fail. Then humans create names and stories for us. These are of little interest to anyone but the humans."

While Crow tried to process this, Simeon spoke up, sounding a bit belligerent. "There's loads of difference between angels and demons in the stories, though. Which is more accurate? And what are the things that keep chasing Crow?"

Now Lo'orush looked mildly annoyed, like a teacher pestered by a particularly dull student. "Some of the tales contain some accuracy and some do not. The ones who wish for Crow to join them are my brethren. They are the same beings as I. But they have made different choices. Much as some humans decide to be lawful and respectful and some decide to be thieves."

Simeon inhaled sharply as if wounded.

And Crow was angry. "Some humans steal because they don't have many other options. But even when they *do* have options, that's nothing like murdering innocent people. Your brethren killed my grandparents, my friends, folks who were just unlucky enough to spend some time near me. I don't really give a shit what you call them either—they're evil."

If this outburst made Lo'orush angry, he didn't show it. "An interesting perspective."

"Look, I didn't come all this way to debate philosophy. I'm not exactly a scholar. Tell me who the fuck I am and how to stop those assholes from hurting more people."

This was not the wisest way to be interacting with his relatives. At best, they would probably kick him out without telling him much of anything. At worst they would squash him—and Simeon too. But Crow's patience, thin to begin with, had worn completely through. He didn't want more riddles and digs at his lover—oh God, Simeon had become his lover, hadn't he?—but instead wanted his decade-long nightmare to end.

Lo'orush sighed. "A fallen angel. If you insist, you may think of yourself thus. Although human blood also runs within you, our essential nature predominates in hybrids."

"Fallen angel." Crow's grasp on religion was shaky at best. Unlike many of their neighbors, his grandparents hadn't been much interested in it. They never took him to church or sent him to Sunday School, and the family Christmases were entirely secular. "Like... Satan?"

That made Lo'orush laugh. "No such being exists. Satan is merely an excuse for certain humans to lay blame for their own bad behavior—or a means to terrify other humans into obedience."

Crow frowned, trying to understand, but Simeon spoke up again. "Miss Aisa—erm, this woman we met in Omaha— said that some of you people go bad. That you've interbred with my people in an attempt to avoid this, which is laughable at best, given what we know about my people. That the bad ones are trying to make Crow one of them."

"That is an oversimplification." Lo'orush steepled his hands prissily. "But it bears some likeness to the truth."

He was quiet again for a long time, but he seemed to be marshaling his thoughts rather than giving his guests the silent treatment, so Crow let him be. While he waited, Crow turned to look at Simeon, who gifted him with a small smile. Until now, Crow had never noticed how *warm* Simeon was. Yes, his skin was as pale as Crow's, but it had a sort of invisible glow to it, the type of glow you got from campfires, not from distant stars. Or angels. His eyes were the most heated part of him, those near-black irises so full of life and intelligence and humor. Nothing like the glaciers of Lo'orush and his compatriots. And yes, Simeon's eyes held shadows as well —how could they not?—but those dark places made the rest seem all the brighter.

*Why am I so lucky?* Crow wondered. Perhaps in this very strange place even a human could read another's mind, because Simeon's smile grew.

Then Lo'orush cleared his throat. "Miss Aisa was correct. Some of our people become afflicted. We do not know why. Once this happens to them, there is no hope and we cast them out. But we had heard from our kind who reside elsewhere on Earth that those who are half human, such as your mother, appear better able to resist. When you water down our foundation with human blood, the resulting beings are able to make a choice that we cannot."

"Seems to me," Simeon said, "that human blood strengthens, not waters down."

Although Lo'orush clearly didn't like this, he apparently couldn't argue with its accuracy. "We had hoped that another infusion of humanity would assist even more, and that the resulting offspring would finally be immune to this... curse."

Simeon opened his mouth to say something, but for once Crow beat him to it. "I'm not a fucking *experiment*! Do you have any idea what you did to me?"

"Would you prefer never to have been born at all?"

Until recently, Crow would have had a ready answer to that. But these days with Simeon had given him glimpses of... a life worth living. He'd realized that despite the deaths, the loneliness, and the desperate rabbiting, he had found pockets of happiness.

Crow sat up straighter. "Fine. I choose not to go to the

dark side. I don't want anything to do with those... demons. I just want a normal life."

Lo'orush's gaze was implacable. "You are not human. You could never have a normal human life."

"I can goddamn try!"

For the first time, Lo'orush's face showed something akin to sympathy, a slight thawing of the ice. His voice softened. "They will continue to pursue you until you surrender to them."

"But *why*? I don't have anything to offer them. Why are they so stuck on having me join them?" Tears scalded the corners of his eyes but didn't fall.

"When it happened before—with your mother and others —we assumed it was simply because our cousins wished to increase their numbers and therefore their power. But now we assume otherwise. What you have seen of them is, I believe, raw strength. But their preference is for subtlety. They could never pass among humankind, but you could. You have. Imagine the damage you could help them cause."

Crow shifted uncomfortably on the pillow. He had an idea of what Lo'orush was getting at and didn't want to hear it. But playing ostrich wouldn't help anything. "How?"

"With their assistance, you could become a wealthy businessman. An influential member of the media. A high-ranking military leader. A charismatic politician. Humans would listen to you, support you. Do your bidding. You could destroy whatever you wished."

It was ridiculous—Crow as doom-bringer, Crow as trigger for the apocalypse. He was just a guy from a small town in Illinois. Most people barely noticed him. He didn't even have a high school diploma, and his entire worldly possessions sat at his side in a damp backpack.

And yet he felt a tug very much like when he wanted to get drunk. He could clearly picture himself standing in front of a huge crowd, giving a speech, staring out at a sea of adoring faces, listening to them roar their approval of his words. He could imagine telling them to do things—not good things—and could imagine them listening. And he *yearned* for this. The power. The adoration. The ability to make everyone suffer just as he had suffered.

This tug made him shudder and convinced him that what Lo'orush had said was true.

"No," Crow rasped. "Please."

"There are alternatives. They are not good ones."

"Then I'll kill myself."

"No!" Simeon cried, catching Crow's arm. "You can't bloody—"

"That is one alternative," Lo'orush interrupted. "However, it is extremely difficult to end our lives. You will die naturally of senescence at some point because your human blood causes you to age. That will be decades from now. In the interim, you are immune to disease and will heal almost immediately from even the most grievous injuries. To be honest, I am uncertain how you could make yourself die. Your attempts would no doubt be painful."

Crow remembered flames burning away his flesh, bullets ripping through his organs, poison eating through him. He shuddered as he tried to imagine what could end him—and what it would feel like to try and fail, again and again.

"Other bloody alternatives," growled Simeon.

Which meant someone cared whether Crow lived or died, cared whether he suffered. That was nice to know.

But Crow's brief spike of happiness was quelled as soon as Lo'orush spoke next. "You could choose the option that your mother did."

And everything dropped away, including Crow's stomach, so that the only thing left in the universe were those words. He started shivering violently. He might, in fact, have vomited, except that Simeon set a hand on Crow's shoulder. That was it—just the palm settling lightly and the fingers curling toward his chest. Then Crow was warm again; his lungs worked.

"What did my mother do?" He was proud of how strong and steady his voice sounded.

Lo'orush looked at him gravely, then stood. "Come. Meet her and see."

# CHAPTER 18

*C*row did not get to see his mother right away, and perhaps that was some form of kindness granted by the angels. Because as soon as Lo'orush's words sank in, Crow stumbled out of the house and puked. Spectacularly, all over the pretty little flowers and his shoes. His legs gave out and he fell to hands and knees, bitter bile hanging in strings from his lips.

The angels stood nearby, watching curiously, as if he were some new form of entertainment. Angels probably didn't throw up. It wasn't until his stomach was starting to settle that he realized Simeon knelt beside him, rubbing soothing circles on Crow's back.

Crow rose up on his knees and wiped his mouth with the back of his hand. "You don't have to play nurse." His throat felt raw. "This is disgusting."

"You think I haven't done the same after too many glasses of bad gin?"

"And did anyone stand next to you rubbing your back?"

"No, but I wish they had."

Simeon stood and offered a hand to Crow, who used it to

lever himself to his feet. He was wobbly, though, and his mouth tasted vile.

"Oi," Simeon called to the nearest angel, a man with a face like a Renaissance painting. "Fetch my mate some water, please." Initially looking dubious, the angel seemed to reach a decision, gave a curt nod, and glided away. All of the others must have decided the show was over and left to do whatever angels did. Only Lo'orush remained. "I will make some brief arrangements. Wait here." Then he was gone too.

"I don't want to talk about my mother," Crow warned as soon as they stood alone.

"All right. Do you fancy being quiet, or talking about something else?"

Silence would be too oppressive, Crow decided. "Like what?"

"Well... what about the birds?" Simeon waved his arm to indicate the hundreds of feathered creatures perched on rooftops and on the ground. Many were crows and ravens, their black feathers shining, but they were joined by jays with their bright blue plumage and jaunty dark crests and another species whose feathers tended toward a gray-brown.

"What about them?"

"Why are they here? Why did they lead us here—and perhaps help us when we were at your old barn?"

"And why do the demons have something going with red birds? I think they can turn into them, even." Crow shrugged. "Not a clue."

It was an annoying mystery, but it was better than thinking about his mother. His stomach lurched again.

Birds. He was going to think about birds.

"I researched them when I was a kid," Crow said. "Crows and ravens. I was trying to figure out why the hell my mother gave me these names." He'd spent hours in the school library digging through dusty books, and when that hadn't yielded much information, he'd gone to the city library instead. Marty had tagged along out of moral support or boredom, keeping himself amused reading snippets of romance novels. The librarian had to keep shushing them.

"We've ravens at the Tower of London. I've never been there, though."

"Yeah, I read a legend that if all the ravens leave the Tower, Britain will fall."

Simeon nodded. "I heard that. So they're protectors, yeah?"

"Sometimes. Odin was supposed to have a pair of ravens that were kind of his spies. In other stories, crows and ravens are creators or tricksters. Sometimes they're associated with war and death and bad luck, probably because they're scavengers. But they also can be messengers between our world and the world of spirits."

"Busy buggers."

"Corvids are really smart. Ape-level intelligence, I guess." Then Crow remembered something. "They're also related to prophecy."

They blinked at each other. It was prophecy that had brought them together, of course.

After a moment, Crow shook his head. "I guess maybe it makes sense that these birds hang around with angels, then. And demons. I still have no idea why I'm named after them, though. Unless it was a warning that I bring death."

Simeon was frowning, deep in thought. "No. Perhaps it's because they do so many things. Your name was meant to be a reminder of all your potential, love. Of all the things you can be."

Except Crow hadn't been much of anything, had he? Sure, he'd spent his entire adult life running, but he hadn't even tried to do anything during those years but survive and escape. Until Simeon had fallen into his life again, Crow hadn't even made an effort to solve his personal mysteries.

Of course, if Lo'orush was right, Crow could give in to the demons, and then he'd accomplish all sorts of things. The idea appealed to a small, nasty part of him. But what if instead he endeavored to do good? He'd never thought about this before: free of the demons, what would he do with himself? Hell, he'd never had much ambition even before he turned eighteen. As a kid he'd assumed he would grow up to be a farmer, not because he had any particular skill or passion for it but because his grandparents owned a farm.

But if he *did* get rid of the demons, he could be someone, couldn't he? Could *do* something. Although he had absolutely no clue what that something might be, even the possibility made him feel warm in much the same way that Simeon did.

He was going to raise the subject, since Simeon would no doubt have a lot of thoughts on the matter, but the angel returned with a clay goblet containing wonderfully cool, fresh water. Crow rinsed his mouth with some and swallowed the rest.

And then he remembered that his mother was here. He didn't need Madam Persephone's powers to know that she wouldn't appear out of nowhere and shower him with nearly three lost decades of maternal devotion.

Luckily he didn't have the chance to be sick again before Lo'orush returned, his expression entirely neutral and his stride measured. He looked like a bored maître d' about to lead someone to their table.

"What did she do to escape the demons?" Crow demanded.

"Follow me."

That wasn't an answer, but because it provided the possibility that an answer might be forthcoming, Crow obeyed. He didn't realize he was holding Simeon's hand until Simeon gave a reassuring squeeze. Although the angels didn't seem especially pleased to have a full-blooded human in their midst, at least they didn't seem to care about two men showing affection. Would his mother care?

They walked toward the far end of the valley, the crushed plants smelling bright under their feet. Angels and birds watched as they passed, blue eyes and black showing intelligence but no empathy. Lo'orush led them to one of the mound-houses, this one larger than average, but instead of ushering them inside, he took them around the building to a little garden surrounded by a white picket fence. Birds perched on the fence. A wooden rocking chair was in the center of the garden among roses, daisies, and lavender.

A woman sat in the chair.

Her hair, the color of farm-fresh butter, cascaded in soft waves that reached past her waist. Her eyes were the color of a robin's egg, her pale skin colored only by a faint rosy tint on her cheeks and lips. Like the angels, she wore a white tunic; hers went to her ankles and was embroidered with shimmery gold blossoms. Her long-fingered hands were laced daintily in her lap. She was beautiful—and her face showed no more life than a statue's.

Just outside the garden, Crow froze. His mother didn't shift her gaze to look his way; she continued to look forward, her eyes unfocused. Though she was in her mid-forties, she appeared much younger. Even younger than Crow. No lines on her flawless face, and no signs of middle-age in her thin frame.

"Mother." Crow wasn't sure he'd said it loud enough for even Simeon to hear.

Lo'orush entered the garden through a little gate and set a hand on Sara's shoulder. It was a surprisingly tender gesture, but she didn't react, nor did she show any sign of hearing when he spoke softly in his language. Then he plucked a lavender spike, waved it under her nose, and tickled her fingers with the end of it. Without shifting her gaze, she clutched at it. He stroked her head before returning to Crow and Simeon.

"She is safe here," Lo'orush said. "And I do not believe she is distressed in any way."

Simeon spoke. "Is she always like that?"

"Yes. She eats and drinks, but infrequently. We help her. We keep her clean, and at night we settle her into bed. But she spends the days here, in her garden."

A bramble had grown in Crow's throat and down his spine, rooting him in place. When he was finally able to speak, he sounded as if he hadn't uttered a word in years. "What did you do to her?"

"It was the other alternative."

"What did you do to her?" This time he screamed it. But still she didn't glance his way.

"We did nothing but inform her of the option. She took action by herself."

Crow had tolerated enough of Lo'orush's slightly smug cool tones. He let go of Simeon, ran to the gate, and vaulted over. When he reached Sara, he collapsed onto his knees in front of her, tears blurring his vision. "Mother? Mama?" He'd never been able to call someone by those terms before.

Her vision remained focused on nothing. She blinked sometimes, but rarely. She was even more beautiful up close, and he definitely saw his resemblance to her, but there was also an absence that terrified him, as if she were the idea of a person rather than the real thing.

He spent some time crying, there on his knees in the garden. She never once indicated an awareness of his presence. He'd heard the word *heartbroken* before and thought he understood its meaning after all he'd been through. But now his heart felt as if it had literally shattered into jagged shards that pierced the inside of his chest. It was more painful than fire or getting shot or being in a bus accident, because he knew this wound could never heal.

"Mama," he said when he could speak again.

When he tried to stand, his legs wouldn't work properly. He was prepared to crawl out of the garden, but Simeon ran over, helped him upright, and supported him as they walked slowly past the flowers and through the gate. Lo'orush waited there, expressionless.

To keep himself from punching Lo'orush in the face, Crow kept going until he was on the other side of the house, his mother hidden from view. He leaned against the wall, welcoming how its nubbly texture bit into his skin. He also welcomed the gentle pressure of Simeon's hand on his shoulder.

Lo'orush sailed over. The three of them stood there in a living tableau, as unmoving as Sara, until a raven broke the silence with its gurgling croak.

"Explain," said Crow.

"It is a… process some of us have chosen rather than becoming afflicted. When we do this, it destroys us completely. When a hybrid such as your mother does it, she still lives."

"Wouldn't call that living," Simeon muttered.

"It does bring about a fundamental change."

"What is it?" Crow demanded. "What did she fucking do?"

"She annihilated her… there is no precise word for it in your language. Her inner, truest self."

Crow pondered this for a moment. "Her soul?"

That produced a shrug. "That is an approximate concept. Soul, spirit, anima, psyche…. The reality is more complicated than those ideas, but I believe they are close enough for you to understand. Certain Jewish mystic traditions speak of the *ruach*, the portion of the soul that contains the intellect and understands the larger aspects of creation. That may be the closest concept, but—"

"She destroyed her soul." Crow had no patience for metaphysical hair-splitting.

"Yes. Her vessel continues to exist. I do not believe she suffers. She may even receive some small happiness out of things such as the scent of flowers. But the person she was, that's gone. And she can no longer become afflicted."

It was perhaps the most awful thing Crow had ever heard of. But he remembered his childhood home aflame, the flashing lights outside the apartment he'd shared with Dee, the desperate way he'd tried and failed to escape the bus before the accident. And he understood Sara's decision.

"I'll do it."

"No!" Simeon stared at him wild-eyed. "You can't do that to yourself, love. You can't."

"I could sit in the garden next to her."

"You're not going to spend the rest of your life sitting in a bloody garden! Look at you. You've spent your entire existence letting fate lead you around on a leash. *I'll be a farmer because my grandparents are. I'll scuttle back and forth because the demons are chasing me. I'll not let myself get close to anyone.* Until now. Right *now* you've decided to bloody *do* something, to take your destiny into your own hands. You can't give up on that now."

Simeon's face was red and tears ran from the corners of his eyes. He was shaking Crow by the shoulders hard enough to clack Crow's teeth.

Crow didn't resist. He waited until Simeon grew silent and released him, and then Crow spoke. "My destiny's never been in my own hands."

"Bollocks! We're all born within a coffin, mate. We can lie there and pretend to be bloody comfortable or we can try to crawl our way out. We might not make it, but at least we can *try*. It's what makes us human, innit?"

"But I'm not human."

Simeon stared at him, face still tear-streaked and eyes gone as reflective as the birds'. His warmth had disappeared; now he was as cold as deep space.

"I can't watch this," Simeon said.

Then he turned and walked away.

Crow watched him: stride slow but steady, shoulders sloped, black hair ruffling in the breeze like a silk shawl. None of the angels paid Simeon any attention; none of the birds looked at him. Maybe it was some trick of the weird light in this place, but he didn't even cast a shadow. Simeon was completely and utterly alone in a way Crow had never been, not even during the past ten years. Simeon had never known his family, not even in the limited and fucked up way that Crow had. He'd never even had sex with the same person twice. He'd left his only real home—the carnival—to join Crow, and now he was stranded in a time and place not his own.

Simeon had steered his own fate, and look where that had got him.

God, but it had also gotten him those moments of joy, hadn't it?

"The process is not difficult," said Lo'orush. "Let us seat you somewhere comfortable and you can begin."

"Fuck you," Crow said and ran after Simeon.

# CHAPTER 19

*W*hen Crow caught up to him, Simeon stopped and turned around, expression bleak. "Can't do it, mate. I'm sorry. I can't watch you destroy—" His voice broke and he started to turn away again.

Crow caught him by the shoulder. "I won't. I'm not going to do it."

It was a lovely thing to see the light return to Simeon's eyes. "Truly?"

"Those fuckers have been destroying my family for three generations. I'm not going to just roll over and let them win."

"You're a stubborn one, yeah?" Simeon looked delighted.

"Runs in the family. My grandparents stayed on that damned farm even though they barely scraped a living off it. And look at Aunt Helen, there with her family and looking to the future despite everything that's happened to her. I need to be strong like that too."

"Bloody beautiful, you are." Simeon reached up and cupped Crow's chin. The contact made heat suffuse Crow's entire body, like drinking a mug of hot cocoa on a brisk winter day.

Ridiculously, Crow felt himself blushing. Nobody had ever looked at him that way, as if there were something special about him—special in a good way rather than in a freakish or dangerous one. As if he mattered. The demons could take all their promises of power and stick them up their collective ass, because Crow would rather matter to this one man than have authority over the entire goddamned world.

"What will we do next, love?" Simeon asked. As if he trusted Crow completely.

"I don't know. If you can't join them, beat them, I guess."

"We fight?"

"Yeah. We'll almost certainly lose, but I'm going down swinging. And look, this is my battle, not yours, so you don't have to—"

"*Our* battle now. They came after me too, remember? I'd rather charm my way out of a corner, or fuck my way out if I need to. But if it comes down to it, I don't walk away from a fight."

It was entirely selfish, but Crow was relieved. "Good, because I need you."

"I'll do whatever I can, but I'm only an ordinary bloke."

"You are the least ordinary person I have ever met." And that was saying a lot, considering some of Crow's recent acquaintances.

Crow had experienced more emotions in rapid sequence on this day than in any he could remember. So when Lo'orush glided over to join them, the most Crow could manage was a sigh. "Forget it. I'm not doing that to myself."

"I see." If Lo'orush was surprised, he didn't show it.

"How do I fight them instead?"

"I do not know."

"Then who among you does?"

"None of us."

Of course not. There were never any easy solutions.

Before Crow could stomp away with Simeon in tow, Lo'orush spoke again. "You realize that we are formidable."

"Yeah, I got that. But it doesn't matter. Gonna fight anyway."

"You misunderstand my meaning. *We* are formidable—that includes you."

They stood and stared at each other for a moment, Lo'orush's expression unreadable.

"Does that mean we stand a chance?" Simeon finally asked.

"All fates are mutable until the final thread is cut."

It didn't appear as if Simeon understood this comment any better than Crow did. And Crow was sick and tired of people being cryptic. "Will you people help us?"

Lo'orush shook his head gravely. "We cannot."

*Cannot* encompassed a lot of territory. Anything from *We'd prefer to avoid minor inconveniences* to *If we help, the world will end.* Whatever the case, Crow had the definite impression that it wouldn't do any good to argue or beg.

"Fine," he said. "We'll do it ourselves. But I want to say goodbye to my mother before we leave." She wouldn't notice, but it mattered to him.

They all walked back to the garden, a dozen or so birds hopping in their wake and commenting to one another with avian croaks and rasps. Crow had the very strange impression that the birds approved.

Sara sat exactly as he'd left her: beautiful and vacant, forever gazing at nothing. When Crow hesitated before entering through the gate, Lo'orush spoke quietly. "She was younger than you are now, with no ally at her side, and she had more to lose. Do not blame her for making this decision."

There was an odd little hitch in Crow's chest as he realized that he *had* been blaming her and that over time his resentment might fester into something ugly. "More to lose?"

"She had you."

The hitch grew into a lump that threatened to stop his heart completely.

But Lo'orush was still speaking. "She spoke of you lovingly, desperately. Her greatest fear was that she would bring harm to you. She pleaded with us to protect you, but we could not. Except for one small way." He gestured toward the nearest birds, who preened themselves proudly. "And that was not nearly enough. But you should know how deeply she cared for you."

Crow nodded mutely and entered the garden.

This time he didn't cry as he knelt at her feet, although his throat tasted bitter. He laid his head in her lap; her dress smelled of lavender and clean linen. "Thank you, Mama," he said very quietly. "I had a good childhood because of you. I was loved. I was happy. And I think... well, I'm far from perfect, but everything good about me is due to you and the family you left me with. I used to think that when you abandoned me, you were being cruel and a coward, but now I understand it was the bravest, kindest thing you could have done. I wish I'd known you even a little bit. The choices I make from now on, Mama, I hope they're things you'd be proud of."

He remained there for a moment, eyes closed, trying to impress into his brain every detail, every tiny second of his time with her.

Then he felt a pressure on his head. He opened his eyes and realized that she'd moved her hand to rest lightly in his hair.

She still stared at infinity. Her face remained entirely blank of expression or humanity. But he felt her fingertips warm against his scalp.

NONE of the angels came to say good-bye, although Lo'orush walked with Crow and Simeon as far as the tree-branch arch. An assortment of corvids followed along.

They all paused just inside the arch. "You'll continue to take good care of her?" Crow meant it as more of a demand than a question.

"Of course. She is our daughter, just as you are our son. We regret that there is not more we can do to protect you."

Crow didn't know whether that was the truth, and at this point he didn't care. "Thank you," was all he said. Because whatever else was true, it didn't seem as if Sara was neglected.

"We wish you a successful journey. May your fate be benign."

Lo'orush turned and walked back toward the houses, while Crow and Simeon passed under the arch and into the forest.

They walked without speaking, although sometimes a crow would caw softly as if encouraging them along. After a time, Crow noticed a familiar smug expression on Simeon's face.

"You stole something from the angels."

"Have to keep my hand in, don't I? Wouldn't want to lose the knack."

"But they're *angels*. Or fairies. Or something."

Simeon simply shrugged.

Crow couldn't completely hide his smile when he spoke next. "What did you steal?"

"Nothing they'll miss, I'd wager." Simeon stopped, reached into his pack, and pulled something out. He opened his palm so that Crow could see.

It was a single stalk of lavender, the florets bright purple against his palm.

Dammit, Crow almost started to cry again. Instead, as Simeon put the flower away Crow cleared his throat. "We need a plan. And I don't even know where to start."

"Well, funds are starting to run low. We could begin with more larceny." Simeon seemed cheerful about this prospect.

Crow was less enthusiastic, but then, he was hardly the best arbiter of moral values. "I don't want to just keep zigzagging back and forth defensively. So the question is, where do we go? And what do we do when we get there?"

Simeon's eyes sparkled in the particular way that made Crow think they should find a private, comfortable spot. God, he wanted to feel Simeon against him so badly. He even considered stripping off his clothing right then and there except the air was misty and you never knew when an angel might come floating by. He wasn't too keen on corvid voyeurs either.

They continued walking, because whatever their next step, it certainly wasn't here. And as they walked, Crow thought. He wasn't usually much for concentrating on… well, anything. The gears were rusty. But if he pushed at them hard enough, they moved.

"What we need next is information," he mused aloud. "That's really what we've been after all along. And we haven't gotten as much as I'd like, but…."

"But we know loads more than we used to."

Crow nodded. "Knowledge is power, I guess. Okay then, where do we learn more? I don't think the Murray Family Agency is going to be useful, and Helen is pretty much tapped out—not that I want to bring the demons near her again anyway. Where's the logical place to do more research?"

"Library, innit? The one in Omaha had loads to say about the Olympic Peninsula."

"That's... yeah, okay. But I doubt they had a section on how to defeat your demon cousins."

"Then we need to find a library that does."

Impulsively, Crow gathered Simeon in for a kiss. "I'm so glad you're here."

"Me too, love. Now let's go find your demon books."

# CHAPTER 20

As soon as they'd developed a plan—tentative and sketchy though it was—Crow was overcome with a sense of urgency. It was pleasant enough to go tromping through the countryside with a handsome and entertaining man at his side, but perhaps sooner rather than later the demons would attack again. If they were smart enough to track Crow everywhere he went, they'd certainly figure out why he'd visited Bayaq.

The birds seemed to agree with his unease. They hopped and flapped from tree to tree, scolding Crow and Simeon for not moving faster.

"How much money do we have left?" Crow asked.

"Enough for a few meals, the ferry back to Seattle, and a night's lodging, I reckon. Perhaps two if we're not choosy."

Crow was not choosy. Still, he worried about funds as they walked through Bayaq and continued onward to Sequim. Maybe he allowed himself to be preoccupied with money problems because they were more manageable than demon problems. Finances were something he had some control over. If nothing else, he was in the company of a thief. But that idea got him thinking about what might happen if they were both arrested. Could the demons come after him in jail, when he was utterly trapped? He shivered.

"Cold, love?"

"Just brooding."

"You're short on clothing, though."

Crow shrugged. Another problem for another time.

Back in Sequim, they inquired at the grocery store about the bus schedule. It was distressing to hear from the clerk—a beige sort of man in his fifties named Gary, according to his name tag—that they'd just missed the last one. "Maybe we could hitch back to the ferry," Crow said doubtfully. He'd never had much luck hitchhiking, presumably because he tended to look disreputable. Simeon's presence—and the coterie of crows waiting nearby—weren't going to help.

But once again, he'd underestimated Simeon, who walked back to the grocery clerk. "Could you give us a hand, mate?" Simeon let loose his 24-carat smile.

Gary cocked his head. "With what?"

"We need to return to Seattle today, but it appears as if we haven't any way to get to the ferry. Can you offer any suggestions?"

"Most people just drive there."

Simeon nodded as if that was terribly wise. "But we haven't a car, you see. Nor horse and wagon, even."

Although Simeon might have been dead serious about the wagon part, Gary didn't know that, and he chuckled. "That would be funny. My grandparents had that, you know. When Grandpa was young, he broke his arm trying to start a car— back when they had cranks, right? Real old-fashioned." He mimed turning a lever. "So he never really trusted cars after that. He had a farm near here and until he got pretty old, he used to ride into town on his horse."

"Did you come with him?"

"Sometimes, yeah." Eyes a little unfocused, Gary smiled at what must have been pleasant memories.

"Did you live on the farm?"

"Nah, we were here in town. My dad learned to be a mechanic during the war, so that's what he did when he came back. But I'd spend time with my grandparents as much as I could. I liked the farm."

"My mate grew up on a farm too." Simeon pointed at Crow.

Somewhat startled at being drawn into the conversation, Crow nodded awkwardly. "Uh, yeah. Corn mostly. Probably pretty different from what you grow here."

A lengthy discussion ensued about crops and growing seasons and irrigation methods. These were subjects Crow could hold his own on, and Gary seemed thrilled to be talking about them. Maybe he was just happy to be doing something other than rearranging canned goods; the grocery store wasn't at all busy. For his part, Simeon chimed in now and then, playing up his angle as a city boy, acting as if the trials of keeping chickens safe from predators were fascinating.

Then several customers came in all at once and it seemed as if Gary might have to leave Crow and Simeon. He scratched his ear. "Tell you what. My son, Dale? I'll give him a call and he'll drive you in to Kingston."

"Are you sure?" Simeon asked. "That's a lot to ask."

"Nah. He teaches high school, which means he spends most of the summer sitting on his butt with a book in his hands. He's got time."

So it was settled, apparently. Ten minutes later, Gary waved good-bye as they rode off in Dale's rattly Ford Escort. Crow sat in the back while Simeon and Dale sat up front and talked about London. Dale seemed surprised at a few of the things Simeon had to say—most of them anachronisms, such as a comment about how soot was thoroughly blackening St. Paul's cathedral and a description of the public bath in Whitechapel. He left them at the ferry terminal after cheery farewells.

The crows and ravens disappeared shortly after the ferry set off. There were seagulls, but Crow didn't think those were part of his entourage. They seemed to want food, not to protect him. Oddly, he found himself missing his black-feathered guardians.

"How do you *do* that?" Crow asked as he and Simeon stood at the boat railing. "Two seconds with anyone and you know exactly how to be their best friend?"

"Dunno. It's much the same as being a thief."

"What do you mean?"

"If you're going to steal from someone, you have to size him up real quick. Suss out what he's got to nick and how to distract him while you do it. Decide if he's a risk worth taking, yeah? And if you want to get along with a bloke, you need to suss out what he wants to talk about. What lights him up. Everyone's got something, so you make some good guesses about what it is and then you're in."

Crow considered this for a moment as he watched the steel-gray water roll by. "Did you do that with me?"

"Might've tried it the first time we met if you'd been a bit older. Perhaps I did, a bit anyway. No real harm in it. But the second time—you punched me, remember?"

"I *pushed* you," Crow said, as if that were any better.

Simeon bashed his shoulder into Crow's. "Berk. Look, I'd seen your future, which scared me half to death. And then you show up all grown and angry, and you pushed me, and I just wanted to know who the bloody hell you were and what had happened. I wasn't trying to get on your good side."

"I'm not sure I have a good side."

Simeon leered. "You do. I've tasted it."

And that got Crow thinking about sex again, which would have been fine if there was any hope of privacy on the little ferry. Which there wasn't.

It was late afternoon by the time they reached the library in downtown Seattle, an old building with big arched windows in the front. The crowded interior smelled like sweat and old paper. First Crow and Simeon wandered aimlessly for a while, then they had a heated discussion about whether to look up books under religion or the occult. That got them shushed twice. Then they decided that either category was possible and they attacked the card catalog with tiny pencils and index card–sized slips of paper. Not surprisingly, they didn't find exactly what they needed. But at least they figured out which Dewey decimal numbers might work, and they headed for the 130s and the 200s.

They'd been browsing for nearly half an hour, and closing time was getting near, when an older lady approached them in the 235s. She was tiny—wizened, really—with her gray hair in a bob. She wore an orange cardigan, gray slacks, and glasses on a chain around her neck. She looked exactly like a librarian ought to, Crow thought.

"Can I help you?" She seemed a little skeptical, as though at any moment the two of them might grab armfuls of books with titles such as *Angels, Elect and Evil* and make a run for it.

Of course, Crow let Simeon talk. By now he looked forward to watching him at work. It was like witnessing DaVinci paint or Baryshnikov dance. "We want to know how to defeat demons," Simeon said. "Or possibly evil fairies."

"Or maybe aliens," Crow added, because why the hell not.

She gave both of them a long look. "Are you playing *Dungeons & Dragons*?"

Baffled, Simeon just blinked and Crow had to step in. "No ma'am. Trying to save ourselves from ruin."

Instead of kicking them out, she nodded. "Physical, spiritual, or metaphysical ruin?"

"Um… all three. I guess."

"I see. I'm afraid we don't have anything in our collection that's likely to be helpful. Our books on the subject are quite general, and it sounds as if you're searching for something more specific."

Simeon gave an emphatic nod. "That's it exactly. We're in desperate need of some answers and we hoped a library would be a good place to look."

That earned him a smile. "A library is always an excellent place to begin. What you're going to require is a specialized collection, however. I know of one that might do. It's small but quite deep, you see. It's privately owned but available to serious researchers by permission."

"Madam, we are dead serious."

"I can tell." After motioning for them to follow, she made her way to a nearby reference desk, where she was almost hidden by the tall front. She used one of the tiny pencils to write slowly and carefully on a sheet of lined paper, which she handed to Simeon. "It's near Portland, I'm afraid. Give that to the owner, whose name I've written along with the address and a brief note from me. That will likely suffice for your entry."

Portland. Shit. Not only would that mean another couple hundred miles of travel, but it was where Dee— Crow shut down that thought at once. He didn't have time for sentimentality.

"Thank you," he said to the librarian. And then, because he was genuinely curious, he asked a question. "Um, our request is a little… out of the ordinary, I'd guess. But you're taking it seriously instead of calling the men in white coats."

She tapped the pencil on the counter a few times, mouth pursed. "Young man, my responsibility is to assist library patrons in conducting research. It is neither my business nor my inclination to judge the worthiness of that research. I find that careful, analytic inquiry tends to rule out the nonsensical, leaving the investigator with… well, perhaps not simply cold facts. I'm willing to accept that truth is sometimes subjective. But it leaves the investigator with something of substance. *Scientia potentia est*."

Crow didn't understand Latin but he appreciated the remainder of her sentiments. "Thank you for helping us."

"It is a pleasure. Is there anything else I can help you find?"

They said no and thanked her, and as they left, she wished them luck. When they were back outside, Simeon clapped Crow on the back. "You were brilliant, love. Well done."

"I didn't do anything."

"But you did. You made it clear that you respected her, and in return she respected you."

Crow hadn't thought about it that way, and he turned the concept over in his mind for a while. Finally he became aware that they were walking down the street. "Where are we going?"

"How far to Portland?"

"Couple hundred miles."

"And how long will that take us?"

Sometimes Crow almost forgot that Simeon wasn't very familiar with modern times. "Three or four hours by bus or train."

"Right. We're not going today, then. You're done in."

Almost as if Simeon's words were a magical incantation, the full weight of exhaustion crashed onto Crow's shoulders. It had been a strenuous day emotionally, not to mention all the traipsing through forests and along rural roads. And the ferry ride. And… everything. His knees started to give and Simeon scrambled to give support.

"A proper meal first, I think," said Simeon, reminding Crow that they'd barely eaten all day. "Then a room."

Too drained to make even a token protest about demons, Crow nodded.

Simeon steered him into the nearest restaurant, which turned out to be a casual Japanese place. His face lit up as he perused the menu. "I've never had any of this. What's good?"

Crow's own experiences with Japanese had pretty much been limited to instant ramen from the grocery store. But of course as soon as Simeon smiled at her, the waitress was more than happy to make recommendations, and soon they were eagerly eating udon noodles, breaded pork, and tempura vegetables. They even tried some sushi, which they agreed was much tastier than they'd expected raw fish to be.

Fortified, they went out into the night.

"You've so many more choices than where I'm from," Simeon mused as they sought a motel. "Things to eat, places to go, clothing to wear, ways to entertain yourselves. It's quite exciting for me, but I wonder if it gets overwhelming after a time."

"I think it can, yeah."

"Still, I'm bloody glad I've the opportunity to experience it all. If I'd known, back when I was a boy, what awaited me, living would have been much more tolerable." Simeon's voice was uncharacteristically soft.

"Have I told you what a miracle you are?"

Simeon scoffed. "Me? You're the bloody angel, love. I'm only an ordinary bloke."

"Well, that's the thing. You are an ordinary human—and yet you've faced so many challenges and shocks and changes with... enthusiasm. Humor. Most people, if they'd gone through what you have, they'd long ago have ended up gibbering in the corner. But here you are, ready for more adventure. Giving me the strength I need."

Simeon stopped suddenly, grabbing Crow's arm and turning him so they faced each other. His eyes were a little damp. "Love," he rasped, "I need to get you naked."

Despite Crow's fatigue, that sounded like an excellent plan.

THEY FOUND a hotel not far away, down near the bottom of the hill. It was an old place, with slightly dusty curtains in the front windows and creaky floors in the lobby. But the clerk, a handsome young man, grinned at them over the polished counter. "Two beds or one, gentlemen?"

Throwing caution to the wind, Crow said, "One."

That made the clerk smile even wider. "Perfect." After he took Simeon's money and handed him a key, the clerk said, "Enjoy your evening." And winked.

Crow didn't really get a chance to survey the room, because as soon as they were inside and shut the door, Simeon was on him.

Last night's lovemaking had been rough, still tinged with the aftertaste of an argument. Which had been entirely satisfying since it turned out that one good way to work out the last of one's angry feelings was by fucking the person who'd made you angry.

Tonight there was no lingering rage, but the mutual attack was just as fierce. This bout was fueled by hunger—a raw, unbridled appetite not for sex in the abstract but for the physical connection with one particular person. Crow wanted to crawl into Simeon's skin and have Simeon crawl into his. He wanted to fill his mouth with Simeon's flavors, to fill his ears with Simeon's moans and grunts and pleas. He wanted every nerve in his body to be inundated with nothing but Simeon.

And God, it seemed as if Simeon wanted the same.

They managed to get their clothing off without ruining anything, which was both a miracle and a blessing, considering how few items they had available. But they didn't make it to the bed. Simeon trapped Crow against a wall, where the textured plaster dug into his back a little. Clutching each other's asses, they rutted fiercely, mouths licking and sucking and biting. Sometimes Crow's head banged against the wall, and the few parts of his brain not otherwise occupied wondered whether someone would complain, but nobody did.

He wouldn't have stopped anyway. Couldn't have. It was like tumbling down a steep hillside, whirling and spinning and cartwheeling and knowing that maybe at the end you'd end up broken, but it wouldn't matter.

What mattered was Simeon's big hands, hot and grasping; His lips, luxuriously lush, and teeth that brought bright sparks of almost-pain to Crow's neck and shoulders and nipples. What mattered were the words Simeon whispered into Crow's ear, some of them sappy-sweet endearments, some the coarsest of profanities, some not intelligible at all.

Crow felt worshiped. Not an angel or a demon but a god made of human flesh and bone. And he was a worshiper as well.

"I want *you*," Crow heard himself repeat over and over, and he knew it was true. "You. You." As if he'd never until this moment knew what *want* meant.

Their coupling wasn't elegant. And there was no penetration. Hell, Marty and Sandy had probably done more than this while cramped in the backseat of Marty's decrepit Pontiac. But what Crow and Simeon were doing was somehow sublime. And when Simeon came with a howl and his hot spend splashed against Crow's belly, Crow fell apart: blind and deaf, breathless, plunging downward in an ecstasy of ruin.

They made it to the bed after that, but only so they could collapse side by side, staring up at the ceiling as they tried to slow their hearts.

"Well, that takes the egg." Simeon's voice was full of wonder.

"What?"

Simeon laced his fingers with Crow's. "I thought you were going to kill me, just then."

"Yeah."

"Wouldn't have minded a bloody bit. Best way I can think of to cut the painter."

Smiling, Crow turned his head to look at him. "You're speaking a foreign language."

Simeon flipped himself over very suddenly so that his body blanketed Crow's and their faces were inches apart. He cradled Crow's face in his palms. "Then I'll say it slowly. Whatever happens to me after this moment, it doesn't matter. It's all worth it, innit? Because it's always been just me—Simeon Bell. And now it's not."

"It's not," Crow agreed, and he smiled.

## CHAPTER 21

*D*rained and satiated, Crow was ready to fall asleep at once, especially because he wanted to get an early start in the morning. But Simeon, after tucking Crow in as tenderly as a doting parent, got dressed again. "Dosh," he explained succinctly.

Oh. That. At least one of them was being a responsible adult. Sort of.

"Do you know how you'll, um, find money?"

"Something will come along. Always does if you know how to look." Simeon's expression grew serious. "What I used to do back in London sometimes… distract a bloke with my mouth or arse so I could lift his wallet…."

Crow felt a pang, but not of jealousy. It was sorrow, because he suspected Simeon had been very young when he'd started that practice. "You had to survive. There's worse ways to get along in the world."

"I expect there are. But I want you to know that I won't be doing that tonight. Not because I give a fig about those blokes. But because tonight I feel as if…." His voice became quiet and tentative. "As if I'm yours, yeah?"

Crow nodded and replied firmly, "You're mine." Maybe not forever, but as Simeon had so recently taught him, even fleeting joy was valuable.

"Right, then." Simeon smiled warmly and left, shutting the door softly behind him.

CROW DRIFTED in a doze for a long time, his thoughts dissolving into wisps before he could grasp them. He heard faint voices, which could have been other guests or ghosts or almost-dreams. He smelled flowers, but that was probably the hotel soap. His body felt heavy, a burden he had been carrying and was grateful to set down.

He suddenly remembered with great clarity an event that he wasn't sure had actually happened. It was the middle of summer, the air thick with heat and humidity and bugs, and he and Marty had spent the day doing farm chores. But now it was after dinner and they'd been dismissed to meet in the Storey barn. They'd climbed into the hayloft and leaned on the sill of the big open window, staring out at the long shadows. They each had a bottle of Coke in hand. They were fourteen, maybe fifteen. Somewhere between boys and men.

"It's beautiful," Marty said, meaning everything they could see. Which surprised Crow because Marty wasn't usually one to appreciate aesthetics, or at least not to express his appreciation.

"Just corn and stuff," Crow had said.

"Yeah, but look at all the colors. And the colors will be different when it's harvest time, and different again all winter and then in spring. You think it's always the same, but it's really not. It never is."

"I guess."

Marty socked Crow in the bicep, making him yelp even though it didn't really hurt. "Look, you can change it if you want to. Stare at those fields real hard and then imagine all those stalks turning into… giant trees. All covered in vines and stuff, like a jungle. Monkeys swinging and snakes hanging down. Hell, maybe you can find Tarzan if you look hard enough."

Although Crow's immediate instinct was to punch Marty back and tell him he was crazy, he instead narrowed his eyes and did as ordered. He pictured the cornstalks rising up and up, the stems becoming broad brown trunks and the tops branching out wildly into a thousand shades of green. There were monkeys and snakes, yes. Also butterflies and birds: blue and orange and red and yellow. A flash of shadowy movement along the ground, which was almost certainly a leopard stalking its prey. And yes, a nearly naked man with long hair leaping off a branch and catching a vine, the muscles of his broad chest— Crow had shied away from that thought.

"Do you see it?" Marty's voice startled him. Crow had almost forgotten he was there.

"Yeah."

"You get it? We think we're stuck here in Chinkapin Grove. But if you try hard enough, you can be anywhere. *You* get to decide where you are."

And then a crow had swooped by the window, calling harshly and shattering the illusion. Crow and Marty had sat down on hay bales and talked about what they'd do with the rusty old Ford truck if Crow's granddad let them tinker with it.

Simeon crept back into the room on tiptoe, but Crow woke up anyway and smiled sleepily. "Success?"

"Yeah."

Simeon spent a few minutes undressing and using the bathroom. He came into bed, smelling like beer and rose-scented soap, and snuggled up against Crow's side. His skin was cool but would warm quickly.

"Capitol Hill," he said through a yawn.

Crow, who'd spent a little time in Seattle over the past decade, lifted his eyebrows. "Gay bars?"

"Yeah. I went there first, and it was beautiful, yeah? Blokes dancing together and snogging, girls dancing and snogging, and nobody afraid the coppers would show up and drag them off to get topped." He mimed being hung, which was useful because that wasn't what Crow had first thought of when he heard the term *topped*. "But it's sad too, innit. Because of that disease. Like they've finally been given their freedom and now they can't use it properly." He sighed deeply. "I couldn't steal from them."

"But you said—"

"Went down toward the water. Found another pub full of toffs. They were throwing money around like nothing. Drinking, inhaling drugs in the loo, nattering on about stock —not livestock, I don't reckon—and some kind of machine with windows. It was almost too easy to lift their wallets. They'll hardly miss what I took, but it's enough to last us awhile."

Simeon looked smug and Crow mustered a frown. "It's still stealing."

"Aye. But I won't lose sleep over it."

Crow briefly thought about trying to rouse some moral indignation but decided he didn't have the energy. "Well, get some sleep then."

Simeon kissed Crow's clavicle. "Will do."

It was Simeon who fell asleep first, his breaths smooth and deep, but Crow followed soon afterward. And at some point after that, he fell into a dream.

He was a bird—a crow, he assumed—flapping his wings among a flock of hundreds, soaring over endless fields of flowers far below. Sometimes he caught sight of a woman sitting in one of those fields, wearing a white dress and smiling up at him. Sometimes there were rivers made of shiny coins or of powdery white cocaine.

"Is that what the blokes in the pub were sniffing?" asked the nearest bird. Unlike the other birds, this one had a white, featherless patch around its beak.

"Yeah."

"They seemed to like it."

Crow made a dismissive caw. "I tried it once. Not my cup of tea. It made everything… sharp and fast. I wanted to dull things. Insulation."

They flew onward for a moment or two before Simeon spoke again. "I fancy this dream. Usually when I fly in my sleep, I end up falling. This is loads better." As if to emphasize his point, he did a complicated series of loops.

"I'm glad, but I didn't choose it. I have no control over my dreams."

"Of course you do. They're yours."

"Well, yeah, but…." Then Crow remembered that memory he'd had of Marty and the faux jungle—assuming it *was* a memory and not a fabrication. *You get to decide,* Marty had said.

Fine. "I'm changing course," Crow said, and banked to his left.

Simeon and the others followed. "Where to?" asked Simeon.

"Enough with the flowers. I want to see the answer. How do we beat the demons?"

All of the other birds began a raucous sound, but he couldn't understand it so he ignored them and concentrated on his goal. And sure enough, soon the flowers disappeared and there was nothing beneath them but a void. That was so distressing that Crow nearly woke himself up. But then the void turned cloudy as if filling with smoke, and the smoke shifted in what seemed like a purposeful way before it cleared, revealing a paper map stretching in all directions.

"Nice trick," Simeon commented. But Crow was trying to read the place names, which at first were too blurry to make out. As they sharpened, he recognized them: Bayaq, Portland, Chicago, Lemont, Ocala, Chinkapin Grove, Hickory, Burlington, Toledo, Minot, Amarillo. And more and more, each of them a place he'd visited within the past decade. Each a place he'd left, sometimes leaving corpses behind him. The cities weren't in geographical or temporal order, but there they were. The map of his life.

And then, as he and his entourage flapped onward, strings began to appear below them: purple lines pinned at one point and stretched to another. Sometimes short and sometimes long, they overlapped one another and went off in seemingly random directions until the map resembled a disastrous game of cat's cradle.

The strings began to unravel. To split. To disappear.

"I don't understand," said Crow. The other birds made noises again—this time they sounded as if they were scolding him for being dense.

"I don't understand!" he screamed.

And then he woke up.

# CHAPTER 22

They took an early train out of King Street Station, their car half full with dozing students and senior citizens, plus a couple of businessmen in suits. Various paper bags smelling of pastries and bacon rustled, cardboard coffee cups steamed, a teenager mouthed the words to whatever he was listening to on his Walkman.

The scenery was pretty, Crow supposed. Simeon seemed to enjoy it. There was water to their left and tall trees on both sides. Sometimes the branches of those trees were heavy with black birds.

Crow couldn't relax. He felt as if someone was watching him—aside from the birds—and that something terrible was going to happen at any moment. Images of derailed trains kept pushing into his brain, the cars jackknifed and twisted on the ground, battered bodies scattered on the tracks.

He'd thought about getting to Portland in some other way, a method that would put fewer bystanders in danger if the demons attacked. But bus travel was obviously no improvement; and if he and Simeon somehow scored a car ride, there was still the potential for horrendous multi-vehicle accidents. That left what? Walking. But that would require days, and he harbored an increasing feeling that time was of the essence.

So here they were on Amtrak, the monotonous clack of the wheels doing nothing to soothe Crow's frayed nerves.

"Did they have trains where you're from?" Crow asked, hoping to distract himself.

Simeon chuffed a laugh. "Of course. I used to haunt the stations on occasion. Lovely places to acquire a shilling or two, if you can stay away from the coppers."

"Did you go anywhere?"

"Nah. Where would I go? My home grounds weren't exactly posh, but at least I knew them. Anywhere else I'd have been nothing but a stranger."

"You're not a stranger now."

Simeon gave him a warm smile. "I've you, haven't I?"

That lifted Crow's mood a little, although it didn't shake his sense of foreboding.

The train was delayed in Centralia for reasons nobody explained. They sat there for over an hour beside a squat brick station with a tile roof. Crow tried pacing the aisles to keep from going crazy, but soon—having attracted worried or hostile stares from the other passengers—he sat back down.

Simeon gave Crow's hand a quick pat. "When I was a boy —nine or ten—I stole a shiny copper tap from the urinal yard at King's Cross Station."

"Why?"

"Was worth five or six shillings and seemed easier than dipping." He laughed at Crow's obvious confusion. "Pick-pocketing, love."

"Oh. So you sold it to... somebody?"

"Would have done, if the coppers hadn't snatched me. I ended up with claws for breakfast."

Crow frowned. "That doesn't sound good."

"Caning. Twelve strokes with a birch rod on my back. I was lucky it didn't scar."

"They *beat* you?" Now Crow felt sick as well as furious at people who'd probably been dead for a century by now.

"If I'd been older it would have been hard labor. This was better. Besides, I was used to it." Simeon said that airily, as if it were nothing, but Crow sensed a foundation of hurt and sorrow. It didn't help to know that afterward, there had been nobody to comfort Simeon or care for him while he healed.

"I'm sorry," Crow said softly.

Simeon shrugged. "Learned my lesson: don't nick anything that'll be so obvious in your pockets. Took loads of fogles after that—that's handkerchiefs, love. They weren't worth much, but they were simple to take and to hide, and it was easy to sell them. And people didn't often notice they were gone, or if they did, they'd reckon they'd dropped it somewhere."

"Did you get caught again?"

"A few times. Part of the territory, innit?"

So now Crow could ruminate on the unfairness of the Victorian criminal justice and child welfare systems, which was an improvement over worrying about when demons might try to destroy him and Simeon. He wondered how he would have fared if, on his eighteenth birthday, he'd been thrust—homeless, penniless, and devastated—into Simeon's London instead of 1970s rural Illinois. Probably not well.

Eventually the train continued its journey, but by then Crow's nerves felt threadbare. He imagined them like the strings in the previous night's dream, unraveling and breaking. If that was all the dream had been—a message from his subconscious that he was close to losing his shit—it needn't have bothered. He could have figured that out on his own.

Simeon grabbed Crow's hand and gave a quick squeeze. "What will you do after?" Simeon asked.

"After what?"

"After you beat your demons."

Crow's mind went absolutely blank. He blinked a few times.

"Love?" Simeon prompted.

"I'm not going to beat them. I can't."

Simeon scowled. "That's a bloody awful attitude. Why even try then?"

"Because... I'm too stubborn to just give in, I guess. And maybe I can buy some time. Somehow."

"Oh, Crow." Another hand squeeze, this one longer. "Is that the best you hope for?"

Crow shrugged. It was more than a lot of people got. More than his parents had been given.

After a moment, Simeon huffed. "Well, I reject your pessimism. I'm going to believe that we'll win. And when we do, you'll need to decide what you want to do with the rest of your life. Have you never considered that? What you'd do if you were rid of your curse?"

No. Crow never had. It seemed as pointless as planning what he'd do if he grew wings. In fact, it was worse than pointless; it was painful. It hurt to reach toward a prize you knew you'd never attain. Better to hunker down and accept your fate.

But now Simeon watched him so intently, and Crow remembered that Simeon had been reaching for that elusive prize for his entire life. "I'd like... friends," Crow said tentatively. "Family. A home—I don't really care what kind. An interesting job, I guess."

"Simple needs," said Simeon, his eyes warm. "They're mine as well. Do you reckon we might find them together?"

"I can't make false promises."

"They're not false promises. They're *hope*. Can we find some hope together?"

What was the point of surviving without hope? Without it, Crow might as well be a living statue sitting in a field of flowers, seeing nothing, knowing nobody.

"Yes," Crow whispered. The single syllable shattered something within him, but in a good way, like clearing a layer of ice and finding fresh water beneath.

Simeon squeezed his hand again.

UNION STATION in Portland was a handsome brick building with a tall clock tower. Maybe under other circumstances Crow would have enjoyed it, but his sense of imminent danger had intensified. Also, the last time he'd been here had been with Dee who, having been fired and kicked out of his apartment, planned to ride down to Klamath Falls to see if his parents would take him in. They hadn't, and a few days later he'd showed up at Crow's door looking frail and defeated.

And now he was dead. Crow wondered where he'd been buried and whether he'd had a funeral. Had anyone else mourned him?

"All right, love?" Simeon's voice was low and concerned.

"Yeah. Just… some rough memories in this city. Let's go find that library, okay?"

They had to take one of the orange-and-gray busses to the center of downtown and then transfer to one that took them over the West Hills and into the suburbs. It was a warm day, and the locals—unaccustomed to heat—looked sweaty and unhappy. For his part, Crow was worried about being on a bus again, although the demons had never pulled the same stunt twice in a row, so maybe he was safe. Simeon seemed content to take in the view through the window.

"A zoo!" he exclaimed. "I've never been to one."

Crow considered. "Neither have I." There wasn't one anywhere near Chinkapin Grove, and once he'd become an adult, he'd never really thought about going.

"Then we'll visit one together after we're free." Simeon nodded as if the matter were settled.

And that made Crow think about how many new experiences Simeon could have, and how much fun it would be to be there with him, to feel his joy. Neither of them were asking for much, were they?

The bus let them off alongside a busy road near a McDonald's. Simeon had never made the acquaintance of Ronald, Mayor McCheese, or the Hamburglar, and since it was lunchtime, they stepped inside. Crow was too nervous to do more than pick at a few fries, but Simeon was quite pleased with his Big Mac and chocolate shake.

After that, it was a short walk to the address the librarian had provided. Crow wondered whether she'd played a cruel joke—maybe to get rid of them—because this was a residential neighborhood with well-kept ranch homes set on large lots. The house at their destination had a deep front lawn overrun with dandelions and clover, and a motorcycle parked in the driveway in front of a two-car garage. The house was painted a nondescript green. Really, the only unusual thing about it were the dozen or more sets of wind chimes hanging from the front eaves, each tinkling a gentle tune even though Crow couldn't feel a breeze.

As he and Simeon hesitated, the lawn filled with silent crows, and dozens of scrub jays landed on nearby trees. They all watched carefully.

"Um...." Crow cleared his throat. "Should I go there?" He was addressing his question to the birds rather than to

Simeon, which was objectively ridiculous. Some of the birds resettled their wings, but that was the only answer he got.

"They don't seem to oppose the notion," Simeon pointed out.

"I guess not."

After a few deep breaths, Crow marched up the sidewalk with Simeon at his side.

There was no sign of a traditional doorbell, only a rope attached to a large bronze bell. It made a startlingly loud sound when he pulled on it. A moment later the door swung open, but nobody was there.

"Um, hello?" Crow called into the dark interior.

A woman's voice responded from somewhere deep inside. "Come in. And make sure you shut the door. I don't want feathers in here."

After exchanging bemused glances, Crow and Simeon obeyed. They found themselves in an entirely ordinary hallway with shag carpeting. There wasn't enough light to make out the colors of the carpet or the walls, but Crow recognized at once the scent of old books—paper, leather, and dust—and was slightly relieved.

"Hello? A librarian in Seattle sent us here. She said you—"

"I know, I know. First door on your right. Look around all you want. I'll be with you in a little while."

Maybe the woman in Seattle had called her, but this was still very strange. On the other hand, pretty much everything in Crow's life was very strange, so he shouldn't be expecting anything different. Trailed by the ever-willing Simeon, Crow went into the first room on their right.

It was much, much larger than it had any right to be. It also bore a closer resemblance to a gothic castle than a suburban tract home: tall arched ceilings, windows of leaded glass, and dozens of ornately carved wooden bookcases arranged in parallel rows. Flickering candles in enormous chandeliers reflected off the polished flagstone floor. Several faded tapestries hung on the stone walls. At the far end, flames danced in a fireplace large enough to roast a buffalo. A big fire was good, because despite the outdoor heat, the room was fairly chilly.

Simeon had the most sensible reaction. "Blimey," he said as he looked around.

Although Crow was overwhelmed by the surroundings, he was mostly relieved at having lost the sensation of being stalked. He began to wander tentatively, peering at the spines of some of the thousands of books, most of which looked ancient. "I have no idea where to begin. We could be here for a year."

But in his usual fashion, Simeon had already plunged in. He disappeared between bookcases, although Crow could hear his footsteps and his muttered commentary. Shrugging, Crow began his own exploration.

A lot of the titles weren't in English. He recognized some of the languages: Latin, Greek, German, Russian. Others he thought were probably Chinese, Thai, and Hindi. But some were in alphabets he didn't recognize at all. Not that he was a linguist, by any means. Of necessity he stuck to the ones in English. He couldn't discern the organizational scheme, however; no Dewey decimal in sight. A volume entitled *The Secondary Haunts of Greater Gloucestershire* was next to one called *Sasquatches: Secrets of their Mating Rituals*, and beside that one was *Walton's Guide to Divinatory Graphology*. If Crow had possessed all the time in the world, he would have wanted to peek at some of these. But since he didn't, he pressed on in search of something relevant.

His heart raced when he found a thick green volume with *The Battles of the Angels* inscribed in gold on the spine. But when he leafed through it, he discovered that the text—in an old-fashioned version of English and hard to decipher—

seemed to be about a war fought in the Byzantine Empire during the twelfth century. If anything in that book was useful to him, he didn't find it after a quick perusal.

He kept looking, sometimes glancing over his shoulder to see if the mysterious librarian had made an appearance. She hadn't. Simeon called out to him periodically but didn't seem to be having much success either.

In a collection of sermons bound in something that looked uncomfortably like human skin, Crow stumbled upon a passage that was dated March 1942 and had apparently been delivered in Locust, Alabama. The preacher, who wasn't named, had gone on at length about the fight between good and evil. And then, according to the text, he'd said this:

WE'RE SEEING *men fight against men right now. Our brave boys have traveled across the oceans to protect the whole world from evil. I don't have to tell you that. Your sons are there, your brothers and your husbands. But let me also remind you that this great struggle between righteousness and iniquity takes place on other planes as well. Angels are in combat against demons, my friends.*

*And do you know how these fights will be won?*

*With strength and courage. With patience. With hope and love. With an understanding of the parts within us that are holy and good. With an understanding that we can and must make the choice to do what's right. We have these mighty weapons at our disposal, and if we use them wisely, righteousness will defeat wickedness.*

THE SERMON WASN'T VERY specific in exactly how people were supposed to use these alleged weapons. It might all be a lot of hooey, some preacher's attempt to invigorate patriotism and faith during a time when people may have been questioning both. But something in those words rang true to Crow. Maybe it was those magic terms: hope and love. Those two things, which for ten years he'd been without, seemed suddenly invaluable.

He was paging through the book in search of more, and not finding it, when Simeon called out. "Oi! Come see this."

Crow returned the book to the shelf, wiped his hands on his jeans, and went in search of Simeon. He found him halfway across the room in the narrow aisle between two towering bookshelves, staring down at the floor.

"What is it?" asked Crow.

"Come see."

There was a purple string on the floor, beginning inches from Simeon's feet, running the length of the narrow aisle between the shelves, and disappearing around the corner.

"What's that?"

Simeon gave him a look. "String, innit?"

"Yeah, but why's it there?"

"Dunno. I reckoned it was best we looked together."

That made sense—or at least as much sense as anything did in Crow's life. Together they followed the purple line around the corner, past the ends of several bookcases, and down another row, where it stopped midway.

"Do you think this means we're supposed to look here?" Crow asked.

Simeon shrugged. "As good an idea as any."

Each bookcase on either side of the string's end held a couple hundred books. Crow started examining the volumes on one side while Simeon took the other. At first this seemed especially fruitless because none of these books had titles on the spines and the pages proved to be completely blank.

And then Crow pulled out a pale blue volume and saw that there was an image of a crow on the front. He almost dropped it. "Simeon," he hissed.

Simeon turned to face him. For several moments they both stared at the book in Crow's hands. It looked innocuous enough. The binding was the same kind of cloth that Crow remembered from his school libraries, slightly fuzzy at the top and bottom of the spine, with a noticeable crease, as if the book had been opened many times.

"What do you think it says?" Crow asked.

"Couldn't begin to guess, love. But it doesn't have to remain a mystery."

Crow loved the way Simeon made suggestions like this—gently, and without implying that Crow was either an idiot or a coward. Just simple words of support, really.

After a steadying breath, Crow opened it. The first number of pages were blank, and he was about to growl in disappointment and return it to the shelf. But then he turned the next leaf and there were words. Instead of being typeset, they were handwritten in black ink. "That's my handwriting."

"It's appalling."

"Yeah. My teachers used to yell at me about it."

Crow hadn't yet managed to focus on the meaning of the words. The hair of his nape stood on end and he had a shivery feeling down his spine: that walked-over-my-grave sensation again.

He closed his eyes. "*You* read it. Sorry. I'm being chickenshit."

Simeon shuffled around and gave Crow's cheek a quick kiss. "It's fine. It's a list of sorts." And then, as Crow continued to hold the book, Simeon began to recite, pausing a little over the worst scribbles.

EVERY LIVING BEING IS BORN *with certain limitations and certain potentials. Within those boundaries lie a host of possibilities, like innumerable islands in an endless sea. Each individual must decide whether their course will be determined entirely by winds and tides, or whether they will take part in steering the ship.*

*Whether demons are internal or external, they will defeat you unless you are in control of your route.*

*Recognize the things for which you bear responsibility. Take agency for those, but do not make your burden heavier than necessary.*

*Disentangle yourself from fate. Assess your weapons. Instead of bemoaning what you don't have, use the powers you possess.*

"THAT'S IT," said Simeon. He sounded confused.

Crow sighed. "Those sound more like fortune cookies than practical advice."

An unexpected voice chimed in. "Wow. You really need it all in bold print, with trumpets."

Crow almost dropped the book as he and Simeon spun around to discover a young woman looking at them, hands on her hips. She looked as if she might have stepped out of a music video—Madonna's or Cindy Lauper's, maybe—with a bright tiered skirt, artfully ripped T-shirt, and lots of chunky bracelets and strings of colorful beads. Her bleached hair was dyed violet and yellow and sprayed into an elaborate spiky arrangement.

"Hello?" Crow said.

She rolled her eyes. "If I hadn't led you to the right book, you'd have been here forever."

"If you knew what we were looking for, why didn't you just show it to us right away? Why bother with the treasure hunt?" He pointed at the string, knowing he wasn't being polite but lacking the energy to care.

"Did you not listen to anything your boyfriend just read? You can't just have everything done for you. Take *some* accountability, Crow."

The *boyfriend* part had sidetracked him, and as he was trying to find a response, Simeon spoke up.

"You're the lady from Murray Family Agency."

That was ridiculous. Why would a woman from an adoption agency in Nebraska—now, only a few days later—be running an occult library in Oregon? Except... there was a similarity between her and the youngest woman at the agency, now that Crow took a closer look. A strong similarity.

She huffed at them both. "You can call me Chloe. Yeah, that works." For some reason, her own statement seemed to amuse her.

Crow decided to stick to the important issue. "Can you help—"

"Help you figure out your shit by spelling everything out for you? Nope." Another huff, this one more resigned than annoyed. "But I can get you something to drink while *you* figure it out. Come with me."

Crow started to follow, but she stopped him with her hand. "Put the book back. It's not a great idea for you to hang onto it for too long."

He obeyed, and only when he slid it into place did he notice the volume next to it, bound in fine-grained black leather. On the cover was a picture of a circus wagon that looked very much like Simeon's.

But there was no time now to deal with that. Chloe gestured impatiently and they trailed her down the aisle, across the stone floor, and back out into the hall. She led them through the next door down, which took them into another large room, although smaller than the library. Its décor was more haunted mansion than gothic castle, and the walls were heavily festooned with spiderwebs. Even though Crow couldn't actually see the residents of the webs, it felt as if thousands of tiny eyes watched him.

Elaborate woven rugs covered the floor, and a large spinning wheel sat in the center of the room, its dark wood gleaming. That was the only furniture aside from a dozen or so chests big enough to serve as coffins.

"Erm—" Simeon began. But Chloe made a shushing noise and took them through a door at the opposite end of the room.

It led into a small and absolutely ordinary kitchen, exactly like someone would expect to find in a modest suburban ranch house. Something fragrant simmered in a big pot on the stove, and the windowsill behind the sink was crowded with potted herbs. Several macramé creations hung on a wall, and a calendar from October 1929 was displayed at the end of a bank of cupboards; it had a drawing of a child and a puppy sharing biscuits.

Chloe pointed to the dinette set tucked into a breakfast nook. "Sit."

They sat next to each other on the brass-framed upholstered chairs. Since the drapes were closed, they couldn't see out the adjacent window, but Crow had the impression that the view would be something other than a suburban backyard.

After fussing at the stove for several minutes, Chloe carried over three mismatched mugs. She put them down on the table, went back for a plate full of Oreos, and then sat opposite them.

"This is very kind of you, miss," said Simeon.

"You don't have to sweet-talk me, honey. Anyway, I don't mind. After a while, it's pretty much just the same-old, same-old, but you two are unique. Makes things interesting."

While Simeon smiled and nibbled on a cookie, Crow tried not to scowl. "I don't want to be interesting."

"That ship has sailed, captain. Speaking of which, have you figured out what the book was telling you?"

Of course he hadn't. He sipped at his mug, which contained something that tasted exactly like the instant hot cocoa his gran used to buy for a treat now and then. This mug didn't contain any tiny marshmallows, however. He glanced inside Simeon's cup and saw milky tea, and Chloe seemed to be drinking… borscht?

"I think," Crow said after the others had waited patiently for a few minutes, "maybe I get some of it. Like the part about not making your burden too heavy. Simeon chewed me out because, well, a lot of bad things have happened around me, and I was thinking of them as my fault. But I guess maybe they're not." He shot Simeon a grateful look.

Chloe appeared pleased. "Good, good. Just because your fate gets tangled up with someone else's doesn't mean you're in charge of them both. Everybody has their own ship. If someone else's sinks, it's not necessarily your fault."

"More with the nautical analogy," said Simeon.

"It's a good one. Because life isn't a train, forced to stick to a track. You can go off in all sorts of directions. But that doesn't mean you won't get stuck in the doldrums or eaten by a kraken." She grinned cheerfully.

Crow scrunched up his face. "Fine, fine. Take responsibility for my own problems and not other people's, and don't make it all about me. I got that when Simeon pounded it into my head. But I don't see how that helps me fight demons."

"Maybe it's just general good advice. Or maybe the better your headspace, the more well-equipped you'll be to deal with your issues."

He could see some logic in that, although he hid it by swallowing some cocoa. He burned his tongue, just as he had every single time Gran made it for him. He'd never hesitated to drink it, though; it tasted good enough to be worth a minor scalding.

Simeon watched him closely, a tiny smile playing at the

corners of his mouth, as if he expected Crow to do something amazing at any moment. Crow didn't feel capable of being amazing. He'd never claimed to be especially bright. Back in school he'd gotten Bs and Cs, and his teachers wrote things on his report card about how he was nice and cooperative in the classroom.

In fact, he'd never been great at anything. He was okay at sports and was never the last to be picked in PE, but he certainly wasn't a star. He hadn't bothered to try out for any teams. He was mediocre at singing, at playing a recorder, at drawing, at working with tools in shop class. He'd always figured that he'd make a passable farmer, hopefully good enough to keep the Storey farm afloat, even if he didn't especially enjoy the occupation. And that was fine; he'd never really considered any alternatives.

And that was it, wasn't it. The thing that Simeon had asked about this morning. Crow had allowed himself to be dragged through his existence like a dog on a leash without ever once thinking about what could happen if he slipped his collar. He had not steered his own ship. Until recently.

"Fate," he said suddenly, slightly startling himself.

Chloe lifted her eyebrows. "Yes?"

"That book was sort of saying the same thing in different ways, and it was about fate. How a person shouldn't just bow to it, I think."

She leaned back in her chair with a broad smile. She had pink bangle earrings shaped like wheels, and if he looked at them too closely they seemed to be spinning. "You're catching on, kiddo," she said.

He thought some more. Understanding was almost there, like a word on the tip of his tongue, and all he had to do was grasp it. What had that passage said, precisely? *Disentangle yourself from fate.* It wasn't simply a matter of girding his loins for defense; he had to take active steps to assert independence from his destiny. The question was how to accomplish that. Despite the urgings of the current First Lady, in this case you couldn't Just Say No.

Crow thought about the string on the floor of the library and the wheel and webs in the room next to the kitchen. "Tangled," he said.

Chloe nodded. "It's handy to think of it that way. Fate loops you in, bit by bit, and if you don't make an effort to escape, you end up trapped. Some get trapped so early in life that they're pretty much helpless—without a whole lot of help, they'll never get free. Some people don't want to be free because it's easier not to be in charge. But fate is never completely inescapable. That's the deal. It's kind of like a game, right? Maybe it's not a *fair* game, but it's like playing the lottery. Everyone has at least a tiny chance to win." Looking smug, she drained her cup. "It's one of the things the Greeks got wrong."

She said something in, Crow assumed, Greek. Then she helpfully translated. *"Fate is mysterious and mighty, and nothing allows us to escape her—not wealth, not fortresses, not war, not the speediest ship.* That's from *Antigone,* and it sounds better in the original. Sophocles was a good playwright, but he forgot that ships are only marginally affected by fate. It's their captains who decide how actively they want to steer."

Simeon, who'd been reaching for another Oreo, drew his hand back. His brow was furrowed. "May I ask a question, miss?"

She gave a regal nod.

"If fate isn't set in stone, how does soothsaying work? Because I had a vision about Crow the first time we met, and it came true." A distressed expression settled on his face. "Could he have avoided what happened if I had told him what I saw?"

Crow wanted to hug him but settled for a squeeze of his

leg. "Don't burden yourself with things you're not responsible for, remember?"

"Your boyfriend gives good advice," said Chloe. "Prophecy is a matter of probabilities, bud. It's like the polls they do before elections—oh, wait. You probably don't know about those." She hummed a bar of "God Save the Queen."

"Probabilities," he echoed doubtfully.

"Right. Oracles have a gift for number-crunching all the data and coming up with a damned good guess about what's going to happen next. It's never foolproof—there's always a margin of error. Before those monsters ever showed up at the Storey farm, Crow could have been gored by a cow or run over by a truck. He could have run away from home. But none of those things were at all likely."

This made sense to Crow, maybe because the pollster analogy wasn't lost on him. During the summer he was seventeen—given all the separate trajectories of various components in his life—the outcome had been more or less inevitable.

Simeon was clearly not convinced. "But if I'd told him what I saw, he could have—"

"Could have what?" Chloe waited, brows raised.

And that was an excellent question. Because if Simeon had shared his vision, Crow would have been scared even more shitless than he had been already and he wouldn't have had nearly enough information to take appropriate action.

At that point in his life, Crow, like most people, had operated under the assumption that the world was ordinary. His problems had been important to him but entirely mundane: bullying, his sexuality, economic hardship. If someone had told him that his grandparents were angel-alien creatures and that he was about to have his family destroyed and existence ruined by bird-demons, Crow would have assumed that person was either lying or insane. He certainly wouldn't have believed a stranger who'd been messing around in a fortuneteller's tent.

Crow gave Simeon's leg another squeeze, this time harder. "There is nothing you could have done to change things. But look at all the good you've done for me. Without you, I'd be... well, not here. I wouldn't know anything more than I did when I was a kid. And... I'd still be alone." He finished in almost a whisper, his voice hoarse.

Simeon took several deep breaths before nodding. Crow spent a few moments wondering whether Simeon had ever been told he was appreciated or been praised for anything besides his beauty. When Crow was a kid, just a few words from his grandparents or Aunt Helen—*Nice job* or *You did good* or *Thanks for the help* or *I'm glad you're here*—had been enough to make up for a lot of misery.

So Crow said it out loud. "I'm glad you're here. Thank you for tracking me down in Mareado and for sticking with me." But even as the words left his mouth, he had a terrible realization, which he tried to hide by finishing his cocoa.

He looked at Chloe, who was watching him intently. She had strange eyes, a sort of gray-green that shifted in hue like the ocean on a sun-chased-by-clouds day. He had the sense that she knew exactly what he was thinking. And maybe she did—she seemed to know pretty much everything else about him, even though he'd barely told her anything.

"How do I untangle?" he asked her quietly.

She gave a sympathetic smile. "It's mostly a mental thing. Unwind those strings from your body. But we're living in a material world, baby, and artifacts help a lot. You need physical representations of the people whose fate got twisted up with yours." And then she gave Simeon an expectant look.

Crow was confused, but comprehension dawned quickly on Simeon's face. He started pulling things out of his pack and setting them on the table. There was the little porcelain figure of a farm boy that Simeon had stolen from the Grove Inn. At the time, he'd said it reminded him of Crow. He put the red feather from the bus crash next to it, and the flower he'd taken from Sara's garden. Then he set down a souvenir magnet featuring the St. Louis arch.

"Where's that from?" Crow demanded.

Simeon looked slightly sheepish. "Aunt Helen's refrigerator. She has loads of them. I reckoned just one wouldn't…."

"Anything else?" Chloe was giving Crow a significant stare.

"Um, what about people who are already dead?" Crow twisted his father's ring on his finger and thought about Dee, from whom he had no tangible memento at all.

She shook her head. "Dead is done. Nothing you do can to change your past—the journey is one-way. Which is just as well, because messing with the present and the future is tricky enough. You can't *imagine* the disasters that happen when you tamper with the past. And that's something you should remember," she added, pointing her finger at Simeon.

"I guess that's it, then," said Crow. Which was a boldfaced lie, and she knew it. But he could not face that particular truth at the moment.

She shot him a disappointed look before shrugging. "Your choice, captain. Okay." She reached into a pocket of her skirt and pulled out a spool of thread. Purple, like the string from the library. She unwound several feet of it, chuckled, and bit it free. "That part's usually not my gig, but I don't think my sisters will mind."

Chloe started winding the string around the objects Simeon had stolen. She didn't simply wrap everything up together, but instead twisted and looped until everything was encased in an enormous knot. The objects looked like the victims of a drunken spider.

She pushed the little bundle toward Crow. "Not here—

that wouldn't be safe at all." She mimed an explosion with her hands. "Take it at least a couple of miles away. Somewhere quiet, away from people. You don't want to cause any unintended side effects."

"What do I do with it?" It was creepy, and Crow wasn't sure he even wanted to touch it.

"Unravel it, of course. You can just cut the threads if you want to take the quickest route, but don't use a tool. Just you —fingers, teeth, toes, whatever."

"And then the demons will leave him be?" Simeon asked.

"Sorry honey, but nope. This is just the first step. The battle part comes later."

Well, of course it couldn't be that easy. Crow remembered the passage from the book. "I'm supposed to assess my weapons."

"Bingo. And don't look at me like that. You figured out the untangling part; you can figure out the rest. Agency and self-sufficiency, right? Otherwise you end up killing your dad, marrying your mom, and poking out your eyes."

Crow and Simeon just blinked at her until she sighed. "I swear, the lack of education nowadays. Crow, put some effort into it. You have some damned strong weapons—all you need to do is recognize them. Oh, and I recommend setting the showdown in a place of power. You can figure out that part too."

Then she pushed the wrapped objects a little closer to Crow and stood. "This has been a lot of fun, boys. We don't normally get to do this. But I have to get back to work. It never ends. I haven't taken a vacation day for four thousand years." She laughed and started gathering the dishes. She handed Simeon the last of the Oreos and winked at him.

Crow gingerly picked up the bundle and stuffed it into his pack. The previous day had been overwhelming, and this one was shaping up to be a doozy as well. He almost longed for the quiet, predictable labor of the farm, where you mostly got worked up over weather or government policies.

Chloe led them out of the kitchen through a side door that opened onto a small garden with a covered hot tub. A narrow sidewalk returned them to the front of the house, where they all paused.

"Thank you," Crow said. "For everything."

"You've been incredibly kind," Simeon added.

"I have my moments. You know, people bitch when we're cruel, but it would be nice if we got a little more gratitude when we're nice. Oh well. I wish you the best of luck."

"Isn't luck the same as fate?" asked Crow.

She rolled her eyes dramatically. "Hoo-boy. Luck is the *opposite* of fate. You know, fate is incredibly personal, but luck's just random. For better or worse, it just drops on your head out of the blue. And that thing dropping on your head could be… I don't know. A winning lottery ticket wafted there by a breeze. Or it could be bird shit. Speaking of which, your friends are waiting."

She gestured at the flock of crows sitting in her front yard. Crow wondered if he ought to disentangle himself from them too but then figured that nobody was forcing them to accompany him. If people had free will, maybe so did birds.

Chloe waved and went back into her house.

Crow and Simeon looked at each other.

"Well," Simeon said finally. "That was interesting."

"It certainly was."

But then Crow realized that his sensation of dread, which had disappeared in Chloe's house, was now back with a vengeance. It was time to act.

He patted his pack. "Let's go cut the cord."

# CHAPTER 23

*P*robably on account of all the ship metaphors, Crow decided that their destination should be near a river. There were two big ones in the vicinity, but the Willamette was closer than the Columbia. Besides, he had in mind a good place where they could avoid other people.

"I'm not completely uneducated." This was Simeon's impromptu announcement after they'd taken a seat on a city bus.

Crow looked at him in surprise. "I know."

"They taught us our sums and letters at the ragged school. I used to nick books when I could, newspapers otherwise."

"I've seen you read. And you told me you used to go hang out at pubs with college students." Crow had no idea as to the point of this conversation, although he was sure it had one.

Simeon chewed his lip, looked out the window at a car dealership, and then smoothed a nonexistent wrinkle in his jeans. "There were lots of bits that Chloe talked about but I didn't understand. Things about Greeks and...." He looked away again.

Oh. "I didn't understand them either. I have a not-quite-complete high school education, and that's it. And unlike you, I've never been much of a reader. Now and then to pass the time, but I haven't exactly boned up on the classics. Anyway, you're a smart guy, Simeon. Way smarter than me. And you've got a lot of other good qualities too. Given half a chance, you could probably take over the world."

The tension melted from Simeon's face, replaced with an eye-crinkling smile. "Tonight you're going to list all of those qualities, yeah? Slowly."

Crow forced a smile. "Of course."

Nothing attacked them as they returned over the West Hills, but despite that, his stomach toyed with turning itself inside out and his throat kept threatening to close up. He wondered whether the heroes in those Greek plays felt like this as they marched—or sailed—off to do their thing.

The bus dropped them off downtown. Before they transferred to another route, Simeon eyed a restaurant. "Fancy a meal first?"

Although Crow would have loved to delay things a little more, he shook his head. "I want to get this over with."

"All right."

They stood at the bus stop, waiting. Most of the pedestrians who walked by seemed to have a sense of purpose. Maybe some of them were tied up with fate as badly as Crow. That unhappy-looking middle-aged man in the suit, for instance. He looked down at his feet as he shuffled along the brick sidewalk, seeming oblivious to the dancing patterns created by sunlight through the leaves. Maybe he'd wanted to be an astronaut, a rock star, a chef, but instead ended up in a desk job he hated. That wasn't as terrible as being chased by murderous demons, perhaps, but it was still miserable. Maybe someday he'd untangle himself. Crow hoped so.

"Where are we going?" Simeon asked after they boarded the second bus.

"Not far. It's this place…. I used to know a guy named Cameron. We were fuck buddies, I guess." He glanced at Simeon for a reaction, but all he got was a gesture to keep going. He should have known Simeon wouldn't be judgmental or jealous. "He had some issues. A pretty bad monkey on his back, actually."

"A monkey?"

"He was a junkie. An addict."

Simeon nodded. "Ah."

"Yeah. Talk about getting tangled in your fate. He tried to quit a bunch of times, but it never stuck. Anyway, when life got too heavy for him, he had this spot he'd go to, and maybe he'd shoot up or maybe he'd just try to exist. He took me with him a couple of times." And yes, they'd fucked there, on the damp and weedy ground, but that hadn't been the point of the excursions. In fact, Crow only just now understood what the main purpose had been: comfort. Two men, each lost in his own way, searching for a momentary escape from their burdens. A temporary grace.

He had no idea what had happened to Cam. The last time Crow had seen him, Cam had looked especially gaunt. That could have been due to the heroin, but between Cam's drug use and his sexual practices, it seemed unlikely that he'd escape AIDS. God, that was cruel. He was a sweet soul, the type of person who tried to be kind to others even when he was strung out.

The bus took them over the river before heading south along Milwaukie Avenue. Crow pulled the cord after only a few stops. Simeon followed him out of the bus and down a couple of blocks along a quiet residential street that dead-ended at a chain-link fence.

"We're going to climb that?" Simeon asked, sizing it up.

"No need." They followed the fence for about thirty yards, squeezing through a narrow space between the metal and tall weeds. The crude path was evidence that Cam hadn't been the only one who came this way. And... there it was. The place where someone had cut the chain link and pushed it away, creating an opening that, if you stooped, allowed you to enter the wilderness.

Because that was what it was, really. There was an abandoned railroad line in there, but that was pretty much the only permanent sign of humans. The remainder was marshy, with trees, brush, grasses, and a lot of birds and other small creatures. Cam had told him that the city had bought the property decades before in order to block its development. But if anyone had originally managed the space, they'd given up some time ago.

Crow could hear the city from here. Traffic rumbling, a rhythmic pounding that might have been a construction project, a rumbling most likely coming from the river, where Ross Island Sand and Gravel had a mining operation. If he looked up, he saw airplane contrails in the pale blue sky. But it was easy enough to ignore those things and pretend that the rest of the world didn't exist—just he and Simeon.

For a minute or two, Crow stood, enjoying the fantasy. But then he saw the crows eyeing him from a nearby tree and the fantasy evaporated. "This way," he said.

He took them to what he thought of as Cam's space: a small meadow surrounded on three sides by trees and on the fourth by a short but steep drop to the water. Cam, who'd possessed a store of specific but somewhat random knowledge, had told him that this was a floodplain, but it was hard to picture it all underwater.

"So green," Simeon commented. He huffed. "I can't get over how different some places are to my home. We had no green."

"Parks?"

Simeon shrugged. "Not for the likes of me. And our river was hardly more than a sewer. They built pumping stations meant to improve the water, but it was still horrible. You know, a few years ago—well, as I reckon time—two ships collided in the Thames near Woolwich. Hundreds drowned. And the ones that didn't, they died later from getting that filthy water inside them."

"I don't know how clean the Willamette is. There's a lot of shipping and industry."

"It doesn't stink."

True. In fact, the air here was pleasant, scented with... growth, a very particular smell that had surrounded Crow during his childhood, regardless of what crops his grandparents had planted. It had good associations for him.

He was going to explain that to Simeon, but then the crows called. Not too urgently, but something had clearly caught their attention. They flapped their wings and shifted from foot to foot.

Crow swallowed a few times before collapsing onto his knees. The soft ground accepted him gracefully, but he would have almost welcomed some pain. He set his pack beside him, pulled out the string-wrapped bundle, and placed it in front of him. Then he stared at it, collecting his courage, as Simeon sat opposite him.

"You're pale as a ghost, love."

"I'm always pale."

"Not like this."

"I just... this is hard."

Simeon nodded gravely. "Cutting ties with your past—I can see that being difficult. But your family remains your family. You can undo these knots, but you're bound to them in other ways. Better ways."

"I guess. But that's not...." Crow closed his eyes. Took

several deep breaths. Opened them again to gaze directly at Simeon. "Give me a couple strands of your hair, please." He was pretty certain that would do it.

At first Simeon frowned in puzzlement. Then his eyes widened, his mouth fell slightly open, and he went very still. "Love." His whisper was barely audible.

"Yes. Love. I love you. Jesus, I never thought I'd say that to anyone again. I never thought I'd feel it. And I'm so incredibly grateful for everything about you. Every damned minute we've had."

"Then why are you doing this?" It sounded like an accusation, but there was hurt in Simeon's eyes.

"I have to. You've been caught up in my mess from the moment we met. The one and only time in your life you have a vision, and it's about me. Then later—much later for me, not so much for you—I tracked you down. I took you away from a place where you were happy, and…." He spread his palms, not needing to describe the rest.

"I told you. Coming with you was *my* choice."

Crow ignored the hard edge of anger that he heard in Simeon's voice. He didn't want to fight with him. "I know. To put it in Chloe's terms, you've done way better captaining your ship than I have mine. But—it's like those two boats that crashed in the Thames. The presence of one sealed the fate of the other."

When Simeon didn't respond, Crow continued. "Have you even noticed some of the ways I've affected you? When we were in that bus wreck, you should have died. Just like me. But neither of us did."

"Isn't that a good thing?"

"Sort of. I mean, being alive, that's good. But I think it means that some of what I am has… infected you. And neither of us knows the repercussions of that."

Simeon rubbed his forehead as if it ached. God, he was so

beautiful. The sun made his hair look like an expensive silk scarf and his lips were—like some cliched poem—akin to ripe berries. He was a miracle, and not just because of his looks.

"I want to be with you," Simeon finally said.

"And that's the hell of it, because I want that too. Desperately. But if I'm going to free myself of my fate, I need to free you too."

"What will happen if you cut me free?"

"Don't know." Crow considered. "Chloe said we can't change the past. So everything we've had together, we get to keep that. And let's face it—I never counted on having a future anyway."

Simeon was crying, dammit. Big tears overflowed his eyes and coursed down his cheeks, but his jaw remained steady. He yanked viciously at his hair and held the resulting strands toward Crow. "Bugger fate. Cut me out of your knot if you must, but that doesn't mean I'll walk away. I'll stay with you anyway. Unless you tell me to go." His stare was full of challenge.

Crow knew that telling him to go was the best thing, the safest thing for Simeon. But he couldn't bring himself to do it. "Stay. Please."

Well, now Simeon was still crying, but now he was smiling too. "You view me as a person of worth."

"I do."

"Right, then. Let's get this over with. But wait." He leaned over for a fast kiss, which tasted like chocolate cookies. Then Crow took the offered strands of hair.

Honestly, Crow wasn't even sure this would work. He wasn't Chloe. He didn't know whether there was a special way to make the knots or if some kind of mojo needed to be injected into the process. But from what she'd said, he had the impression that the physical objects weren't the most important part of the task, so maybe all that mattered were his intentions. *It's the thought that counts.*

He took the dark, silky strands and tucked them among the other objects. And then, because the crows were growing increasingly restive, he brought the entire mess to his mouth and bit the string. Not very elegant, but he wasn't an elegant sort of guy. The string proved surprisingly sturdy. While he gnawed on it, he did his best to direct his thoughts and intentions in the appropriate direction.

*I am the captain of my ship. I control my future. I choose who I'm connected to, and I recognize that they are responsible for their own journeys.* Suddenly he remembered a song that had come out a few years before, and he smiled to himself even while continuing to tear with his teeth. *I have chosen. Free will.*

The string gave.

He wasn't sure what he'd expected. A puff of smoke, a ringing of celestial bells, a lightning strike out of the clear sky. What he got was... nothing. The little collection of objects tumbled into the grass. The string disintegrated into little pieces and fell from his fingers.

Wait. Perhaps there was something after all.

An odd sensation tingled beneath his scalp and down his spine. His chest, meanwhile, felt constricted as if a belt were tied tightly around it. It wasn't bad enough to make him panic, but he took a few deep breaths experimentally and something inside him seemed to snap. The tightness went away, replaced by a pleasantly warm feeling.

"You all right, love?"

Crow smiled. "Yeah, I'm—"

The crows began to scream.

Simeon and Crow shot to their feet, frantically looking around to identify the danger. There was nobody else in sight. The sky remained innocent and clear. There were no flames. No gunshots. Nothing at all except green things and the swooping, whirling birds.

And then Crow heard it.

It was a low, rushing rumble, and his first thought was that a train was going to come flying off the nearby tracks. Then he realized that the sound was coming from the opposite direction. From the river.

He turned to look at the water, and his heart nearly stopped.

"Run!" he bellowed and grabbed Simeon's arm, dragging him back toward the chain-link fence.

But no human can outrun a tidal wave. Even if they're a hundred miles from the ocean, even if there'd been no rain, and even though the Willamette had looked as placid as a swimming pool just a few minutes before.

When the wave hit, it felt like being run over by a truck. The collision was the first shock, followed swiftly by the inability to breathe. The water lifted them, and although they were clutching each other, it tore them apart. When Crow tried frantically to reconnect, his hands closed on nothing. He'd lost Simeon.

Crow was blind. He heard nothing but the water. He tried to surface but couldn't tell which way was up, and now he was being violently tumbled with no more control over his movements than a cork in a whirlpool. He screamed—stupidly, instinctively—and his lungs filled. Although he was floating, he felt impossibly heavy. And he was cold.

*Simeon*, he thought. Desperately. Full of grief.

Then he bashed headfirst into something solid, and he thought nothing at all.

# CHAPTER 24

*If a tidal wave crashes in a meadow and nobody's there to see it, was it really there?*

Crow's first thought was nonsensical, but it was better than the agony that descended a split second later. He tried to put a hand on his head to assess the damage, but he couldn't move. Couldn't feel, in fact, anything but his head. Which wasn't fair because his head fucking *hurt*.

He blinked a few times to clear his vision, but there was nothing to see except some green and dark brown. He must be lying on his belly with his face against the muddy grass, he concluded. Able to twist his head and look sideways, he saw only the broad trunk of a tree. Most likely the same tree he'd collided with.

"Simeon!" he called. Or tried to. Nothing came from his throat but a weak rasp.

Broken neck. Head injury, possibly serious. And the rest of him... who knew? He might have massive internal injuries and a hundred broken bones. He might be missing his limbs. No way to tell.

Nothing he could do.

Except cry. It turned out he could do that fairly well.

THE PAIN in his head faded eventually. Or maybe he just got used to it. He still couldn't move or feel anything else, so he concentrated on the sensory information he did have.

Scent. Mud and that growing-things smell. His own blood. Water—either the river or remnants of the wave.

Hearing. Engines, big and small. Birds twittering—not corvids but songbirds. Buzzing insects. The slight whisper of leaves in a light breeze.

Taste? Ugh. Blood and mud.

Sight. The tree trunk. Close up, the brown came in dozens of shades and the texture was intricate. He couldn't tell what kind of tree it was, not that it really mattered. A line of ants was trooping up the trunk. He hoped they weren't on his body too. He really hoped they wouldn't come to investigate his face, because he wouldn't be able to brush them away.

As if magically summoned by that thought, a maddening itch attacked his nose. It was a stupid torture, but torture nonetheless, and he was about to scream with frustration when something landed between him and the tree, making him call out in alarm.

It was a crow. It cocked its head this way and that, examining him, and made a small interrogative sound.

"Simeon. Where's Simeon?"

The bird clacked its beak. Crow had no idea what that meant.

"Please. Simeon. Where is he? Is he all right? Can you get help to him?"

Another enigmatic beak click. The bird hopped very

close, and for a moment Crow thought it was going to peck his eyes out. Instead, it softly scraped a claw against his nose. The itch stopped.

"Thanks. But please, Simeon?" The more times Crow asked, the more frantic he felt. He couldn't do anything, trapped here in his broken body, and the bird just stared at him. Crow thought it looked sad—something about the slump of its shoulders, maybe—although it was really hard to read a bird's emotion.

After a moment, the bird seemed to sigh. Then it tucked itself under Crow's chin and settled in with a small crooning noise that was oddly comforting. More birds came and arranged themselves around his head. Maybe around the rest of him too; he couldn't tell. He wanted to cry again, to rage, to do *something*. But instead he drifted into sleep.

HE WOKE to the song of crickets. Night had fallen and the crows were gone. And God, he *hurt*—a whole-body ache that made him want to curl into a ball and moan.

But wait. He felt pain everywhere, and he was actually able to curl up, and those were good things.

Moving slowly and with great care, his body creaking and protesting, he maneuvered himself into a seated position with his back propped against the tree. He looked around, but there was very little light. When he called for Simeon a few times, there was no reply.

Groaning, he took stock of his injuries. If he hadn't fractured his skull, he'd sure as hell banged it good, but it felt solid and intact. His clothing was in tatters, and his skin displayed a host of fresh scars. They were all tender, and some of them, such as the one across his belly, were big. But he knew from experience that they would fade rather quickly.

His skeleton felt slightly wrong, as if he'd been assembled by someone in a hurry. Weird cricks and kinks in his hip, his shoulder, his back, and his left leg. Those would probably fix themselves too.

In other words, once again he'd live. But that was of little solace when Simeon was lost.

"Do I blame myself for whatever's happened to him?" he whispered through a dry throat. "I'm the one who chose to untangle us. I thought it was the right thing to do."

After a few minutes, using the tree for support, Crow stood. He still couldn't see anything except lights on the river. He couldn't tell whether they were from boats or maybe something on the islands. He managed to take two limping steps before his legs gave way and he crashed back onto the ground. Too soon for walking, apparently, and even if he *could* walk, he'd probably trip over something and break his neck. Again.

Although he didn't want to, he'd have to wait until morning.

He lay down and made himself as comfortable as possible. He was thirsty—ironic, having been attacked by a wave. But far worse than thirst or any of his other physical woes was the tearing sense of loss, the gut-clenching anguish about Simeon's fate.

And there wasn't a damn thing he could do about it right now.

As Crow lay broken in the mud, he thought about solitude. It was a reasonable thing to think about now, with Simeon missing, Crow's fated connections broken, and no other people nearby. Over the years he'd sometimes considered running off into a true wilderness and staying there forever. Hidden away in a forest somewhere, he'd no longer endanger anyone else. He researched survival skills and had even attempted to follow through on this plan a couple of times.

But he couldn't stick to it. After a couple of weeks, the lack of companionship became oppressive, bearing down on him like an ever-growing boulder. Each time he'd given up and returned to civilization, he'd berated himself for his weakness.

Now, however, he reached a realization: no matter how hard he'd struggled to remain an emotional island, Crow had the fundamental need to... care. To let other people inside. Not just his family and Simeon, although those people lived deepest in his heart. There had been Marty. And Julie. And Dee and Cam, and Zen the hippy roommate, and dozens of others who'd never known who Crow truly was but nonetheless had made at least some connection with him.

And this wasn't a weakness. It was, in fact, a strength—possibly the greatest strength he possessed.

He was still thinking about what that meant as he fell asleep.

THE FIRST THING he saw in the morning were two red feathers, vivid as splashes of blood, on the ground a few feet away. Two instead of one, so he'd know for sure this wasn't just the feather that Simeon had picked up after the bus crash. The demons had left a very specific message. Well, fuck them. He was still alive, so he'd assume there was still hope.

Nothing remained of his physical injuries except some lingering soreness, and he supposed he should be grateful for that. He spent a good couple of hours searching the area for any sign of Simeon but found nothing. Finally admitting that to look any longer was futile, he decided it was time to plan his next steps.

He had nothing but the filthy, bloody, torn clothes he was wearing. Even his shoes had disappeared at some point, and his pack was long gone. But to his surprise, when he checked his back pocket, his wallet was still there. He was even more shocked to find it full of fifties and hundreds. Over a thousand bucks, all told.

"Dammit, Simeon. Pickpockets are supposed to *take* money, not give it."

All right, so he had funds, which always made life easier. But he knew he looked far too awful to be seen in public, and that complicated things. Also, he was really thirsty and incredibly ravenous.

Not far from the meadow was a small pond, where he and Cam had once watched dragonflies skim the surface. Now Crow used the water to wash up as best as he could. Even without a mirror he could tell that he wasn't very successful. Due to his self-healing abilities, he wouldn't have to worry about getting sick from any bacteria in the pond, although he didn't go so far as to actually drink the stuff.

The next step was clothing. If Simeon were here, he would have found a way to steal or charm some from someone. But of course Simeon wasn't here.

Crow ended up walking almost two miles up to Powell Boulevard. People stared as they drove by, probably figuring that he was a crazy homeless guy—more or less true, in fact —so they let him be.

There was a thrift shop at 28th Street. Dee used to go there to find improbable outfits for clubbing, and occasionally Crow would tag along to pick up a few cheap basics for his wardrobe or household. He nearly crumpled with grief—

over both Dee and Simeon—as he stood outside the door. But then he pulled himself together and walked inside.

The store had just opened and there were no other customers. The two employees gaped at him. "Um," said the big young guy with an unruly mop of curls. He seemed unsure what to say after that.

Crow tried to look harmless. "Had an accident. I know I look awful, but I just need something to wear. I'm not going to cause trouble, and I promise I can pay." He remembered some of Simeon's tips for getting along with strangers. "If you're not busy, maybe you could help me find a few things? I'd appreciate it. Then I'll get out of your hair."

The young guy glanced at his coworker, a woman of similar age who resembled a short Grace Jones. She shrugged. "Sure," said the man to Crow, although he didn't appear to be especially enthusiastic.

After they'd spent several minutes together and Crow hadn't morphed into a homicidal maniac, the man, whose name was Todd, got into the spirit of things. "It's like being a personal shopper," he said. "People don't usually want those here."

"I hope it's okay with you."

"Yeah, it's fun. Um, if you don't mind… what happened to you?"

"Rogue tidal wave brought on by vengeful demons."

Todd chuckled. "Yeah, all right, none of my beeswax. C'mon. Jeans are this way."

In the end, Crow ended up with two pairs of jeans, a couple of T-shirts, a blue-and-white-striped button-down, and a hooded sweatshirt, along with a pair of surprisingly good hiking shoes in excellent shape. He even scored a few pairs of socks and some tighty-whities, all of them still in their original packaging. He used the dressing room to change into one of the new outfits, and when he glanced at himself in the mirror, he looked almost normal. The rest of his purchases he stuffed into a nice backpack that Todd had also found.

Todd seemed slightly surprised and more than a little relieved when Crow, as promised, handed over cash to cover everything.

"Thanks," said Crow, making eye contact as he pocketed the change.

"Glad I could help. Good luck with… whatever you've got going."

With a final wave to Todd and Grace Jones, Crow left the store.

He walked the mile west to the Hotcake House, another place he sometimes used to visit with Dee and Cam. It was open twenty-four hours, and Crow and his friends had usually ended up there in the wee hours, when the tired-looking waitresses would set down plates in front of students, junkies, hookers, truckers, cops, and other denizens of the night. The mid-morning clientele was less colorful, but that was fine. Crow ordered enough food to feed four men and gobbled it all much quicker than he should have.

Then he got on a bus, rode downtown, got on a different bus, and stepped off near Chloe's house.

The first thing he noticed when he arrived was that the wind chimes were gone, as was the bell outside the front door. He rang the completely ordinary doorbell three times before the door was opened by a sleepy-looking teenage boy wearing PE shorts.

"Yeah?" The boy yawned.

"I need to talk to Chloe."

"Who?"

"Chloe, the librarian who—" Crow craned his head to see past the kid. The hallway he'd seen the previous day was gone, and now he looked straight into a living room with a brown fuzzy couch, a reclining chair, and a television with a potted plant on top. "I'm looking for Chloe," he said again, weakly, knowing it was fruitless.

"Dude, there's no Chloe here."

"Do you have... a library?"

The boy blinked. "Uh... there's one downtown, I guess. My high school has one but it's probably closed for the summer."

"Of course. Sorry to bother you."

Crow wandered back to the main road. Deep in his heart, he hadn't really expected Chloe to be here. After all, he'd rid himself of fate. But it was still disappointing.

He tried the police next, with a fabricated story about going swimming with a friend and losing him. But the cops seemed more focused on finding out why he'd waited a day to report it rather than on making any effort to find Simeon themselves, so Crow gave up. As far as he could tell, the police didn't know anything about Simeon's whereabouts.

He tried hospitals, with no success, and by the time it grew dark, he was heartsick, footsore, and exhausted. He ate some dinner, stopped at a drugstore for a few grooming essentials, and booked a room at a cheap but decent motel near the edge of downtown. The shower felt nice, but the bed felt far too big.

He lay under the blankets, huddled at the edge of the mattress as if leaving room for someone, and he reminded himself how fortunate he was. He was clean and well fed, resting in a comfortable room, and fortified with a sizable stash of greenbacks in his wallet. He'd met his mother—sort of—and learned a great deal about his family history. He'd untangled himself from fate and, for the first time ever, had some small hope of ridding himself of the demons. He'd spent long days and nights with an amazing man. He'd fallen in love.

That last bit was the problem. Ever since the night of the fire that killed his grandparents, Crow had thought of himself as indestructible. He had survived all kinds of horrors that would have killed anyone else.

It turned out, however, that Crow was vulnerable after all. Simeon had torn a hole in Crow's essential self, and unlike wounds from bus crashes, bullets, or trees, that hole would never heal. He felt it with every heartbeat.

He remembered every kiss and caress. Every thrust. Every moment of Simeon smiling, laughing. Every time Simeon marveled at some ordinary thing that was a wonder to him, or grinned smugly after stealing something, or watched Crow with those dark, bright eyes.

The wound, Crow decided, was worth it.

# CHAPTER 25

*L*ocated close to the train station, the Multnomah County medical examiner's office was in a concrete-and-glass building that gave little indication of its grim contents. Crow took a few strengthening breaths and went in.

A man in uniform sat behind the reception desk, his face displaying a neutral expression. "Can I help you?"

"I...." Shit, this was hard. "I'm looking for someone. He's.... I can't find him."

Now the man looked genuinely sympathetic. "If you'd like to file a missing person report, you'll have to go to the police bureau. We can't do that here."

"I know. It's just, it's possible he may have drowned yesterday. We were at the river and then he disappeared." Which wasn't untrue.

"I'm sorry to hear that. But the police—"

"I was there yesterday and they weren't very helpful." Crow took a shaky breath. "I'm sorry. I know this isn't supposed to be part of your job. But... I care very much about this man and now he's gone."

The uniformed man regarded him for a long moment. The inside air was chilly, raising goosebumps on Crow's bare arms. The logical part of his brain said that well-circulating cold air was probably a good idea in a place that stored corpses and performed autopsies. He shivered.

Then the man sighed. "I understand, you know that? I really do. I wish I could help you. But I can tell you one thing: we haven't received any drowning victims within the past few days."

Crow's shoulders slumped with relief. This didn't mean that Simeon was still alive, of course. He could have been washed out to the Pacific by now or be stranded somewhere along the way, in another county. His body, once warm and full of life, cold and empty.

"Thank you," Crow said. "I appreciate it."

"I hope you find him alive and well."

Crow nodded, turned away, and took a step toward the door. Then he froze and turned back. "There's one other thing. Please."

"Yeah?"

"I had another friend. He died in April. He didn't have anyone." Oh, it hurt to say those words. "Can you tell me what happened to, uh, his remains?"

The man didn't make any snide comment about Crow's seeming habit of losing friends. He picked up a pen, clicked it open, and let it hover over a pad of paper. "What was his name?"

Crow had to think about that for a moment, which was awful. And then he remembered that Dee hadn't known Crow's real name at all, which was worse. "Darby Walsh."

"Walsh. Okay." The man finished writing. "Come back tomorrow afternoon and I'll let you know if I found anything."

"Thanks again."

As soon as he stepped outside the sun felt unrelenting, even though it wasn't a particularly hot day. He trudged back to the downtown police station; different officers were on duty, but they weren't any more sympathetic. "He's an adult," said a thin-faced cop. "Adults can disappear if they want to."

"But he didn't want to. He told me that."

The cop, probably realizing that Crow and Simeon had been more than just buddies, looked as if he'd confronted a bad smell and took a step back. "We can't do anything for you. It's time you left."

Crow spent the rest of the day haunting the banks of the Willamette, to no avail. Even his avian entourage had evaporated, leaving him utterly alone. He'd been on his own for the past decade, so he should have been used to it. He wasn't. As he made his way back to the motel, the city felt bigger than it was and strangely soulless, as if everything and everyone were only the background scenes in a dull movie. The colors had drained from signs and cars, the sounds of engines and voices muted as if passing through water. Crow's lunch had been as tasteless as sawdust.

He rested for a time, propped against the headboard and staring at the wall. He didn't go out again until after dark, when the businesspeople and shoppers had gone home, leaving mostly those on the margins of society. Several people offered to sell him drugs. A skinny girl who couldn't have been past her mid-teens asked for a cigarette and, when Crow said he didn't smoke, suggested that, for a price, she'd put something else in her mouth instead. A woman of indeterminate age, dressed in far too many layers of ragged clothing, smiled at him and told him he had pretty hair. Crow asked all of them if they'd met a man with long black hair and an English accent, but none of them had.

That night, Crow dreamed he was in a canoe, lost at sea during a tempest, trying to row with a giant black feather because he had no paddle. Simeon was not in the dream. Nobody was except for Crow himself, although the wind and water seemed almost animated.

The police were still no help the next morning, although at least this time none of them treated him like a leper. Simeon was still not at the floodplain where Crow had lost him. The world remained hollow.

Late enough in the afternoon so it didn't seem pushy, Crow returned to the medical examiner, where the same uniformed man met him with a small smile. "Have you found your friend?"

"No."

"Well, he's still not here. Which is generally a good thing, you know?"

Crow nodded.

The man held out a folded piece of paper. "But I did find Darby Walsh."

After a brief hesitation, Crow took the paper and tucked it into his jeans pocket without looking at it. "Dee. He hated being called Darby."

"Understood. My parents saddled me with Horace, which is why I go by my middle name. Anyway, you were right—nobody claimed Mr. Walsh's remains. Once the police finished their investigation, he was released to the funeral home listed on that paper I gave you. The state has a program to pay the expenses for indigent deceased, but it's pretty much up to the funeral home to decide what to do with them."

"Dee was a good guy." Crow wasn't sure why he was saying this to a stranger. Maybe because *someone* needed to know. "He was smart and funny. He liked to dance. Once he surprised me when I got off work—I was on graveyard, and when I clocked out, there he was with a box of donuts and this stupid red scarf with snowflakes on it that he made me wear." Crow's voice caught like fabric on a nail and he had to stop.

The man gave a small nod. "I'll remember that, okay? I'll remember him. Dee Walsh was the kind of man who'd brighten a friend's day with a nice surprise."

And that was something, wasn't it? An acknowledgment that Dee had existed; a slightly bigger ripple in the pond.

Crow thanked the man once more, and after leaving the building, he opened the folded paper. After only a brief bus ride across the river, he located Elysium Funeral Home in a gray-and-white foursquare house, its front porch converted into a small storefront. A bell on the door chimed softly as he entered, and a moment later a woman came through a door at the back of the room.

She wore a gray trouser suit with an orchid-hued silk blouse, and protruding from the breast pocket of her jacket was a small silver ruler and a carnation that matched her blouse. Her graying hair was pulled into a neat bun.

He wasn't remotely surprised at her remarkable resemblance to the middle-aged woman at the Murray Family Agency.

"Can I help you?" she asked pleasantly.

Crow decided not to ask unnecessary questions. "Yes, please. I'm told you handled arrangements for a friend of mine back in April. He was indigent." God, he hated that word. It was Dee's epitaph, but it said nothing about who he'd been as a human being. It made him sound worthless. Disposable.

"I see," she said, her voice soothing. "We do often provide those services."

"I'd like to pay my respects, so I was hoping you could tell me where he is. I doubt anyone claimed him."

Maybe it was simply a professional mask, but her expression conveyed sadness and sympathy as well as understanding. "I'll see what I can find out. Can you tell me his name, please?"

"Darby Walsh. But he went by Dee." Crow knew the last part was irrelevant, but it still felt important that he say it.

"All right, Mr. Rapp. Please make yourself comfortable while I do a little search. It may take a bit of time. Just call out if you need me. My name is Miss Lacey."

He nodded his thank you, and as soon as she went back through the door, he sat down on a love seat facing the front window. He was absolutely positive that he hadn't told her his name. He also hadn't mentioned it to the guy at the medical examiner's office, so there was no chance that the man had called here to give Miss Lacey a heads-up. Whatever. Just one more weirdness among many.

The view out the window was of the Village Inn restaurant across the street and cars going down Broadway. Since that wasn't very exciting, Crow turned his attention to the interior of the room, which was a cross between a doctor's waiting room and a grandmother's parlor—the one that only guests were allowed to use. The carpet pattern was in somber blues, the wallpaper an understated cream floral, and the windows surrounded by elaborate curtains. There was his upholstered love seat and a matching couch, plus a large round coffee table. A chandelier hung from the ceiling. A white-painted cabinet with doors covered much of one wall, while on another hung a tranquil seascape and an elaborately carved clock. Despite the traffic outside, the only sound here was the clock's steady ticking, perhaps meant as a reminder to visitors that their life was finite as well.

Nothing in this place was the least reminiscent of Dee, who liked bold colors and lots of noise. Who, before he became skeletal and weak, used to sprawl on the most inhospitable-looking surfaces, such as kitchen counters and concrete floors, and yet somehow manage to look supremely comfortable.

Miss Lacey returned twenty minutes later holding a cardboard box and a manila envelope. She set both items on the coffee table, sat down on the couch, and angled her body toward Crow. "Those are his cremains in the box," she said gently. "I'm sorry the container isn't nicer. The state pays us very little in these cases."

"There would have been no one to see a fancy urn anyway," Crow said bitterly.

She leaned back and settled her palms on her thighs. "You know, humans have been doing elaborate burials for thousands of years. I suppose that sometimes those burials were partially successful, in that people still admire those tombs. The pyramids from the Kingdom of Kush, for example. The Romans' elaborate sarcophagi."

Maybe she was trying to talk him into springing for something expensive to stuff Dee into. "I'm not buying an urn."

"Of course not," she said with a chuckle. "But you didn't let me finish my point. People admire those burial places, but the people who were buried within them have been mostly forgotten. Even the emperors and empresses are hardly more than fancy grave goods and a few written tales that may bear little resemblance to reality. The things are here, but the people—even when their bodies remain—are long gone."

That made Crow think about Sara in her chair among the flowers. He nodded.

Miss Lacey straightened the crease of her trousers and continued. "What we do with the body, that's for the peace of mind of the living. Sometimes someone's vanity gets involved too. It makes no difference to the deceased. And I believe that the most important memorial isn't a shiny urn or an elaborate grave marker. It's what the name suggests:

*memories.* The pieces of that person that are carried on in the hearts and minds of those who knew him and cared about him."

"That's an interesting philosophy for someone who owns a funeral home."

Her laughter was a rich contralto. "Well, let's just say this place is more of a hobby than a business for me. Now, I have a suggestion for you. Spend as much time as you need sitting here and saying goodbye to your friend. Then leave the cremains here—they're nothing but ashes, and they'll only weigh you down. But take his personal effects, if you like. They're in the envelope."

Twisting the ring on his finger, he remembered two other envelopes. The contents of those had proved incredibly precious.

"Thank you, Miss Lacey."

She stood and took a step or two before pausing and turning back. "When Dee died, he wasn't on the streets or in a cold institution. He was in a friend's home, and he knew that friend loved him enough to take him in. His death was a terrible thing, but I believe you gave him some small measure of peace and consolation."

The sound that escaped from Crow's throat was suspiciously like a sob. He clamped his jaws shut before more could follow.

Miss Lacey smiled warmly and gave his shoulder a little pat. "I'll give you some privacy. Take your leave whenever you're ready and not before." As she left the room, the door closed silently behind her.

Crow spent a long time sitting on the love seat and remembering the exact sound of Dee's laughter as well as the sharp anger that could appear in his eyes. He remembered the way that, before Dee felt sick and when they still used to fuck, Dee would hug Crow afterward as if Crow had given him a treasured gift. He remembered the expression of pure pleasure when Dee smoked his clove cigarettes or dug into a piece of strawberry pie. He remembered the cheerfully filthy lyrics he would make up as he sang along with the radio.

Dee had been in college before he ran short on money. He was a good student—on the dean's list every semester despite having to work two jobs. He wanted to be a social worker.

"I loved you, Dee," Crow whispered. It felt good to say it. And then he added, "I'll remember you."

The envelope contained only three things. One was the digital Timex watch that Dee always wore, but the crystal was shattered and the strap bloodstained; Crow slipped it back into the envelope. The second item was a cheap gold-toned necklace with an enamel Pac-Man pendant. Dee used to wear it all the time. Now Crow put it around his own neck. And finally there was the orange nylon wallet that Dee had bought one weekend from a booth at Saturday Market. It was bloodstained, too, and contained nothing but Dee's driver's license, his college ID card, and the high school photo of the boy who'd been Dee's first crush. Crow put the wallet with its contents into his back pocket.

He looked at the box but didn't touch it. The label stuck on the front had Dee's name—including the hated Darby—his dates of birth and death, and a string of numbers that probably referred to a file somewhere. "None of that is you, Dee. Miss Lacey is right." Crow patted his chest. "You're in here."

He stood and, without looking back, walked out into the sun.

CROW WAS RESTLESS THAT EVENING. He strolled past some of the clubs that Dee used to go to. People in their late teens through late twenties were gathered in small clusters on the sidewalks, outfits monochromatic or neon-hued, hair sculpted extravagantly, clouds of clove-scented smoke trailing away. Even though some of them were Crow's age or just a little younger, he felt ancient, as if he'd been plodding around since before Simeon was born. He would have envied their laughter, but he suspected that in many cases the happiness was a brittle cover over dark memories and trembling fear. He wished hope and joy for them, imagining he could sprinkle those gifts like fairy dust as he walked past.

The warm evening had an edge to it, a subtle reminder that summer was nearing its end. When he was a teen, this time of year had always unsettled him. It meant long hours of labor on the farm. It meant having to turn his head away from other boys, shirtless and tanned as they horseplayed on the banks of Lick Run. It meant knowing that school would begin soon, with the numbing coursework and the taunting by other students.

August was also the time of year when the carnival would come through town.

Leaning momentarily against a brick wall in Old Town, Crow allowed thoughts of Simeon to fully catch up with him —but only the good ones. If Crow had been forced to name Simeon's single paramount virtue, he would have said openness. To people—that was the root of Simeon's magic charm. To adventure and new experiences. To *feeling*. He wasn't afraid of making himself vulnerable.

A turtle that retreated tightly into its shell might be safer from attack, but it wasn't going anywhere or doing anything. It was alive, but not living. What was Crow open to?

Well, maybe it wouldn't hurt to start with a bit of education.

The libraries had closed hours ago, but Powell's Books was still open and only a couple of blocks away. For a time he wandered the long aisles through the maze of rooms without any specific goal, but eventually he found himself in the Greek Classics section. There were a lot of books there, most of them well-worn paperbacks that he imagined had once belonged to students. He browsed a bit, selected a few, and then made his way to the café at the back of the store.

Dee used to come here. He had liked to drag Crow along, and if Crow complained that he wasn't the literary type, Dee placated him with graphic novels and baked goods.

So now Crow bought coffee and cookies and sat down with his stack of books. He quickly decided that he should be looking at the Cliff's Notes versions instead of the originals, because he had a lot of trouble following the texts. He'd never really learned to be a good student. He'd always figured there wasn't much point in learning how to parse sentences or remembering who signed the Treaty of Ghent, not when he was going to be a farmer. Now he found himself wishing he'd paid a lot more attention in English class.

Since Chloe had mentioned *Antigone,* one of the volumes he'd picked up was *The Theban Plays.* He sort of understood the first play; even an uneducated lout like him knew about Oedipus and his mom. What he gleaned from the second play was mostly that Oedipus had as many problems with his kids as he did with his parents. Crow did, however, get a general sense that the old guy made some kind of peace with the role of fate in his life—before he dropped dead. And then there was *Antigone* itself, with a female hero, which was nice, even though she died too. None of the plays seemed to give him much guidance for his own drama, however.

Sighing, he reached for *Orestes.*

"Mind if I sit here?"

Automatically, and without really glancing up, Crow

mumbled an affirmative and cleared some space on the table. But when his new companion cackled, he looked across at her.

It was impossible to tell whether she was truly plump or if that was an illusion caused by her many layers of clothing. Tunics, sweaters, and scarves, all with a handmade look, were piled on with no attempt to match colors or patterns and with no regard for the season's warm temperatures. Her gray-and-white hair was such a wild and knotted explosion that he half expected to see forest creatures peeking out of it. Her deeply tanned skin held a topography of wrinkles, a sign that she'd spent a great deal of time outdoors, and her long fingernails were curved like claws.

He recognized her face, although it had changed, and he gave a surprised exhalation. "Miss Aisa."

"I'm Atty." She sounded as if her voice had been scratched by lions.

"All right. Hello, Atty." Noticing that she eyed his remaining piece of shortbread, he scooted the plate closer to her. "Help yourself."

"That's a dear." She hauled a nearly overflowing plastic basket of books onto the table next to the plate. Although he could see only a few of the titles, he noted a knitting pattern book, something by Peter Straub, and a textbook about X-rays.

For a short time, she nibbled on the cookie and he frowned at Euripides.

"You needn't bother, you know," she said. "More family issues. It has a more or less happy ending, though, so there's that, although it takes a deus ex machina to achieve it."

Crow closed the book with a sigh. "It's not going to help me, is it?"

"None of the Greeks will. They were still struggling with free will. Although the concept of hubris might resonate."

"Pride?" He'd heard the term *hubris* thrown around now and then, but he didn't consider himself especially prideful.

Atty waved a claw-tipped hand. "That's a more modern interpretation of the word. Sophocles meant it differently—to him it was a mortal who was too self-important."

Crow thought about that. At first he couldn't see how it applied to him—he'd always considered himself insignificant, a man who ran from shadow to shadow. But then realization dawned. "Blaming myself for everything that goes wrong around me is a type of hubris, then?"

Her grin revealed sharp yellow teeth. "Bullseye, sonny."

"Okay, but I'm working on that. I mean, I get that I was involved in some terrible things, but they weren't really my fault. I was just as caught up in shit as everyone else."

"All people are caught up in shit. It's part of being human."

"But I'm not—"

"Close enough."

He had to concede that. And he found it comforting to think of himself as a member of *Homo sapiens* and not the result of a science experiment conducted by angels. Or aliens.

"Got it. Tone down the hubris."

She looked at the empty plate and wrinkled her nose. "Get me more sweets, boy. No raisins."

He wanted to roll his eyes but decided it might be unwise. Instead he got up and stood in the short line by the counter. He had plenty of cash for now, so why not make her happy. He suspected it was a wise idea to stay on her good side. Atty, leafing through her books, paid no attention to him. If anyone else thought she was a little odd, they didn't show it and concentrated instead on their own book stashes.

After purchasing a brownie, a slice of lemon pound cake, and more shortbread—might as well give Atty some options—Crow made his way back to the table. She cackled again when she saw the plates. "Good boy." Her praise made him feel ludicrously proud.

She ate the entire brownie, smacking her lips approvingly, before she spoke again. He waited as patiently as he could, figuring she'd speak when she was good and ready. Finally she pointed at his stack of plays. "If you wanted a somewhat more useful guide, I'd say look to the Elizabethans rather than the Greeks. Othello, Lear, Faustus—their problems came from their own weaknesses and choices, not from the will of the gods. And even poor Macbeth, who should have known better than to base his decisions on prophecies."

"Can any of those guys teach me anything about power?"

This time she laughed so hard that several people sitting nearby turned to stare. She almost knocked her basket of books off the table, and she sent some crumbs flying. "Oh, kiddo. They knew all about power. They sought it in ways they shouldn't and used it in ways they oughtn't, and that was what destroyed them. Again—their own actions, not the gods'. Certainly not fate." She laughed again, a little more softly.

This was all going over his head, as incomprehensible as anything Sophocles had written. Crow sighed. "It's all Greek to me."

Atty's expression grew serious and she leaned toward him. "Then let's stick closer to home, shall we? This is a puzzle, Crow Rapp, and you have all the pieces. You just need to put them together. And you have to do it yourself. I can't do it for you."

"I'm my own captain."

"Yes." She reached for the lemon cake, broke off a big chunk, and ate it. Several bits landed on her purple scarf, but she didn't seem to care. "You know, the lovely thing about free will is that hope remains until the thread is cut." She mimed a scissors motion with her fingers; for some reason that sent a cold shiver down his spine. "So the key is to act before then."

She stood and smoothed her skirts and then smiled down on him. "You have the capacity to be a very good man. I hope you use it."

"I'd like to try. But Miss— Atty? Can you tell me what happened to Simeon?"

She shook her head. "No. Not my tale to tell. I wasn't involved."

He hadn't expected otherwise but he'd had to at least give it a shot. "Thank you for…." What could he call it? "Counseling me."

Atty gave an appreciative little hum. He thought she'd leave then, but instead she scooped up his tragedies and dumped them into her basket. Before he could protest, she'd pulled out one of her own books and dropped it on the table. "This won't help you much more than the Greeks or the Brits, but you'll find it a lot easier to get through." With a final cackle, she picked up her basket and sashayed away.

Crow picked up a shortbread cookie and looked at the cover. *Something Wicked This Way Comes*, by Ray Bradbury. According to the blurb on the back, the title came from a line in *Macbeth* and the story had something to do with a traveling carnival. That hit too close to home, making Crow shudder.

But also, according to the book jacket, the novel had themes related to the power that people's minds implanted into objects and ideas.

*The power of objects and ideas.* Crow thought about the bundle of items that Chloe had tangled together. Artifacts, she'd called them. Because we live in a material world.

Hesitant as the first warm breeze of spring, a plan began to form in Crow's mind.

# CHAPTER 26

*C*row spent a couple more days in Portland, alternating between visits to the floodplain and the police station, without any word of Simeon. One of the cops finally took pity on him and filed a report, but by then Crow's hope had dwindled. If Simeon was still alive, Crow wouldn't find him here.

He bought a train ticket to Chicago, and with a backpack of freshly laundered clothing, a wallet still thick with cash, and Atty's book, he checked out of the motel and boarded the train.

He wasn't too worried about another demon attack as he chugged eastward. In the past, they'd only showed up when he was with someone he cared about. Because killing Crow wasn't the point. Coercion was the demons' primary goal, and they pursued it by harming those close to him. And now he was traveling alone.

Crow settled more deeply into his window seat and prepared for the two-day journey. Although he'd traveled by train before, the trips had usually been shorter. And he generally spent them staring blankly at nothing, trying not to think about whatever horrors he'd just fled or what he'd do with himself when he arrived at his next destination. He had, in fact, showed no more enthusiasm for those journeys than if he were someone's battered old suitcase.

Today, though, he looked out the window and discovered beautiful scenery. The first leg was along the Columbia Gorge, with the Columbia River and waterfalls to the right and forested hills to the left. A son of the Midwest, he'd never truly become inured to the wondrous sight of vast swaths of evergreens blanketing steep slopes. They still seemed almost magical. Which was ironic, because they were entirely real and mundane whereas his personal biography was like something out of a twisted fairytale.

It was a clear day, which meant that, as the locals liked to say, the mountain was out. The phrase referred to Mount Hood, the glacier-capped peak that gleamed white even at the end of summer. It was believed to be a dormant volcano, and experts predicted that it might erupt in the not-too-distant future, just as its sister, Mount St. Helens, had five years earlier. Crow wondered briefly whether the demons could speed things up, if they were so inclined, but the prospect didn't particularly trouble him.

Around dinnertime, after the terrain had become drier and the riverbanks steeper, the train stopped briefly in a tiny town called Wishram. A young man with shaggy hair and an enormous backpack boarded and took the seat next to Crow. Normally Crow would have given the kid a terse nod and then studiously ignored him. But today he possessed a bit of Simeon's spirit and he smiled instead. "Have you been hiking?"

"Yeah, man, it was great. I was so stoked. And I did some windsurfing in the gorge too. You ever tried that?"

"Never."

"You should. It's totally rad." Then the kid, whose name

turned out to be Xavier—"But everyone calls me X, dude"—gave a long soliloquy on the joys of hurling oneself down the river on a polystyrene board. Surprisingly, Crow enjoyed listening. Not because he had any intention of taking up the sport himself, but because X was so enthusiastic and because Simeon would have been fascinated by the discussion. Presumably, nobody surfed the Thames during the nineteenth century. X was very much the captain of his own ship, Crow decided, even if that ship wasn't very big.

Eventually the conversation turned to X's destination, which was a university in Spokane. He was about to begin his third year as a biochem major, which sounded very impressive. He was passionate about that too; and about his girlfriend, who wasn't the outdoorsy type but was super smart; and about his dog, who was currently staying with the girlfriend; and about his job at an awesome pizza place; and about… being alive. Surely he must have had obstacles in his life, disappointments and losses that chipped away at his soul. Yet X greeted the world with eagerness and joy. With hope.

"How about you?" X asked sometime after darkness had fallen. "Where are you headed?"

"Illinois."

"Cool! I've never been there. You going there for work or tourism or…?"

Crow considered for a moment, and then smiled. "I'm going home."

IT WOULDN'T BE accurate to say that the rest of the trip sped by, but it didn't drag either. In fact, Crow lost all sense of time and began to feel as if he'd always been on the train and would always be there, a sort of purgatory on rails. Had that been the case, he wouldn't have minded, really. After X disembarked, he was replaced by a retired Montana rancher who'd been visiting his grandchildren, then a woman from the Fort Peck Reservation who'd been working for the park service in Idaho but had grown homesick. All the way from North Dakota to Minneapolis, Crow's neighbor was a little girl whose mother and younger brother occupied the seats across the row. She was a serious child who drew pictures of horses for an hour before falling asleep; she woke up shortly before the train pulled into her station. A tourist from Germany got on there, the sort of robust middle-aged woman who looked as if she'd cheerfully clamber over the Alps. She was spending three months exploring North America by train and was having a fantastic time doing it. She got off in Milwaukee and the seat remained empty, but by then they were nearly in Chicago.

Crow slept along the way, ate, admired the scenery, and read some Bradbury, but mostly he listened. Sometimes his companions asked questions about his life, and he answered with carefully edited versions of the truth. He found it much more interesting to hear about them. Every last one was fascinating. None had done the kinds of things that people wrote books or screenplays about. Not a single one had experienced adventures like Oedipus or Antigone or the boys in *Something Wicked*. No prophecies. No malevolent supernatural beings. Just the small dramas of everyday life. But none of those dramas exactly resembled another, and all of them were *important* to the people involved. Which meant, Crow realized, the events were important, period.

Sometimes when Crow was talking to one of these people, he'd mention Simeon in passing, as in "my friend Simeon and I went to the top of the Sears Tower" or "my friend Simeon used to work in a carnival." He found this unexpectedly easy to do, and although each mention brought a pang of grief, it also warmed his heart.

It was just after one of these mentions—telling the German woman that someday he'd like to visit London—when Crow realized something else: Simeon had never completely left him. Yes, he might very well be dead, and he was certainly somewhere far away. Perhaps in some *time* far away. But he'd left an impression on Crow's skin, on his soul. It was like one of those fossil footprints archeologists found. A person walks across sand or mud, which hardens into stone, and thousands of years later the shape of the foot is still there, unmistakable.

Crow's body could feel Simeon in every spot he'd touched—which was everywhere. Could taste him. Could, if Crow inhaled just right, smell Simeon's unique personal scent, which was a little like smoke and cotton candy.

Although their fates had been untangled, Simeon still lived inside of Crow.

The train arrived in Chicago close to dinnertime. Crow walked to the bus station and discovered he'd have to wait until morning, which was fine. He checked into a hotel—not the same one where he and Simeon had stayed—and spent a couple of hours just wandering the city. It wasn't the same as being there with Simeon, but Crow enjoyed it nonetheless. It felt good to be walking instead of riding, and he liked watching the passersby, each of them so intent on their own story.

He had deep-dish pizza for dinner, because why not. And it was good.

Back in his high-rise room, he stood at the window for a long time, gazing out at the city lights and contemplating the sources and uses of power. Then he stripped, showered, and got into bed, paring down the wealth of pillows.

It was a nice bed. Too big for him alone—after Simeon,

every bed would feel too big—but exactly firm enough and with smooth, crisp sheets that cooled his summer-warmed body. With the lights out, he could stare through the window and imagine himself floating in the night sky, a bird gliding on a thermal, a wisp of cloud, a dream not quite formed.

But he couldn't sleep, so after a while he propped himself up, clicked on the bedside lamp, and returned to the book that Atty had handed him. A piece of folded paper, slightly tattered, fluttered onto his lap. A place marker from the book's previous owner, perhaps. With mild curiosity he unfolded it.

It was a page torn from a different book. An older one, he thought, the paper yellowed and brittle at the edges, the typeface old-fashioned. *Walt Whitman* was the heading on one side and *Leaves of Grass* on the other. Ah. Poems.

Poetry had never interested Crow, and his recent dips into Greek tragedies hadn't changed his opinion. He was going to set the paper aside, but a word near the top of one side caught his eye: thrusting. So he read the whole thing, which seemed to begin mid-poem.

*From plenty of persons near and yet the right person not near,*
    *From the soft sliding of hands over me and thrusting of fingers*
    *through my hair and beard,*
    *From the long sustain'd kiss upon the mouth or bosom,*
    *From the close pressure that makes me or any man drunk,*
*fainting*
    *with excess,*
    *From what the divine husband knows, from the work of*
*fatherhood,*
    *From exultation, victory and relief, from the bedfellow's*
*embrace in*
    *the night,*

*From the act-poems of eyes, hands, hips and bosoms,*
*From the cling of the trembling arm,*
*From the bending curve and the clinch,*

HE HAD to turn the paper over to read the rest.

*FROM SIDE by side the pliant coverlet off-throwing,*
*From the one so unwilling to have me leave, and me just as*
*unwilling*
*to leave,*
*(Yet a moment O tender waiter, and I return,)*
*From the hour of shining stars and dropping dews,*
*From the night a moment I emerging flitting out,*
*Celebrate you act divine and you children prepared for,*
*And you stalwart loins.*

OH. It was a sex poem. And it was... surprisingly hot. He read it again, more slowly, thinking more deeply about the way the piece was constructed and about its imagery. *Act-poems of eyes*, yes, *the bending curve….* If Miss Davis had asked the class to read this instead of *Little Women*, Crow might have actually paid attention.

Another poem began after the first, so he read that fragment too.

*I SING THE BODY ELECTRIC,*
*The armies of those I love engirth me and I engirth them,*
*They will not let me off till I go with them, respond to them,*
*And discorrupt them, and charge them full with the charge of*
*the soul.*

. . .

ELECTRIC WAS RIGHT—CROW felt as if he'd been struck by lightning. He cried out and for a moment couldn't see anything but a corona of orange-and-yellow brightness. Jesus Christ, he was literally seeing the light.

And for the very first time, Crow believed that defeating the demons was a real possibility.

# CHAPTER 27

*H*e was too keyed up to fall asleep after that. Instead, lights out but curtains open, he jerked off while thinking of Whitman's words—*plenty of persons near and yet the right person not near*—and of Simeon's hands and mouth and cock. But Crow didn't pretend that the touches on his body were not his own. Rather, he imagined that Simeon was there with him, embodied in him, joined in moans and gasps and thrusts.

Afterward, sticky and catching his breath, Crow shed a few tears. They were sweet rather than bitter, however, and afterward he slipped gently into soft nothingness.

Unsurprisingly, he dreamed he was on a train, an image which probably also had something to do with sex. Thanks, Dr. Freud. He was the only passenger, and no matter how many cars he walked through, the train never ended and he saw no one else. At first he didn't mind, but after a while, it grew somewhat frightening. Then, for the first time, he thought to look through the windows, which had previously been nothing but gray blurs. When he focused his gaze there now, however, he saw trees and rivers and plains and cities. And people. Their images were blurry and indistinct but they seemed familiar even if he couldn't recognize them. None of them looked at him, not even when he waved.

Crow walked the train cars for a while longer before suddenly coming to a halt. "Boat, not train," he announced. And lo and behold, he stood on the deck of an old-fashioned sailing ship with multiple masts and a great many sheets of canvas bellied by the wind. He peered ahead and saw that the ship's figurehead was a carved black bird, which made more sense than most things in dreams. The landscape around him, however, remained stubbornly terrestrial, as if his ship were scudding along a road rather than a waterway. The indistinct people were still there.

He found the helm, grasped the wheel's spokes, and tried to change course. At first he couldn't turn the wheel at all, and when he squinted, he saw that it was tied in place with nearly invisible purple threads. After a few moments of tugging, he was able to clear those away and the wheel turned easily.

But now he was headed toward a dire-looking storm. While the sky overhead remained faultless and blue, dead ahead brewed a massive, seething cloud the color of basalt. He knew that kind of cloud: it meant sheets of rain so heavy you could barely see in front of you, hail fierce enough to ruin crops, lightning that would blow out power lines, tornados that could flatten entire towns.

Crow snorted. "Yeah, I get it. Not very subtle symbolism there."

As if in answer to Crow's words, a black bird flapped down, perched behind the helm, and fixed its bright eye on Crow. "Nasty weather ahead," the bird commented in a Midwestern accent.

"I can see that."

"Sure you don't want to go back on your original course? Much sunnier."

"It only looks sunny. It's actually way more dangerous."

The bird clacked its beak. "Not for you. Only for them." It gestured with one of its wings toward the people near the ship.

"Maybe. But they're important. I care about them." Crow continued to aim for the storm.

He could have sworn that the bird smiled, which was dumb because creatures with beaks *can't* smile. Then he remembered that this was a dream, and it made more sense.

"You're okay, kid," said the bird. It hopped into the air and flapped up to one of the masts, where it disappeared inside a bucket-like structure.

"The crow's nest," said Crow. "Of course." Without taking his hands off the helm, Crow twisted his neck and tilted his head—almost painfully—to get a better view of the crow's nest. A man stood inside it, gazing into the distance through a telescope. His face wasn't visible but his long black hair, waving in the breeze, was unmistakable.

"Simeon." Crow said it with a sigh, because this wasn't like his previous dreams where Simeon had been truly drawn in. This was only a figment, a manifestation of the yearning in Crow's subconscious.

Right?

Sighing again deeply, as if trying to fill the sails with his own breath, Crow turned his attention back to the looming storm.

316

THE CROWDED BUS creeped through Chicago traffic and then, seemingly, stopped forever at every town in Illinois. Crow tried to read his book instead of jittering anxiously in his seat, but he wasn't very successful. His fellow passengers kept casting worried looks in his direction.

It wasn't that he was afraid. Well, it wasn't that he *wasn't* afraid either, not entirely. But in at least equal measure, he was eager. He imagined that this was how a top-class athlete must feel right before an Olympic event. Bristling with nerves and yet also knowing in his core that he was among the best of the best—and feeling impatient to prove that to the world.

Sure, maybe Crow was making a huge mistake. But if so, it was *his* mistake, his choice. Not a consequence of his strange family history or of fate as a puppetmaster. And for once he was running toward a confrontation rather than away from it. That felt good too.

By the time he got off the bus in downtown Chinkapin Grove, it was late afternoon. The farmers, who tended to rise early, eat early, and go to bed early, would be getting ready for dinner soon. Crow briefly considered doing the same. He could have meatloaf and mashed potatoes at the B&R Café, maybe with peach pie for dessert, and then book a room at the Grove Inn. Spend another night thinking about Simeon and Walt Whitman, maybe with some Greeks or William Shakespeare or Ray Bradbury thrown in for good measure. A solo literary orgy. He could get an early start in the morning, and—

No. Enough waiting, and far too much doing nothing. A full decade's worth. Now was the time to act.

Crow adjusted his pack more comfortably on his shoulders and began the walk to Aunt Helen's house.

This time Jamie wasn't out front playing and Helen

wasn't tending her garden. She was likely getting ready for dinner too. Crow could picture her standing at the kitchen counter, chopping carrots while gently instructing Jamie on how to set the table. They might be singing along to the radio. Maybe they—

Maybe Crow should stop imagining scenarios and just ring the damn doorbell.

Helen answered, her face registering shock as soon as she saw him, but a split second later she was squeezing him in such a tight hug that he could barely breathe. "You're okay! You're back home, and you're okay."

He returned her hug and then managed to gently extricate himself. "I'm not staying."

Her expression grew serious. "What are you going to do, Crow?"

"Face my demons." His chuckle sounded only slightly hysterical.

"What's wrong?" Now she looked worried, which only intensified after she looked past him and saw that nobody else was there. "Where's Simeon?"

"It's a really long story. One I don't have time for." He remained just inside the threshold, resisting her gentle tug as she tried to urge him farther inside. Slightly tinny television voices wound their way to him, making him smile. "Is that *Gilligan's Island?*"

"Those old reruns are Jamie's favorites. She likes— Crow, what the hell is going on?"

"I've learned a lot of things in the past days, each one less believable than the next. And I hope that soon I'll get to sit down and tell you everything. But I can't right now. I just stopped by because I really needed to tell you that I love you."

Her face was grave and she looked older than her years. She gave a quick glance over her shoulder as if to make sure Jamie wasn't listening. "You're going to fight those birds."

"You know, it turns out that the crows have been on our side. They've protected us from something really bad. But yeah, I'm going to face the really bad things. If I don't, they'll never let up."

"What if they kill you?" she hissed, but in a low voice that she probably hoped would be unheard in the living room.

"Then I die. And people will be safer than if I do nothing. I'm okay with the possibility. I've made my peace with it." He shrugged. "It's what I have to do." Every word was the absolute truth.

Helen pressed her lips together and took a few noisy breaths. "Fine. I'm going with."

Crow was overcome by such a deep wave of affection that he almost cried. "And you'd give 'em hell. But you know you can't. There's Jamie."

She opened her mouth as if to argue and then gave a defeated sigh.

"Look, Helen. You'll definitely be there in spirit, okay? Just knowing you're here and that you know I care about you, that gives me exactly the strength I need to face them."

"I care about you too, Chick." Oh, that old nickname, one he'd forgotten. She used to tease him with it when he was very young, and although he'd get angry, he knew even then that it was born of fondness and love.

She pinched his cheeks, as if she were his grandmother instead of an aunt not much older than he was. They hugged again, even more fiercely. He was going to step away, but then he thought of something. He pulled out his wallet and held it toward her. Several hundred dollars remained.

"Keep this for me. If I come back tonight or tomorrow, you can return it. If I don't, use it to start a college fund for Jamie."

Although her mouth was tight, she took the wallet without argument and then stood there clutching it, arms crossed. "You better come back. Jamie needs to know her cousin Crow, remember?"

"I want to know her too. And watch her grow up. That's one of the reasons I need to do what I'm doing."

She gave him a tight nod, followed by the ghost of a smile. He smiled back, turned, and left. He felt her watching him for a long time as he walked in the direction of the Storey farm.

HE'D MADE this same trek probably thousands of times, the modest houses petering out and giving way to fields. At this time of year the corn stood tall and proud, the soybean bushes heavy with nearly ripe beans. As a boy he'd run or plodded, depending on his mood and whether he was on his way to town or returning. Today he took the journey in long, steady strides, the sunshine warm against his back.

Only a single vehicle passed him, a battered pickup also heading out of town. Crow didn't catch a glimpse of the driver, but he imagined it was a farmer running late from some errand, his wife impatiently holding dinner. The driver didn't slow for a better look at the tall blond man with the pack on his shoulders. If he had—if he'd glimpsed Crow's face—maybe the man would have recognized him. Or maybe not. Crow felt like a completely different person from the boy who used to walk this path.

The boy who'd never known his parents and had been teased about his odd name and about being a bastard, but who was entirely confident of the love from his grandparents and aunt. Who sat quietly in school, doing his work well enough to slide through without much fuss. Whose best friend, Marty, would sometimes drag him a little out of his shell. Who assumed that he'd grow up to become a comfortable cliché—the bachelor farmer—and that he'd be content enough in the role.

Yes, that boy was gone.

But then, so was his successor: the fugitive man who rabbited from place to place, desperately lonely but terrified of becoming connected to anyone. That man never planned, only reacted. Never hoped, only dreaded. Never dared to open himself up, and never noticed the world's small joys.

As Crow neared the old Storey farm, he looked up at the gathering flock of birds whirling overhead and decided that he rather liked the person he was now. There was room for improvement, to be sure. Lots of room. But *this* man, this Crow, knew who he was and what he could do, and he held a sweet heavy burden of love that made his heart feel too big for his chest.

"If I survive today—if I'm successful—I think I'll have an interesting life."

He smiled at the prospect. He wasn't sure what he would do next, but that was due to a wealth of possibilities rather than a lack of interest. Maybe he'd save up some money, get a passport, and go to London. He didn't expect to find Simeon there, but he might learn things that would help him know Simeon better.

Or he might… well, anything. Until the thread is cut, hope remains. And for the moment, at any rate, his thread was intact.

Crow paused when he reached the overgrown remains of the old gravel driveway. There was no sign of the house from this distance, which he expected. But now the barn lay in ruins as well. Grandad had taken great pride in keeping the barn in good shape, annually checking the integrity of its roof and walls and refreshing the red paint regularly. It had been his domain while the house had been Gran's. On the rare occasions when he and Gran had argued, or when the memories of his lost daughter became too painful, he'd retreat to the barn's workbench and putter around with his tools.

But now as Crow stared at the rubble, he realized that Grandad was still here, as were Gran and Sara and every other member of the Storey family that had lived and worked here. When people had such a strong connection to a place, they could never be completely removed, which meant a part of Crow would always be here too.

He smiled. Yes, this was his place of power.

After a few moments, he walked onto the property itself. He kicked his way through the weeds, past the remains of the house's foundation, and neared the edge of the barn. Some crows settled on the barn's broken bones and many others landed on the patch of bare ground between him and the cornfields.

One of the crows strutted toward him. It was the same size as the other birds, with the same glossy black eyes and gleaming purple-black plumage. But it was… odd-looking. Its head was less rounded on top, as if it were wearing a small helmet under its feathers. And the beak was gray edged with white. Its difference made Crow uneasy, even though none of its feathers were red.

It moved forward with a great sense of purpose, as if it were the spokesbird for the flock and intended to make a speech. Maybe it did. Crows could certainly talk in Crow's dreams, so it didn't seem like much of a stretch for them to begin conversations in real life.

But the bird stopped when it was seven or eight feet away. Never taking its gaze from Crow's face, it resettled its wings a few times. It bobbed its head. Then it made a terrible screech and... grew. Very suddenly, like a balloon pumped rapidly full of air. And as it grew, it changed. Feathers turned into pale skin, wings to arms and hands, beak to nose and a full-lipped mouth. The feathers atop its head elongated, becoming glossy hair.

"It turns out," Simeon said calmly, "that I'm a rook."

# CHAPTER 28

*A*lthough Crow didn't faint, his knees gave way and he fell hard onto his ass. Simeon ran forward, arms out, probably intending to help him up, but instead Crow pulled him down into a fierce embrace. Neither of them said anything—Crow couldn't possibly manage words—but they didn't need to. Not immediately.

Eventually, however, Crow became aware that Simeon was naked, that several hundred birds were watching, and that just a few minutes ago, Simeon had been....

"A *rook?*" Crow demanded. Perhaps not the most important question at the moment, but nonetheless pertinent.

Simeon climbed out of Crow's lap and finally helped him up. "*Corvus frugilegus*. Closely related to crows and ravens. You haven't any in America but they're quite common in the UK."

"But—"

"In retrospect, I expect it was quite obvious, really." Simeon brushed dirt and leaves off his legs.

"Obvious?" Crow was still dazed.

"Neighborhoods like the one where I'm from are called

rookeries, you know. And the birds themselves are known for being talkative and sociable and intelligent." Simeon was marking off these characteristics on his fingers as he spoke. "Rooks can be thieves as well—they steal one another's sticks when they're building nests. Also, it's not unusual for rooks to be friendly with other corvids. Such as crows." He grinned widely at the last sentence.

Crow realized he was opening and closing his mouth like a landed fish, and he tried to engage his brain. "But you're a man."

"That as well. Love, can I borrow some clothes? Flying is lovely, but it's hard to bring along luggage, and rooks haven't any pockets."

Nodding mutely, Crow handed over his pack. His jeans wouldn't fit, but Simeon seemed satisfied with a pair of exercise shorts that Crow had bought in Chicago and a plain gray tee. He didn't seem to mind remaining barefoot. Clothed, he looked more real, although Crow touched his arm a few times just to make sure.

"I don't understand," Crow said. "This isn't possible."

"If you can be an angel courted by demons, I don't see why I can't be a rook. At least rooks are objectively proven to exist, whereas angels are fairytales, religious dogma, and conjecture."

Crow, who had the feeling that Simeon was teasing him a little, frowned. "I believe in rooks. But rooks who are also men? Were-rooks? It's not even a full moon."

Now Simeon was laughing, and despite Crow's ongoing confusion and shock, that was a lovely thing to hear. He'd never expected to hear Simeon's laughter again, or see the way his eyes sparkled with humor. "Sit down, love. I'll tell you what I know. Which isn't much, really, and anyway I expect you've other matters to take care of soon."

Right. Demons. Funny how Crow had almost forgotten about them.

As instructed, he found a grassy spot and took a seat, with Simeon settling in beside him. The surrounding flock settled too, although Crow couldn't tell whether they wanted to hear the tale or were simply waiting patiently.

Simeon took Crow's hand, interlacing their fingers. "Right. Here's what I know. I lost you in that wave."

"And I lost you."

"And I'd like very much to hear what happened to you next, but you can tell me later. I was washed away. Don't really remember that bit—just tumbling through the water, and I couldn't breathe, and I reckoned I was drowning. When I woke up, I was on a rock in the ocean, soaking wet and bloody cold."

"The ocean is a hundred miles from Portland," Crow pointed out.

"Aye, and there's no such thing as evil red birdmen."

Crow capitulated with a sigh. What was one more improbability in his life right now after so many? "A rock in the ocean."

"No land in sight. Just gulls who weren't pleased to have me as a guest. It was too foggy to see far anyway. Stranded on a rock in the Pacific is an unlikely end for a lad from the East End—at least, one who's never been a sailor—but there I was. Waiting to be dinner for the gulls. But then I'd an idea."

"To turn into a bird? That would totally occur to me right then."

Simeon bashed his shoulder into Crow's. "Berk. I'd lost my pack in the flood, but I was still wearing my jeans, yeah? And I'd a few things in my pockets. Such as an empty wallet."

"You unpicked my pocket!"

"You needed the dosh more than me. I can always nick more."

True in general, yes. "But not on a rock in the ocean."

"But money wasn't what I needed then, was it? And I had two more things as well. One of them was Miss Aisa's spool of thread."

Crow had completely forgotten about that. Simeon hadn't produced the spool when Chloe told him to hand over the items he'd stolen. "Miss Aisa told you to use it wisely," Crow said, now with some inkling where this was going.

"And I did."

"What did you steal from me?"

"A work ID card from a bloke named Cliff Robertson. He's an employee at someplace called Corrucorp. Looked quite handsome in the photo, he did." Simeon had a smug expression.

"You took it when you put the money in."

"Nah, long before that, love. And there on my rock, I wrapped that little card in purple thread, and I—never been much for prayer, and I'm not sure I'd call it that—I *willed* us to be entwined again." Simeon drew back a little, looking apprehensive. "Are you cross?"

"No! God, no. I never minded being bound to you, Simeon. I just didn't want it without your consent."

"Well, I bloody consented my heart out on that rock. And then I turned into a bird."

Crow shook his head. "See, there's where you lost me. You just... poof?"

"Not exactly. Hurt like the blazes, and I reckoned I was dying. But when it was over, I just rose into the sky, easy as that. And that was bloody *marvelous*."

Simeon closed his eyes for a moment, his expression one of pure joy, and Crow tried to imagine what it would feel like: marooned, earthbound, imprisoned by sea, and then suddenly free from it all. He could *almost* feel the wind tickling through wing feathers.

Then Simeon opened his eyes and continued. "Didn't know what sort of bird I was until I found my way back to land and saw my reflection in a pond. We hadn't any rooks in the city, but I'd heard of them, and I saw them when I was with the carnival in the UK. So at least I knew what I was. It's not bad at all, as birds go. Better than being a pigeon or a buzzard."

Crow nodded at that. He also wouldn't want to be a pigeon. "So all you had to do was make a wish—or do the string thing—and you turned into a rook?" That seemed far too easy.

"No." Simeon frowned thoughtfully. "When I'm a rook, it feels as if… as if the possibility has always been there, but I didn't recognize it. Like hearing a song that's familiar even if you can't place from where. I was always a rook, Crow, but it took being washed away and then tying us together to bring it to the surface. And I've no more explanations for how or why I can become a bird, so no use asking me. I simply can."

Well, it was weird. But Simeon had always accepted Crow, taking him exactly as is, and Crow could damned well do the same. "Maybe we could… do some research. Like we did for me. If you want."

That brought Simeon's widest smile. "Brilliant. After we've finished this business here. Which is *my* business as well as yours, yeah?"

"All right." And Crow had to admit, it was comforting to know he'd have someone at his side when he faced his demons. "But what happened after you figured out you were a rook?"

Simeon shrugged. "I flew back to Portland and looked for you. I was going to wait for you at the spot where I'd lost you, but I wasn't sure how much time had passed. I didn't see you. And your crows convinced me to join them and come here."

"You can talk to them?"

"There are ways to communicate without words, love. It's a long flight from Portland to Chinkapin Grove. I'm glad I got here on time."

Crow remembered that old, stupid joke—*I just flew in from New York, and boy, are my arms tired*—and chuckled. "Were you a bird the whole time?"

"Mostly. Easier that way, on account of the lack of clothing. I didn't mind, but it feels good to be back in this body." He flexed his shoulders a little.

And suddenly Crow yearned to rip the clothing off Simeon and explore all the wonderful possibilities of that body. Now, however, wasn't the time. Among other things, he had a few more questions. "Did you always know so many rook facts?"

"Nah. Before I left Portland, I nicked a shirt and shorts from a clothesline, popped into a library, and read up." When he cocked his head, he looked exceptionally birdlike, even in this form. "One more thing I learned. Not sure how you'll take it, though."

"What?" Crow asked warily.

"Rooks mate for life."

"Is that... a proposal of some kind?" Crow had experienced a lot of emotionally dizzying days, but this one headed the list.

"Of some kind. If you want one. We can't get married properly, but...."

Crow took Simeon's hand, brought it to his lips, and kissed the knuckles. And then a thought struck him. He removed his father's ring from his own finger and slid it onto Simeon's. "I do," Crow rasped.

Although Simeon didn't cry, his eyes were big and glossy. He had to swallow twice before he spoke. "Yeah?"

"You're extraordinary, Simeon Bell. And not because

you're a bird. I've had more change, more progress in the short time we've been together than in my whole adult life. You've shown me how to be myself." Crow paused to sniffle, although he wasn't quite crying. "Because of you, I can imagine having a future. I can love. Whatever you want of me, whatever you'll have of me... I *do*."

They kissed after that, naturally. Long and slow and sweet as a funnel cake, and it was like flying, only it was Crow's heart that was swooping and doing loop-de-loops, his soul that was soaring so high that it might brush against the sun. He held on to Simeon as if their lives depended on it —Simeon doing the same—and Crow knew that however many bad choices he'd made in his life, they were still the right choices if they'd gotten him here.

# CHAPTER 29

*I*t was nearly nightfall when Crow and Simeon stood up and brushed debris from each other's skin and clothing. They hadn't made love, but that was all right. They'd have time for that later if they survived. Maybe Crow should have sped things along and gotten down to business more quickly, but he figured the universe owed him and Simeon a short, blissful intermission.

But now shadows had grown long and the sky was streaked with cotton-candy pinks. Crickets had started to chirp. The crows and ravens and jays—hundreds of them—were restlessly waiting.

"What do we do now?" Even with his hair mussed and lips kiss-swollen, wearing nothing but a thrift-store T-shirt and nylon shorts, Simeon looked like a warrior, his chin firm and his eyes sparkling with anticipation.

Crow smiled. "I call on my armies."

"The birds?" Simeon, obviously puzzled, glanced at the gathered flock. "No offense intended to you or them, but I don't think they can help much. Last time we were here, all they did was herd us into the barn."

"The birds are only part of it. Feel it, Simeon: we're on my turf now. I've been attacked twice here, but I wasn't prepared. Now I am. This farm is *my* place."

Crow stood still, eyes half closed, and imagined himself as a tall stalk of corn, his roots spreading deep into soil that had nurtured five generations of Storeys. It didn't matter that he wasn't related to them by blood; they were his family. It also didn't matter that none of the Storeys had ever prospered here. They'd never starved either. They'd always had enough, and they'd loved one another.

He could feel it: his bone-deep connection to this land. He'd always loved it. Even when he was a boy and felt as if he might be imprisoned here for the rest of his life, he'd been a willing captive. In the decade since, when he'd traveled so far, he'd measured every place against this one. Although it wasn't much—a flat bit of acreage in the middle of nowhere, at the edge of a town in which the primary attractions included a creek and a moderately attractive post office—he loved it anyway.

"Erm... Crow? Look."

Crow opened his eyes and followed Simeon's gaze. The barn was back. Not physically—the weathered boards still sprawled in ruins—but the structure was there, like a ghost, yet as bright and believable as Crow himself. "Do buildings have *souls*?" Because he was pretty sure that was exactly what he was seeing.

But before Simeon could do more than shrug, another spirit-structure appeared, this one on the foundations of the house. It included the wide porch with its gently moving swing. And there was the front screen door, which always slammed shut with a bang if Crow wasn't careful, earning him a scolding when Gran was inside. There were the orange and pink and purple dinosaurs that Crow and Helen had drawn on the white siding in colored chalk one afternoon when Crow was five—it had been Helen's idea and the results had made Gran laugh. She'd allowed the artwork to remain until rains washed it away. There was the window in Crow's attic bedroom, the lower sash lifted and the yellow curtain fluttering out with the breeze.

Simeon moved closer and slung an arm around Crow's shoulders. "Bloody gorgeous."

"Isn't it? Isn't it the best house you've ever seen?" Crow meant those words.

And the wonders didn't cease, because moments later shadowy figures rose out of the ground. Their faces were indistinct, but Crow recognized his grandparents. There were other people as well, dressed in antique clothing, and he guessed that those were more distant generations of ancestors. Closer to him, a man appeared, tall and dressed in a white uniform and paper hat, like an employee at an old-fashioned diner. "Larry," Crow sighed, because it had to be him. And then Larry was joined by a woman also dressed in white, her pale hair in a long braid. She held Larry's hand.

"What's happening, love?" Simeon's voice was low and reverent but not afraid.

Crow, who'd never in his life memorized a line of poetry, said, "The armies of those I love engirth me and I engirth them."

More figures appeared. Marty was there in the ridiculously flared jeans he'd been so proud of. And there was Cameron, thrumming with energy, looking around with what Crow sensed was approval. And God, Dee was there. No longer emaciated, he wore his hair in a blue-dyed Mohawk and bounced up and down as if waiting for a dance club to open.

Some people were less distinct, such as Zen, his one-time hippie roommate. And Ximena, who owned the little market near his home in Mareado. Julie, who'd been his sort-of girlfriend, and Sandy, who'd dated Marty. And more: room-mates, friends, acquaintances, co-workers. X and the little girl and the other temporary companions from his recent train ride. Even the man from the medical examiner's office and Todd from the thrift store. And God, there was Aunt Helen with little Jamie scrunched up next to her. As far as Crow knew, all of these people were still alive, so what he was seeing weren't their ghosts. They were the bits of them that remained with him when he'd opened himself up a little. Souls were like chalk, and if two of them rubbed together even briefly, they exchanged traces of themselves.

From this place, from these people, from the birds, from his remarkable lover standing beside him, Crow drew power. And the wonderful thing was that, because his army gave willingly, he didn't drain them. If anything, the more he relied on them, the stronger they grew.

And perhaps what he did next was melodramatic, but if any moment in Crow's life called for melodrama, this was it. He widened his stance, raised his arms, and lifted his chin.

"Come get us!" he bellowed. And then, miraculously remembering a line from *Antigone*, he added, "And even if I die in the act, that death will be a glory!"

The sky went dark very suddenly, as if someone had switched off the sun, but there were no stars or moon. A sort of grayish glow appeared, its source unclear, but it was enough for Crow to see well. The temperature dropped, and instead of the light sweat of an August evening, his skin produced goosebumps. Simeon must have been even colder in his shorts and tee, but he didn't complain.

The birds began to call—the ravens croaking the loudest but the jays and crows more strident—and they all took wing at once, wheeling in the eerie light as if they were bats. Now the gooseflesh along Crow's nape and spine wasn't due to cold. The air carried the scent of something like old carrion.

Three birds the size of ostriches dove downward, oblivious to the attacks of Crow's flock. They had feathers the color of fresh blood and each wingspan equaled that of a Cessna. They landed gracefully a few yards away, and after a moment they shimmered and became three tall, thin beings in red cloaks. Hairless and beak-nosed, their faces were not identical yet resembled one another in cold cruelty.

"You will join us now," said the middle one in a deep, throaty voice.

"Go fuck yourself." It might have sounded better in Greek, but it got Crow's point across. Next to him, Simeon was tense but silent. The corvids had stopped making noise, although they continued to circle in flight, and the spirits of Crow's loved ones waited and watched.

When the middle demon strode closer, Crow stiffened but didn't back away. The demon held out its hands, palms up, as if offering something. Crow distractedly noticed that the creature's fingernails were actually talons. He wasn't sure what to expect, but certainly not what appeared: a crystal ball very much like Madame Persephone's. Simeon gasped, but Crow—against his will but also curious—gazed into it.

He saw himself, although he was barely recognizable because he wore a suit. The last time he'd worn a suit was to Aunt Helen's wedding, and that one had been purchased on sale from the Sears store in Carbondale. In the crystal ball, Crow's clothing was expensive and perfectly tailored, a gold watch shining on his wrist and his hair expertly cut and styled. He sat in a restaurant, the kind with gleaming wood and brass and with waiters in black vests and bowties. He had an enormous steak in front of him, but he was talking rather than eating, and his companions at the table, a dozen men and women, hung on every word.

The glass became murky, and when it cleared Crow was at a party, still dressed to the nines. A highball glass in one hand, a cigarette in the other. He was laughing, and so were the people surrounding him.

Outside of the glass ball, standing on the dirt of an old farm, Crow felt a deep pang. The future version of himself seemed happy, and he clearly belonged. He didn't so much blend into the crowd as lead it. None of his companions questioned whether he was smart enough, rich enough, interesting enough. If they knew he was gay, that he'd been abandoned as an infant, that he came from a hardscrabble farm in a nowhere town, they didn't seem to care.

*That* Crow didn't spend his days toiling at mindless jobs or his nights alone in a cheap room, silently aching for someone to hold him.

The ball clouded again, and now the future Crow stood on a stage with a podium and mic, speaking to a crowd. He was confident and articulate, his movements smooth and natural, his expression suggesting he was as comfortable here as he might be on a couch in his living room. And the crowd listened, leaning forward in their seats, eyes wide and mouths slightly open. Many of them were nodding. They didn't just agree with whatever he was saying, they believed in him.

After the fog moved through the crystal ball once more, Crow in suit and tie sat at a large wooden desk flanked by two flagpoles. Elaborate gold curtains framed the windows behind him. Of course Crow recognized this office—he'd seen it on television many times, most recently with Ronald Reagan holding a stack of papers and smiling at the camera. The future Crow smiled too, a mass of men in suits looking on as he signed something in a black leather folder.

*Think of the things you could do*, said a voice. Crow wasn't sure if it came from the demons or his own head. *Think of the power you would wield.*

The power, yes. There was a cracking sensation inside

Crow's chest, as if there were a giant wishbone in there and children had snapped it apart. He understood that all things came at a price. That in order to become this confident, popular, authoritative Crow, he'd need to be pulled apart piece by piece and reassembled into something quite different. But maybe that wouldn't be such a bad thing. It would be like stripping Grandad's old Ford and putting it back together as a Ferrari. Wasn't that an improvement? That truck couldn't even run, but a Ferrari could go fast and far.

Crow could change laws. He could make the country— the world?—into what it should be. A place where farmers didn't struggle to have food on their tables, where bright boys didn't waste away and die rejected and alone, where—

Once again the scene inside the ball shifted. Now future Crow stood on a giant stage, like at a rock concert, with dozens of cameras pointed at him. In front of him, tens of thousands of people knelt with their foreheads on the ground, chanting something he couldn't hear but knew was his name. They didn't simply like him or want him—they worshiped him. He filled their dreams. Their only desire was to bend themselves to his will.

God, he could do *anything*.

A dozen or so men appeared from offstage, all naked, every one of them as beautiful as any model. Glistening skin, glossy hair, erect cocks. They fell in front of him and vied to be the most alluring, the most perfect, the most—

"No!" Crow brought his fist down on the crystal ball, smashing it into tiny shards. He felt the sharp sting of cuts and the warm trickle of his blood, both of which he ignored. "I don't want that," he growled.

The demon, unperturbed, gave an icy smile. "It doesn't matter what you want. It is your future. The less you fight it, the less damage you will cause to others."

But Crow remembered what Chloe had said. "Prophecy is

a matter of probabilities. There is always a margin of error." In fact, Crow now recalled something Gran used to say whenever Grandad was dead sure about something and she was dead sure he was wrong. She would give a surprisingly evil smile and remind him about the 1948 presidential election. Now Crow echoed her: "And Dewey defeated Truman, right?"

The demon may or may not have been familiar with American politics, but it understood the gist. Its grin turned into a snarl. "There is no error. You will join us."

That spurred another of Gran's favorite sayings. "When pigs fly, motherfucker." The last word was Crow's personal addition.

"Then die instead." The demon threw back its head, opened its mouth wider than humanly possible, and emitted a sound so terrible that Crow's knees nearly buckled. Simeon did begin to collapse, in fact, his hands held against his ears, but Crow caught him and hauled him upright. The demon's screech sounded as if every bird on earth were being torn apart. *Crow* was being torn apart, cell by agonizing cell. He lost all his senses except hearing and pain, which right now were the same thing. He couldn't breathe. His heart couldn't beat.

But he could feel someone's hand on his arm. Simeon.

Crow pulled energy from that point of connection—and Simeon eagerly fed him more. So did all of the corvids and all of the spirits around Crow, until a sort of armor enveloped his entire body. His cells rebuilt themselves; his organs resumed their vital work. Although he could still hear the demon, it was now no more painful than listening to "We Are the World" on repeat.

The demon shut its mouth and stepped back to join the others. They spent a full minute glaring at Crow. Apparently they hadn't expected him to put up a fight, especially after he'd spent the last ten years turning tail and running.

But of course they weren't ready to give up either. All three of them waved their arms synchronously as if starting a dance routine. And everything went up in flames. The fire started in the ghostly house and spread quickly to the barn, the rows of corn. And, horribly, to the birds and Crow's loved ones and, God, to Simeon, before finally latching on to Crow as well. He remembered this agony very well. It had been coupled so tightly with terror and grief, and now the flames licked at his skin and devoured his bones.

He'd survived that fire, however. And nothing as simple as combustion could annihilate his love for his home and family and Simeon. Those feelings would remain even if Crow were nothing but charred bones and a pile of ash.

Besides, he was the captain of his ship, and that meant... water.

There was a well not far from the house. When the farm was first settled—generations before Crow was born—Storeys had to carry all the water from that well for drinking, cooking, and washing. Eventually, of course, they got indoor plumbing, but the household still drew from that well, and the well drew from an underground aquifer that was probably connected indirectly to the Mississippi.

So Crow drew on that.

Not the actual, physical water, but its essence. Because just as the soil from the farm was in his bones, the water was in his blood. It was a part of him too.

Ignoring the heat of the fire, Crow created an enormous ghost wave, far bigger than the one that had washed Simeon away. Cool and clear, the wave engulfed the entire farmstead and quenched the fire at once.

Crow and Simeon stood tall, as did all the spirits. The house and barn remained intact.

The demons were furious.

After a few moments of silent snarling, they attacked for a third time. And this time, Crow felt sick.

The paint on the house peeled like poorly healed scabs, the windows cracked, the roof sagged. The rows of corn withered and died. The barn collapsed. The birds plummeted to the ground like a morbid hailstorm, feathers falling from their bodies, leaving them pallid and naked. They lay there, panting weakly. Crow's friends and family grew emaciated, sores formed on their skin, and they crumpled to the ground with heartrending moans.

Simeon uttered a pained sound between clenched teeth. His skin, always pale, went white as bone. His eyes clouded, and he slumped against Crow, who struggled to support him despite his own illness.

But he couldn't. Crow fell to his knees, taking Simeon with him. Soon he was on all fours, vomiting, shaking, his body cold as ice yet burning with fever. All his muscles seized into an excruciating cramp; his bones weakened and threatened to crumble. Crow's mind blurred as hallucinations and terrors pushed away reality. Memories faded like old photographs. He was losing himself.

"Crow." Simeon's voice was barely more than a ragged whisper. It sounded as though his throat was torn.

"I'm sorry," Crow managed. "I'll stop. You can—"

"Fight, love."

With what may have been the last of his strength, Simeon gave Crow a psychic shove. Perhaps it was a physical one as well; Crow couldn't tell. In any case, it was enough to loosen some of his will from the demons' contaminated influence. Crow tried to pull some energy from his host of spirits—but nothing happened. He lacked the strength. He tried to vomit again, but his stomach produced nothing but strings of bitter bile.

He was too weak. The demons were going to destroy him. They would demolish everything and everyone important to him. There was no point in struggling any longer and prolonging Simeon's pain. It was useless. Crow was useless. He should have found a way to end himself long ago, or buried himself in a cave to rot.

No. No, that wasn't right. If he'd done that, he never would have seen the fog roll in from the Pacific at sunset. Never tasted wild blueberries still warm from the sun, just plucked from the bush in the barrens of Maine. Never danced with Dee in a crowded club, forgetting to feel awkward while in the presence of Dee's effervescence, laughing as sweat plastered his hair, as the scents of cloves and pot permeated the air. He never would have gone to the top of the Sears Tower. And he never would have met Simeon and fallen in love.

Despite everything, he had so many bright jewels of joy in his life. Those were worth fighting for.

Crow drew on his powers again. It was terribly difficult, like hauling a boulder by a chain. But concentrating on those joys, he felt the boulder budge, first a fraction of an inch and then a bit more. And then Simeon was pushing and so were all the spirits, and the birds grabbed links of the chain in their beaks and tugged along with Crow. The boulder moved.

Rising to his feet, Crow took a gloriously deep breath as the sickness receded and health returned. Beside him, Simeon coughed, laughed, and stood upright. The spirits recovered as well, and the birds, refeathered, took to the air. The house and barn looked as sound as if they'd just been built.

"Nice try," Crow said to the demons. Simeon followed up with some cheerful British insults.

Even as relief surged through him, Crow came to a realization. So far he hadn't been defeated, but the demons would keep at him until he was. Next time when his strength waned, he might not recover.

"A stalemate won't do it, love," said Simeon, who'd apparently reached the same conclusion. "We have to win."

Fair enough. But how? Today and over the past years, the demons had attacked Crow in many ways. Even if he could muster flames or sickness or hailstorms, Crow was fairly certain that none of those things would destroy the demons. He had no idea what weapons he possessed, let alone which would be effective against this enemy.

Taking advantage of his hesitation, the demons pressed close to one another and again waved their hands. Their eyes were black, like Simeon's, but entirely without luster. High above Crow's flock, clouds gathered like clots of moldy cream.

Arms hanging at his sides, Crow nearly sobbed in defeat.

"Thread's not cut, love," Simeon said.

Crow nodded at him and smiled. "Hope remains."

Once again, that snippet of poetry came to him: "I sing the body electric. The armies of those I love engirth me and I engirth them."

Well, his weapons were right here. And they were mighty: hope and joy and love. Which, when you look at them closely, are really one and the same.

Crow pictured himself as a lightning rod, attracting all of the hope and joy and love that the spirits allied with him had to give. Every affectionate smile and tender memory, every daydream, every laugh and caress and fond tease and late-night plan and carefully chosen gift and home-cooked meal and postcard and hair-mussing and midnight drive and salty tear and crayoned artwork and tickle and shared book and concerned advice and spring bouquet and warbled birthday song and….

Everything. All of it. Flowing into him like rivers flowing into the ocean, filling him. Engirthing him. Becoming him, because wasn't he the sum of all of these people, all of the times he'd spent with them, all of the things they'd shared?

Crow overflowed with these gorgeous, precious weapons. He lifted his arms and pointed his entirely human hands at the demons, making himself a transmission tower. Hope and joy and love ran into him, through him, and then out of his hands in powerful streams, the glowing white threads arcing toward the demons. The threads twisted around them, first gently, then tighter, and the more the demons struggled and screeched, the more ensnared they became, until almost nothing of their red cloaks was visible. Their dark eyes became covered, their talons useless.

When Simeon let loose a raucous, delighted squawk and landed a messy kiss on Crow's cheek, the demons and the electric threads momentarily glowed so brightly that Crow was almost blinded.

And then the demons were gone.

The weird glow disappeared, replaced by the deepening purples of a beautiful sunset. A warm breeze ruffled Crow's hair. The corn stood tall and nearly ripe in endless rows.

He collapsed onto the soft ground, Simeon falling halfway on top of him. They were both laughing, as were all the corvids, who began a dizzying show of aerial acrobatics. The windows of the house glowed softly, as if a family inside was preparing for the evening, and atop the barn, a rooster weathervane did a slow dance. All of the spirits looked at Crow and Simeon and smiled. A few of them, including Dee, waved cheerily.

The ghosts faded away with the last of the sun, leaving Crow and Simeon lying between the weedy house foundation and the rubble of the barn. The birds started settling in to roost.

"They're not gone, though," Crow said, filled with wonder. "The spirits, I mean. I can feel them still a part of me. They always will be."

"Aye," replied Simeon, combing fingers through Crow's hair. A new warmth began to gather under Crow's skin, and it had nothing to do with demon fire.

"It's weird. I used so much energy to destroy those demons, but I don't feel depleted. In fact, I feel great." Happy because the long threat was over, of course, but also strong. He could have run at top speed all the way into town and back without being winded. He could make love to Simeon until the sun rose.

Simeon smiled as if he knew the contents of Crow's thoughts and shared the same sentiments. "It's the nature of our weapons. It's not like bullets—you shoot them and then you're out. The more hope and joy and love you give, the more you have."

"I have a lot right now." Crow gave him a hard hug and a kiss.

"As have I."

"And we have… God, we have a whole future together. One that *we* choose."

Simeon squeezed him back. "We'll steer our ship together, my Crow."

# EPILOGUE

They raced back to Helen's house like a pair of rowdy boys, jostling each other and laughing the whole way. When they arrived, Helen fell on both of them with embraces and kisses and tears. She introduced them to Jamie as Uncle Crow and Uncle Simeon, which wasn't exactly accurate from a genealogical point of view but seemed to satisfy the little girl. "I have two uncles!" Jamie sang, dancing around the living room. "Two, two, two uncles!"

Helen had been in the middle of making dinner, but she abandoned those efforts and started a frozen pizza instead, much to Jamie's delight. She sang a new song, this one about not being forced to eat broccoli.

After Jamie finally settled down and was tucked into bed —Simeon told her a bedtime story that had something to do with a Queen Jamie and her best friend, who was a dragon— Simeon and Crow told Helen everything that had happened. She gaped and sometimes cried, but she never questioned the truth of what they said. It was late by the time they finished, but neither Crow nor Simeon was tired.

Helen, in contrast, yawned. "Let me go get the spare bedroom ready," she said. "It's not a big bed, but I bet you'll manage." She made a sound somewhere between a giggle and a snort.

Crow put a hand on her shoulder. He was blushing madly, but if he could face demons, he could also make a vague allusion to his sex life. "Um, I think tonight we'll get a room at the Grove Inn. We might be, um, loud." His cheeks burned worse than fire.

Eyes sparkling, Helen tried to contain her laughter, probably so she wouldn't wake Jamie. "I got it. Privacy is precious. But will you come back tomorrow? I want to know what your plans are. And man, it's so good to see you. Both of you." To back up her assertion, she gave them both mighty hugs.

They ran even faster toward downtown than they had to Helen's, arriving at the inn breathless and nearly overcome with laughter. Darrin Spiegel was on duty again. If he'd noticed before that Simeon stole a knickknack, he didn't mention it. In fact, Darrin seemed delighted to see him. "You're back!"

"We had such a lovely stay last time, we reckoned we'd do it again."

"That's great. I've lived here my whole life and I've always thought it was pretty boring. But maybe not?" Darrin looked as if he wanted to be reassured that his hometown had some value.

Crow surprised himself by stepping in. "You know that golden light when the sun hits the cornfields just right in late summer? And the way everyone gathers when the high school has a football game, even if they hate football, and it sort of feels like one big family? And those old farmers who park themselves at the B&R Café every morning like they're part of the furniture?"

Darrin nodded, wide-eyed.

"Hold on to those things, Darrin. They're precious and they're yours. You won't find anything exactly like them anywhere else."

After they paid their thirty dollars, received the key to room 306, and made their way into the cozy little suite, Simeon gave Crow a slow smile. "You waxed almost poetic just now."

"Ode to Chinkapin Grove," Crow said with a chuckle.

"Quite a change of heart."

"Not really. Somebody just taught me to open up my heart and notice what's in it."

Simeon correctly interpreted that as an invitation to attack. They both got their clothing off without ripping anything, and then they were all over each other. Bouncing off walls and furniture, ravenous with mouths and greedy with hands. When Simeon pinned Crow in place against the closed bathroom door, Crow felt delighted to be pinned, to feel safe and adored and *kept*.

"You're a bloody marvel, Crow," Simeon panted breathlessly as he rubbed their bodies together.

"Right back at you, rook."

The bathroom door was fine—God, *anything* with Simeon was fine—until it burst open behind Crow, sending them tumbling to the floor. It took them a while to untangle themselves, mostly because they didn't try all that hard, and then Simeon dragged an unresisting Crow to the bed.

Crow opened his body just as he'd already opened his heart and soul. And it was glorious. He lost himself in the writhing and the thrusts, in the commingled whimpers and moans, in heated skin against heated skin, in hair like silk, in a mouth both soft and sharp, in the bright perfection of their union.

Some of the electricity from earlier must have remained

within them. Crow's nerves crackled and fizzed like uninsulated wires. Simeon's eyes glowed like lanterns meant to lead lost souls out of darkness. More lines of poetry came to Crow, and he gasped them out loud whenever he had enough breath.

*SINGING the muscular urge and the blending,*
*   Singing the bedfellow's song, (O resistless yearning!*
*   O for any and each the body correlative attracting!*
*   O for you whoever you are your correlative body! O it, more than all*
*   else, you delighting!)*

and

*HARK close and still what I now whisper to you,*
*   I love you, O you entirely possess me,*
*   O that you and I escape from the rest and go utterly off, free and lawless,*
*   Two hawks in the air*

and

*FROM THE MASTER, the pilot I yield the vessel to,*
*   The general commanding me, commanding all, from him permission taking.*

. . .

AND THEN SOMEHOW CROW AND Simeon were laughing and crying and climaxing all at once in a magnificent tempest of emotion and sensation.

They trembled and laughed some more when they held each other afterward.

"For life?" Simeon whispered.

"For life."

THEY SPENT the next day at Helen's house, swapping stories with her and wearing out Jamie so thoroughly that she took an afternoon nap for the first time in years. Helen's company was wonderful—and so comfortable, as if they hadn't spent a decade apart. She must have felt the same way, because at one point while they sat at the kitchen table with coffee and cookies, she leaned forward. "You boys know that this is your home, right? Wherever I am, that's always your home."

Simeon cocked his head at her, birdlike. "You don't mind that we're poofs? And, erm, not exactly human?"

"You're family, Simeon. Exactly as you are."

Well, that led to hugs and, in Simeon's case, a bit of an emotional breakdown because, as he managed to say through tears, he'd never had a family before.

After hugs and Kleenex and more cookies, Helen leaned back in her chair. "Do you know what you'll do next? You're welcome to stay here as long as you want. We can get a bigger bed for the spare room."

How warm was Crow's heart now? But he took her hands in his and shook his head. "Thank you. I'm incredibly grateful. But I think it's Simeon's turn to get some questions answered."

Simeon, still a little sniffly, managed a grin. "I'm a mystery, I am."

Helen seemed to understand. "Do you know where you'll start?"

Crow and Simeon exchanged looks. They hadn't talked about this yet. "In London, I think," Crow said. "Since rooks don't seem to live on this continent. Is that okay with you, Simeon?"

"Yeah."

Nodding, Helen stood and cleared the empty dishes. "You'll need money for that. I know that's sort of not a big challenge for you, Simeon, but...."

"But perhaps I might give my light fingers a rest for a bit. For Crow's sake."

Crow wouldn't have asked this of him, but he was relieved by Simeon's decision. Not that he wasn't thankful for the previous thefts, which had saved them both, but he'd prefer to avoid larceny if possible. "We can look for jobs somewhere."

"Not many available around here, I'm afraid." Helen returned to the table with a frown. "The farms are mechanized, the businesses all dried up. I mean, I can ask around...."

"We'll find something somewhere." Crow was confident of that.

"Okay. Just promise me one thing? I have the feeling you two might sort of disappear for a while. Not a prophecy, Crow, so don't worry. Just an educated guess. And that's fine. But if you do, send me a postcard now and then. Or something. Let me know you're doing all right."

They promised to do their best.

Helen's husband Paul arrived home around dinnertime. She had forewarned him, so he wasn't shocked to find that

Crow had reappeared with a lover at his side. Paul didn't know their whole weird story because Helen thought it might be better to explain it to him later, in person. "I might need to tone down the details a little," she'd told Crow. "Paul's the best, but he's also sort of... a realist, I guess. Imagination isn't his strongpoint. He'll need to learn about you two gradually."

Paul looked... well, ten years older than when Crow had last seen him. Balder, pudgier. But he looked happy as well, and he greeted his guests with what seemed like genuine enthusiasm. He didn't insist on learning the details about their pasts and didn't seem to care that they were a couple. The five of them had a nice dinner together, full of good food and laughter.

That evening, they gathered in the living room. The windows were open to let in a cooling breeze, another hint that summer was drawing to an end. Simeon was as relaxed and happy as Crow had ever seen him, and Crow felt... replete. And yet oddly eager for more adventures.

Paul stood and stretched. "Anyone want more coffee?"

"Me!" shouted Jamie, who'd been watching a *Webster* rerun on TV.

"Sure, pumpkin. Caffeine is exactly what you need. How about some moo juice instead?" He bent down to tickle her.

She giggled. "Moo juice!"

He returned several minutes later with a plastic cup for her and a refilled mug for himself, then settled into his BarcaLounger. "You know, when I was coming into town, it looked like someone was setting up a carnival. Maybe we can go tomorrow."

Crow momentarily stopped breathing, and Simeon gripped Crow's knee hard enough to hurt.

"They, uh, might only be here for one night," said Crow. His voice sounded weird, but Paul didn't seem to notice.

Paul shrugged. "Oh well. We'll find something else fun to do."

After the sun set, and after Jamie recruited Simeon to tuck her in again, Crow and Simeon prepared to leave. Paul shook their hands and went off to clean up the kitchen. Helen hugged them at the door, her eyes knowing.

Crow said, "If we don't come back in the morning, Paul and Jamie…."

"I'll find a way to help them understand. Just remember your promise."

"Of course."

The last round of hugs was a little tearful, but Crow didn't have the sense that this was a final farewell. Helen— and Jamie and Paul—were a part of him now.

Crow and Simeon strolled through the warm night, hand in hand. "They're lovely," said Simeon. "Your family, I mean."

"Our family."

They heard the sounds long before they reached the carnival: delighted screams, the familiar chords of Queen and Lynyrd Skynyrd. The scents of beer and popcorn and sugar and trampled grass reached them soon after.

"Do you fancy being a roustabout for a time, love?"

Crow squeezed Simeon's hand. "Yeah. I think I'd like that."

Inside the brightly painted entrance booth, the fat man with the unlit cigar gazed at them silently.

"A dollar each?" prompted Crow.

The man waved impatiently. "Nah, that's for the cake eaters—the locals. Not for you two."

The grounds became crowded by a steady stream of people keyed up with excitement. Little kids danced instead of walking, teenagers and young adults strolled in pairs or little groups, older adults looked younger than they should have. Crow imagined sweaty dollar bills crumpled in fists and pockets, stomachs growling in anticipation of corndogs and giant soft-serve cones. He imagined the residents of Chinkapin Grove stepping into tents to watch the acrobats and the strongman, the knife-thrower, the magician. Some might walk to the quiet end of the midway and enter a tent the color of summer irises, where someone might be waiting to tell them their fate.

Simeon let go of Crow's hand, but only so he could tuck an arm around his waist. Nobody else seemed to notice their intimacy—and screw them if they did.

"What do you reckon will happen to us next, love?"

Suffused with joy and eagerness, Crow grinned. "Only one way to find out."

Together they walked beneath the red-and-white-striped arch. *Welcome Traveler*, it said. And now, with Simeon so close beside him, Crow felt very welcome indeed.

THE END

# ACKNOWLEDGMENTS

The plot bunny for this particular story has been languishing for years, sometimes hopefully pricking up its ears, only to be ignored once again. I am very thankful to Ari McKay for inviting me to join the Carnival of Mysteries series, which finally gave the bunny its chance.

I'm also thankful to Thea Nishimori and R.L. Merrill, both of whom took the time to read this story and give me very helpful suggestions.

Of course I owe deep gratitude to my wonderful editor, Karen Witzke, and my eagle-eyed proofreader, Allison Behrens. Any remaining errors are mine alone.

Finally, while the Fates might take center stage in this tale, the Muses played a strong role behind the scenes. Thank you to my literary muses for this tale: Ray Bradbury, Sophocles, Walt Whitman, and Neil Gaiman.

# ABOUT THE AUTHOR

Kim Fielding is very pleased every time someone calls her eclectic. Winner of the BookLife Prize for Fiction, a Lambda Award finalist and three-time Foreword INDIE finalist, she has migrated back and forth across the western two-thirds of the United States and currently lives in California, where she long ago ran out of bookshelf space. She's a university professor who dreams of being able to travel and write full time. She also dreams of having two daughters who fully appreciate her, a husband who isn't obsessed with football, a cat who doesn't tromp over her keyboard, and a house that cleans itself. Some dreams are more easily obtained than others.

Kim can be found on her blog: http://kfieldingwrites.com/
    Facebook: https://www.facebook.com/KFieldingWrites
    and Twitter: @KFieldingWrites
    Her e-mail is kim@kfieldingwrites.com

# CARNIVAL OF MYSTERIES

Welcome, Traveler! Join us for a series of M/M fantasies by a talented group of both new and established authors. Whether you enjoy mystery, action, danger, or just sweet romance, there is something for everyone at the Carnival of Mysteries!

Kim Fielding * L. A. Witt * Kaje Harper

Megan Derr * Ander C. Lark * E. J. Russell

Morgan Brice * Sarah Ellis * Kayleigh Sky

Nicole Dennis * Elizabeth Silver * Ro Merrill

T. A. Moore * Z. A. Maxfield * Ki Brightly

Rachel Langella